Seasoning Fever

Seasoning Fever

A NOVEL

Susan Kerslake

∽

The Porcupine's Quill

NATIONAL LIBRARY OF CANADA CATALOGUING IN PUBLICATION DATA

Kerslake, Susan
Seasoning fever / Susan Kerslake.

ISBN 0-88984-234-5

I. Title.

PS8571.E76S42 2002   C813'.54   C2002-902250-9
PR9199.3.K427S42 2002

Canada

Published by The Porcupine's Quill
68 Main Street, Erin, Ontario NOB 1TO
www.sentex.net/~pql

Readied for the press by John Metcalf and copy edited by Doris Cowan.
Typeset in Minion, printed on Zephyr Antique laid,
and bound at The Porcupine's Quill Inc.

Represented in Canada by the Literary Press Group.
Trade orders are available from Stewart House Distribution Services.

We acknowledge the support of the Ontario Arts Council,
and the Canada Council for the Arts for our publishing program.
The financial support of the Government of Canada
through the Book Publishing Industry Development Program
is also gratefully acknowledged.

ONTARIO ARTS COUNCIL
CONSEIL DES ARTS DE L'ONTARIO

Canada Council   Conseil des Arts
for the Arts   du Canada

Thanks to Rich Cumyn and Sandra Barry for their enthusiasm.

Prologue

This was how they got there: through soothsaying old women, blizzards and births, shape-changing, gender-juggling, sheer will and circumstance. Despite it and because of it. But mostly through the stretch and yaw of the imagination. How they left the low and slow thinkers behind and set out to match their dreams. What was *de rigueur*, and what happened along the way, and what was left in the end but the big stain of story. So you wink and believe it.

One

This way and that, she pulled the black shawl around her body as if it were the lost night, that last night when she had stood at his bedside, refusing offers of a chair to sit on, cups of tea, another warmer shawl, watching him sleep when she hadn't thought sleep still lived in the world. 'My son,' she'd said, moving the candle to the edge of the table so that the soft light washed his head.

Carrying that last night with her into eternity, the woman was there again showing her photograph. What had been stylish clothes were now deranged rags, twisted and tied in unlikely places around her body. Mud on her shoes, in the laces – she couldn't ever take them off. The startling vibrancy of her hair, electric curls snarling out from under the dingy hat brim. Snapping curls permanent as teeth. The wolves would dig up her bones and that hair. She wore gloves without fingers, clutching the edge of the photograph. Her nails were carefully done in blood-red polish. Thick fingers, a wedding ring. But delicately around the edges, around the face of her son, her fingers held the paper as if it were part of him.

Hawking up and down the platform between the trains, she said, 'My son, have you seen my son? Look here, this is a photograph of him. Oh no, not too long ago. Before the war. But he's not changed I'm sure. The war would not be long enough to do that, to change him so much I couldn't recognize him. A mother can always recognize her child. He looked like this ... Maybe he had a beard?' She covered the lower half of his face with her finger. 'Like this, like this, but the eyes, they'd be the same, lovely eyes and the shape of the eyebrows ... He was just fourteen. He's coming home any day, today! You might have seen him? Did you see this boy?' Thrusting the palm of her hand. 'Have you seen ... my son, my beautiful ...'

Steam lapped in the hem of her skirt, coating the black iron of the locomotive until there was no difference between oil and water and the reflection of shadows in the mirrored surfaces. Against the tide of exhaustion, weeping children, people seeking each other from the frayed ends of separation, the woman worked her way like an old splintered log broken off a sea wall, bobbing on the wave, pointing out to the horizon.

Hannah watched her swirl in the steep spokes of sunlight that let down through the glass and grid roof of the station. She said to herself, she came in the sun, she came again, every day in the sun, the sun hanging down like chains from the ceiling, ropes lowering her still squirming into this tomb. The thoughts were clear, the image sharp. She had been watching the old woman for years and it was suddenly clear to her that the woman was dead. In every way that counted, dead: mourning, crying dumb wasteful things, spreading herself between the sharp claws of martyrdom, singing proudly of her empty breasts, that her life had stopped, her love was lost in the moment of the past. Hannah knew he was dead, her son, that all the sons were dead now. No one waited for that train any more. There were no more coffins in the boxcar riding between the molasses and the silk. No more boys to go into that special corner in the cemetery. She wouldn't be able to steal flowers from the fresh graves any more to make wreaths of her own for dead dollies that sprang alive after the festivities to wear the wreaths as crowns for their May weddings. To wear on her toes, on the end of her nose, on her flat chest, around her belly button. In the dark grove where no one could find her. 'Coming, Mama,' she had called, throwing her voice to the clear sunny hill where children romped in elfish games for all the adults to see. 'Coming, Mama.' Called away. Mama smoothing her springy red hair, wondering why it didn't bleach like the other children's on the hilltop, ringing with shrill excited colour. Pressing the little Hannah to her skirts. Proud, indifferent little child, pretending. Already crossing her fingers and her toes so it wouldn't matter what she said.

Hannah got right around in front of the old woman to try to see where the sound came out, the breath of death calling for her dead son. She saw a small blue wrinkled mouth. It looked like her grandfather's anus the time she'd been too close and Mama was wiping him up.

She said, 'Stop it!'

'Have you seen this boy, dearie?' Her eyes searched inside Hannah as if she were a big sack that looked empty but might still have what she wanted at the bottom.

'Well done,' said Hannah, looking at the photograph that was a rare thing.

The woman was using her up. Hannah turned slowly, not lifting her feet. She watched the old woman melt down into a corner, out of the sun to live on the dust and her own devotion. Hannah watched because she still couldn't believe it.

Matthew was there for a timetable for trains west. He was going away, he said, this time for sure. It was what was on his mind until he saw Hannah.

After all that time she had changed. Or it could have been overnight. One day he'd seen a winged creature, bird bones, hollows, hard parts. And the only reason he'd seen that much was that she was apart, sitting up on the high fence around the butcher's yard, her heels just clipped into the cracks between the wide boards that hid the killing yard. Her knees were open. It looked as if there was blood on her stockings, but it must have been mud, spotting the sun-bleached white of her thin thighs just like blood. She had been holding on to the top of the fence, waggling her knees open and closed.

'La la, ha ha, la la,' singing a brisk crackling breathy song she'd made up. Phonemes dropped on his head like hail and the thick wind coming from under the fence, from the last breath of the animal being slaughtered, of the man with the axe, the smell of manure and urine.

Steam rose as far as the top of the fence. Hannah fanned it with the apron of her skirt. Later she would say she was sending smoke signals out across the fields into the pastures far and near, 'warning all the animals about what happens in the yard behind the big fence'. But she didn't see him. 'La la ha ha la la ha ha.' Beating the air and her knees.

He didn't want her to see him. He backed up into a shadow. His eyes shone out of the shadow with blue longing. It was the first time he wanted something for which he could see no use.

And until he told Hannah, he never told anyone what he had seen. It was the first time he had kept private something that seemed to make no difference.

He couldn't see the look in her eyes, the one that watched the old lady draw an opaque silence around herself. The way the sun covered Hannah's whole body, ladling on her eyelids, throwing the stark shadows of her lashes down her cheek like terrible tears. Spreading a pool of mystery at her feet. Her dress itself shifted suns, rainbows of colour. He couldn't quite see, and thought he might be missing something important, something that might change his mind.

'She meets every train coming in,' said the man in the ticket cage.

'Every one!' he echoed, furrowing his brain against some small image, some prophecy.

'We figured she'd die before this, but she's still here meeting every train.' He leaned forward on the ledge through the window, indicating the corner. Pigeons were walking over the old woman's shoes. 'We got rid of her a few times, but she kept coming back. Then we gave up.'

'What?' he said, tangled in the slough of the official's boredom. Sweat trickled inside his shirt. He looked sideways. Hannah was gone. Columns of light dusted the empty platform.

In five steps he grabbed the station doors, threw them open and ran out into the still white street. Choking, gasping for breath he pulled open the collar of his shirt. Tears clogged his throat. He felt weak, his clothes too tight. The one thought pierced his brain. Anxiety drugging his muscles, he bumped into the air.

'What have you done!' he shouted, turning around, looking for the only thing he lived for. Out of his sight? Dead? His heart plunged. He couldn't lose her before they'd even begun. 'They' had always been someone else. 'They' were other people with their clothes on all the time, riding children on their hips, grandchildren on their knees, old stories, the war, deaths and escapes. Things shared in time, the only way, along time, the narrow path, the moments, at the moment that fled, and only she remembered how it was. When we were. You remember how it was. Remember when we. Remember when I. And the night. And the morning when no one else was up but you and me. We watched the sun come up. Such a beautiful day after the terrible night. We were awake all night, lamplight, moonlight, light in each other's eyes. We who had chosen. In such a moment as this, blinding bright with truth and certainty. He had to find her, she would fill the raw cave, the hunger gaping and gnawing within him. This hollow, this space startled him, its depth, breadth, dark. He survived on hope, and although hope was an endless source it rang around the rim of his despair, singing in that shrill pitched glassy note, echoing endlessly over the empty place. 'They' had always been someone else. It was his turn. His life depended on it.

He thought he saw her between porch posts, ducking into the hotel, the grocery, the livery, hiding behind a black buggy parked in front of the bank.

'Hannah!' In sight then. The minute shrug. A sass of her hips. Following her down bright streets, lulled in afternoon silence, he could

12

hear himself breathing. The warm rich scented summer air sustained him. That and the slipstream of his desires. She was in sight. Her skirt caught between her legs.

Hannah's mother used to have a long witchy switch. She chased Hannah round and round inside their fenced yard. 'Stop, stop right now. Hannah. I'm going to catch you, you know.'

Matthew was walking down the middle of the road thinking about his father's guns, especially the hunting rifle he was going to be allowed to use as soon as, as soon as, as ... The bullets were on the top shelf out of reach. Even one was heavy. It lay in his palm, cold, shiny, mute. His father stood one of his guns up on its butt. Matthew wandered over, that far, then a little bit farther, to measure himself beside it. He was smaller than the gun. He put his finger on the gun barrel. Reaching up he could just fit his finger into the hole up to the first joint. In his daydream he hoisted the gun to his shoulder with no effort, the deer, the rabbit, the bear flashed in the tall, weedy grass, the forest of his imagination. He stopped, pointing his body, listening for the telltale creak and crack. Instead he heard Hannah's mother.

'You can't get away, Hannah, you're going to learn to do what I tell you. And when!' Smoothing down her skirt, she started down along the back fence. Hannah screamed. Her apron caught on a splinter. Grabbing a wad of cloth with both hands she pulled and wrenched and yanked and screamed again, this time too late. Caught.

'And listen to me when I tell you something.'

The switch was on her calves and ankles. Dancing, screeching. Tucking her feet up, hopping on one foot then the other.

'Oh no you don't!' growled her mother, avoiding Hannah's sharp teeth. Grabbing her by the clothes at the back of her neck, beating at the fronts of her legs then, Hannah yelling, reaching down to protect herself, her hands in the way, getting hit, the sharp thin whippy stick hitting the backs of her hands. Blood smarting up.

Matthew's body stiffened, skin quivering at each cut of the stick. Hannah's shrill shrieks. It was awful and exciting. He couldn't stop watching. Hannah's face twisting, her mouth purple, eyes glaring. The white body of her mother avenging, white like the terrible angels of God, white bloodless angels interpreting the laws, making the rules. Hannah was down on the ground then, her skirt lumped up around her waist.

Matthew was surprised by thin, white, bare skin. Kicking. Twisting her head from side to side, mouthful of grass, dirt mushed on her lips. Trying to holler, but it was more like crying, sobbing wetly into the ground. Trying to turn over. Then her mother put her knee across Hannah's back, her skirts flounced, shifted. Hannah's arms stuck out from under it. Her arms and legs stuck out like thorns. He could hardly see the stick, it was going so fast, up and down, up and down, the white storm of her mother's arm, sleeve whipping back and forth.

Suddenly Hannah's scissoring legs caught the switch and it see-sawed between her knees, calves, ankles, toes, and flipped into the blue air.

'Is it going to stop now?' he wondered, but Hannah continued to thrash beneath the monstrous white will of her mother, until she realized she wasn't being hit any more. Her mother rolled off her, lurching, exhausted, having trouble getting to her feet.

'Get up, child, do what I tell you. Get up.'

Hannah propped herself on her elbows. She didn't look up. She picked at a reedy strip of grass, twisting it one way, then the other. Then she rolled over and sat up, bending her legs at the same time. Matthew could see her eyes, bloodshot, glossy with tears but fierce, unbroken. She held her knees tight together.

'Get up, Hannah.'

She stood up carefully and did not move. Her mother came over to untuck her skirt, shake it out, pat it down. Then, putting Hannah's head under her arm, she bent her over to look at the backs of her legs. All around them the crushed grass swaggered up. Matthew thought Hannah's head looked like a doll's, swaddled in the soft wrap of a mother's care.

'Come with me, I'll put butter on you,' she said, taking her firmly by the hand, walking too quickly through the sharp grass. Hannah wincing in the keen-edged blades.

Matthew didn't move. He could see shadows in the summer kitchen, the shadows of Hannah and her mother, the mother's voice telling Hannah to hold still, to stop, but the sound did not echo with anger any more. Matthew thought that his mother would never do such a thing in public. There was no audience to the trials in his family. Doors were closed, curtains pursed, lamps lowered. His mother and father spoke clearly, their big words cleanly dividing the air. There was no blood. No one screamed. Matthew swallowed his tears. Later when he was all by himself he coughed them up.

Hannah came outside. She was very quiet. She leaned over the porch railing, letting her arms dangle over the edge. She stood with her legs apart and stiff so they wouldn't touch anything. He wasn't sure she was even breathing. The springs on the screen door were broken, so when Hannah's mother came out quickly, the door flew too hard against the side of the house. Quickly down the steps in the heat of the day, she was looking for something. The switch wasn't broken. Picking it up she waved it at the nameless little boy in the middle of the road. Matthew ran away.

At a distance, in daylight, he followed her into the summer he was twelve. Slipping into the trough she cut in the sunlight, getting in before it closed up. Following just so far back in the sweep of her long skirt. He didn't care where she was going. Across the bridge, boards popping, hopping up off the chains and steel beams. Keeping his eyes down to see the lush blue-green rush of the river singing underneath. Up on the wide road until the traffic of tinkers, icemen and dangerously lurching caravans drove Hannah into the ditch and Matthew followed. He saw nothing on either side. Ahead in the soft dust her feet were like beetles scurrying under the umbrella of her skirt. Hannah, not letting on, was watching for snakes in the tall grass weeds. She loved to fling her shadow out over the tops of the grasses, into the grass stalks. If she could only do it all. If only, if only...

He wanted to follow her back into the hills at dusk, catch her eyes on a hook. Beckon her dreams when she didn't know what they were herself. He wanted her to bring him all her unhappiness, her grief, her secrets, most of all her secrets, which would be the same as his. He knew it, they were the same. Why else would he feel this way?

'Hannah,' he whispered across the whole history of man and woman. The woman's name sounding like honey on his tongue. The beautiful sound of the lover's name. A name never thought of before as special. Hannah in rhyme, in mime. Scribbled in the sand. Hannah, used by the teacher to illustrate a name that can be spelled backwards and forwards. Hannah, called across the night air by her mother. A name like no other. 'Hannah, my darling, come home, come home to me now.' She turned. The words were so familiar, but the voice was different. Not so tired, not so long and thin, this sound spilled and spread around her. There was enough left over to cover the hill behind her, to coat the grass. The heat rubbed against her legs like an old cat. 'Hannah,' he purred. The field trilling with insect song. Flowers watched through thick pollen.

'Hannah.' She stood tall listening to the voices that might mean chances.

Matthew hid in a clump of bushes. Above him the wind played high in the old oak tree. The branches swayed this way and that.

Hannah thought, 'He's made wind in the trees.' Leaves twitched, tangled, turned belly up then down. Had she seen him following her, was he more than breath and sound and heat? Was he what she wanted after all? Closing her eyes, she imagined.

'Hannah.'

'Don't bother me.'

'Hannah.'

'I'll never give in.' She put her hands over her eyes. It was wonderful to have someone call her name. The sound filled her up.

'Are you very close? I can't see you.'

He pulled in his breath. The wind dissolved. He was remembering every moment as if he were dying, as if his whole life depended on this. He must never lose sight of her. All the promises of the past were simple beside this. Yet, as simply, was this God speaking to him. Here were no sides, no edges. His heart tilted. His soul walked on thorns. There was no one he could ask for directions. He was the last man on earth.

'I know where there are berries ready.'

'I'm not hungry.'

'You can watch me.'

And she could, bent in the bushes, conspiring in the dusk, at the edge of the farmer's patch, reaching into his crop of strawberries, handing them to her and she planting them in her apron that hung between her knees. Brushing the hair back out of her eyes as she huddled over the deep red ripe berries, until she had a bellyful and stood up holding the corners of the apron together, high, just under her breasts, poking her lumpy berry stomach at him. Teasing, catching her lower lip in her teeth, catching shadows, catching him. Cradling the berries as she ran after him, the getaway in the imagined barrage of bullets, waving brooms, shouts, threats. When actually the air parted reluctantly, caught as it was in nightfall.

'Don't spill them, we'll never find them in the dark.' Laughing, bolder then on the other side of the hill, going down a steep slope. And when they stopped, heaving against the dark, the first stars let themselves down.

She shivered. 'Star light, star bright, first star I see tonight ...'

He wanted to touch her.

'Let's see.' He indicated the clutch of fruit.

Slowly she opened the white apron. Opened her arms to balance the dark berries on the spread of cloth. Leaning against the dark, she invited him to take some.

'Don't you want any?' he asked. 'Here,' offering her the best, 'this one,' putting it to her lips. 'Smell,' rolling the strawberry gently across the skin under her nose. She waggled the tip of her tongue out and took it, while he held onto the starfish stem. The taste spilled in her mouth.

'Shhh,' he warned. Dogs barking. A rough sound, tumbling over teeth, tearing up the ground. 'They're going hunting in the hills,' he whispered. 'They hunt the deer.' He stood over her as if it would help. He put his hands on her ears, muffling the howling, the pursuit behind the veil of night. She listened instead for the sound of the sea inside his hands. Strawberry juice as dark as blood stuck in her hair. Later when she would pull her hair across her face, remembering, she would smell the stain of berries, the night, and the salt of the inland sea in his hands. It might be what she wanted. He was looking over her head for the dangers that might sneak up behind. He was keeping her warm. She saw his throat shining. She saw his lips move, but couldn't hear what he said.

His hands were tangled in her hair. 'It's all right, it's all right,' he told her, although it wasn't. It was going to be better. Tangling her in his life. Bruising her lips. Covering her with his hands. Later. Later. Now. But he put his arms down. Laughing, dipping in the apron of berries. Feeding her. Himself. Her.

Hannah sat behind him in school, behind and to the side, on the girls' side. When she leaned down over her work he couldn't see her because the stove was in the way, but when she sat up and tilted her head just so – inquisitively? bored? – he had a clear view. She was looking at the old empty-headed poppies lopping against the window.

'Matthew, read from the bottom of the page.'

He slid out of the seat and stood up. Luckily he had read this very passage to his father last night as he sat and smoked in front of the fire.

His father had said wistfully, 'I remember studying that.'

His voice floated out into the hollowed space.

'Speak up, Matthew, I can hardly hear you.'

When he finished he sat down. While other children were being rehearsed, drilled and heard, he could sit still and think. Sitting on the school bench was almost as good as kicking stones on a dusty road in summer, fishing in the deep pond that elbowed out of the river, or hiding on the stairs. Peculiar solitary sounds rustled in corners. The jittery shrill bungling voices of the children blurred after a while, and he was left alone. He was thinking about the fact that no one had died in his family. He had been born after the burial of his grandparents, who were misty word memories, story and smoke told in the evenings when all work was done. One great-grandfather was still alive, a blurry, gnarly figure.

He was also thinking about going away. No one would expect it of him, no one would expect it at all. He tried out the idea. There were plenty of children, one could go away and do something new. One could go and the hole would not be very big. His mother said that when all the children were gone the house would be empty. He used to think that meant his parents would die. The house would be empty. Derelict, old-rot, listing and damp, the house fell over in his mind like an abandoned chicken coop. As long as his parents were there, nothing like that could happen. No one had died in his house. In all the other houses, the mothers limped through mourning songs.

'You would have been the one, the one to die, the youngest always dies, the babies, before they get started really, so you would have been the one, but you didn't, so here we all are, all alive,' said Molly, wiping the dishes, her hand swathed in white cotton, going faster and faster around and around the plate. 'Anyway, it's not going to be me, I'm not going to die.' Matthew was convinced. Later he would wonder why he had not died after all, why he was allowed to stay.

'Mama, why?' But for the first time she didn't know the answer.

That was not why he was going to leave.

He didn't tell anyone because he didn't know the answer himself. One day he had gone down to the train station with his father to collect a parcel. There was an old woman there rubbing her shoes on the floor. Matthew stood too close to her and she asked him a question he didn't understand. Just as the woman reached out her hand to touch him, his father rescued him. 'Would that have been a bad thing, Papa, would it have been bad for that lady to touch me?'

'She's waiting for someone else, son, you mustn't get in her way.'

Matthew looked around the station. It was empty. He slipped his hand inside his father's and looked again. It was like a deserted church. Dust full of sunlight slowed and smoked, lazily snowing on the bare benches. A bitter smell of coal, pinched steel, displaced horses. Dust settled on the old woman.

His father was talking with the freight officer. He owed a little more money and wanted to see the bill. Papers unravelled over Matthew's head. Once he had been wide awake. Now he was sleepy. Maybe the lady was a witch. He held on tighter. Maybe she was the queen and this was her castle. Well, bad times had come and her castle had been turned into a train station.

'Who, Papa, who's she waiting for?'

'I'm just trying to see where the charges were added, where in the processing.'

'Who's she waiting for, Papa?'

'Shhh, just a minute ... shhhh.'

'Papa ...' Tugging on the long minutes.

Harris took his son's head in his hands, one cupping around back, mussing his hair, the other muffling his mouth. Matthew started giggling. The next thing he was supposed to do was to try and get free. It was a game they played when he got fidgety. He could pull his father off balance now by pulling, then suddenly twisting to the side. When he got loose he laughed and laughed. The old woman lifted her head. A dull look came out of her eyes and stretched across the space between them.

'Are you coming home, my boy, are you coming home to me? I wasn't through with you. They took you before I was finished and now I'm too tired. Hurry, hurry home ...' Her words zigzagged, falling in the dust. 'Hurry. Now. I'm waiting, I'm waiting.'

'Papa, Pa-pa.' He was hiding a little bit now, behind his father. 'Papa, is she talking to me?' He didn't know if he should be trying to catch those firefly words. Hannah had said the dead come back in other bodies. 'Is that my grandma?' he wondered.

Harris handed the bill of transit to Matthew. 'Carry this for me, please.' He took the parcel of books under his arm. 'Come on, let's go.'

That night, when his mother was tucking him into bed (he was the first to go, everyone else still up, everyone! Scraps, slips, bits, echoes shuffling at the door sill) he sat up one more time and asked, 'Mama, are you finished with me?'

'Why no, of course not, you're my boy yet, I'm not finished with you.'

'Mama, will you let me know when you are?'

'You think such a time can ever come?' she said, talking to the air, hugging him as if she ever could tire of him, as if she would hold him forever. As if she could.

That was not why he was going away either.

Another night Mama was telling him one of her stories about him. 'Then you said, Mama, what's your name? Your other name.'

'Did I say that?'

'Yes, you did. And after I told you, you asked what Papa's name was.'

'And then what did I do?'

'You said Mama was a better name than Una.'

That wasn't so funny. He wondered why she was laughing in that private folded-in way. Reaching up, he patted her cheek. When he touched her lips she became very quiet. Then, though she wasn't looking at him, he knew he was all her thought.

But that wasn't the only reason he was going away.

'Papa, why did you come here to this country?'

'I came because I was the youngest. The first son inherited the land. The second son went to the church. The third son to school, but the fourth son had nothing. I was supposed to be the girl.'

Matthew wrinkled his face. 'The girl!'

'Nothing is simple. Nothing happens just the way it is supposed to.'

'You weren't supposed to come here?'

'Yes, I was. Now we'll wait and see.'

'See? See what?'

'See what happens next. See what will become of all my children.'

'Well, I'm going to play in the symphony,' declared Molly. 'It's what I'm supposed to do, I can feel it in my bones!' She swooped down beside her father, pecking him on the top of the head, her hands firmly on his shoulders. He ignored her.

'It's true, Papa,' she hissed in his ear. 'Nothing could be truer.'

'I'll wait and see.'

'Yes, you do that, you wait and see.'

Matthew watched her go out the door into the bright evening air. As soon as she was clear she stuck the violin under her chin and began to play.

'You're going to wake up the birds,' her brother shouted. 'It's not my fault, it's not!'

His mother caught him teetering on a chair at the window. 'Come down, come down.'

Neither was that why he was going away.

'Come on, Matthew, come on.'

'Matthew, the bell's rung, didn't you hear it? You can go out for recess now.'

Pebbles and poppy seeds were strewn around the front steps. He rubbed his shoes on top of the stones until the seeds filtered down to the hard ground. Hannah, in the middle of a shout of children, scooped up a handful of rocks and started throwing them out into the field. He grabbed her skirt.

'Hey, hey you!' She shot him a fierce look, then yanked him up with her and out into the loud game.

'It's going to rain tonight,' Hannah said again.

Matthew picked up a handful of dust. Parting his fingers slightly, he sieved it through. 'If you insist, I'm sure it will!' He sprinkled the last of the earth over her shoes.

'Hey.' She shook her feet, then stomped a wave of dust at him. He jumped back. 'Hey you!' Smiling, trying to catch her eye, she said, 'Look at me,' as she put her hands on her hips in mock outrage. The lush garden of her lips curled in on itself. 'Look at me, look at me for a moment,' she insisted, the smile fading.

She laughed. 'Rain, rain,' she said, shaking her hands in the air above her head, conjuring. Rolling her eyes back to seed the sky with her dark clouded stare. Behind her, the trees, tissue-thin and flat as grass, waited for the cooling water.

'Hannah,' he said, reaching for her head, her wild hair. Dangerous then, static condensing on the curls, the coils. The excitement. Inviting lightning. 'Hannah, I want you to …'

'Ho ho!' She glimmered and shone on the hot skin of the afternoon.

He wanted to pluck her off.

'Stop, stop, I want you to stop.'

Suddenly her face flattened and grew dark. She leaned towards him. Softly she said, 'Tell me again.' Matthew thought that he would never refuse her if she came to him like this, bending her body, letting back her head, throat vulnerable, divine. 'Tell what it is you really want.'

'Just you?'

'Nah, that's too simple. What do you want forever?'

As if to find help in space, he looked over her head, but it was not as far as the distances in her eyes. 'I think I'll be going away from here. I want to do something on my own ...'

'What, what?' Tugging on the collar of his shirt.

'... all by myself.'

'Without me?'

'If you can really make it rain, I'll take you anywhere, everywhere.' He smoothed the tangle of her hair.

'Going away,' she echoed wistfully, though she'd never entertained the idea before. It might be the answer, after all.

Rummaging a moment in her thoughts, he found a deep pond, its black sleek surface mirroring the sky, clouds, the lean of trees, the world he could already see. But invisible, under the water, his feet sank in velvet mud, slipped on slimy rocks, felt fish and eels bumping into his legs. Wondering, in that cold thick world of hers, wondering what he was. Too dark to see. Too close, he was too close.

'We are alone, there are no others.'

'We are alone, there is no other.' And they touched so that there would be no distance between them. Breath to breath. The heel of his hand in the hollow of her throat, his fingers on her chin, cheek, ears. A small incendiary darkness.

Hannah thought, 'This is what it feels like to have a man touch me, these are the things he likes to do.' She closed her eyes. It didn't matter that it was Matthew, he was any man, every man. She didn't care who he was.

Colouring the sunburn in the shallows of her shoulder blades.

Her lips with a milky moustache of perspiration.

Tickling the signature of her ear with a damp curl of her own hair.

His eyes soothing the curves of her face.

Taking her hand, turning it, tracing up and down each of her fingers, circling the knob of her wrist, finding the heat beneath her hair.

As long as it was summer, she need never talk to him again. This was enough. This was everything.

Two

Matthew held her hands, then he smoothed one of her hands, palm side down, on his, looking intently at the back. Between the tendons and the veins he hoped to find the thin white scars of the switching her mother had given her that day so long ago. He proceeded to her other hand and did the same thing. But there were no signs.

She didn't know what he was doing. She looked at her own hands as if they might be valuable after all. Light dappled by clouds and leaves scattered on her skin.

In the static-charged air, leaves shivered, turned over and back again, fluttered, held the air still, and waited. For a moment it was the only sound. The birds sang only in the cool of the morning. He had stopped talking.

He's really serious, she thought.

Crickets started, their chatter fretting the edges of the clouds. To avoid this, clouds huddled, bumped, and mounded against each other until thick cumulus anvils formed in the accommodating sky.

But Hannah, in a moment that could not be more commanding of her attention, had drifted away. Often she felt this way, a visitor in her own life, participating with one eye on herself, the other, perhaps an inward or third eye, seeing something quite different, something she had never seen before, a place, time of day, person. With dream-like sight she gazed through walls, beyond horizons of hill and leaf, past the sharp quick grip of people. She narrowed in to her own stare in the mirror, hoping to find, in her own eyes, a crystal ball. Looking and looking. There was nothing there. Mirrors and eyes, shining at each other across a small space ... his eyes. She looked carefully. There, in the black centre, her face, a tiny clear dream. She couldn't see her eyes. Her face framed in the light sky-blue iris of his eye. He held her there.

She had broken the mirror. Her father smacked her. 'I'm too big for you to do that to me any more, stop it!' He smacked her again then helped her puzzle the pieces back together and paste them down to a board. She took the mirror to her room. Her mama said, 'Your own room, imagine that, having a room for your own self at your age. What a marvellous country this was. So much space. Everyone can have their own room!'

'But you don't, Mama,' Hannah teased.

The cracked ice surface of the mirror distorted the planes of her face. She couldn't bear to look at the fractured whole, and concentrated instead on each part as it appeared in an irregular shard of glass. She looked in the mirror again. How many of her were in there, trapped?

'Matthew, I feel so peculiar.' It was the perfect thing to say. He was pleased, flattered. Being together like this seemed to give him great pleasure. Hungrily he sucked her lips, kneaded her arms, pressed his fingers in the small of her back. She rolled her head around. 'Oh, to be ... to be ...' What was it she should be feeling?

Behind them in the bushes they heard someone giggling. Shaking loose, swivelling around, Matthew shouted through his haze, 'Who's there? Come out. Now!' He pushed Hannah away, but held her there at arm's length. No one moved. He listened. There was not a sound now. For an interminable moment, they waited. 'Let's get out of here.' He was alarmed and flushed. Hannah started to smile. She had never been spied on before.

His energy detoured, Matthew pulled her down into the gully, further into deep shadows, pretending they were walking and talking.

'It's okay,' she said, rubbing his arm. The muscle was rigid. He didn't answer. She saw the furrows that would eventually dress his face. It started to rain. 'I was right! I knew it would rain.' They ran. Up on the road they saw a boy neither of them knew. Matthew wanted to get him, but Hannah held him. 'He might not be the one. He might have gone up on the other side of the gully. You can't just grab a kid off the road.' Matthew continued to clench. She said, 'What d'ya think about the rain?' Which was falling faster now. 'Did I do it or not? You'll take me with you now, won't you, like you said. You say you want rain and I'll do it. Just like this time.' All around her, rain drops were raising dust when they splatted on the dry road. Across the fields, up and down the roads, people were scurrying for shelter. Hannah looked as far into the distance as she could. It was a habit she had. Overlooking.

He is so serious, she thought. Her mother was drying her hair and directing kitchen traffic. Hannah sat by the window. Her mother stood behind the chair, towelling her head absentmindedly. Hannah was glad she didn't have to talk. The rain was falling steadily. Now and again the thin muslin curtain puffed in across her face, making her close her eyes. Then it snapped out, dragging against splinters in the window frame, billowing on the whim of the wind. It held her thoughts in its shadowy belly for a second then flung them into the streaming rain. Where the yard was tramped down even beyond the hope of a weed, vapour rose like a wraith.

She thought about the way his eyes grinned into her soul. Boys had come along on her heels before. She had laughed at them, but with such a shivery nervous sound that they sucked on her breath excitedly, held her head up to catch the fire, stamped uneasily on imagined embers at their feet. She liked being followed, but when it came time to turn around she had always closed her eyes.

Thinking, for just a moment, how maybe he did astonish her. His eyes were liquid, feverish. For me, she remembered, he was looking at me. Under her hands, his had trembled, but it didn't seem to be a fear of her as much as a fear of himself. His face wasn't used to wrinkling from the inside out. Hannah was curious about strong feelings. They made Matthew sweat circles and stripes.

Aaron fed the stove for supper.

'Did you get paid today?' her mother with purse strings asked.

'Oh yes, here,' she said, digging out two coins.

'So what did you have to do?' Her mother hung the wet towel over the stove.

'Oh, some sweeping up. I put some new stock on the shelves. Things like that.' It was another life, one belonging to the girl who sat here under her mother's hand, who was old enough to start contributing to the family welfare, who could fit her shadow into her mother's and serve supper, bathe the children, clean up, open and close windows, scold, chase, caress, and kiss the kiss that sealed the soul against the onslaught of night. Someone who could do all that but who climbed into bed shoving the coverlet down in both sides of her body to protect herself because she was alone, still alone, though until she had met the boy in the offbeat woods, she hadn't known it. On each side, already asleep, lay her other selves: daughter, employee, sister. Each night she unleashed the thoughts and dreams peculiar to herself, believing that she was alone, believing this was the first time such desires had ever been realized. Her thoughts blossomed, exploded, coalesced and filled her until she subsided like a tide pulled back before it discovered its own strength.

He was so determined, sure of himself. Though he was older than she, he was still in school. He would probably go to university. But what was it he said about going away? About wanting to do something all by himself? The moon, sullen and invisible, wouldn't answer.

At Matthew's, the dining room was on the west side of the house. Sunlight clattered in bowls on the table, shone on silverware and revealed corners. Matthew's mother, Una Brede, marvelled at Hannah's clean skin and red sun-drenched hair.

'How old are you, my dear?'

'Fifteen, ma'am.' The sun in her eyes blinded her.

'My son says you're working in the general store?'

'Yes, ma'am.'

Matthew looked at his plate. There was no reason to be surprised, but in fact he was proud of her.

'And you live over on Old Mill Road?'

'Yes, ma'am.'

Shoving the swinging kitchen door open with her ample hips, the serving girl entered backwards balancing a tray with three large covered bowls. Mrs Brede took the bowls by the handles and placed them in front of her. Another girl brought a platter of baked ham scored and pierced with cloves at the intersects. A cider and syrup baste glazed the flesh and fat. Mr Brede flourished fork and knife. With organized precision of long practice, they handed the plates round from one end of the table to the other, returning them with slices of perfect pink ham, orange brown-sugar glazed carrots, green peas, cauliflower and new potatoes. Mrs Brede clamped the lids back on the bowls, which steamed in the late afternoon sun.

Hannah reached for a crystal glass of water. She wondered if Matthew was worried about how his mother would receive her, and if he wanted to protect her. She sat straight. Everyone bent forward for grace. Steam moistened their faces. God was indeed a full plate. Hannah took the moment to look around above the heads. Printed wallpaper chambered the room, finishing the effect of oriental rug and mahogany furniture, the dark wood unmarred by dust. None of the stern portraits staring down from the walls looked like Matthew.

Where are you going, anyway? she wondered. It was so quiet, she was afraid someone would be able to hear her thoughts. Pointedly she noticed how beautiful Una Brede was, how white and soft her hands. Hannah didn't care who overheard.

Immediately after prayers the meal began. Windows and doors were thrown open. She could smell the salt of the sea far away, feel night on a desert, hear the lisp of tongues and laughter.

Hungrier than she'd been for days, she ate every bit on her plate. Unprepared for the lively worldly conversation, she was thankful no one forced her to talk. She caught Matthew smiling calmly at her across the table. He was so sure of something. It had made his eyes deep and open, trusting. It's me he believes in, she realized. He's counting on me. She would let him near so that she'd belong. That's what it would be like, what she wanted. She belonged to no one and no thing. She wanted so much, everything. At that moment she had every reason to believe that the world resided in Matthew Brede.

After supper his sister Molly played a fiddle. Not just the jigs and struts of foot-stomping, knee-slapping, clapping tunes, but something Hannah had never heard before. It reminded her of church, but was more complex, more joyful and unresolved.

'A delicious heathen sound,' Mr Brede leaned over to whisper in Hannah's ear. He patted her knee, his hands huge and beautiful. Quickly he leaned back, returning his hand to his own thigh. Yellow stains between his fingers. Idly he tapped his knee. Hannah looked straight ahead at Molly, but she could feel his eyes on her now and again. Molly finished one piece and started another. She twiddled her feet on the floor, shuffling this way and that, swinging her skirts. Hannah felt overwhelmed. She had no talents, no prospects, no ambitions, but she knew she didn't want to be an audience forever. She wanted to do something wonderful. Molly had closed her eyes. The music swirled round and round her head. Hannah could almost see it. She could imagine Molly all by herself, not needing anything else in the world but her music. It was as if the wings folded in her back were good for this life, too. Matthew came over to stand behind Hannah. In order to whisper in her ear he put his hands on her shoulders. She couldn't hear what he was saying. 'It wasn't anything,' he would say later, 'just an excuse to touch you.'

It was getting late, but no one moved. In the pauses, sounds from the kitchen filtered through to them. A cupboard door, a ring of glass. Windows creaked and she heard the little dry scritch of drapes being drawn across on rings. She could smell the grass dampened with dew. Deep shadows flooded the dooryard, climbed the trees and waited in the high branches for the sky to give in.

'Do you like your work?' Molly asked, draping the chair she'd pulled up beside Hannah. 'I love to play my violin. It's going to be my life's work,' she confided. 'I'm not exactly sure how yet – don't tell Papa that, he thinks I know how I'm going to do it, but I'm going to play music all day long, forever! I just finished school, you know, eighteen and just, if you can imagine it, though this last year I was mostly helping the younger grades and actually most of the work I was doing was just finishing off for university. I'll go stay with my aunt in the city next year. It's terribly exciting, don't you think? Mr Bartelli, the famous musician, is at the university. I'll actually be studying under him. It's going to be wonderful, I just know it. I …'

'Come on, Hannah, we'd better get you home, it's dark,' said Matthew, extricating her from Molly and the family, who rose in the saturated air to remind themselves of her.

She thanked them for their hospitality. Mrs Brede held her by the shoulders and gave her a little kiss on the cheek. Mr Brede put his finger under her chin and kissed her lightly between the eyes.

As they approached her house, Hannah noticed dull, low lamplight filling the kitchen window. Inside, her mother sat slouched against the back of her chair, as if she'd tried to stay awake but had succumbed to weariness. Hannah leaned against Matthew. It was unusual for her mother to be up. Something was wrong. 'It might have something to do with me, though.' She started to rush forward, stopped, turned to say goodnight and thank you.

'Don't you want me to come in with you?' he asked, but she didn't want him to find out what was wrong at the same time she did.

'I'll tell you later.' She ran ahead. Matthew waited in the wet grass by the fence.

'Mama, Mama, are you all right?' Rattling the door open, waking her mother suddenly. 'Why are you sitting here like this?'

'Grief, born to grief!' Hannah reached for her face. Before fresh tears threaded down her mother's cheeks, Hannah saw the salt tracks of earlier ones. 'Mama, have you been crying all this time?'

'Ohhh.' Tears streaked and streamed down her face. 'Oh, oh, my darling girl, I thought, I thought, I couldn't find you. I looked in your bed and you weren't there.' Clasping her hands, she leaned forward, lifted her fists up to her lips, then buried them between her knees. 'I thought you were kidnapped, I thought you were dead, I thought ...'

'Mama, I'm right here. I went to Matthew's for supper, I told you that.' Alarmed, she turned the lamp up, discouraging hostile shadows. Picking up a shawl from where it had fallen in a woolly pool beside the chair, she comforted and stroked. Her eyes wandered out the window. She wondered if he was still there. If he were, things might be all right. If only she could ask him to come in.

'Mama, what is it, what's happened, really?'

'You died. It was terrible. It was all dark except for the glow coming out of the cracks in the stove. It was quiet everywhere, everyone asleep, you know, and then this thing came into my mind, this thought, a sort of dream picture. You were falling down through a dark sort of tunnel or cave. There was your face and the darkness, your face was all light like a ghost's, as if you were already dead, but you had to die all over again. You were screaming. I couldn't do anything, I couldn't reach you, you didn't even know I was watching, you thought you were all alone, I started to be able to know all your thoughts, you were calling to me in your thoughts, calling for your mama, wondering why she wasn't there, why she wasn't helping you, why she had deserted you, why she had left you all alone, why ...' Her voice shrivelled and she began sobbing again, deeply shuddering, inconsolable.

'Papa,' Hannah called carefully so as not to wake the others. 'Papa, come here, something's wrong with Mama, Papa come here ...' chanting until her mother curled and closed over her own lap, clutching the shawl. 'Mama, don't go in that dark again.' She got up and ran into her father's bedroom, pulling the coverlet from under his chin, shaking his shoulder. 'Papa'

Groggily he sat up, swung his leg out. 'Having a spell, was she?' He swallowed.

'What do you mean?' Had he heard? 'It was a dream, she was describing a dream,' said Hannah, fitting it into what she knew.

He knew what to do, gathering his wife under his arm, wrapping the shawl to keep her warm because her clothes were wet through. He repeated her name. 'Adele, Adele ... my child, I'm so tired of this, my child.'

'Luke,' she pleaded.

29

'Go to bed, Hannah,' he said, as if she could sleep when the sight of her mother had sheared a film from the surface of her eye. Hadn't she seen this before, in the middle of a night long ago, waking in her bed or crib, watching alone or with the others, all the still fearful heads poised on the pillows, eyes wide open in the owl dark? Had that been her mama lying on the floor? Was that her papa swinging the lamp to make awful shadows on the wall? But the morning changed everything back again and what had been unable to survive in the bright daylight seemed impossible. The floor had been full of table legs, crumbs, toenails, dust balls, cats and sunlight.

Hannah turned to watch them go. Her father's nightshirt was stained, the edge ravelled. He didn't talk to her any more. They had moved on and it was she who didn't belong any more, she who was bereft, she who wasn't finished, and yet they were making her leave. Her part wasn't over and they were changing the rules.

She blew out the lamp, and looked into the night, which was bluish and smooth. She stood helplessly at the window, unable to beckon, afraid if it wasn't Matthew it might be someone else. It was difficult to remember him, as if she were a horse after a hard run, washed and scraped of sweat and no longer feeling the weight of the rider on her back. From the stains on the hem of her dress came a tart crushed smell.

Enveloping her was a silence she felt was both indifferent and profound, a place that denied its secrets while beckoning her. Out there was the green garden, the roost of chickens, old bottles, some new kittens, an airing of laundry on the line. She'd seen them all when she had left in the evening slant of the sun, the long shadows, the dim dusty gathering of hens in the coop, the reflections from shiny coils of wire, and in the warm yellow breath of air a loft of sheets beginning to lie down. Now night had furnished the yards with a darkness and a silence. Hannah wrung her hands. There was nothing she could do. She stood at the edge of her life, love and death on each shoulder, whispering in her ears, drearily, their half truths, while out there, in the other side of night, was another truth.

Behind, in the bedroom, she heard the muffled sullen consolation, almost an argument, but a practised one. She couldn't hear the words, but they had a smooth rehearsed quality. So complete was the circle of words, it began to sound like a song. She pictured their dance of shadowy gestures swaying on the wall, and imagined a ritual unique to her and Matthew, something they might do alone, touching fingers and lips, speaking comfort in their special language.

'Matthew,' she whispered into the night, but he had gone.

The next day Adele received a telegram informing her of her mother's death. In the kitchen, in the broad spill of afternoon heat and haze, the children called to each other as if they had seen a green tornado sky, and they cowered in corners.

Hannah came home for lunch. Adele handed her the telegram with its peculiar typed letters. It was just like the dream: 'Mother died falling into the well.' It was the dream, only it wasn't supposed to have been her. Hannah took the heavy family Bible from the shelf and opened it to the inside cover where the small sketch of her grandmother shuffled among other dignitaries. Holding it up she looked for the resemblance, for what would have made Adele confuse the two of them.

'Did she have red hair like me, Mama?' It was the first thing she'd ever been told.

'Her hair was still red, red like yours.' In her mind she saw wet matted hair, head scraped, bumped, banged on the side of the well, scum, bugs. Quenched sizzling red hair.

Vindicated by truth, Adele momentarily rejoiced in its terrible perfect beauty. She called the children, who emerged and clung to her resurrection. Joel wept excitedly, caught up in the drama.

'Stop being such a goose.' Hannah pushed him aside. 'You didn't even know her!'

He stared at her. 'Doesn't matter, does it, Mama?' Reaching back for her.

But Adele disengaged the children one by one and propped them up in front of her: Aaron the next biggest to Hannah, Sally next, then Joel. 'Aaron, the stove; Sally, the chickens; Joel, the woodpile. Hannah, something is burning,' she said with a pointed gesture towards the pots. There wasn't time to do everything. She'd have to make time later. 'Hannah, go tell your father, tell him I'm taking some money, then you go to your boss and tell him you've got to stay home for a few days because of a death in the family. Let's see what else ...'

When Hannah returned, the bags were packed and waiting by the door. Adele stood in front of her bedroom mirror as she pinned on her hat. Hannah had seen it and the black dress before. On top of the blankets in the trunk were her black purse and gloves.

'Don't you think it's peculiar, Mama, I mean your dream last night and now this. I think it's very peculiar. A red-headed person in your dream and you thought it was me, but it was Grandma. Do you wonder what time it happened, I mean if it was at the same moment as your dream? Do you really have the power to dream things and make them happen, Mama?'

'What, Hannah, what are you saying? I'm sorry, I wasn't listening.' She gave a last adjustment to the veil that hid her face. Walking quickly by, she started to pat Hannah on the head, but couldn't bring herself to touch her hair. Instead she took her shoulders and kissed her through the veil, a dry textured kiss. Hannah's stomach was cold. She watched her mother call the others together and admonish them one more time. Then, taking Aaron with her to carry the bag, she was gone. Sally and Joel stood on each side of Hannah. They watched until their mother was extinguished by distance. Joel said, 'I still see her don't I, isn't that her, just there, yes I'm sure it is, it's still Mama. She's so tiny.' He pulled Hannah's skirt around himself.

'You heard what Mama said.' She didn't want his small sticky fingers on her arm, but she let him sit next to her on the back steps. Sally went to play with the kittens, who rolled in the grass and struck at the string she dangled between their paws. Hannah wondered how long her mother would be gone, how long she would have to be off work, why this had had to happen just now.

As long as the sun shone they drowsed and daydreamed. Hannah tried to imagine what it would be like if her mama never came back, if she suddenly became an orphan. If there was an accident at the shop and her father was killed. If they lost their house and, like the Parkers, had to live in a shack on the edge of town. If she had to take care of Aaron and Sally and Joel for years and years. If.... Just then she saw her father coming down the road. He had bowed legs, she noticed, startled, as if she'd seen him naked, compromised in some way. It made him look older or vulnerable like a child with rickets.

'Papa, you're early.' She got up quickly. 'Nothing's ready.' She was afraid he'd be disappointed in her.

The children went to bed after supper, even before dusk neutralized the shadows of the posts lying on the porch.

'I want you to go talk to the neighbour lady,' her father said.

'Why do I have to?'

'Go tell her what's happened. She'll be over here wanting to know, it's better if you just go now.'

'All right, all right.' All the time she needed for herself was being swallowed.

She thought she saw Matthew walking beside the abandoned Carter barn down where the road split, but it was only the Arn boy, who was about the same size but not the least like Matthew. She was disappointed, having expected him to come. Little wild flowers stretched and closed at her feet along the fence. Did she really want him to know everything, even things she hardly knew herself? Wary of toads in the grass, she walked in the middle of the road.

Despite the heat, which made the children sweat in their beds, Luke sat inside, his sock feet up on the table.

'Papa! It's not cleaned up yet.' The supper dishes, crumbs, crusts, spills, crushed napkins, all remained strewn on the table top. Hannah sighed. As she was about to stack the plates, he spoke to her.

'Sit down, Hannah.' She looked at him. His voice was different in some way, though she couldn't figure out how. He took his feet down and tucked them, ankles crossed, under the chair.

'What is it?' Sitting heavily, she emptied her hands and opened them on the table, showing the white palms in a strange gesture of supplication. Her gaze drifted out the window like a long slow net. She saw Matthew in the net, but he swam through, laughing. 'What is it?' she repeated absently, placidly, looking through the percolation of the sunset.

'It's very likely that your grandma's death was not an accident,' he said in a thin, tight-rope voice. 'Your mother won't want to tell you, but I think you should know things like this. You're not a child any more.'

Hannah glanced at him. He was knotting his fingers uneasily. She looked back out the window. 'In fact, you do know what it's like. Old man Harper who …'

'Mr Harper! He killed himself.'

'That's right.' He looked over at her. She bit her lip. He waited, watching the lights flit and fan over her face. 'Adele's mother was confused in the last few years. There is no doubt in my mind that she stumbled into that well on purpose.'

Hannah closed her eyes to try to see her grandmother again. She was no longer sad. Done in a stupid messy way, it was a glorious gesture. Her passion, her integrity, her will! It was hard to imagine that small tidy person pressed in black and lace rising so successfully, up from plush cushions, skeins of wool, breathlessness and bony eyeglasses. Up out of a world she must have known so well. Maybe too well, without challenge or excitement. Hannah decided she admired the spirit of her grandmother. Was it what she herself felt in her blood, this dissatisfaction? She was tired of looking at the same people, doing the same things. Only her daydreams delighted her now.

'Is that what's wrong with Mama?'

'There is nothing wrong with your mama.'

Hannah left the dishes in the sink and went to bed, leaving her father smoking. He had put his feet back up on the table. The stove went out and the breeze wandering around the rooms was scented with the sultry night instead of wood ash and smoke. She sat on the edge of the bed, a thin coverlet over her knees, chewing on her nails. When she fell asleep, thoughts flew around the top of her brain, out of control. She curled into a ball.

In the morning she sat at the table. She hadn't started chores, nor had she made the children do theirs. Opening the back door, she sent them down to the creek. She didn't warn them about the danger of falling in, or tell them that they had to be back for dinner. Joel ran back from halfway down the road just to stand silently in front of her, just in case there were instructions.

'Well, what is it?'

'Nothing,' he said, dipping his head.

'Go on then, I mean it. Scoot!'

When they had gone for sure, Hannah set a place for herself at the table. She pulled the loaf of bread towards her from the centre, and got the honey pot, the jam jar, some leftover porridge in a bowl, a cold meat plate and a strawberry pie. Making a hot fire in the stove with kindling, she heated the kettle and brewed tea. Hunger always surprised her when she woke in the morning. She hadn't eaten much since supper at Matthew's. She sat with her hands spread protectively around the food, then began to eat. Ravenously beginning with bread and honey, she slowly, deliberately moved through the porridge to the meat and finally to the pie, plucking strawberries from inside the crust. Her mind was blank.

Mrs Forbes appeared at the window, pointed to the door, and came in. 'Poor child,' she said, plunking a covered basket on the table. 'I thought you might need some help with the cooking. Here's a casserole, a pudding and some cookies. Not a great deal, but it'll help a little. I'm sure you're busy with the children.' She looked around. 'Where are they?'

'Oh, out fishing, Mrs Forbes.'

'By themselves! Well, I suppose it's all right, the boy's pretty big now, I suppose, hmmm.'

'Big enough to be going to work in a couple of years.'

'Oh my, isn't that something. Well, tell your mother I came by. When will she be back, by the way, have you heard yet?'

'No, not yet, but I expect we will today. Thank you for the supper. Papa will be so pleased it's not my cooking again.'

Alone again, she peeked under the cloth, stuck her finger in the pudding and took a cookie. A spice cookie and a cup of tea in the plain brown peace of an empty kitchen.

When Matthew finally came by the house, she was sweeping. She said, 'Oh, I thought you'd already gone.'

'Gone? Gone where? What are you talking about? What's happened?'

She told him everything while she swept the dust and crumbs between his feet. Before she had finished he took her shoulders and, smoothing back the fiery wisps of hair, kissed her face, on which he tasted the faint tang of jam. Her shoulders boned up into his hands. She smelled warm and a little dirty. There was nothing he could do at the moment, she needed room and the right balance of sunshine and shadow. She forgot to ask if he had stayed that night and had seen her standing by the window. He took her hand and idly patted a small scarred hollow on her wrist. She never told him what had made the mark.

Adele didn't return for another few days. Hannah hadn't expected any change in her mother. Adele went immediately to her room. Aaron put the suitcases on the bed. Hannah made the little ones wait. 'Mama wants to change her clothes first,' but they broke free and dashed into her black skirts, 'Mama, Mama!'

There seemed to be nothing she could tell her daughter, though her feelings were so strong they made her stagger. She wondered at this. Why was she being assaulted by all these things, why was she being pierced and burned, why was she all alone? There was small comfort in the pure bodies of her children. She touched them, their hair tousled and dried by summer, their skin soft and perfect, but the house seemed strange when she wandered around in the dark of night. Someone had moved the table, and the chairs angled out in new directions. The pump handle rested lower. Pots were too close to the edge of the stove. She went and stood over the beds of her children, listening to their breath overlapping one on another like the game they played, hand over hand: don't pull your hand out until it's on the bottom, then quick as you can to the top. She adjusted the covers.

Hannah was asleep too, listless, limp, deeply asleep as if making up for something. Yes, Adele thought, I'm home now, you can sleep the child's sleep again. Her face was pale and ghostly, her hair lay like an aura, and she had to remind herself that it was red.

Luke called gently into the night, 'Come back to bed now, come back.'

'What did you bring us, Mama, what did Grandma send us this time?' Crowding around her knees, darting little hands into the paper in the box, withdrawing just as quickly – snakes! What did it matter what she gave each of them. Perhaps they would treasure something, take care of it, create a keepsake and a memory where none existed. 'Grandma sent her love to each of you.' Liar, thought Hannah. She took the cameo and examined it, the chiselled profile. 'Is this Grandma?' Adele smiled indulgently at her. Well, it could be, thought Hannah, why not, it had to be someone. 'Is that all?' said Sally, whose drawer was already full.

Just Adele and Hannah were left in the kitchen. 'Mama, you seem very tired.'

'Yes, I am.' She looked at her daughter. It was easy to see resemblances, that small tilted smile, swimming in her blood.

'Do I remind you of her now more than ever?'

'Yes, you do.' Cold and a tightness in her back made her sit upright. She thought about becoming helpless, an infant in the hands of her own daughter. What would this child do to her?

'Everything was fine, Mama, while you were gone.' Hannah reached over and touched her mother's hand. 'Everything was just the same. We missed you. There was lots of work to do, but I didn't forget too much. We missed you. Don't worry, it's all right now.'

For a few days the children returned to her often, reassuring themselves, rubbing against her, leaning into her stomach with their faces upturned.

Hannah went back to work the second day. Molly sped by with condolences from the Brede family. She seemed uncomfortable talking intimately across the counter in the store. Hannah tried to put her at ease. Molly hesitated and rounded the end of the counter. 'Hannah, do you, do you and Matt, you know...?' She waited expectantly.

Hannah listened, but wasn't sure what she was saying. 'You know what?'

'You know, do you and Matt, when you're alone, do you...?' She mouthed the word. Hannah watched her eyes, which were shining, and so she missed it. Molly did it again: KISS. Hannah pulled back and looked at the floor.

'I knew it!'

'Why?' Hannah asked, startled. 'What does that mean?'

'Oh nothing, nothing, it doesn't mean a thing.'

Ho ho, she thought, it does too, it means everything. But when Matthew caught her behind the store at closing time, with his laugh and his joy, and kissed her in daylight, she wondered if he really did mean it. She held him at arm's length. Over her shoulder she could feel Molly, her words thrumming like mosquitoes. 'Matthew, what are you going to do with me?'

'Do with you?' Not comprehending.

'Yes,' she said, poking her chin out at him.

He stepped back. 'Well, nothing, I'm not going to do anything to you.'

'Not *to* me, *with* me, what are we going to do with each other?'

Under a deep breath, Matthew took his hands back and put them in his pockets. 'This isn't the right time to talk about it.' His voice was fuzzy.

'Why not, is it too bright?' she said, her hand pushing back the broad lazy late afternoon sun.

'Don't.' He was bristling now, and for a moment she was frightened. Matthew turned to face the wall, spinning away before he did something from his blind spot. Through his fist he continued. 'Do I seem like a person who doesn't know what he is doing? Do you think this is a game?'

'No.' Painfully her lips lingered after the word. She pressed them shut behind curled fingers. 'I didn't mean ...' but she didn't know what she'd meant. A shadow was sniffing at her shoes with the snout of a larger darkness, a black river that could burrow between them.

'Have I done anything to, to … to mislead you, have I …?'

'Please, Matthew,' his name dust in her mouth, 'I didn't mean anything, I didn't mean to …' It was awful the way her hands shivered in the air. She was so unexpected and intense in her feelings, in a shame she hardly recognized, that she hurt all over. She had no idea it mattered so much that he not leave her.

The alley was a flood of bleached dust and sunlight. He said he was sorry, but she felt he was still on the other side of a great expanse from her. He said it was the wrong time, the wrong place to talk about this. He didn't tell her about the distances, about needing more room.

She wanted to ask, When, when will it be time? but he didn't look at her. She thought, It doesn't matter any more. What made me ask such a stupid question? Who cares, anyway? Not I. Not I for sure. She turned and began to run.

He couldn't call her back or follow her or answer the questions she asked or answer his own. He did want to lie down with her in the dark. She knew it, that much she did know. He had felt her stir inside his hands, seen her skin flush. Her body was opening to him even if her mind wasn't.

For the next few days she peeked warily around corners to and from work, blended in with the morning and evening crowds, and kept busy, but still he caught her at the crossroads: 'How long are you going to keep this up?' And on the hollow wooden sidewalk: 'Hannah, don't you think this has gone on long enough!' On the highway: 'I have apologized, what else do you want? Enough is enough!' Just outside the gate, grabbing her arm because she wouldn't wait: 'You know what they say, the course of true love never runs smooth,' harshly, letting go before she wrenched free.

It was so hot the pale sun hid behind a damp spongy haze in the sky. There had been rain every night, slow, steady and soft, rain transforming to thick mist in the morning, diffusing the dawn. The walls of rooms sweated, laundry hung limply behind the stove for days. Bed sheets were cold and soggy even after being left open to air all day. Bread turned mouldy. Joel broke a glass because it was too slippery to hold. No one was hungry. The children put their elbows on the table and couldn't lift them off. Sally cried and complained of stomach ache. Finally Adele just sat. Between her legs, her skirt hung down laden with sodden vegetables she was trying to rescue. Mud marred the floor. Luke walked through it in sock feet. In the cracked mirror Hannah noticed that the high humidity had made her hair twirl about her face in tight little curls, and her skin glowed.

Puddles couldn't evaporate or soak into the saturated ground. Wagons stopped, mired on the road while horses tried to claw through the mud. Cows stood knee-deep in wet grass, and when they walked they looked as if they were swimming.

Hannah continued to sneak around to avoid Matthew, but then, when she didn't see him, she went to his house. 'He's not here,' Molly told her in the front hall. He'd gone to visit a relative in the next county. Hadn't he told her?

'No! Of course not .... It's all your fault, too!' she said, swinging the door wide open, throwing Molly's protest back in her face.

This was unbelievable. She had thought ... well, she hadn't even had to think. He'd never done anything like this before. It wasn't like him. There was no reason for him to take off without letting her know. He mustn't have had a single thought about her. All the times he'd stopped her with whirs and whispers. Even the last time, he was only speaking roughly because he was upset, because he did care despite everything. She had been counting on it. He must still care for her, he must.

She ran until she was out of breath. The air was strangling. Soggy clouds squatted in the hollows. She leaned on a pasture fence, getting her elbows wet on the rail. Her shoes were soaked and slimy with mud. No one who didn't have to be was outside. A slow plod of oxen passed behind her. The creak and groan of the cart taking its time seemed to calm her. After it passed by she looked over her shoulder and, standing up, saw it begin to sway from side to side in rhythm with the load of hay. 'Dum-dum, dum-dum,' a small appropriate song. Drops of water flicked off her swinging hair.

'Go home, Hannah, you're soaking wet. Go home,' Mrs Bilton called across the backs of her wet cows. The cows thought she was talking to them and began to move towards the barn.

Matthew hitched a ride out at night, and since he wasn't getting any sleep in the back of the wagon, when old Samuel asked him to drive for a while he took the reins. They stopped at the next village inn, where they persuaded a night clerk to get them each a draft of ale and a bucket of water for the horse. Old Samuel drooped his moustache in the foam in his mug, then wiped it with his tongue, one side then the other. He mumbled. Matthew nodded, hoping nothing the man said required an answer. The flickering lantern light was hypnotizing.

'Better not let the dew settle on Apollo,' Samuel said, tucking the empty mug in by the door. 'Come on then,' climbing in behind the seat where a heap of old horse blankets cushioned him from the buck of the wagon. Samuel snored and snarled, and at times Matthew heard a whinnying sound. In the strange light that pooled down from the lantern, first on the back of the horse, then on the road, he saw Apollo turn one ear around listening to its master.

His mind should have been full, there was so much to think about. Instead, the lush warm landscape of night spread like honey inside his head, and his body found a comfortable tripod position propped up by the edge of the darkness. He turned the lantern lower and lower until the pale glow of moonlight rivalled it. Neither was strong enough to show shapes. The old horse travelled this route twice a week, and knew every rut and wrinkle, each stone grinding under his hooves. Fences stalked along beside the road. Farther out, a blur of hills and trees, a horizon of infinite variety, soft, close, deep. Friendly. So much to think about and his head was empty.

Old Samuel slept until dawn. They switched places and Matthew fell asleep on the rotten horse blankets and did not awaken until they were in town.

He'd come to see his great-grandfather. Some silly notion he had, some memory of climbing up knees like woolly mountain peaks. The old man living to be a hundred, a thousand. The old stories were sunk in Matthew where he could feel them but couldn't remember the words, not the right ones. They might be what he needed. Up to now, perhaps, his life had been a necessary interruption in the grand schema, a time to learn and practise. Here he heard the old stories, saw them rise like flags and ride the horizon like magic horsemen. He felt like shouting, 'I know what I'm supposed to do, where I'm supposed to go!'

He walked through the town in the bright morning. Goodbye to snug harbours, the advantages and amenities. The boredom, small-mindedness. The arbitration. He could feel his life grating its teeth under his skin.

'He's in there.' His cousin pointed to the closed door and shrugged. 'Likes it that way.'

Matthew turned the knob. 'Is there anything I can take in to him?'

'Nah.'

He pushed the door open just enough and stepped into the sick-room. It wasn't what he'd expected. A violent stench, at first indecipher-able, separated into stale tobacco, urine, sour flesh, dried sweat, medicine, feces. The accumulation of life without air. He started to breathe through his mouth. At first he couldn't see anything in the drench of gloom, but gradually an oppressive jumble of dark furniture outlined itself against the walls. He shivered. He remembered a back porch cluttered with apples, kindling, and straw flowers; the woody edge of his great-grandfather's chin; stories scudding out from between his lips. Hot early afternoon sun. But in here it was cold and he couldn't find the old man. In the corner was a small black stove. A shuttered window let in a barely discernible pattern of light that lay corrugated on the floor in front of an old high-back rocker. The hunched, dirty husk of a man sat chewing the ragged fringe of a lap rug. 'May I fix this for you?' said Matthew, but he couldn't bring himself to touch it.

'Who?' said a voice he didn't recognize.

'It's Matthew,' he said hopefully.

'Who?' hooting into his velvet night.

'I just need directions, Great-Grandfather.'

'I don't have to apologize for anything!' a thunder using all his breath, requiring him to lean aggressively forward in the chair to catch it back. He was poised over the rug of striped light. The chair creaked threateningly. Wading through the fetid air, he got around in front and pushed the old man back into the chair. The sick smell enfolded him. On the floor at his feet was a puddle of drool, some of it on his boots. The face was gutted, spread like a fish. Cataracts slandered the surfaces of the eyes. Matthew remembered the bandits in those eyes, as icy blue as the mountain tops in stories. He touched one of the claw hands, the cracked shredded nails, paper skin silky like an old woman's. There had been bushes of bleached hair on the backs of his fingers. He had done rope tricks, knifed a bear, whittled rattlesnakes, birthed his own chil-dren. Now these hands struggled to hold on.

'Why did you go west, Great-Grandfather?'

'What!' Angrily.

'How did you say goodbye?'

The old man was crying or oozing.

'Tell me, tell me something.'

'Kak, kak,' he said, calling ducks and deer. Come out little birds, big animals, come out so I can kill you. I'm hungry, come out.

Faint seam lines in the skull, old maps and murders. Death's head shining like a tombstone. Matthew felt that peculiar dread of walking on the ground of the dead, remembering the time in the old graveyard when he had run over the mounds, testing the ability of his six-year-old legs to adapt to the rise and fall, and suddenly his mother had shouted, 'Stop! Don't run over the dead!' And he had stopped on the edge of the next hilly grave, his heart thripping, his stomach sucked up in his throat, a cold sent up out of the earth scuttling his amazing mortality. 'It's just not respectful,' his mother continued, but that wasn't it at all, he knew. She had forgotten. It was too awful. He knew that once upon a time a man had stepped on the raised mound of a grave and been pulled in.

Holding onto the dome of the old man's knee, Matthew stood up. It made him doubly tall to stand with his head in the rare cold thin air, looming over this shrivelled figure of the past. His height made him uneasy, but it was easier to stand than lie down, easier to run than walk, easier to go than stay.

'Perhaps you should never have come back, Great-Grandfather.'

Since they were alone, the rules were laid aside, the formalities, consolations. There was no one to exchange subdued knowing glances with. No one to pat on the shoulder, no one to remind him that a world existed outside, though he had come to recall another and had found this third world instead, timeless, suspended. Perhaps his great-grandfather had done all this on purpose, gathered around himself those things necessary for transition. Forgetfulness, separation, lack of desire, disinterest.

'Can you give me anything?' Matthew asked. 'Anything at all?' Despite the disappointment, the evident frailty, the faint edges, the betrayals to memory, despite the hopelessness, the raging complex of odours, the sullen cold, the voice that crackled, not like dry autumn leaves but with the strange condensed sound of fire, there was that firm shape of the ancient head and the places scattered all along it, marks on a map. He had walked ahead, and the footprints were still visible.

On the way home, Matthew remembered thinking, with wonder, He did nothing to make me feel sorry for him.

Hannah and Matthew sat facing each other.

'What do you want, Hannah?' He was looking into her eyes, calmly, gently.

Shyly she dropped her eyes and shrugged, her mouth in wry indecision, taking it lightly because she was thinking about right now, but he took his hands from hers and she felt as if her skin had been ripped off, as if the world were melting away beneath her. Shocked, she blurted, 'No, really, I don't know what I want, that's not a crime,' reaching for him, her fingers pleading on his thighs. 'I want to go with you, I really do. Please let me. Please.'

She was so close, warm, her hair burned his hands when he touched it. 'Please.' He loved the look of her head in his hands, the way they protected her, the tangle of damp curls at the back of her neck covering her ears, smoothing her forehead, her eyes, her cheeks. He would do anything to keep her safe and close. 'Of course, of course, I won't leave you behind.' How could she have imagined otherwise?

She felt the tear sliding down her cheek. How peculiar. She was trembling, desperate. If she stood she knew she would fall. Who am I, she wondered, this person in his hands? Why did she need his breath on her like this?

'Are you frightened?'

'No, I'm never frightened,' she said, forgetting the instant when, at the end of his voice, she would be dangling in a new element.

'You really do want to come with me, don't you?'

All around were the same rocks and trees, the same streets, same people. No matter how hard she tried she could see only things she had seen countless times before.

'Where?' Catching his eyes. Catching her breath.

'Can you keep a secret?'

'Yes,' she said, looking over his shoulder. 'I don't have much practice keeping secrets.' Why was everything so mysterious? As long as he let her in on it.

Anxiously, breathlessly, pausing in unlikely places, creating a strange sense of emphasis, he began to describe his ache. 'They call it the Garden of Eden on the posters. The West. There's room out there. I've never felt

43

there was enough room for me here. Sometimes I can't breathe.' He'd never said it out loud before. The words sounded leaden. In his mind they had been so beautiful. 'I want to do something all by myself.'

He's talking about me, too, Hannah assured herself. If I go with him something will happen to me.

'Out there is this huge space.' He held his hands up. 'You can do anything out there with no one watching you, no one.' His eyes narrowed. 'No one expecting you to do what they want.'

Back snug in his hands she said, 'Yes, yes.'

'I don't want to be safe, you see, I want more.'

She didn't know what wide open spaces were like, what cottonwood or sage or the mud of a dry riverbed smelled like, and yet a heady, thrilling odour filled her nose, intoxicating her.

'I feel old here, already old!'

Suddenly she was not afraid to milk the blood out of the veins in his hands.

'There are no lines, no boundaries. Out there you draw your own.'

'Someday.'

'It's not going to be someday, Hannah, I'm going next spring. Will you follow me?' At that moment he couldn't hear, wouldn't have been able to remember if she had answered him, didn't care, because he was drunk on dreaming. He couldn't focus up so close, could only feel her holding on to him.

Her life was going to start soon. Follow him? Of course she would. But she couldn't say it out loud just yet. He didn't wait. They had already collided. The chance to turn aside, to turn back, was past. They held each other, the collusion of their hands clasped between them.

Three

'What have you got of your own?' He wanted to make a list. Overhead, as thin as the paper in his hands, autumn leaves scritched and scraped on each other, then fell all around, small tongues of fire. 'Well, what have you got of your very own?'

She went home to look.

'Is there anything here mine?' she asked her father, who was chopping wood.

'What do you mean, yours?' He looked at her curiously.

'You know, like this dress is mine, right? Well, for instance, is my bed mine?' Hands on hips.

'While you need it.'

'But not mine so's I could take it away.'

'Take it away?' He stopped splitting a small log. 'You're wanting to take your bed somewhere else?'

'No, no, but what is mine?' Careful, Hannah, she thought.

'Nothing is yours, my girl, nothing.' He was serious now. Putting the head of the axe on the chopping block, he rocked it back and forth. He had started with nothing but a knapsack, blanket roll, good boots and a comb. Now he could walk around his own house, uncover his wife when he wanted to, pinch his own children. His axe, his home, his gun, his wife, his children, his dog. Hannah belonged to him. That was the way it was.

He was becoming far-sighted in his middle age. He could bring the parameters of his world into focus, but the ground beneath his feet blurred. It made him uncomfortable to see what was there. How the fence guarded his ownership, but let the grass run under it. Along the road the picket fence was a sharp gauntlet of drawn swords. Children knocked sticks, clack-clack-clack, along its boards. Most of the time he didn't mind. It meant they were outside, going by. Besides, he had done that when he was a kid. Fences, bottles, stones. Touching, kicking, batting, moving and changing what he could reach of the world.

Closer, in the froth of weed, he could barely see his own shoes. Daughter, touch my feet, he wanted to say. Bend down here. Put your

45

knees on the ground and slowly, carefully lean forward. Place your hands, one on each boot and bend over. Put your face close and smell the leather and the mud, now your cheeks, your lips, kiss them, lick them. Let your hair fall free. His heart beat wildly. Tension like St. Elmo's fire pulsed through the axe handle and electrocuted the bladed head. Overflowing with peculiar energy, he felt as strong and bold as a king. Something shone in his eyes, a blast of sun thrown up from wire or glass, and he lost his thoughts.

'Nothing at all? Nothing belongs to me?'

'Ask your mama if she's started a hope chest for you.'

'But I would know that!'

'Don't you think there are any secrets in this house?' he said, hoping this was one, then wondering if it really was, and if he didn't know about this one, what others there were. His house indeed!

She ran to the house.

'Mama, do you have things put away for me, for when I get married?'

Adele was sitting quietly at the table. Her eyes were uneven as if she were looking at something different with each eye.

'Did you hear me, Mama?'

Adele could smell the salt sweat from her daughter's skin, the autumn sun on her skin and folded in the wrinkles of her jumper.

'Such a bright child.' So shining, impatient.

Child! Hannah wailed inside, I'm not a child. But she hesitated to shout, Woman! I am nothing like you, Mama, and I never will be.

'Mama …' She repeated the question.

Adele nodded sadly. 'Yes, I know, I don't have much myself. You were never interested in handiwork. You're supposed to do it yourself, you know, the embroidery, table linen, towelling.'

'Did you do it, Mama?'

'Some, when I was your age, I did some thread work. It's a nice quiet thing to do. I made the dresser scarf in there.' Pale small puckered flowers in a lattice of grey-green, rose, blue, lavender. She leaned to open a drawer in the sideboard. 'You've seen these things,' taking out a few hand towels, napkins, tea towels. She shook each out, then refolded it, reversing the crease lines. 'And you've seen the handkerchiefs,' gesturing to the bedroom, but too tired to pursue. She'd had a lot of that since her mother died, just too tired to go beyond necessities, which were plenty, anyway. Thank God for Hannah's energy, she thought, as if working not only agreed with but invigorated her. A slippery child, parts of her old, knowing, able to arrange things in her favour, parts of her baby-selfish, innocent of the lessons of life, stumbling. Like a wind, gusting, blowing, eddying in whorls, then, dying down, thickening heavily with a close humid smell, she could become irritable and rebellious. 'Don't, you'll stick to me,' she would warn the little ones.

One night she'd seen Hannah bathing herself in her room. She couldn't remember how long it had been since she'd seen her daughter's body. It had been the body of a child. A draft pushed aside the curtain to Hannah's room. A single candle burned on the small box dresser at her side. The window curtain, worn thin like gauze, was closed but let in a creamy soft light that gathered on her skin. Baby's skin. Reaching up she let down her hair, which fell in a shower, shuffling sunlight in its waves and curls, begging for a hand to touch it. She remembered Hannah at her knee, and vigorously brushing her hair into a swarm on her lap, thinking about how she had brushed her own mother's hair, how it had been a treat, an honour, her own hair thin and colourless, best drawn back from her face, not calling attention to itself. Once her mother had stood behind her, chin on top of her head, and let her hair fall around Adele's face. She had been so shocked; it hadn't suited her at all; her face had looked odd. She felt better afterwards in her centre part and tight braids. Luke liked her to undo the braids and spread her crinkly hair on the pillow. But it was not alive like Hannah's or her mother's. Hannah leaned forward to splash water on her face. Her slip fell loose to her hips. When she raised a towel to dry her face Adele could see the curve of her breast. She felt extraordinarily peaceful. I did that, she thought. My child, she's growing up, she'll help me now. She does help me now. She was strong, look at her back, the small hard stepping stones of her spine, the span of her wings. Petals of muscles that barely cover the breadth of ribs. Her movements are not economical. She must be thinking about something else, singing, humming bits of tunes. She was happy, Adele thought, absorbed and happy. She sleeps well, eats well, gives me all these signs of her well-being. The candle flickered. Hannah was almost finished then, prowling around her room, setting things just so, throwing the wash water out the window, checking her bed for spiders. Adele saw the slight tensing, the shiver as night air stroked her daughter's damp skin.

'What do you want, Hannah?' she said, leaning placidly forward, her elbows on the table, folding her arms protectively over the labour of her hands.

'I want to know if anything here is mine.'

'Everything is yours, everything here belongs to all of us.'

Of course this wasn't true, but she didn't know how to ask. 'Don't you know what I mean, Mama? I mean, what would I take with me to my own home?'

'Your own home!' This was her own home.

Hannah sat down heavily, hopelessly. She reached inside the nest her mother had made around the tea towels and napkins, pulled the linens out and pretended to admire them. Then she found that she really did. Some of the stitches could barely be seen. Steady and even, the threads slipped in and out, never disturbing the material. Her mother was right, this was nothing she would have the patience or the interest to do.

She returned to Matthew. 'What kind of stuff do you mean?'

'Money, we need money.'

'They take my money.'

'What do you mean?'

'They take my money. All the money goes into the purse. Everybody's.'

'And you don't get to keep any for yourself?'

'If I want something I ask Mama for the money.'

'Well, start asking.'

Matthew thought he had it all figured out. He would not involve Hannah until the end, until it seemed inevitable, and people started asking questions. Continuing in school permitted him time to plan and daydream, because he saw less and less of a connection between what he was studying and what he needed to know. He found pamphlets on survival, booklets of suggestions for homesteaders. Personal recollections, adventures, the diary of a trapper. Broad sheets of expenses. Costs. Handbills on steamboats. The advantages of rail travel. Sights and sounds. Overland routes, the Santa Fe Trail. 'Big Muddy.' Indian Sign Language. Buffalo. Buckshot. Covered wagons. Cavalry. Gamma grass. Sawyers. Prairie dogs. Rattlesnakes. Jackrabbits. Pronghorns. Sloughs. Chinooks. Tornadoes. Kansas Hotwinds. Soddy. Buffalo chips. The names on the land, the territory of heroic adventure. Words like plums in his mouth, dark, mysterious, round. He looked at one side, then another and another, turning the temptation this way and that.

His stomach turned over in a terrible gulp of fear. He wouldn't be able to go. Something would happen. Someone would stop him. His own fear would stop him. What the hell did he know about oxen and tornadoes, snakebite or bloated rivers? What do I know about anything! Oh Hannah, I need you. You know about me. In his daydreams she was always there beside him, silently, lovingly, or if not at his side then she stood on the hill in the open door of his house. Or she would stop him! In some untenable betrayal she would turn her back and let the snake strike. He couldn't understand where these thoughts came from.

After school he hustled jobs wherever he could. Then when his studies began to suffer, he stayed up late and, yawning, read the lessons in bed. The house was so quiet with Molly gone. They had all gone to the station with her, wishing her well, stacking and rearranging her trunks, hatboxes, baskets. 'That one is lunch, don't let the porter take it with the others.' She was beautiful. Everything was plastered down, curls screwed onto her cheeks, ribbons tied and sewn flat, yet she rustled defiantly inside the dark blue dress and looked like a grown-up lady for the first time. She talked differently, too. 'All part of the new musical Molly,' she said. 'You won't laugh at me any more.' That wasn't why, though. Matthew had great faith in her. Faith in all of them. The belief that they could do whatever they put their minds to. Molly hid from nothing. She felt marvellous, expansive, forgiving. Loving her mama and her papa. 'Here's a kiss for you … and here's two for you … Matthew, where are you? Come and get your kisses. Where are my gloves?' The filthy engine started up and a down-draft dumped soot on them. Whining, winding up. 'Goodbye, Mama, goodbye, Papa, goodbye, Matthew. Goodbye!' To my old life.

The ache in Matthew. Left behind. It's not your turn yet. All his life. Wait. You're not big enough, old enough, clever enough. Wait. Wait till next year, Matthew. You can do that like Mama's big boy. My turn next. Something so spectacular! Beat this, Molly! Sorry, Mama, but you said it was my turn.

Molly waved from inside. She had a good window seat, but the window wouldn't go down or up. Pressing herself to the glass, she made faces. They were supposed to be funny. Harris checked once more to be sure the baggage was in the boxcar. Una took Matthew's arm and waved softly but bravely, whispering to him. The noise of the train overrode the words but not the intimacy of her slender grip in the crook of her arm. White smoke: farewell! Beneath their feet the platform rumbled. The train jerked around a bend and was gone. Lingering noise rolled behind in a wake.

Harris walked on one side of his son, Una on the other. They started talking about Molly as soon as they could hear the sound of their own voices again. Their darling spirited Molly. Her enthusiasm had been catching, everyone said so. Barring the unforeseen, she would do well, attracting the right people and giving all she could. Everyone loved Molly.

Matthew felt as if he were eavesdropping, not that they said much he didn't know about. It was their tone, a quality of intimacy, the posture of confidants. The air wafted across Matthew's skin as they turned and talked and nodded. There were no demands on him. Strangely, he was being supported between them, on the power of their words, the heat from their bodies. Ghostly and immaterial, he was surprised how easily he had disappeared.

Would it be the same when he was gone, would they clutch each other all the closer for his absence, for the shrinking space between them?

Molly continued to consume their thoughts and conversation. They waited for her first letter with impatience and anticipation. She wrote that no one sat next to her until the train had pulled out of town. Her second, anxiously. Her third, in an atmosphere of gathering calm. Every phrase, every word savoured, deciphered, looked under and behind, lines read between, analysed. Over teacups with friends, at the front gate, in front of the fire. Then there were no more letters for several weeks. Just when Una was about to board the next train, a small, scented note arrived telling how busy she was, how wonderful were the boys, girls, classes, professors. A dream come true. 'Does she miss us, Mama?' Matthew asked innocently. Will I? he thought.

He got used to her not being there. All the things that had hidden behind her quickly filled the obvious space that had gaped open when she was first gone: the chair she sat in to play the violin, her place at the table.

Letting the book fall forward on his chest Matthew started to daydream again, but in no time at all he was asleep. In the middle of the night his mother checked on his sleep. He had left the lamp on again. He was not quite the same boy this year, but she didn't exactly know what was different. He was purposeful but secretive. He might wake up now if she pushed back the lock of hair from his face or pulled the covers up over his shoulder. He might wake up and accuse her. He was frightened when he woke suddenly. She used to have to hold him tight in her arms to keep him from crashing off the bed, or hurting her without knowing he was doing it. His face would become so distorted, plump, swollen with sleep, unable to fit the terror coming out of him. She remembered. And now he filled the bed from head to foot, her tall thin boy who used to fit in a picnic basket, nestled under the gingham cloth, flap of the top down to keep the sun out. Dogs sniffing curiously at the strange smell in the familiar container. Children sneaking a peek. What a beautiful baby. Sometimes she could not bear it. His beauty stole her breath and she would lean over and suck up the air he exhaled. She would lick the drool from his chin. It sustained her. She would uncover him when she was all alone and look at his penis. She put out the lamp and crept back through the quiet empty house without touching him.

A first light frost clutched the thin hollow stalks of grass, but it slid into the ground in the break of early sun before anyone saw it. Small brown spots blemished the leaves. In another month hard frost would stripe the trees and shrivel the hardiest weeds down to their roots. Wagon wheels crunched in the ruts. Ice slid into the pail and the crust had to be broken with a small axe. Windows were closed, heavy drapes put up and fires fed until the boards shrank in the floors.

Hannah loved having a secret, as did Matthew. They met under a chandelier of icicles. No one knew of their plan.

'Have you started to ask for your money yet?'

'I find it hard to do that. If I ask for some, Mum says, What for? And then, if I say such and such, she'd expect me to come home and show her. What am I supposed to do?

'I don't know. Ask for a raise and don't tell anyone.' He held her gloved hand conspiratorially. 'I'm keeping all mine. In a new sock in my top drawer. I lock the dresser now. No one's noticed. I've got all the stuff in there, too.'

His secret life in a locked drawer, the one Una was picking at with a hairpin. She looked over her shoulder, glanced out the window, listened for footfall. The sun was wrong. She could see little of the dark lock. Her fingers trembled. Finally it yielded.

She found a jumble of paper and a lumpy sock. In the sock was money, quite a bit. Lifting the papers she shuffled them in her hands. Almost dropping one she placed them nervously on the edge of the bureau. A breeze suddenly came through the crack in the window, twitching the pages. What in the world was all this? She'd never seen these things in her house before. Where did they come from? She picked up a pamphlet and began to leaf through it. The paper, sharp like a blade, cut her finger. She dropped it on the floor, where it shuddered in the undercurrent of draught. She listened, but no other sound followed. Weakly she picked up the pamphlet and threw it back in the drawer. She couldn't remember what order his things had been in, and piled the rest as they were. Why did he have these? Her stomach was upside-down. When she closed the drawer she held onto the top of the dresser to steady herself. Her head was spinning. Why? Why these, but more to the point, why had he hidden them? And the money. He'd never had to hide money from them.

'What are you finding out?' Hannah asked, but she felt a great emptiness, the kind that happened when her ears were full of water or while she swam under the surface, wondering at the faint roar, the sound of her own brain. Then with a soft pop, as if there were small doors made of petals in her ears, she began to take soundings off irregular surfaces, the bark of trees, the hollows in hills, weathered cracks in rocks. Matthew was talking over all this, his words dancing tiptoe on top in the cold air. All she heard was his excitement. What was it going to be like there? her soul was asking, yearning, having been chilled in the early morning. She needed words to break through the chain of her unease.

'Open and wide, the sun coming down without a thing in its way, land stretching farther than you can see, a land that's alive.' Hannah crept forward to be under his protection. New to these dreams, she glistened in anticipation and ignorance. She wouldn't admit feeling afraid, though fear was moving closer now as winter approached. All her emotions were growing stronger, like tides and quaking pulses she couldn't control.

Matthew had another picture in his mind. Inside the endless land overgrown with grass was his nest. In the very middle, the sun shining right over his head, was Matthew arranging for rain, making his own way, making things happen, the prime mover. The same boy who could not imagine life outside himself, who sat in the middle of his toys, ordering them, who made a tree house to hold his daydreams. He would go to the virgin land of his imagination and find ground waiting to be turned, opening itself, rolling waves of soil aside the furrow, the wake of earth broken by sun and frost, readied by rain, the earth waiting for him to realize it. It was promised him, right there in the pamphlet, it said so. Doubt was such a puny thing he could barely feel it.

Hannah listened to his every word. Surely she could hear his thoughts as well, see them in his eyes, his face. His intention would be visible in his face the rest of his life. He held her hand between his, but it wasn't enough. Pulling her forward, he fitted her between his legs and put his arms over her until she disappeared and became a warmth inside him. Without shape, without name, she was his, penned in the corral of his mind.

Una wasn't used to mysteries. Those small bits she kept hidden she didn't call mysteries but things in protective custody, things better left alone, best not known. But when she could hold back no longer, she consulted Harris, then confronted Matthew with his locked drawer, shaking him awake one morning, closing the window that let snow in a tiny drift on the floor, wrenching back the curtains. The bright hard day approved of her. She gave the drawer one more tug to be sure it was still locked.

'Have I made a mistake? Was it an accident?'

'Huh?'

'What are you hiding in there? Why are you hiding things from us, from me? I'm your mother!'

'What are you talking about?' Sleep talking. 'What's wrong, Mother?' Was something wrong with her? Was she having a spell, as Hannah's mother had?

'What is this!' Triumphantly tackling the drawer, rattling it back and forth, from side to side. 'Why is this locked in my house?'

Matthew sat up in bed suddenly. He was naked. She hadn't known he slept this way. 'That's my drawer,' he said. 'That is mine.' His voice was level and dull with contempt.

'Look at me, Matthew.' She sat on the bed in front of him. She thought to soften him in this way, with her weight beside his, her hand on his arm.

'Don't.' He pulled back, reaching for a flannel shirt hanging on the bed post behind him, gathering the blankets and quilts up to his chest. 'Are you sure you want to know?' And maybe she didn't, not yet, not so soon. 'What have you done, Mother, have you looked in there?'

'Yes.'

'And what did you see?'

Is this my boy, she was thinking, talking to me like this? What had happened to his voice, where was the arresting little quiver in his throat that betrayed him when he was caught doing something he shouldn't?

She stood. 'How dare you talk to me in that tone of voice. Your father will …' But she was unsure of this. As if a feather were stroking her cheek, she wondered if this time Harris would, indeed. This time might be different, a camaraderie of men, an understanding. Harris might say, Oh yes, I thought about going west once. I wanted to and couldn't. It's like you're going for me, son, taking on that old dream. Had she ever heard him talk about it? Long long ago, when they both talked about their dreams. If her husband had ever had the same dream, he would never understand how she felt about the betrayal contained in Matthew's secrecy. Her gaze wandered away from Matthew's face. When she looked back it seemed he had been waiting. What was it he had asked? She touched the dresser nervously. 'I found money.' It made her angry all over again. 'Why do you feel you have to hide money? None of us had ever touched your … your …'

'My what? That's the point. I've never had money or –'

'You've never needed money in this house.' They both stopped. She left it in the air.

'I've worked for every penny in there.'

'Why do you need money now?'

'If you looked at the other things in there, then you know what I have in my mind.'

'But why?'

'What do you know, Mother? What do you know of me?'

'I know you better than anyone else.'

'Now. What do you know of me now, today?'

'I know you better than you do yourself.' Coming closer as she always had, as was her habit.

'You know nothing!' Proudly.

His life was all in front of him. He was watching this happen from a great distance. This wasn't important. His mother looked very small. Old. There were fine wrinkles on her face. In the winter light they filled with hard shadows. Her words were a blur. She'd said them once too often. This time he couldn't hear.

Snow had melted into a puddle on the floor. He was suddenly chilled through and began to shiver violently.

'Put your shirt on and come downstairs to the stove.' She wondered why she had taken it so seriously. He hid a plan for body-building under his mattress once. Another time his report card. There was nothing to worry about, she thought, busying herself with breakfast kettles, a pot of simmering porridge, brown sugar. How Molly loved coarse brown sugar. Una caught herself the moment before she knew she would start crying by banging dishes on the table, knocking the chairs aside, opening the stove to shove in more wood. It is my right, she decided, some things are my right.

Hannah worked at the store every day from early in the morning until just after dark at six. She tried to worry about the money they needed, but she couldn't. She told Matthew she was trying, and did succeed in holding back a little each week, calling it pocket money, persuading her mother that it was what the other girls were allowed to do. She had even made a little drawstring purse out of a scrap of linen and lined it with a musty rose silk. When there were enough small coins, she changed them for a silver dollar. When the dollars began to drag her down, she bought paper money and held it with a paper clip.

She watched the people come and go. They moved too slowly, scraping the floor, dragging in mud, loitering. Why did they stand around, the men hogging the stove, melting boots dripping, women huddled under hats, inside muffs and shawls on the other side, warmed by bolts of cotton, unfaded rainbows of ribbons, fresh threads, lace and feathers? They were warmed by the flickering of tongues. Ruddy faces broke and brightened as the men recalled last summer's tales, Ho ho ho, and the ladies embroidered the edges of small white stories. They never talk about me, Hannah observed, I never hear them tell on me. I'm always in broad daylight. If they only knew my secret. I could give them something to talk about.

Mr Comus told her there was always something else to do, no need to stand around. Giving her a soft flannel he told her to dust each of the jars on the far shelves. She lifted the first one. It was cool to the touch, full of a dark purple syrup. Slowly she began wiping and thinking. There had been so much time already. She couldn't think so far ahead. Time stretched out as if it wasn't real. But this wasn't real, either, this inch-by-inch creeping. It took no imagination to live her life like this. She was too safe; there was something else; she thought it would take a different form. Things came into her mind, but they were presently without shape. She couldn't name them. None of the old definitions fitted, and in the end she lost them as she did her morning dreams. Surely she had something special to do. Within her was a milky pool of secret humours, the colour of pearl. Nothing was reflected. She had no idea how deep it was. The surface had always been dead calm. Underneath, hiding, was her secret truth, the messages telling her what she had to do.

Round and round, her cloth traced the metal lids on the jars. There would always be alternatives, choices. She could tag along with Matthew and find out what they were. Other possibilities. He said he would take her with him on his adventure, according to his desires. His will was steep and fast like a waterfall breaking down the rocks in an old soft hill. There was a way to do everything, anything, if you wanted to badly enough, he said.

She placed the jars on top of each other on the floor. Hard fast little thoughts. What did she really want? If there was time to think, would she decide to turn back? Would she deny him, trust him less? Take away her arms, her eyes. Might he make her cry, she who never cried? She'd never asked him to do anything he didn't want to do. The thoughts came on like the trains, approaching steadily from a distant speck, closer and closer without sound, then suddenly they were upon her with wind and alarm, knocking her over in a thrill of noise, the whistle blast deafening, rushing through her, then, shuddering, gone.

Someone shoved open the door. It caught on the hemp mat put down to scrape mud. Outcries accompanied the struggle to get the door shut. Meanwhile, the cold poured in, down the corridors, over her hands. Her thoughts turned on her as if to say, Don't think, don't think, just do! Follow him. Do something. Do whatever you can, whatever it takes. But I am, she reminded herself. Why do I need to? Why was there a problem? Had she not heard him in her last dream, the night before, when his voice coiled up in her ear and it struck her as perfectly natural that her life and his were to mesh? 'Yes,' she said in the dream, 'yes,' as she had decided to say yes to him forever.

On warm days, the ice melted in the shallow ruts and puddles. At night it froze, and the mornings, though light when she rose with her mother, were bitterly cold, all the more so for her expectation of the power of the sun. Opening the curtains to her room, she stood in the full glare, waiting. It was almost the end of the waiting now. There in the early naked light she had the odd feeling that her first prayers had been answered.

'Have you told your parents about us?'

'Not as much as there is to tell.'

'What will they do?' She shrugged, but she knew. 'Will you come with me?'

Last summer there had been too much time. Now it was late winter and they would be leaving soon. If need be they could go as far as one of the river cities and wait there, working to get the rest of the passage. They would be close to the beginnings of the trails. A little farther on the train, perhaps, then north. Or upriver on the boat, then overland. His mind was shivering.

Though it was now light when she left work, they were standing in the dark. Always brave in the dark, she said, 'I'll follow you.' His eyes were flat. Perhaps it was the second-hand light.

'You are a stranger to me, daughter.'

In the kitchen, the children were gathered around Matthew. He thought for a moment they were going to touch him with the tips of their fingers. As tension built in the air their faces froze in concentration and the breath was stopped in their chests. Not one of them had red hair, he noticed.

'I do not know you.' Adele went to her bedroom. Hannah followed. 'Mama!' She was ill at ease. It was the room. She'd crept in here countless times, in between the dreams of her parents, separating them in the bed with her enormous need, crying, Keep me, keep me safe, and they did, under that old poke-holed quilt, the one she had made herself. Now it lay still and smooth, forgetting her, sighing under the weight of her mother, forgetting her already. Moving over, she stepped on the creaky floorboard, she knew just where it was, but this time it refused to make the sound.

'Mama, I want to go so bad, I have to go.'

Adele turned her back. Hannah stroked the quilt with the back of her hand, that gesture of gentleness and love.

'Mama, I'm going with him, I am.' Was everything going to fall away from her? Was this house going to dry up, a relic in her memory?

'You are too big for me.'

The children filled the doorway. Hannah turned around for a moment. She looked over their heads to Matthew and gestured helplessly. Mouthing the words, he asked, What do you want me to do? She ran though the children, scattering them, and pressed her hands on him. For the time being it was all she seemed to need. Was this all there was to it? Could she gather such strength from just touching him? 'Go home, Matthew.'

'Do you want me to come in the morning? Do you want me to stay somewhere around here?'

'No, no, I'll be all right.'

Behind her, like a little fortress, the children had surrounded their mother on the bed.

'Don't you come near my mama!' warned Joel, monkeyed up against her. His clenched claw fingers scratched the air.

'Don't you dare do that, stop it, all of you, stop it. Don't threaten me in this house, I belong here as much as you do. I'm not doing anything wrong. I just want to go away, I want to be with someone, I have to be with him, I have to go with him, I can't help myself, there's nothing I can do about it, nothing anyone can do. I shall go even if you all hate me, even if you take everything I leave behind and burn it, even if you wash me out of all the rooms with lye and even if you say you will never speak my name again, I will go, I must go. I would go even if I was going all by myself.'

Was that true, would she go alone? The faces blurred. Tears smudged her sight. Her hands tingled. She slammed the door on them and fled to her own room. The curtain would keep no one out. She stood in the dark. This old house, she could break it up and burn it in a bonfire. Plucking at the edges of her sleeves, tugging open the neck of her jumper, she tried to get rid of the heat of her rage. Back and forth, pacing to the corners of the small rug, silently, she was as excited as a hunter, as frightened as the prey of fate. She began to hear every sound. A door opened, chairs scraped on the floor.

'I want the pie first,' she heard Joel decide. She smelled dried fruit and spices.

'No.'

'Well, just put it right here by me, I'll keep an eye on it.'

'You'll eat your supper first. Sit down, all of you, sit on your hands if you need to, your father'll be back in a minute, we can wait for him.' Then, despite all the people in there, there was not a sound but that of the fire pecking for sap pockets in soft stove wood. They were staring at Hannah's empty place.

In a while he wouldn't have to leave her anywhere. He wouldn't have to wait out in the weeds and woods, getting cold, denying what he was, what they were together. Why did he have to peer over his shoulder, periscope corners, provide excuses? He knew every hiding place. From out here in the shaggy alders he could see Hannah's silhouette beating like a shuttle back and forth across the narrow frame of her window. Soon it would be his turn. He'd take her home with him one day, one night, and never give her back.

Suddenly her father was at the gate. Matthew hadn't even heard him coming. Luke didn't see him. In the dark, Luke took up an armload of wood. Once on the porch he dumped it by the door. Hannah froze at the sound. When she moved again Matthew couldn't see her. Luke went back in the house. Nothing happened. Matthew grew cold and hungry. It was getting late, he had homework and a job to do for a neighbour.

In the morning, as soon as she was clear of the house, he was there by her side, pulling her into the Pattons' barn, which was still with disuse. The musty stale air took his breath away. Cobwebs sparkled in the thready sunlight. She unbuttoned her coat and removed it.

'Tell me what happened.' He couldn't believe the way she looked.

'I heard him come in and Mama told him, then he asked where I was and she told him I was in my room, so he stayed out in the kitchen and ate supper. Then after supper he came in my room.' The side of her face was swollen and discoloured.

'You're not surprised, are you?' Disbelieving, standing far back.

'Of course not.'

'Did you expect me to be able to stop it?'

'No, no. Matthew, it had nothing to do with you. Mama likes you a whole lot. It's that we're going away.'

He wanted to see. She wanted him to see. Did he have wounds like this to prove his dedication, hive-like welts, a cross-hatch of red and brown lines? Rolling up her sleeve, she showed him the bruise on her arm. 'This is where he grabbed hold of me.' She was breathless. How brave she must have been sitting there in the dark of her room, waiting for him.

'How could your mother let him do this?'

'She said it had nothing to do with her, it's between him and me. She said I was too big for her to beat so it was up to him. I'll never be bigger than him.'

I'll be bigger, thought Matthew, I'll be bigger than him one day. But then they'd be gone and it wouldn't matter. The only thing they could do was run. If they had to they would run away. As if this was easy. Maybe it would be. People disappeared from time to time. He had been out beyond. Hannah hadn't, though. He knew what happened when the last fence was passed, how the trees closed up behind.

'... so as long as I'm there that's what he'll do.'

'What did he say to you?'

'He didn't say anything, he doesn't talk when he's mad.' Why was Matthew so interested in those things? 'Look at that!' She pulled up her skirt. It was as if her body were separate from her soul and she didn't feel the pain. She wore the stripes on her thigh like a medal. Turning, she displayed the crisp thin lines that would soon turn muddy, but which for now were brilliant on the stark startling white of her skin. He couldn't bear it, helpless with admiration and disgust.

'Did you cry?' Looking for stains and traces on her cheeks, kissing, licking, tasting for salt.

'No. I don't cry. I don't.' Hadn't he noticed?

His face in her hair. I will make you cry, he thought, and was ashamed to think it. Dropping to his knees, he wrapped his arms around her hips. She didn't see that he could cry. He pushed the cloth of her skirt up, burying his face in her thighs, caressing her.

She gasped. 'Gently.' His lips sucked the heat from the marks as if they contained poison. And beneath, she felt the sweet leap of his bragging blood.

'Anyway, it's done,' he said. 'I can go anytime.'

Matthew was looking at his father's face. They had just finished supper.

Una was supervising the clean-up and rearranging the dishes on the sideboard and cupboard as they came back from the kitchen. She was humming a wistful little tune to the clatter of glasses and pots in the sink. His father seemed to be taking the pulse of the candles as they flickered in the draught. He didn't look at Matthew nor did he seem aware that his son was looking at him. They were at such a distance that Matthew couldn't see clearly. Search as he might for the faces his father had shown him in the past, he couldn't find them now. It was as if each time he looked, his mind had peeled off what he saw at the moment and had pasted it on the face in his memory. Bit by bit he had built his father in his mind. This would be the last time. What changes will come after I am gone? he wondered. I don't look like him, I look like Mama, her bones squared and thickened slightly. When I look in the mirror I'll be able to keep an eye on her, but how will I remember his face? Matthew lifted his hands from his lap and placed them on the table in front of him. Momentarily the blood drained, then returned.

'Nothing is ever resolved. If I stay here I'll never change.' The long argument, having circled itself, was coming to an end.

'That's what you think now. You're seventeen years old, for God's sake, you can't see anything farther than the end of your own nose. What makes you think you know how the world works?'

'This world!' he said, his hooked finger jabbing at the door. 'I've seen nothing else but this world every day of my life. If I don't know how it works by now, I'll never know. Don't you see, I've seen what happens to people who stay here. They stagnate, they go crazy, they kill themselves. Their children die.'

'You have not died.'

'Not yet.'

'We are not crazy.'

'I feel like I am.'

'What's made you so angry, so dissatisfied?'

'I don't want to stay here!' Pleading on the edge until Harris remembered that the boy had said the same thing when he was seven and was being dragged into the doctor's office with a fish hook in the back of his hand. 'And so you go away and then you find out it isn't so great out there either. Then what?'

'How do I know? At least I will have tried. You must have wanted to go somewhere, sometime. You were my age.'

'Your age! When I was your age, I had no chance to go just anywhere I wanted. I had to ...'

'I've heard that story. I know that you had to come back. I know all you had to do, but I don't have to stay. You don't need me. You can't keep me here, you can't make me stay.'

'No, I can't.'

You don't care, either, do you? Matthew thought. You won't help me. You won't even wish me well. Just 'Goodbye.' Nothing like Molly's departure brimming with your approval. Nothing like that for me.

'Your father loves you so much. It hurts him when you talk like that to him.' That was how she began, the blade covered with putty, sitting on the edge of his bed, wearing a hole in the bedspread, worrying a hole in him. 'You won't know how it feels until you have a son of your own.' He stopped listening. The same, the same, he told himself. You dig the trench deeper and longer and then put me in the trench with a shovel and tell me to dig and dig and dig.

'You are indebted to him,' she continued. 'You should do what he wants you to.'

'No, not this time,' he said, shaking his head, 'I'm going to do what I want. He taught me that, didn't he?' And it was true. Somehow it was true.

'You're making a mistake.'

'It's my mistake.'

'What have I done? What have I done to make you...?'

Downstairs, Harris brooded over his wife in the flickering light from the hearth fire. 'I am willing to have him go, you know. He's right, it is his turn.'

But to Una this was a basic threat like sickness or war. Her head could ride along with Harris, but her heart balked at the vagaries of life. She wanted to keep an eye on everyone she loved.

'In the old days,' she began.

'There are no old days, Mama. You know what the old days are? Childhood. Your own, mine. His.'

The fire tumbled and disintegrated. Una tucked a rug around herself. Harris listened to the house as it adjusted to the seasons of their lives, as it shaped the sounds of their living. Molly's room was hollow now. Once Matthew was gone, silence would investigate the empty space he left behind. It would scoop out his echo and absorb his scent. Eventually it would take over, and he and Una would sit in front of this fire in the evenings, listening, with what they had remaining between them.

Four

'Goodbye,' said Hannah. To the tree at the corner where the fences met. 'Goodbye,' to the iceberg rocks in the road. 'Goodbye, Joel. You won't see me ever again!'

'Not true, Aaron says we can go see you anytime we want.'

'And how are you going to find me?'

That was not his problem. He ran off in his big rubber boots. Spring rains had puddled the roads and fields. Knee-high grass waded through the gullies.

By now everyone knew they were going. Old school friends ran up to her on the street, grabbing her hands in theirs as if they might share the excitement or absorb her peculiar courage. 'How can you?' or 'What are you thinking of? People did that before the war, that's what my uncle said. Hardly anyone's still going from around here.' But the thrill, the unknown. 'You'd never get me out there!' What did she know? 'Oh my Lord!' blurted Mary. 'How did you keep it a secret? Are you mad? You must be mad.' Clutching, clucking.

'Goodbye, I really must do some packing now.' She didn't even have a suitcase. Matthew got her an old duffel bag, which she hung over her bed post. From behind winter clothes in the bottom drawer she retrieved her old doll. She smoothed the straggles of yarn hair, picked at a loose thread, buttoned the small shawl across the pleated bodice of her best dress. She wrapped the doll in a small soft rag and packed it in the very bottom of the duffel. It was the first thing she packed.

The house was quiet. Out in the garden, her mother was puttering with the weeds, which had come clamouring for the strong spring sun. How could life go on normally? Though she tried to look at everything with the difference it deserved, because this was after all the last time, she couldn't, and her gaze slipped and slid, focusing on nothing. She flung herself on the bed. This soft place, home of all her dreams. What would she be sleeping on next, where? Where do you sleep on a train, a wagon? Would they stay in a hotel? Or a tent? She rubbed her cheek on the soft cotton. As silence widened and deepened around her it unearthed distant sounds that were transformed or disguised:

64

something like the chord on a piano or harmonica, a windmill, a waterwheel, things from the far side of town.

Rolling over onto her back she reached out to the sides of the bed, feeling the angle, pinching the coverlet up into her fingers. She smoothed her hands in close to her body, then out again, all alone. Again, stroking her stomach through her dress, then out across the vast empty space to the edge. What would the new arrangement be, sharing her bed, her sleep, mixing the air above their heads, the warmth between their bodies, sharing secrets, time? How much of her did he want? What did he expect?

They filled the train station: family, the mothers already paired, friends, well-wishers, idle spectators, hangers-on, truants, passengers. The children, who had never been here before, discovered the sound of their own voices in the hollow building, and ran from corner to corner shouting vague commands in different tones that swooped and curled in the air like carnival streamers. In the confusion and excitement, stirred-up dust accentuated the sun sweeping in from the skylights, and shuddered like the vapours of dry ice along the floor. People rushed in the door afraid they wouldn't be able to get a ticket. Others idled on the long dark benches. Hannah saw one man watching his own foot as it lopped back and forth on the fulcrum of his heel.

Out of the corner of her eye Hannah saw the old woman in black. She could only sit now, her legs withered up under her, ankles plugging the holes in the tops of her shoes. Bruises mottled her arms as if she had been carrying things that were the wrong shape. Burns festered the ends of her fingers. Her skin was scaly. For just a moment Hannah saw memory displayed on the woman's body. Each incident had drawn itself across her skin, hanging on, clawing, clutching, desperate to stay, parasitic on her life. Shifting from indifference to intent, but going too far, killing her: ghouls, nightmare beasts crawling around under her clothes, pinching, snipping, clipping bits of her skin, gnawing under her heart, sucking on her soul, wading through her mind, leeches on her soul. The woman turned to her and began sucking on her thoughts, chewing, draining her of energy and direction. Stop it, she thought, you old ... The thought grinding between her teeth, but there was no word for it. What was not happening here was a process of forgetting. The woman couldn't forget. Nor could she forgive herself.

It made Hannah feel hard. Her skin thickened. She saw all this to be a warning against weakness. Before she could start thinking about it, and about mistakes, their departure was announced. She looked ahead, then turned around and raced over to the woman. 'Do you have anything to say to me?' she asked in her new hard voice. But the woman was living without seeing, without hearing. Hannah smelled the confusion of odours. Perhaps dust and soot, never cleansed, just moved around the body, having placated the sweetish scent of decay. 'If you have nothing to say to me, then stay away. I can only do one thing at a time. I don't want to know, anyway. You have nothing to do with me.' She ran back, grabbed Matthew's elbow, hurried him along the platform to the outside where the train waited. Everyone went with them. The children stopped in their corners, then ran ahead so they could see everything. 'Where is our car? Hurry, Matthew, where is it, where?'

Without seeing them she kissed her mother, her father, her brothers and sister. Without looking at them she kissed Matthew's mother and father. His father patted her chest as if she had no breasts at all. Then her own mother again, a hug to the tight unyielding body that she didn't recognize. She looked in order to be sure. The conductor put his hand under her elbow to help her up the steps. She thought she would burst if she didn't get inside away from all the hands fluttering in the air, all the mouths opening and closing.

'Hannah, don't you want to stay for the circus?' said Joel, unable to believe that they were leaving on this very train, this very minute.

'The circus!' whispered Hannah. Life would continue here without her. Exciting things would happen and she would miss seeing them. She'd miss seeing Joel's face at his first circus. A circus probably wouldn't even come to the prairie, wherever they might end up. Turning quickly, she looked at Matthew standing behind her. 'Don't they want to see you? Come on, get here beside me.' Moving slightly, cocking her knee up onto the seat, she made room for him. 'Here beside me.' She looked at him, looked out at her life beyond the window and here behind this pane of glass, squished into a frame. Her whole life had come to this moment, this point of standing here, waiting for the train to move. Why didn't it start, why did they have to wait, waving, making faces, smiling, trying to figure out the mouthed words? I'm dying, she thought, they look as if I'm dying. Turning to talk to each other while I am standing here. This is the last time they will be able to see me. Hannah leaned forward, banged on the window with her fist. The sun in her eyes, she retreated into

66

shadow. The train eased forward, jerked, stopped, jerked, jostled, and began finally, steadily, to move.

Matthew checked his watch. Just a couple of minutes late. He put the watch back in his pocket, running his fingers along the golden chain. For a moment he was so frightened he felt he might lose control of his bowels. A noxious chill drifted around his stomach and inside his skin and sweat began to spring out in the small of his back. He put his hand up under Hannah's hair, that warm dark safe place. He felt better already. She didn't move. She must have felt his hand, but didn't acknowledge him.

How small everything looked from this height, she was thinking. Old bird's nests sat in the rotten gutter on the station roof. Along the platform people were moving too slowly ever to catch up. 'It's too late,' she whispered. 'It really is too late!' She put her cheek to the glass for a last glimpse. Then they were moving too fast to see the faces. Streets whipped by like the spokes in a wheel. That street, down there's the store, she thought, and this one, the hotel. Where was her house from there? A dog raced up to the train. At the major crossroads the semaphore flag was down, holding back three wagons. For a second she saw the faces with shocking clarity and for a while would remember them better than those of her own family. And the horse, lobbing its head up and down, froth dangling from its mouth, a limp blue hat on its head.

Abruptly the landscape changed to farmland. The fences zigzagged, houses hid in old elms, and cows lumbered away from the engine, though they saw it three times a week. Inside the coach, the noise had subsided as the car steadied and began to rock rhythmically from side to side.

Hannah was shaking. 'It was awful. I thought it would be different. I couldn't hear what they were saying. What if it was important?'

Matthew hovered beside her. Despite their being married, he didn't feel he could touch her in this public place. Consoling with his voice, not hearing his own words, he said something about letters. As soon as they got to a town they'd send back a post box address. She had never received a letter of her own. She settled into the seat and looked out the window.

Matthew sat back in the plush, dusty, tobacco-smelling order of the seat, and laid his anxiety down under the long whistle of the train. The chuff and deep rocking motion lulled him. The car was almost full. He wondered where all the people were going, where they had come from. For some reason he expected he and Hannah would be the only ones on this ride, that everyone else would be at work or home where they belonged. Some must be businessmen, he decided, the commercial travelling kind who sleep soundly and immediately, peacefully ignoring noises and, having posted their tickets like Indian feathers in their hat bands, the attentions of the conductor. Having seen these men in action, audacious, convincing, flushed with heat, liquor and excitement, he was now surprised and disappointed. It was not such a great life after all that left one sprawled ungraciously in broad daylight in the coach seat of a train. Behind him two women were chattering. He would have eavesdropped, curious about each person's reason for travelling, but all he heard were bursts of breathy laughter. Strange voices, strangers all around him. He would be glad when Hannah turned to him again. For the moment he couldn't remember what she sounded like. He couldn't remember a single thing she'd ever said. A shivery sensation overwhelmed him. What was she thinking about?

'Pardon me, sir, I see you and the missus – off on your honeymoon trip, are ye?'

'Well, not exactly,' said Matthew. 'We're going to homestead.'

'My congratulations! A big step! Newlyweds heading out together to their new life. You'll be building a home out there. The winters – have you been told about the winters? You have. Capital! I myself represent the Fuller Stove company of ...'

Smiling wearily, Matthew asked the man how far west his company delivered its product.

'You just tell us where you are and we'll get it to you,' he said, patting his chest, cleaning out his ear, loosening the skin behind his neck with a vigorous scratch. 'Oregon, California, you name it. This is my life. I love it. Wouldn't do anything else, even for more money. It's a great land, this country of ours,' and though the thought of travel appealed to Matthew, the idea of doing what this man did for a living never entered his head. What passion could there be unless a man could sell himself, his brain, his muscles, his sweat? Perhaps that was what the man felt he was doing, equating some black beast of a stove with himself. Quickly starting, long burning, stays hot for hours on hardwood, me. Easy to keep, attractive, decorates any room. Safe, sure, dependable, me. Buy me. You won't be sorry. I'm guaranteed for twenty-five years.

Matthew listened. Except for the jostling of the train, he was sitting still. That so much could be happening around him while he only watched amazed him. It was like being an infant. He felt no responsibility. People walked up and down the aisle. He didn't have to do a thing. Another man stopped to tell him a story and to eye Hannah. Matthew listened as before, but had no desire to respond. His curiosity was delayed and discouraged. He felt as if he were sleeping with his eyes open, lulled and languid, the late morning sun leaving his knees, pulling a blanket of shadow after it.

'*Your missus.* Did you hear him say it?' Matthew looked at Hannah, who looked back. They giggled.

A vendor sloshed by offering cans of beans, crackers, apples from a box. Hannah thought slowly of all the things she had never done for Matthew. Rolling them over in her mind, she tried to see herself taking care of him. Isolated images yawned lazily before her closed eyes. Hannah carrying a hot dish in her apron, steam flushing up her body, he waiting hushed with hunger at the table. Someone else, still named Hannah, who sewed buttons on shirts and darned socks by the fire, a transformed Hannah who inspired yeast and soda, soothed curdling cream, revived souring milk. Transformed by what? Love, devotion, duty? Nonetheless, Hannah sitting on the front porch, sorting seeds for the summer fields, with her husband, or side by side, his arm over her shoulder, supporting him in his exhaustion from some unknown calamity, holding his hands between her breasts, their shadow long and singular before them.

At first she had been uneasy inside the train because there was no relief from the noise of the wheels on the tracks and she couldn't hear anything else, but now she was comfortable. More than that, as if she had lost her body or had given it temporarily to the safe keeping of the thick seat, she wondered if she could get her body to go under Matthew's.

Outside, nothing but trees. The way they strained light, breaking it into packets between themselves made her dizzy. As yet few leaves adorned the bare branches. She was relieved when it was noon and the sun was above the car and out of sight. Cooler, she felt hungrier and wider awake.

It took three days and two nights to reach the end of the line. There they crossed the river and got on the Pacific train bound for the fort town where they could get outfitted. They slept in a cloud of cigar smoke and the gathering gloom of their own bodies. At town stops they had a few minutes to find a vendor to supplement what they had bought of bread, cheese and dried fruit aboard the train. They packed their blankets at the top of their bags so that they could be easily withdrawn. The stove at the end of the aisle was maintained during the night, but its heat was negligible. Once a day they heated a little water to wash with, but dust had grown like a skin on everything.

They arrived at night. Matthew couldn't get his bearings in the dark. Which way was the river? He could smell it, or something peculiar, stagnant. Dead fish, chips of yellow moon, manure, waves? Crowds thrashed. They were in a funnel, a whirlpool. A funeral party laboured down the middle of the street strewing tulips and jonquils and dirges, sad bad songs in memory of old times. Wagons creaked and shuddered with midnight cargo. At the end of the street were the mountains of goods that had to wait, while the ice and the spring floods receded, for the steamboats to make their way down the river. On the other side were goods waiting to be loaded on the trains going north and west. Lanterns astride the darkness burned and smoked and beat like frantic wings. Someone touched Hannah through her skirt. Faces slurred around her. Breath fast with booze flashed in her face, warm by her ear. She didn't even have her hands to deflect blows because they were tight on Matthew's arm. When she opened her eyes someone was staring at her. Blood from a chicken freshly beheaded in the street spattered the front of her dress. 'Matthew, I'm sick.' He couldn't hear her. There was no place to fall. She slipped in something slimy.

It was the middle of the night. They had to make sure their things were off the baggage car. When they got there, men were hauling crates onto a wagon. 'Who are you?' the man in charge demanded. The numbers corresponded. Matthew carried two bags, Hannah the third. 'Don't hang on me, I can't walk when you do that,' he snapped. They headed down towards the end of the train where there seemed to be a break in the crowd. A tail of red light lay on the track behind the caboose. Inside, all by himself, a man sat with his feet up and head lolled back, dead drunk. A boy was pilfering the trainman's hat from his head. Hannah and Matthew hurried through the light and disappeared into the darkness on the other side.

It was cooler, and they figured they must be nearer the river. Matthew wanted to see it before he slept. The thick brown mucilage of water swallowed light and reflected legends. Wending their way down a steep, surprisingly deserted street, they came to a slip. Oily water lapped beneath their feet. 'For God's sake, Matthew, why are we here?' On the edge.

'Just listen for a moment, and smell.'

How could she avoid it? Smoke, oil, bilge, hemp, a tangy odour like crushed insects. 'Is that it?' But he was ahead of her, at the edge, as if an old dream had come true. And though he could see nothing for sure, he heard the soft current in the middle of the milky river. It made him immortal for a moment. Then he was reminded of the cold, late, shrouded hour. Hannah, slumped against a post, clutched her duffel.

'You're lucky I'm so tired,' she said.

'Didn't you hear it?'

They still had to find a place to sleep. The first hotel they tried was full, but the proprietor suggested another, which turned out to be a large old private home in the centre of town, inhabited by a spinster lady who said she would have been unable to keep the house if she didn't take in lodgers. The hotel owners passed their overflow to her as long as the guests seemed to be decent people. Matthew thought she was telling them this more for their peace of mind than her own, as she was a formidable woman with bristles and large feet and wipe marks that were unmistakably stains of blood on her apron.

'We need a bath,' said Hannah, but the best that could be done at that late hour was an extra hot water bucket.

'Pay in advance,' she said.

Hannah was asleep as soon as she lay down. Matthew hung on for a few minutes thinking about the river and Hannah beside him. The two intermingled in his mind. He wanted to look at her, but they were in darkness like the river, and all he could do was listen to the brown rhythmic current of her breath.

In the morning he leaned over her, quietly because he thought someone might be listening. They were so far from home. Behind their eyes they each wondered if anyone there was thinking about them.

After some coffee and bread downstairs they carried up hot water for a bath.

Hannah said, 'I want to go first,' ducking behind the screen, stripping down, sitting in the tub, ladling water over herself as if she were a piece of fountain statuary, again and again, the warm water soaking through, undoing her hair down her back, running down her face, her shoulders.

'Hurry up, I want to get to the land claim office here and see what they say.' Hannah was to stay behind to keep an eye on their things. She sat by the window, which looked out on a side street, but even that was busy with people taking what looked to be a short cut. Broad flat sides of buildings seemed pasted one behind the other as far as she could see. Windows gaped open. In the one across from her the curtains were tied up in a big knot.

'Are you staying another night?' the woman asked at the door. Hannah couldn't remember her name and didn't know how to ask again.

'I don't know.'

'Well, if you'll help me take the bath water out, that'd be good, something for you to do.' She is treating me like her daughter or a drudge, thought Hannah. If I were a grand lady, she wouldn't ask me to help her! But it did give her something to do while she waited. She wasn't used to doing nothing.

'Where are you from, dear?'

'Nowhere near as big as this.'

'Where are you going?'

'We're going to homestead on the northwest plains.' Just words to me, she thought.

The woman looked at her crossly as if she were impatient and fed up. After she left, Hannah sat waiting for Matthew to return.

'What did they say? What did you find out?' she said, rushing to him when he returned.

He had copied it down. 'We have to go out and what they call squat on a piece of land. That means mark it with a foundation of four legs,' he shrugged, 'for a cabin, and put up a board with our name on it. Then we go back to the nearest office and file a declaration of intent to homestead on the quarter section. Then we have to build a habitation eighteen by twenty and when the land comes up it's ours. Or there's something called a pre-empt: when the land comes up we pay $1.25 an acre for it. There's also land along the railroad for sale. Sometimes people can apply for an additional section, and there was something called a tree claim, where the government bets that if you can grow ten acres of trees in ten years on one hundred and sixty acres you can have that land, too. That's a new thing they just started up.'

Was he finished? In another second she asked, 'Well, so what do we do first?'

They needed each other desperately. Within sight, smell, touch, across the small restaurant table, nudging the sunlight aside, their sharp elbows jutting out to the edge, they held onto the lifeline in each other's eyes.

Almost past lunch time, they were served the scrapings of a stew pot, bread, a pot of coffee, their first hot sit-down meal since they had left home. When they started to eat, a sharp surprise of hunger bolted loose in their stomachs like a live creature they couldn't control. They'd never imagined anything like this, a vulnerability that made them nervous and fragile, when they had always thought of themselves as strong. They ate and took seconds of everything that was left, and began to feel better, heavy and full with a gracious sense of well-being, of extraordinary fatigue, so much so they hardly kept their eyes open. Going back to their room, they held on to each other while the strange city surged around them. At home they knew everyone. People here didn't say hello unless they wanted something. Matthew and Hannah kept to themselves and tried not to let anyone bump into them. They bumped each other instead, hips, shoulders, heads together, walking fastened at the ankle as if in a three-legged race. Aggressively immune, porcupines of sharp love, they walked on peg legs past goats and raggedy beggar boys. This is all we need, they thought. We are all there is to each other in this world. Locking the door to their room, they drew the curtains against the alien city.

A knock came at the door. 'If you're using the bed again I'll have to charge you for another night.'

'We're staying the night,' said Matthew, and he paid her on the spot.

'Is she all right?' asked the woman, peering in at Hannah's pale face.

'Yes, we're both just very tired. Thank you.'

Hannah lay flat on the bed, unravelling.

'Don't you go to sleep on me,' he said.

'Let's sleep together, just for a little while, just like this. Come here, closer, like that, closer.' In the low, laced light she gently stroked the present, his surfaces, and though she held him close, pressing her damp fingers on his soft hollows, her breath like stay lines across his body, his brain raced ahead, out of her arms, out of this dim place towards a future he could only imagine. It was a place without accident, storm, anger or sickness. Without rips or tears in the fabric or doubts imbedded deep under the surface.

A little dust blows from the ground when he cuts it with the plough. Rain fills the ditches, soaks the roots, fills the well. Sunlight beckons the stems up out of the dirt. A balance of dark and light. He walks confidently upon the land, coaxing, demanding, subduing. The land, like a woman, lies in wait for him. Incomplete, uncertain, the earth waits for him to direct and design, to make it matter.

Beside him Hannah stirred. He couldn't see her clearly as she settled into sleep. Her breathing shifted, spending itself in the air above her. Unless he put his hand over her mouth, he couldn't feel it.

After supper he said he was going to try to find some work for the evening.

'Where?'

'Down at the river.'

'Why?'

'We're going to need all the money we can get.'

'You're going to leave me.'

'You can't very well come with me, can you,' he said, holding her shoulders. She wasn't as big as she sounded. 'What do you want to do?'

In answer she caressed the back of his hand with her cheek. 'I don't know, see the city. Something. I don't want to sit in here.'

He left just when the city was changing for the day, when women and children were closing doors and the children cried because they suspected the world was going on without them, and the women swatted them on their suspicions and sent them to bed and turned to the men, who had been smoking and reading the papers. And the men without women opened all the doors they could to let the women in.

Hannah lingered at the window, leaning against the cool painted wood, flicking the curtain out so she could see. Perhaps Matthew would cut through the alley so she could see him one more time. In the building across, the knotted curtain had been undone. Wrinkles persisted in it. The dark came quickly and someone inside lit a lamp. A woman walked back and forth, her shadow dusting the walls. She went to the window and looked down into the alley. The bodice of her slip was untied, and Hannah could see her skin way down even though she held a shawl together just beneath her breasts.

To pass the time, Hannah hauled out the duffel bags and began unpacking the first one. She'd not seen Matthew's things, these clothes, separate from him. Overalls, trousers, socks, shirts, long johns, hand-kerchiefs. She unfolded the clothes. His mother must have done that, washing, ironing, carefully folding, smoothing the cloth. Hannah shook each item vigorously, making it snap out. She put them on the bed and returned to the window. Two people were there now in the room across the alley. She couldn't see them, but their shadows melded curiously. Distracted by street noises, she looked down to see if anyone could see her. The shadows moved away.

Picking out a pair of trousers, she pulled them on and stuffed her petticoat into the waistband. Over the bodice she tried on a wool plaid shirt. The sleeves hung down over her fingers. It smelled brand new. The creases were clean and sharp. In the three-way mirror, she could see all around herself, two sides at once. Spying a soft cap she tucked her hair under it and pulled it down close to her eyes. 'What a fine boy you are!' she said to the image, smoothing her hips, turning around to look at the crease between her legs. She stood with her legs apart, squatted, switched her hips from side to side, put her hands at her waist, swung her arms around. Poking her chin out, she rolled up a piece of paper and stuck it in her mouth as she would a cigarette. Keeping her teeth together she talked tough. Her image was barely visible, it was so dark now. Dropping the hat and shaking out her hair, she went to the window once more. It was a man with the woman. They were naked. He was pushing her up against the wall. Hannah shivered as she watched. Her body opened and closed, loosening flesh, but her joints locked beneath, holding her there, not letting her move. The woman's face appeared over the shoulder of the man. She was gasping as if she were drowning or strangling. Her fingers held on to the man. Laughter burst up from the street. The man slumped to the floor as if he had been scraped from the woman's body. She looked down, then straight ahead. She touched her throat in a convulsive movement. In another moment she covered her-self and disappeared. Hannah could still see the shape of their bodies. The wallpaper where they were pressing was now stained. In the alley, lanterns wavered like fireflies. Thick liquid flows of people moved smoothly back and forth, heads and hats floating on a viscous surface. Odours of grease, perfume, smoke, urine, manure, but not the river. Where was Matthew? What if something happened to him, an accident,

75

murder, amnesia? What if he never returned? What would she do, where would she go? Stripping off his clothes, she shoved everything onto the floor and jumped into the middle of the bed, gathering the quilt up against her. It was cold. The curtain wavered. She thought she saw someone peeking in. She decided she would pretend to be asleep when he came in. In the morning they were going to cross the river and leave on the last stretch of the journey. There was no point hanging around here. They could get a tent and a wagon and camp out from then on.

It was so late when Matthew came in, he was afraid he wouldn't wake up in time, and so he left a note for the landlady. Hannah was already asleep. He stumbled over the pile of clothes on the floor, but was too tired to wonder why they were there. He could have worked all night under the lamp glare, its ghostly slick on the muddy water. Despite the cold of these early spring nights, all the men were stripped to the waist while they worked shifting barrels, boxes, bales, crates. They had warned him to arrange to be paid on completion of his work instead of agreeing to wait until tomorrow, which might never come, and so he now had a couple of dollars in his pocket. He would be relieved to have his wagon, horses and tools instead of the money to worry about. A half-bucket of water was beside the washstand. He hung his reeking clothes over the screen to air in front of the window. The room across the alley was still lit. Standing aside, he poured water and washed thoroughly with a rough rag cloth until he began to shiver. He climbed into bed, envisioning a quick drop into the oblivion of dreamless sleep; instead, his eyes remained open, disinterestedly registering the smear of pale light from next door on the ceiling. At home he never lay awake in bed, and had often fallen asleep while the lamp was still burning. His mother would creep into the room to extinguish it. He wanted to tell her everything, but right now he didn't own a piece of paper. He scribbled his letter to her in the parchment air.

They got up early before the coffee had been brewed. Having dressed in the grip of dawn, they made their way through the refuse of the night's streets, the half-frozen drunks. 'Is that a dead person?' Hannah pointed. They passed a stable and heard the disgruntled stomp of animals waiting for feed. A pile of manure smouldered and steamed, digesting itself. The false fronts of the hotels, warehouses and sheds on the way were pale and flat awaiting the sun to yellow them.

They were among few passengers standing in line for the ferry at that hour. Most had crossed the day before and had found accommodation near the outfitting station. Matthew and Hannah stood at the stern to have a view of the receding shore and the odd whirlpool the propellers stirred in the soupy brown water. Matthew hunched over the rail, hypnotized in the rigorous chill and sleepy streamers of steam. Crossing in the cold smother of river mist, they saw the water only briefly and occasionally through the vapour. It was like being on a cloud. Perhaps they had died and this was that other river. The ferryman, just visible at the bow, shouted unearthly commands under the engine noise. Hannah spread her feet when she felt the deck shiver, her hand numbing with the vibrations of the handrail. She began to wake up. The grey and dusty towns on each side beckoned and teased each other, extending piers and breakwaters like fingers or tongues. They heard about plans for a bridge. The buildings, pouting at the water's edge, pushed back the lush shore. White houses winked high in the greening bluffs.

From the middle of the river Hannah could see around her in a circle. A great energy inside her demanded release, but she couldn't open for it. Her hands clenched, her legs stiffened. Sweat burst in a flash as if she were on fire. Her eyes felt like they might explode. Noise burned in her ears. Thoughts snapped off before they began and the stumps smoldered. The marrow melted deep inside her bones. She felt the dread of some amorphous evil, and longings reaching into the past of some unremembered dream or a dream yet to come, and a yearning for something still unknown. And more: the excitement of the battle, the chase, flight. She stood rooted, waiting for it to wash over her, to sweep her away in whirlpools and mud flows. If she could only see where they were going. Her thoughts began like the bubbles of water in the spring house, slowly soaking her brain. Don't let me be cast off, she prayed. The river stretched away, so empty in the middle, dirty with mud and rust. Why did Matthew want to go into a land that made its rivers so filthy? Who would drink that? She felt sick to her stomach, but her stomach was empty.

Matthew pulled her along the side of the boat towards the bow to watch the docking procedure. He listened intently to the commands as if it mattered that he know how it was done. He did that, she had noticed. He was always paying attention and thinking about something important in the future, as if the future were a big puzzle and he must gather every piece that might fit along the way, carrying them no matter how cumbrous.

He had hardly spoken to her all morning. His face was sideways to her, the profile sharp as if ice had slid away from a rock face. He was fixed on the grey blur of the shore. He was beautiful, his bones shining through, calling shadows to themselves. She wondered if he would be so beautiful without her, if he would shine so. If she were suddenly to disappear over the side to be drowned in the mud, would he continue to look the same?

The ferry was made secure. They walked off before the wagons and carts. It was half a mile to the train, and soon they saw it, burly and black, glistening with dew. A man was polishing the brass knobs. He was glad to see them and immediately entrapped Matthew in conversation. After a few minutes Matthew interrupted to ask where they might get a cup of coffee. The man wiped his hands, which were green, disappeared around a corner, and returned moments later with two grimy mugs steaming with strong black coffee. He was pleased when they accepted his offering so eagerly. Matthew felt his mind clear. Hannah sat on one of the duffel bags and held her mug with both hands. Without the coffee she felt she might fall asleep in a minute. She felt she had been awake forever and had run a gauntlet between unrecognizable forces. Matthew laughed politely at something the railway worker said.

The sun rose over the bluff. The small office opened and Matthew bought two tickets. Magically a line of sleepy people formed behind him. Conductors, engineers, flagmen appeared, and the vendors loaded each passenger car with boxes of food, wood for the stoves, and water. As soon as they were allowed aboard, Matthew and Hannah found seats and huddled under a ledge of fatigue. The sun was on the opposite side of the car. They turned towards each other and tried to sleep.

The other passengers adjusted their surroundings according to the length of the trip. Some families were going to ride for four days all the way to the coast, arranging blankets, canteens and food boxes around them. Women nursed babies under their shawls. Strong tobacco smoke rolled down the long aisle. Gun barrels stuck out from under the seats. A pale girl was already standing at the stove heating a thinned porridge. For the moment voices were low and polite. No one had begun to tell a life story to the stranger in the next seat over.

Outside, the land began to change. Trees clumped near water. Along the tracks garbage rotted in on itself. Piles of buffalo bones bleached in the sun and mysterious funnel-shaped fences led up to platforms so close to the passing train they looked to be in danger of being knocked away. Long grey-green fields stretched out behind railway shacks and the occasional trading post. In the distance, houses stood riveted at the conjoining edges of land and sky.

And beyond, the land opened like the wings of an albatross, indifferent, inattentive to the newcomers. Without form, it was unconcerned with the tickle of the plough, the prick of a deep well. It was deaf to the sound of the gun, unmoved by the soak of buffalo blood, this land in its unquestioning trance, still rebounding from the weight of ice, still attentive to wind and rain after eons of amorality.

Matthew woke with a start, disoriented. In his dream he had been wedged at the foot of his bed between the mattress and the foot board. The man in the seat ahead of him shoved the window down and poked the barrel of his rifle out to shoot into a small herd of buffalo. The sound of the shot signalled all the men with guns. They pulled out their weapons and, moving the women out of the way, rushed to that side of the train. Excusing himself, a man leaned over Matthew, forced the window, and began yelling excitedly. He fought with his dirty gun, wrenched the cock back, whooped and fired. The burning powder charge sprayed into Matthew's lap, and he jumped up, pushing the man away and brushing off the hot gunpowder. The man rushed to the rear of the car and tried to get out on the platform. 'Did I get him. Did I?' The herd was hidden behind the dust of their stampede. The men continued to fire. Blue gun smoke, a sharp exciting smell, blew back into the train. Hannah leaned across Matthew and out the window. 'Hey!' he cried, grabbing her and pulling her back inside. 'Don't do that, you'll get your head shot off.' She couldn't stop looking. Where the dust had cleared, several brown lumps receded on the plain. The men slowly returned to their seats, swinging their guns by the trigger loops, laughing, sweating, back-slapping. She looked at them for a moment and then back outside. The buffalo were gone before she had a chance to see them. The dust made a soft yellowy cloud that roamed. When it settled, exposing the plain, Hannah tightened her grip on the window's edge.

'How do you tell where you are out there?' she asked, leaning back in her seat. Beyond the windows on the other side of the train were bare hills, as swollen as rising bread. A little dust fluffed off their tops, and off the far side was a haze of green that she thought must indicate trees. She had never seen so few trees. Where had they all gone?

'Most were cut for railway ties,' said Matthew, 'and for those homes out there.' He pointed to a speck and then another on the next hill, a reddish dot, perhaps a barn.

Hannah's shoulders were cold and slivers pierced her joints. If all the trees were gone, what would they use to build their house? What would they burn in their stove?

Matthew asked the conductor how fast the train could travel.

'Forty mile on the hour, average.' Matthew was impressed, the officer proud.

It didn't seem as fast, though, as when he rode that old skinny devil of a racehorse that belonged to Bill Boyle down in the bottom land. That shiny horse had run its socks off. Bill used to rub its legs every night with a gooey concoction of slippery oils and secret ingredients, and in the morning, ride until that horse steamed like a gutted deer in winter. On Saturday mornings Bill let Matthew ride, showing him how to do everything, how to read the horse's ears and clean his feet and get the last best try out of him. He had big black bulgy eyes that could look right around at you while he was running forward. He'd tilt one eye back to see if you were going to hit him, but mostly Matthew talked to him up close, in behind those swivelling ears, talking him up the headlong hill out of the river bottom, through the steeple trees and out on the flat poor land sticky with tough weeds, where soft mice slept, and the dust flew out behind and got stuck in the trees and that horse wore the ground right down three inches, and when the gully filled up with rain Matthew would start another path. Sometimes he would slow the horse down and stop at a certain place, and they would stand there in the quiet air. The horse was warm, glistening, his muscles still, and he would flutter his skin to get rid of a fly, and look around, sticking his nose up in the air and blowing out his nostrils. Matthew would start talking again, getting him ready, and the horse would leap and snatch at the ground, pulling on it, clawing it until he was free of that sleepy inertia, the wind a whine in his ear, a song. Matthew hung on, thinking the horse was going to come apart in the middle, he stretched out so, like a lean dog sliding, snapping back, muscles bunched over rib and sinew, while beneath him beat the terrible drum of hooves. Matthew clung to the mane. So fast, so close to the ground, the wind, the smell of crushed weeds and clean sweat, that wonderful speed.

The wind blew stronger when they arrived, piling up against the bleached bump of a town. The street was almost empty. Men wore ban-dannas pulled up over their mouths, the women, a corner of shawl or handkerchief gathered to their faces. Those disembarking from the train gathered at the baggage car, and they milled, sandwiched between the train and a flat ugly wall peppered with posters, handbills and broadsides, all covered with dust and unreadable. Hannah noticed deep burns and depressions as if the signs had been shot at and pelted with rocks. She wiped the grit from her face as best she could.

They had to get in out of this wind. The first public building they came to was the wagoner's shop. Immediately distracted, Matthew walked around each model. Hannah stood at the open doors watching the cold wind blow by. Her clothes were heavy with dirt. They would have to get a room so they could bathe before setting out in a wagon. There was supposed to be a river around there, maybe she could jump in it.

Next door was a stable, one of three on the edge of town. Blacksmiths, farm equipment, saloon, land claims office, grocery, saloon, hotel, restaurant, cooper, saloon, pharmacist, general store, hotel, saloon. They ducked into each establishment, out of the dust, dragging all their belongings. Each place was more utilitarian than the last, rough warp board floors and canvas curtains for doors. People were everywhere, whole families taking up corners, children lying on benches, asleep, wetting their pants.

'What are you waiting for?' Hannah asked the woman who appeared the least exhausted.

'Waiting out the dust storm.'

'Do you live around here?'

'Not too far, a half-day's trip up the northeast.' By now the woman was looking more closely at Hannah. She had been there for three years and hardly ever saw the same person twice. People arrived, flickered and disappeared, even the red-headed ones. Tomorrow or the next day, she and her man, that slip-switch, whippy-thin boy, would be gone out to the land and she'd never see them again. It was lonely out there. Even through the dirt the girl looked lively, intense, as if she might suffer from loneliness more than some, more than those whose feet were broad and flat, who had more flesh on their necks and on the backs of their hands. She would suffer, that one. Not a trace of sadness in her eyes, no betrayals, no children, no dust storms. No pain slowing her down yet.

Once upon a time, the woman began to think, but just then one of her children tugged her blouse loose and put his head underneath. He looked like a mouse. She deftly shifted him from one breast to the other and counted the heads around her.

Hannah looked around. Everyone was bored with waiting. Some groups were gathering up anyway, going home before they got stuck there overnight. Touching her elbow, Matthew led her to a spot where they could talk. She told him the only thing she wanted to do was take a bath. That was possible at the hotel, without their having to stay overnight, but the bath was expensive, the rooms vastly overpriced because there was no real competition. What he had in mind was to buy a wagon promptly and get it hauled to a campground where they could stay until they made their other purchases. 'As long as I can have a bath,' she repeated with a closed-lip smile.

By nightfall the wind had died down and they were sitting face to face in a wagon. On a small mat between them were two tin plates, two mugs and a measure of milk. Hannah had heated a can of beans at someone else's fire. They'd have to get a stove or a grate. The duffels made a back rest. Dogs came sniffing around, one putting his feet up to have a look in, but no one was paying attention to him. The lantern shone in his eyes. With a yawn he left. Matthew was thinking about tomorrow.

The wagon had ash-wood arches bowed over the top, the front one tilted forward to provide a roof over the driver. A white canvas was flung over the arches and tied down. Hannah had hung a blanket over the front opening. The back could be shut by a drawstring like the Conestoga prairie schooners. They couldn't stand up straight, but there was plenty of headroom when they sat like this.

When they had finished eating, Hannah washed the dishes at the water supply, then made a bed for them. She used two duffels as a mattress, evening out the clothes inside. The third she shoved under the front seat from the inside so that no one could steal it. She put the lantern down by their feet and pulled the drawstring to close the canvas. It was too cold to undress. She had on the clean clothes she had donned after her bath. They tucked themselves in under four blankets and two plumped quilts. They were lying in the middle of the whole world. In a white bubble like the moon they held each other and listened to the soft sounds of life all around them, the creak of wagon as someone shifted, hungry cries of nursing babies, a sleepy scolding. Hannah wondered if anyone was making love, if anyone had the energy. Matthew was asleep beside her, his hand in her hair. Something moved outside, maybe that old dog.

Early the next morning Matthew was talking to the men on the grounds. They had no reason not to tell the truth. Some had come this far by wagon, bringing their belongings and animals. The man camped at the far end might have a cow for sale, Matthew told her. A ranch just out of sight beyond a low bluff was the place to get horses or mules.

Hannah heated water and cooked porridge at a neighbour's fire.

'Thank God the wind's down. You can't imagine trying to cook with that dust. It gets into everything, smothers the fire. You're eating it! I have to put gauze over the baby's face. You have to cover everything and still it don't make a bit of difference.'

Hannah carried the water back to their wagon and poured some of it into a teapot, saving the rest to wash in, then returned with the porridge. The back flap of the wagon could be dropped. They sat adding molasses and dried apples to the oatmeal, swinging their feet a little. Work had begun in earnest all around them, their neighbours shaking the dust from bedding, washing clothes, stringing up drying lines, cooking in stove kettles or bake ovens, milking cows and goats, overseeing children; wagon repair, harness splicing, gun care; a line-up had formed at the blacksmith's shop. The air rang with shouts, clangs, neighs. Hannah tried to remember the dry wind. She woke around the strong tea, its bite in her stomach, smelling first its fumes, then the sweetish air mixing in. The twitch and spill, the scent of grass pushing aside snow, sloughing through mud. And above, the sky was peculiar: translucent, pale. She had no sense of its size, there was nothing in it to hold on to. Their bright future was an empty sky. The thought made her sit still, not in fear or anticipation, but as quietly and with as little expectation as the air awaiting a whim.

For a while, after Matthew went to the stables, she wandered around listening to and talking with the other women. Once she had to run back to the wagon to stop a boy from stealing their kerosene. After that she stayed close, guarding their belongings. Watching from her cave, she made a list of what they'd need: flour, lard, sugar, tea, coffee, baking powder, custard powder, cornmeal, crackers, beans, dried fruit, bacon, matches, candles, soap, washtubs, a stove, kettle, bake oven, butter churn. Matthew was probably making a list of tools, farm implements, seeds, all the things he knew about.

He didn't return at noon. Hannah had watched everyone do everything a thousand times. She had rewritten her list on both sides of the wrapping paper, remade the beds, washed their clothes in the neighbour's tub and hung them over the wheels, which were new and clean. Nibbling on bread, drinking cold tea with more sugar, she waited with nothing to do. Napped, woke up. Some people packed up and moved on. New families arrived, occasionally young couples like themselves. Shyly they asked each other where they were from, where they were going. New pots and pans, the bridal quilt, a wedding ring were soon exhausted as conversation pieces. They became homesick and uncertain, only daylight bleaching out the fear they slept with. They didn't want to listen endlessly to little stories about someone else's home, they wanted to cling to their own, and soon soft tears stained their cheeks, and they drifted away behind sad smiles and drawn aprons. The children in the camp stared curiously for a moment; being grown up might have some drawbacks, they decided.

In the next three days Matthew accomplished everything he thought needed doing. He told her that the vendors made it easy for him to buy. After all, that was the purpose of the town. They acquired their necessities bit by bit until the only thing they didn't have was a hay stack. To the side of the wagon Matthew tied a walking plough, shovel, spade, rake, saw, axe, rope and water barrel. Under the wagon he hung an iron pot and several buckets. He bought a trunk, medicine, seeds, grease and groceries. 'You forgot the churn,' Hannah complained. But he hadn't forgotten the cow, who was due to calve in a month. Last, the horses and harness, leaving enough money to pay for registering the claim and for the camp rental. Besides the money Hannah had hidden in her clothes, the purse was almost empty. Matthew was relieved to have it done. It would be harder for a thief to rob them of these bulky things than to abscond with their cash. Besides, once they were alone out there, money would mean almost nothing. Out there he'd put money in a tin on the shelf. Later on he'd be able to repay his father. No hurry. After all, in the end his father hadn't been able to do enough for them. 'What's it for, if not to help your children? What's it for?' he'd said.

That night, in the ember glow of their fire, their heads at the end of the wagon, Matthew felt too long for his bed. Unable to sleep, he peeked out under the canvas and saw the horses tied near a bale of hay, the cow, the stove and trunk. What was that? Was someone outside touching his things? He got up. Nothing was going to wake Hannah tonight. He walked all around. The horses, two big steady animals driven all the way in from the East, tough and calm from the trip, were already getting used to him. A gelding and a mare pregnant with her second foal. The seller couldn't make him pay much extra for something that was less than a sure thing, but if it worked out Matthew would have another horse. He checked the tools and the buckets underneath. There was probably not a lot of theft here, he reasoned, with things out in the open and people so close to each other. Still, he decided to tie the cowbells on the plough and the saw. The fire's red embers glowed under ash. Hunkering down on his heels he put his hands out over the fire.

He tried to pretend he was all alone, but there was always movement. A woman awake with an infant circled her fire. She was so tired she was in danger of burning the bottom edge of her skirt. A man with trouble stood with his back to another fire, his body a bizarre, bloated, twisted silhouette. He appeared to conjure a reddish smoke that floated his head and touched him here and there, making guesses about him. Matthew didn't feel pity for him but rather a shapely awe as if in the presence of a minor god, someone whose body had been deformed by misfortune, someone who had a special purpose and resided in remote corners, feeding on flame, conserving his strength.

Next morning he and Hannah were the ones to leave. The goodbyes had a frantic edge, though said to strangers. Matthew knew he would probably return to this same office to register their claim, but by then the faces would have changed.

'Even the dust will have changed!' yelled one of the old women, who was thinking that it wouldn't keep her covered when she needed it, but would blow away, leaving her up for grabs.

'Good luck then.'

'And you too.'

'Take care of yourselves.'

'Come by if you're on your way.'

As long as they could see, Hannah was the last to let go, leaning out the side, waving a washrag at men, women, children, dogs, horses, mules and fence posts, anything taller than the grass bowing as they passed. Matthew pointed out the map in a box under the seat.

'Never lose that,' he said. 'Don't start a fire with it!'

'Or use it as toilet paper,' said Hannah. She touched it. 'Does it tell us where our future lies?'

Under their chatter was the clomp of hooves and creaking wagon joints. Fully loaded, they bellied much nearer the ground, and saw the slow stages of the passage ahead.

'Is that the river?'

Matthew looked at her from the edge of her eye. 'A mile wide and an inch deep.'

'That's what they say, I hear.' She sang. Already the going had soothed her. She slipped her hand in the loop of his suspender against the thick wool of his shirt and leaned her head on his shoulder.

'It's deceptive, they say. Those shallows are full of quicksand, and if you go to sleep near the edge, you can wake up in the water. It's between floods right now. The river ice was broken, but soon it'll swell up with run-off from the mountains.' He talked on, lulling her with the sounds in his voice. She loved the breathy aura around each word as if he were amazed by what he was able to say. Besides that, though, there was a space around each word, as if it might mean more. She listened and leaned. The river leaned a little towards them. With a soft lick some sand fell into its stream.

Soon they were alone on the trail. The horses walked on the packed footprints of the thousands of oxen that had gone before. Matthew said, 'We are only alone because we can't see far enough.' He was afraid that right now someone was looking at his land. At ten o'clock they stopped for the cold tea and biscuits someone gave them as they were leaving. They watered the horses and let them graze in harness. The lonely cow ate the new grass. Matthew studied the map, which had fine drawings of such landmarks as unusual rocks. Hannah went back to the cow, and crouching down near the animal's big face she sniffed. The cow sniffed up a clear mucus running down her muzzle, and licked her rubbery lips. Hannah had no sense of ownership. It was as if they were two creatures who had come together to discuss mutual benefit, to find the common ground between them. 'Not too fast now,' she said in her damp voice. 'You and me.' Big windmill ears swivelled. 'You're a nice clean cow, I like those spots, and those ones. I can see your teeth when you bite. You're enjoying that prickly new grass, aren't you. I think it's going to be harder for us to find food than for you.' The cow stamped her broad hoof. 'What's her name, Matthew?' she called over her shoulder.

He shrugged. 'Didn't say anything about her name.'

'We need you, cow,' she said, tucking her hands under her chin. 'When can we touch you? When the mystery is all gone? It's different with people, you know. We like to touch each other when there's something hidden. We want to uncover each other, we want to open ourselves right up to the bone. You might be lonely now, but pretty soon you'll have your calf. And we'll have your milk.' The cow looked at her blandly, a shiny curtain of glaze falling across her eyes. 'Well, you know what's important.'

They continued on their way until they noticed a wagon stopped ahead, pulled off the road at an angle as if hurriedly. Someone was holding the heads of the horses, keeping them quiet. Others were huddled around something on the ground, shoulder to shoulder, heads bent forward. As Matthew and Hannah got closer they heard a disturbing sound, one that shouldn't be outside, exposed in the open air. Matthew stopped the wagon. Its groans soaked into the ground. Now they heard clearly the raw flayed sobs, and saw over the tops of the heads the body lying still, someone about to cover the face because they had stopped listening for the breath, stopped looking for its fog on a mirror, stopped praying for it. The distance they assumed by stepping back was respectful and fearful, as if death might need the extra room.

Hannah put her hand on Matthew's arm. 'Wait … can we? Can we wait and see what happens?'

In a few minutes a man came over and asked to borrow a shovel. It was the first job their shovel would do.

'They aren't going to take the body with them?'

'How can they?'

Spring had softened the earth, but it was still not easy to dig down. Nothing grew in a strip on each side of the road, the feet of women and men and children and dogs and cows walking beside the wagons having packed the earth into a hard spine across the land. They walked farther afield with pickaxes, shovels and spades, and heard the sound of boards being nailed together.

The women prepared the body. 'We can't leave her here, I know what happens, I've seen the broken markers, the bones dug up. They're probably watching right now, waiting for us to get through and leave. The minute we're gone they'll come. She won't even be cold. Oh, God, I can't go on. The desecration. Why are we in this godless place, why did we come? If we were home she'd be buried in the old churchyard with all her friends. This isn't right. I can't leave her here, I must stay.'

The other women whispered, patted her back, wiped her eyes, and took her by the hand, so that before she knew what had happened she was back at the trail. 'No, I want to stay, I want to go back.' Some things they didn't want her to see.

'What did she mean, the bones are dug up?' asked Hannah.

'Scavenger animals dig up the bodies.'

'And eat them?'

A small wind hooted in the canvas. When it had filled the cavity it made the wagon rock from side to side. Hannah turned around, but no one was there, only the wind fluttering the blanket corners. I will never die out here, she promised herself, her flesh, her eyeballs, her tongue.

Several men carried the body to the shallow trench.

'Keep the blanket, the baby will need it.'

Hannah was uneasy. Why was she the only one who was continually surprised? How did Matthew know all these things? What would shock him?

When the shovel wasn't returned, Matthew went to retrieve it. She watched him standing with the group of men. He was not the biggest. Would he be big enough to keep them from harm? Under this sky everything was dwarfed.

Stowing the shovel, he climbed back up on the wagon and clucked to the horses.

'I can't stop looking,' mumbled Hannah. The hunch of mourners was shrinking in the distance of grass and sky, faster than it should, as if Hannah and Matthew had jettisoned some great weight from off the wagon.

In the late afternoon the sky backed up against an invisible wall of air. Within the hour the wind dropped and the grass stood straight up with a quiver that came from inside the blade. The horses became agitated, pulling and pushing in the harness. Stretching her neck out, the cow bawled. The sound didn't travel far in the charged air, but lay like a brown package in front of her face. Hannah brushed at something near her head, but nothing was there. She couldn't sit still. Clouds climbed higher in the sky than she had ever imagined they could, then boiled and spilled, darkening the earth around them.

Matthew slowed the wagon, picked a spot and pulled over. Unharnessing the horses, he hobbled them, threw the harness inside the wagon, then secured the cow. Frantically Hannah climbed back into the wagon to drop and tighten the cover. She called to him, 'Hurry, hurry,' her voice pitching the words. They stuck in him. She hauled him through the last crack in the cover and clutched him to her with her white hands. Dust shone in her hair. Her touch was electric. It was hard to breathe inside the hot wagon. The limp canvas glowed white even though the sky was black. The air had a strange smell. His arm was numb where she had hold of him. He sat back on the duffels and drawing her across his lap began to rub her back.

'I'm so afraid.'

'It's only a storm.'

'No, afraid I'm going to hurt you. Sometimes I feel peculiar, as if I've done something terribly wrong and something is going to happen because of it. I don't know what it is, I can't find out, but I feel there is this judgement.'

He rolled her over. She had tears of perspiration on her face. It didn't matter to him where they came from, he thought the shape of her tears was beautiful. He kissed her, licked them up, holding her face between his hands, sticking himself to her. But her body was rigid. She fought to get up, out of his grasp, out from under his lips. The wagon box was too small. She scrambled up, pulling at the neck of her blouse, undoing it, trying to catch her breath, mumbling, giggling, shivering.

Lightning burned the air. They could smell it. Thunder ground between its teeth, but nothing moved. He put out his arms to catch her should she fall between the strikes. The air suddenly drained out, sucking the canvas close to them. Then the wind was released, roaring in through the cracks, billowing the canvas out like a balloon, and the thrum and slither of rain brought abrupt relief. She glanced out the slit at the back to be sure what was happening was really rain, that nothing else was falling on them. It was just rain smacking the backs of the animals, drumming on the ground, which spat back dust for a while, then succumbed. She cupped a handful and brought it in, catching the water as it dribbled from one hand to the other, finally rubbing her face and his. He held her shoulders, nuzzling the hollow at the bottom of her throat where the rainwater had trickled, and from there down as she wiped her hands in his hair. They were deaf to each other, the storm squirrelling, clamouring over top of the canvas. Having forgotten her confession of fear, he was thinking only of the blue static thrill of her skin, her ability to arrest him mid-air, to change the direction his blood flowed, to bandage him in night at high noon.

It was dark inside the wagon but lighter outside. The rain fell straight down. The animals stood dully, ears turned over. He didn't want to stay out there for the night. According to the map, a few more miles would get them to a trading post. His logic escaped her; soon they'd be out there alone in the open like this for good. Parting the canvas enough to look out, they watched, chewing on stringy jerky and dried fruit. The rain slowed and stopped.

'We're off,' he declared, handing her a piece of towelling and a stick. They scraped and wiped the horses, harnessed them, and turned back onto the road. For all the violence of the rain, the ground dried quickly. The river was clumsy, its small tidal assaults on the banks undermining roots and spilling seedlings. But the air was fresh and clear. Their bodies were damp inside and out, relaxed, precious, otherly. The horizon reappeared. Behind them the storm moved away to the east. The grass shone wet and dustless in the white air. The wagon cast a long shadow behind it. Against the watery sunlight Matthew pulled on his hat and Hannah closed her eyes. The sun had no warmth, but she could taste a sweet scent in the air, purple with some yellow.

Approaching the trading post they caught up with a siege of travellers, traders, farmers, soldiers. Men and boys were drying horses and oil machinery. Frittering children held onto their mothers, who stirred smoking pots and tried to make up for the time lost to the rain. Soldiers idling in wet clothes poked their fingers into the ends of their guns and eyed the scuff of Indians squatting with their backs to the wilderness.

A rack of gutted elk, the horns, the skulls. Brown rabbit skins. Black-brown skins of unknown small animals. Entrails. A live coyote chained in a stupor of fatigue and starvation, the children throwing rocks at it as they passed, screaming with the thrill of taunting its teeth that were mere stumps broken against bitten steel links.

Soldiers who had not found Indian women amused themselves by firing their rifles into the night. Children woke crying, but the soldiers were too far away to hear. They had plenty of bullets, and Matthew bought some from them cheap. The soldier who took him into a small tent for the transaction asked him if he would like to share the squaw sitting in the corner.

Hannah waited for him. In the grim light of red fires laundry shuddered in slow dances. There were no stars to be seen through the smoke, and blurred sounds of strenuous drinking masked the wilderness just beyond. Once more she looked at the cow, who dozed because she had never smelled or been smelled by a wolf. Sleepless, pensive, Hannah was without two true thoughts to rub together. Her thoughts of old comfort were at an end, but nothing new replaced them. She admitted a thin, elusive feeling of loss but no regret. She didn't know how to recognize regret.

Next morning they turned north away from the river. For three days they followed the spidery trail on the map. In the beginning Hannah said, 'What is that called, and that, and that over there?' itemizing the landscape into bumps, stumps, bluffs, breaks, knolls, cuts, draws, passes. She didn't take her eyes from the trail for long, memorizing the purple rocks, that gnarled old tree, memorizing the way back.

The air dried her face in a tight mask. The territory was becoming a limitless land dotted with huddles of sod huts, herds of stringy cattle, rickety windmills, unsmiling women. Everything named was significant, every person puny upon the land, speechless, from somewhere else. What was there to say? 'You won't be staying'? 'We need all our strength'? A pillar of dust rose behind them.

Hannah and Matthew sat side by side in a silence the land seemed to demand. But the land didn't even feel them, they skimmed so quickly over its skin.

On the second day she asked, 'Matthew, do you know how to shoot a gun?' He was surprised because he had just been thinking of this. 'Enough to feed us, I hope. Do you see something?'

'Something over there,' she said, pointing to a shallow scoop of water speckled with shiny ducks.

'That's too far away.'

She was disappointed. 'Prove it before tonight!'

But that night they camped near a small settlement of related families. The women showed Hannah how to tend a fire made of buffalo or cow manure. They thought she would find it distasteful to handle the dung, but she didn't seem to mind. One of the women talked about the others. They listened. Matthew was leaning over the back of the cow, the men, against the wagon. They shared tobacco with him. The air was unusually warm. Before the firelight pushed back the dark, everyone went home.

91

By late afternoon of the third day, they knew they should be at their destination. Matthew stopped the horses and looked around. The road, which was becoming overgrown, continued in the direction they'd been travelling. By the map they knew they had to head east around a sand hill and look for a creek that twisted through a clump of cottonwood and willow. The horses were reluctant to leave the trail. Matthew got down and led them out into the grass, which bent down before them, but they didn't like the feel of it on their legs or the fact that they couldn't see what was underneath. In an hour they hadn't gone far. He had thought they would be there before dark.

On the fourth day he woke Hannah just enough to tell her he was going to ride out on one of the horses to find out exactly where they were. Sleepily she agreed to stay put and not wander in the snake-hiding grass. It was still night as far as she could tell, a thin chill swimming in dark airy lines on top of her. When he was gone she heard something else. The horse snorted. Something else. She held her breath. The cow ripped grass. Hannah lifted her head. The flaps of the canvas flew open and a face peered in. Another face, smiling. The Indians chattered to each other, then reached into the food box, took a bag of dried fruit, and were gone. She jumped up and peeked out. As she climbed down they were already riding away on scruffy ponies. She heard laughter, giggles, nothing from the ponies, then nothing except the grass stirring in the dawn breeze. She hunted through their belongings, saw that nothing else was missing. Her feet were soaking, the bottom of her nightgown wet. She gathered her shawl closed at her throat, backed up against the wagon, sat on the edge, and tucked her feet under her.

When Matthew returned, Hannah refused to come out. He made the fire and prepared breakfast. 'After all, nothing really happened. That's supposed to be something they do, just come around to have a look-see. I doubt if they expected to find you! They probably were watching and when they saw me leave they thought they'd come on over.'

'First of all, you never told me that might happen. Secondly, if there's no trouble around here, why are there all those soldiers? What do we do when they come back and start stealing from us on a regular basis?'

'It's all right, it's safe now. Come on out.' He wanted to reassure himself. There were strangers out there, outlaws, Indians, wild animals. Women were spared because they were harmless or killed because they were weak. This was what he had heard, but found it hard to believe. He couldn't convince himself of a personal danger. He was too good a person. He believed that those around him shared the umbrella of that goodness. Hannah would never die. If anything, if the Indians stole her they would make her a goddess. They would pluck strands of her hair while she slept, weave them into bracelets or use them to decorate arrows. They would ask her important questions and breed magic children from her breath.

'Come on, come and sit with me.' He harnessed the horses and smothered the fire. It was not far now. 'Come and see what I found for us. I want you to share this with me.'

This was how it began on that sunny morning: his idea, this promise. It touched him: the first wind, the first sky. He heard the first sigh. He wanted to hold her hand. The land was dry and cool. The grass murmured anticipation. He wanted to show her that he brought more than the sun, the rain, the frost, the simple seed to this land. He brought a heart on this first day. The earth below and the sky above met in him. His hands were empty. He opened them to let the earth smell his intention. On the second day the furrow of his plough would leash the land. Be not afraid, he would say, let me put this seed here, let it grow and then give me its fruit. Let me take it, I promise to put it back. I will take nothing you cannot give. I promise.

'Take my hand now.' He helped Hannah down into the middle of a great emptiness. Walking to the front of the horses, they stood as if they were all alone. They were all alone. They had walked a million miles and Hannah was as much a part of him as was his own arm. And he was as unconscious of her as he was of that limb hanging at his side.

'Well?' he asked tenderly, a whisper. He didn't imagine talking to the earth so much as caressing it, rubbing it between his fingers, sifting it between his toes.

Is this it? Is this far enough? she wondered. This land of flat lines, hitchless, domed by an empty sky. Only ripples in grass to break the monotony of space. She saw the wind everywhere in the grass, but couldn't feel it on her skin, and its breath was quieter than her own. The air, bone dry, too thin to digest, parched her throat. The liquid light deceived: at the same time she was too tall and too small, her shadow scattering in the grass.

Is this it? Have I come far enough? I believe, I believe, she said to herself. Why is it harder? It should be easier now that I am close. I've had

93

practice and time. I should be more comfortable, not less. What does he see that I don't? He is rapt, even blissful. He sees things that aren't there.

'Just you and me now.' His prairie raged gold, purple, greens, brown before him.

The answer to all my prayers, she thought. But it isn't wonderful, isn't anything. There must be something else. She scanned the horizon. What is it? I thought it would be here. Maybe it is and I can't see it. I thought I would recognize it right away. Not this vagueness, this haltered step. She slipped her hand out of his.

Five

Matthew slept the deep slumber of one who had arrived to a home-coming. He had dropped off the end of a journey that had kept him awake even while he slept, dreaming this day over and over, the strangeness of it, the promise running ahead of him in the grass. The grass would thicken, closing behind him in warm darkness violated by a knife of light, his own star squinting his eye, crimping his sleep. Now he owned the sweet air of an open night, the stars standing where they belonged in the sky, bedding and boards under him, and beneath that the skin of the earth, as good as any mother. Turning, turning over, rolling softly across him, on and on, the breath of his wife.

In the morning Hannah climbed out of the wagon. Down in the tangle of grass was a bloom, a white tulip-like petal folded around a cluster of yellow stamens. She had thought there would be no flowers in this harsh hazy place.

They stripped down the wagon so that Matthew could use its flat bed for hauling sods from around the buffalo wallow where the roots were dense. He rode out to borrow a breaking plough and a team of oxen from a neighbour, the use of which he would pay off in work at harvest time. When the clevis was adjusted, the blade cut three inches deep, two feet wide, and turned the sods over in a curl. He cut them into two-foot lengths, loaded the wagon and returned to the site. Each sod weighed fifty pounds.

By moonlight they laid out the foundation, sighting on the North Star to get the proper alignment north-south and east-west. The blocks were arranged grass side down and alternated like brickwork.

It took more than an acre of sod and a week of dry weather to build the walls eight feet high, and above that the gable peaks. When this small fortress, twelve by twenty-two, was complete, he drove the horses to a grove of cottonwoods to cut roof poles and corner pins.

Hannah stomped the dirt flat into a floor while he was gone. All the while she planned where she would put things. The sun was hotter now. Using a branch she brushed back and forth. She let her thoughts go to the gap where the door was going to be, and they peered out like mice.

There was nothing out there. Cold shimmered against the sky. The absence was a great wall without seams. She saw no way through.

Matthew was coming back across the flat. Before he was close, the sun shone on the buttons of his white long johns, making it look as if there were holes punched in his throat and chest and some bright substance had been let out. He was panting. A skin of sweat on his cheeks. When he stopped, his pelvis tilted forward making his belly pot out.

Until he could get back to town, the ceiling was made of clean peeled poles and sky. A blanket hung across the door. He cut a window through the south wall. At night Hannah covered it with newspaper. In the starlight, for a moment before she slept, she imagined the stove there against the west wall, the buttery in the southwest corner beside the window. In the window, a geranium. In the geranium a blossom. In the blossom...

Time was short. Matthew returned to sharpen the plough share. He ploughed another day. Ten hours a day, twelve miles, one and a half acres. And another. He returned to sharpen the plough. Two more days of breaking ground and he had to sharpen the plough again. Two more days. When he looked back, the weeds and grass were growing up out of the turned sods.

Before he returned the oxen and the plough to their owner he broke an acre for a kitchen garden close to the house. Hitching the horses he drove back to borrow a stirring plough that the horses could pull to cultivate the ground. Before leaving he sharpened the share of the breaking plough and each disc of the disc plough.

East, west, back and forth, north, south, up and down, the small tough acre succumbed. Hannah followed to touch the earth behind the plough.

In the evening, while the sun was still warm and the air still, she walked with Matthew to the creek. She rinsed the caked mud of sweat and dust from his shirt and overalls. In just this short time he was brown where the sun had got at him. In contrast was the white flesh of his thighs. She washed his back while he crouched hunched between his knees, his feet sinking into the warm sand. Uncupping his hands he spread them open. They seemed enormous to her. The blisters were breaking one by one, plastering the leathery top skin to the layer underneath. He hardly recognized his own skin, which was dark, rusty, the nails broken down to the quick. The water cooled his burning muscles. He thought he might just stay there forever, wallowing in the smooth wet sand, but she was already towelling his hair. She had brought a long shirt. He moved close to her.

'Who will see?' he said.

Her hand on his arm was softer than the air.

Afterwards, while they held each other, he decided he would go to the mill in the morning. He'd need lumber for the door, the roof, the window frame, the well. He'd need a latch and hinges, nails and stovepipe joint to go through the roof. It was early enough that they were sure to give it all to him on credit. It should take only five days round trip because the wagon would be empty on the way in and he knew the way now.

They worked as long as there was light in the sky. Chances were good there was potable water between the house and the creek. Walking about twenty-five feet out they looked for ants. His neighbour, Lewis, had told him that an anthill was a good indication of water. Using a pickaxe he began to dig, loosening the sod and soil. Beneath the mat of roots the soil was crumbly, but a little deeper he had to go back to using the axe. Hannah shovelled the dirt away as it piled up at the edge. When they could no longer see what they were doing she helped him out of the hole. He checked the animals, pegging them on the other side of the house, not wanting them to wander into the well hole.

Just before they lay down for the night he told her he was going to town the next day.

'I'll go to Lewis's,' she said.

'What if someone steals our stuff? And the cow.'

'I'm too tired to think about it.' She fell asleep to the sound of his voice.

While he ate oatmeal and molasses, she rummaged through the duffel bags. 'You mean we don't have a single scrap of paper, not even one piece? What did you do with it? I've got to write a letter home!'

'I'll do it when I'm in town.'

'I want to do it!' She was incredulous.

'Well, you can't, can you. Tell me what to write. I won't forget.'

'Well,' she began. It was almost impossible. He wouldn't remember the way she said it. How was as important as what, maybe more.

She'd never listened quite so carefully to the sound of the wagon. As

97

it receded, each creak of dry wood, rattle of chains, squeak of leather strap rushed in her ear like the echo of her whole journey. And then as if swallowed the sounds grew thin and disappeared. She could still see the wagon, the small dust behind it, the wobble of the grass tops, but it moved in silence. Her eyes burned because she didn't blink. Because the land was flat and treeless, she watched until the image changed from real to imaginary.

As soon as he disappeared, she grabbed her skirt and ran around the house to see what the cow was doing. She didn't seem to have noticed Matthew's departure and remained placidly exploring the grass within her tether. 'Let's go for a walk,' Hannah suggested, taking up the rope, undoing it and looping the end over her arm. The cow, Lettice, was not sure. After all, she hardly knew this girl. Still, she caught a whiff of creek water and greener grass.

The creek was not very far. After they both drank deeply, Lettice moved up the opposite bank to sample the weeds there. Hannah pulled on the rope though she was hard pressed to leave the protective cuff of brush and tree. The air was warm and thick with the scent of mud, quicksand and soft earth. 'Come on.' It was easy to forget how close the night was. Climbing the low bluff, she expected to see the homestead of their neighbours, but the plain was empty.

She stopped. Lettice dropped her head. 'You must be nearsighted, you old cow. Don't you ever look at the sky?' Which was beginning to blaze blue through the last haze of morning. She looked for signs of their wagon's passage, of the oxen breaking down the grass, but the prairie had closed over. It must be that way, she decided, looking into a shudder of wind revealed on the back of the grass. 'If I go that way but always make sure I can see the creek …' But she didn't move. 'He wasn't afraid to leave me alone, even though … Maybe he told Lewis to check on me, to be sure everything was all right … Maybe when he comes I can go back to their place with him.' Above her the trees netted the sun as it rose over them and there was a little fresh noise from the creek, the crackle of some animal from its cover of dense bush or its hole just underneath.

The longer she stood still the more life resumed around her. She thought it might grow right over her. She felt cold danger awakening in some old spot, spreading along the bottom of her stomach, tingling in her hands. Organs she didn't know she had tightened. Is this the way it's supposed to be? Aren't I supposed to be able to be on my own, to be by myself, even here?

The land had an almost imperceptible rise to it. When the sun was overhead, she and the cow had gone far enough, and she could see the tarpaper shanty of the neighbour. In the distance a tail of dust unwound and flattened behind the man, Lewis, and his plough. From there he looked like Matthew, like everyman in his field, leaning as everyman had since the first sharp stick was stuck in the ground to make a seed hole.

The ground opened bloodlessly. Thin spirals of dust, no more than smoke, rose from the thin cut. The earth didn't make a sound. Hannah could hear Lewis gobbling to the oxen, who swayed this way and that. She switched her mouth from side to side, stretching her dry cheeks. She rubbed her eyes. From there she could see everything. Lewis didn't look up. She decided from now on she must keep an eye on the horizon. Someone just might be ...

An old woman appeared in the doorway of the little house. She saw Hannah and shouted, beckoning her to come. Hannah pulled the cow's nose out of the buffalo grass silvering in the sun. She forgot the distances, the blind spots. Another person was calling to her. She was so hungry.

From behind the woman came small children. Their easygoing eyes floated. They had the sweet smell of a home on them. As the woman tied Lettice to a post, Hannah noticed her hands. They looked like her mother's. Inside the shanty the children moved aside, making room for Hannah to sit on a chair at the table. Their eyes roamed over her, skimming the dull parts, lingering on her hair. The littlest one was close enough to touch it. She reached up, but the woman knocked her hand aside.

'I'm Addie, there are my children: Tully, Rosa, Nellie. And here's another one,' she said, patting her belly. *Her* children. But?

Addie shrugged. 'Well, what can you do?'

Hannah sat between two worlds. She could still run with the children if she wanted to. Couldn't she? Yet Addie was talking to her as if she knew what grown women were. She didn't know if people were allowed to inhabit both worlds at the same time.

'Oh, my dear, you can't stay here. Not that you aren't welcome, but you mustn't leave your things alone. There are thieves.'

'I'm not much, I wouldn't be able to stop anybody.'

'There are thieves and thieves.' Addie handed her a tangy drink in a fragile blue china cup.

'We have no china,' Hannah said, running her finger around the rim. She sniffed the solution and dipped the tip of her tongue in it.

'Ginger water. Maybe I could lend you Tully for a couple of days, seeing as we're neighbours. He's a good boy and he can shoot straight.'

'Shoot!' She looked at Tully, who shrugged and raised his eyebrows.

Tully was still picking over the possibilities of change and adventure when he saw the unfinished house. 'I sure hope it don't rain,' he said.

He snared a rabbit (Hannah had yet to even see one), making her watch as he bled, gutted and skinned it. He was surprised she had no cat or pig to eat the offal. Guilelessly he showed her its sex. The ears, tail and skin he kept for himself. He showed her how to prepare and cook it in a pot, outside, where men did their own cooking. They sat on the ground. The night swelled around them. Because she seemed to appreciate him, he told her proper fireside stories flavoured with wood smoke while the rabbit stewed.

'How old are you, Tully?'

'Thirteen.'

Small, she thought, for thirteen. He could have just turned thirteen, four years younger than she was. Four years ago, what was she doing? She tried to remember.

The stars were close, the moon howling with a wide-open mouth. Tully said, 'It's letting the light through from the other side,' voicing her very thought, as if it were some universal concern of children to worry about holes. His face was rubbed with firelight. The night held him loosely, unable to penetrate the wrap of light. How much darkness would it take to swallow the fire and get him, get them all?

She began to separate the bedrolls. For a moment she thought he wanted to sleep outside the walls, but he arranged himself like a dog across the door opening. She was sure he was making something up to go along with the little rituals. He kept the gun beside him on the dirt floor and he wasn't talking.

Hannah lay back in the dark. She hadn't imagined being alone out here and wondered what else Matthew hadn't told. A small persistent pain bathed her stomach. It might have been the rabbit, but she knew better. For a while the night was so quiet she couldn't sleep. Her breathing shallowed to a point where she had to hold her whole body still, waiting. She thought she'd never be able to sleep again; she dreamed of rabbits.

First thing in the morning Tully broke the spine of a rattlesnake that had coiled itself just outside the door. Hannah backed into a corner.

He chopped its head off with the axe. 'It's safe now.' He sawed off the rattle. 'Six this time,' a good trophy, though he wondered aloud if the snake had crawled near him in the night to get warm. 'You need a good dog, lady,' he said without looking up. With the sun lighting him he looked bigger than he did last night. Now he was staring at her because she had only her petticoat on and her feet were bare. 'Always wear shoes outside,' he said.

Each morning he went home, returning before dusk to stay the night with her. Addie sent along corn muffins and jam.

On the fifth day she heard the wagon creaking through the shadowless grass.

'I knew it, I knew it was you.' She held him, his arms, his large warm hands. She held him at arm's length to be sure he was the same. 'You smell like wood and sunshine.' She felt the tug of gravity in her loins, making her feel heavy and peaceful.

He had brought newspapers, circulars, a small packet of paper. But instead of both talking at once, trying to get it all in, all the adventures, neither of them spoke of the last few days, as if they could no longer see them in their mind's eye, as if they were ashamed or the time had been unimportant.

Everyone nearby who was able came to help. Hannah made coffee and dried apple pie on an open scrub brush fire. 'We all started in the same place,' said one of the men. Hannah considered her neighbours as they were now. Once Addie started to talk, Hannah forgot about the way she looked. Now she saw that all the women, the men, even the children, were wiry weed dry. Dried-up men, milky dusty crinkly women.

'How many years?' she asked each one. 'How many years for you?' Brown smoky burnt skin. Dust on her lip. Tight lariat loops of words. 'How long does it take?'

'Shhh.' Matthew touched her lips lightly, gently. Quickly, but as if to make an impression, he moved behind her and sat his hands down on her shoulders, his thumbs in that tight place between the blades. Imperceptibly she tilted her head back. They were looking at her. If it weren't for Matthew ... Look at me, go ahead, she thought, scuffling the dust with her feet. Look at us. He leaned his hips into her. If these people hadn't been there, he would have slipped his hands around to her breasts.

The light shone through her hair.

The men went to work on the roof. On the tamped-down gable ends they positioned the peeled ridge pole. Poles were laid also on the tops of the walls and one across to make a ten-by-twelve area at the rear of the house. The cheaply cut rough boards were laid side by side the length of the roof. Tar paper was unrolled on top of this. Later, Matthew would cover the whole thing with sod. The window frame was inserted, then the window. Matthew wanted to watch how to make a door. The stove was positioned and the stovepipe attached, run out the roof and fastened. They talked about making a chinking plaster out of clay from the well mixed with ash and straw. Many in this district had made a floor cover of the wagon tarp spread over straw.

The women stood for a few minutes by the pile of things they had removed from inside the house. 'You're lucky to have a wood roof, the dirt won't be such a problem. When we first came, the first year, there was no mill. We had to wait a whole year. The ceiling was straw and tar paper. Straw dust in everything.'

They took the dishes to the creek. 'Tell me the whole story,' Hannah said, watching the reflections break in the water. If she could figure it out, she could arrange it so that things didn't happen to them. Conditions could be altered, things could be different.

'The snake come through the wall into bed with us 'n' the kids. One of 'um says, Quit bothering me, and the pa says, Shut up, and in the morning the kid's stone cold ...'

Mice. They told her they'd bring her some kittens out of the next barn batch.

Lice and nits. 'Strew wormwood and silver sage in the bed robes. Then in the summer spread them over anthills and let the ants eat the bugs. In the winter build a smudge fire of sagewood and sweetgrass and hang your bedding over it.'

'Chew plantain and rub the spit on to take away the sting.'

'Kerosene for bugs.'

'Get a toad out of the slough to eat the bugs under the house.'

They didn't have an under-the-house yet. One less place for the bugs to go.

'It's still so nice and cool, the mosquitoes aren't out in full force yet.'

One of the women yelled at the children to play downstream from where they were washing up. Hannah had forgotten about them. 'Do you ever forget us?' she had asked her own mother out of curiosity, but Adele had laughed so hard she'd been unable to answer, and then her gaze had wandered off as if she were thinking about a time long past.

There was little wind that night. Matthew burned some brush and cow patties to see how well the chimney drew. They closed the door and pulled the latch string. The wind stroked the window. The stove was breathing. They cuddled together and listened to it. In the dark the roof felt close, cocked open like wings catching small heat, holding it over them. He was thinking about what he had done, about how this had all happened. He hadn't thought the roof would make such a difference. Or a real door. While he was thinking, Hannah fell asleep.

For a while Matthew went out every other day to work off what he could of his debts to his neighbours. On the days he was home he dug in the well and built a crib to line the hole. It was deep enough to strain water out of the quicksand. The water was sweet, thank God. He built a well head cover to keep the animals from falling in.

One morning Hannah said, 'There are no trees. Get me a tree, Matthew.'

'Get me a tree,' he mimicked.

'No, I mean it. I can't live out in the open like this.' She crossed her arms, tucking her hands in. She was uneasy. Something was different. In all this space did she feel a tentative stretching of those wings folded in behind her shoulders?

Riding out, he found an old dead hackberry tree, which he cut down and dragged to break up the clods in the field. Hannah planted her seeds. She hadn't much hope for them that year. Each row was won from the grass. Each sod had to be ripped apart, the dirt shaken from it, the grass dried quickly and burned in the stove. Because there'd been no rain the earth blew around. She caught it on the hem of her skirt, in her hair, under her fingernails. She stomped and hoed and poked small holes to put the seeds in: peas, lettuce, cucumbers, beans, tomatoes, turnips, peppers. All this work engendered more: watering, cultivating, scaring away birds and rabbits, discouraging moles. Every day the animals had to be watered and moved to new grazing. They put in posts for a fence. She wanted a table, a bed raised off the ground. She needed a post for a clothesline. Chickens. An outhouse.

In late May the creek swelled with mountain run-off stirring the sand, but when it had settled, the water was like nothing they'd tasted before. Cold, tart, bright, it froze their teeth and made them think of explosions. She washed bedding and it smelled like lichen and icicles.

'Will we ever see the mountains?'

Or oceans, icebergs, tropical islands, the North Pole? The other side of the moon!

He trickled water over her face as she tipped it up and stuck out her tongue to catch the drops. Would everything she wanted come to her here? Would it find her? How would it? How would she know for sure that this was the right place for her, that the taste in the water was more than merely this moment?

The night was hot and humid. A burnt smell caught on the edge of the house and crept inside, making no sound, but waking Matthew nevertheless. He thought it was the end of a dream, something disappearing when he opened his eyes on the dark, which was deep enough to hide in. His body was too heavy to move. He was suffocating, sweating, shivering where he lay. He'd thought that what he'd been doing was the important thing and that he'd been doing it the right way, but now all he felt was exhaustion, desolation, dirt. All over his body his muscles trembled. The persecution of the plough, the endless spectrum of dust. Nightmare sloughs of time. Long-tongued laughter forked him up. He tried to twist away from it. With grim blunt teeth a different kind of hunger gnawed on his insides. He thought of the seeds suffocating in the ground. Soft hills flattened, furrows slithered with an empty sound.

In her dream Hannah wanted to ask, 'Why did you bring me here?' but Matthew took her hand. It was the last night in May or early in the morning. Dew and a smooth black earth-sky. Silences that lived in the dimensionless dark had been disturbed. She felt them snuffling at her feet as if they were trying to identify her. She didn't want to go outside, where wolves lurked. Matthew put his jacket over her shoulders. He was ahead of her, his skin too hot to touch. As if fireflies had been smeared on her skin, her arms flared and glowed, the details of her face lost in a halo of white. 'Hurry, hurry,' he said, but she wanted her boots laced up so the snakes couldn't bite her ankles. He crouched. In the blackness she could see the shape of his back floating. Like a prince he fixed her slipper. She held up her petticoat, the edge brushing across his face, so close to his eyes. A pure light, white, laced with sage dew. The smell of her warm body bleeding from beneath the hem of her gown. She lifted the skirt over his head, cloaking him in snow. She faced the dark by herself, letting it hear her breathing. 'Come and get me,' she whispered.

He held on to her body. He was keeping it, holding his breath. His fingers climbed the backs of her knees. A pale early shadow began to form out of dew and leftovers. 'Hurry, hurry,' he said, before the real dawn, taking her hand, her petticoat twisting between her legs, blowing out behind her, snagging his knees. He pulled her along beside him, jostling her when he slipped in the dirt, steadying her on the broken ground. 'This way, this,' hissing, urgent. His feet sank in the soft treacherous ground. 'Hurry, hurry,' intimate, softer than a whisper, disturbing the layers. 'Listen to me.' The blind night listened from out in the middle of the field, jellyfish darkness pulling its tentacles back down the long furrows. 'Here, here,' he insisted, nervously stamping at the ground, scratching, turning round and round. She stumbled in the deep cut, deep in his fantasy, and before she could look around he covered her face, his hands holding the smells of everything he had done. She knew his flesh, but his eye was hooded, secret like blood, and when it spilled it was dark, shapeless, ineffectual, a dead dream on the blanket. She couldn't wake him, she didn't want to as he laid her down in the dirt. But now his hands were tighter, his fingers pressing deeper, his breath burning. He nuzzled the ground beside her head, licked the dirt up into his mouth, tasted it on the sides of his tongue. Beneath him the deep furrow twisted and hungered, split white, fabric, earth, skin. He opened it, a sound coming up against him. 'I hear you, I hear you.' He needed to rub her all over to make sure the surface was alive, sweet, warm. Making sure, taking handfuls of soil, cloth, skin. She might have been dying bit by bit. He might have found cold scaly spots. He plucked out a stone and it made him want to cry. There would always be stones down there, unseen, making the horses stumble, stubbing his toes, breaking his knees and teeth, ripping the webs between his fingers.

Sweat soured his skin. Gathering her hair, he wiped his face. He sucked on the hairs curling around his tongue, spit them out before they could wring his tongue from his mouth. He wrapped his arms and legs around her, tightening his grip, but she melted, and he was drowning in the mud she had made out of his sweat and semen, the stuff of dreams and earth, which she knew without knowing.

105

He listened. A sigh. He sucked it up. A cry, dissolving inside. The sky slipped, separating, gathering itself up from the earth, colouring itself gold and green, leaving the shredded darkness behind. Rag ends of twilight, this dawn-scooping shadow.

They could barely see each other on the shallow furrowed prairie. He had hold of her elbow, balancing himself as well. His legs weren't strong enough. He turned to her to suck her lips. More, more, but she cried because her mouth was sore and smeared with mud. As she walked across the garden, her petticoat discharged a brown dust that powdered the small seeds. A sweet thin scent of morning bathed them, the air warming, auroral light moving between them, dividing their dreams, draping them in the wreckage of ritual and memory.

Work on the well continued. Hannah carried water to the garden while they waited for rain. She gathered lamb's quarters for greens, made tea from horsemint and catnip. Matthew travelled to get wood. It took him two days, but he killed an antelope. They shared the meat with Lewis, who showed them how to cure the hide, which was thin and not much good, but would do for laces and leggings. They saved the fat for tallow. Tully taught Matthew how to snare partridges, how to recognize their dry little paths to the slough. Hannah saved the feathers. Matthew sawed, split and stacked firewood. Hannah took the wagon out to gather dried dung for fuel.

As if someone were pulling up a tent, clouds unrolled over them. Hannah had been feeling uneasy for some time. The boundless sky was empty and full, thick with sunshine, thinned with blue. She waited for the little winds to be let out. She turned her back to it. They needed rain on the dry hard little seeds. The cloud cover spread across until she felt warm and even cozy tucked in by its dullness. It was thick and lumpy underneath. She called across, 'Matthew, Matthew!' to hear the sound of her voice slowed by the dense air.

He was far out with the axe planting sod corn. Chopping a slit in the jungle of roots, he dropped in three kernels of corn and kicked the root mass back with his heel. It was a way to get something out of nothing in the first year. He had learned how to let the axe fall so it did the work. The rhythm felt good, but the back-bite vibration through the handle of the axe stung his hands. No shadow strained his eyes. He forgot about time. He had been doing this forever right under God's eye. The cloud rolled lower, bringing Hannah's voice. He waited for the warm rain, his seed bag almost empty.

Without warning the rain began. Hannah ran to cover the well, then retreated to watch from the doorway. The animals huddled together in the old postures. At first the drops spattered dust. She stood with a hand on each side of the doorway, thinking, This is my house in the rain. So far she had only played in it, fussing with corners, wiping the window pane, repositioning the sleeping mats, folding the bedding. She smelled the cool clean dirt, the rogue hint of dung ash, the sharp tang of tar paper sneaking through the cracks in the roof boards.

Matthew scurried in soaking wet, his hair curled into ringlets. He showed her the empty seed bag, pleased with himself. She felt differently towards him. She had never been curious about his ability to make her safe, but now she was thinking about him that way: he had done something important. She found pleasure in leaning back, considering him from a distance. Crossing her arms and fitting them like a shallow shelf under her breasts, she watched him strip off his wet clothes. She couldn't take her eyes off him.

The storm grew darker and warmer.

She said, 'I don't know to do anything. I hate that. I hate having to ask. I want to know from the start. I want to be able to figure it out all by myself and I can't.' But what she was really feeling was that she couldn't do enough for him. This surprised her, this slight and new concept of taking care of another. It made her eyelids feel heavy, sluggish, as if those thoughts were weighing on them. As if she were going home after a long absence and seeing all the old things changed from pebbles to pearls, and her muscles had locked so that she wouldn't thrash and hurt herself reliving her life. This new way of seeing things would take getting used to. It stirred her hands and she saw that they were still too soft to wring soup out of a stone, that they were sore and sotted with blisters.

As if being warm and dry were unreal, they stood in thrall. The rain was all sound masking sound, an odourless scent, light hiding light. It leased itself to the closures of the earth, its inclinations, surfaces, temperatures, confining itself momentarily to the sloughs, the rivers and the deep furrows. It continued gently through the night, pattering on the tarpaper roof. They pulled the sound over themselves as they might a handmade coverlet.

In another day the first shoots of green appeared above the ground.

Matthew stripped the bark from some poles to make a rope bed and scythed grass from the slough, which had no hay needles, for Hannah to use to stuff a canvas mattress. In the fall she would make a new one from corn shucks. She remembered the story about the rattler crawling out of the sod wall, and so their bed stood free.

Between putting in fence posts they built a shack for the chickens Addie had promised. Several times a day Matthew rode out to chase the crows and reset rabbit snares. He couldn't waste bullets on them. Hannah weeded, watered the animals, cooked, cleaned.

In a few weeks he was prepared to go to town again. This time Hannah stayed alone because Tully had too much work to do at home. This time Matthew was looking for work. He needed a whetstone. They needed salt, molasses, flour. He needed rope, stove black, lineament, kerosene, disinfectant, and tools to fix harness. Thread for mending, talc, pannikins for soft soap, tin buckets for lard and berries, milk pans, clothespins, cheesecloth, fly paper. He hated to leave his fields. At the creek the crows ignored him, yawning, dropping down one by one for a dip and a drink. Cocking their wings and puffing out their feathers, they looked larger than they were. And surely, there, in the long rough grass, furry ears were tilting.

Just as he was about to leave, Hannah handed him the long letter she'd been writing. He was to check first at the post office and if there was a letter for them, to open it and add a postscript so their families would know that theirs had been received. She looked up, but it was hard to see him: a blinding halo of light bound his head, pinching his face into darkness. Indeed, she had not really seen him for some time. Even when they'd stood side by side they'd been too busy to look at each other. Once when she had to look way out to the edge, it didn't look like him. What would she do if a stranger came back in his shoes and knew just where to touch her? Would anyone doubt her word? Where could she go? 'It's just you and me,' he had said, though she'd never heard of such a thing. She had replied, 'There's all kinds of people behind us, my family, your family, and sideways Lewis and Addie and those other people who came to help you with the roof,' but she knew he was still all by himself.

After he'd gone there was nothing between her and the sun. Where it struck her skin she burned, she broke out in a sweat. That night a prickly-heat rash speckled her chest under her blouse. Folding the old newspaper she fanned herself. It was too hot to lie down. She walked back and forth in front of the door. Night like deep warm velvet smothered the stars. She lit the lamp, but turned it down to a whisper. Still it shone on the white side of Lettice tethered within sight. From the door she could hear the cow nuzzling dust in the yard. She decided that if a wolf came she would bring Lettice right into the house. She began hearing unidentified sounds. When Matthew was there, one of them was always making some kind of noise. Now there came a flood of small sound: chicker, thrum, scritch, distant roll, cow coo, mosquito humm. Some of the sounds began but were never resolved. Others wandered through the night as if they were lost, like the snatches of lullaby her mother used to sing, to people the dark for her. 'Birds and butterflies, beckon out your eyes.' That's what she thought the words had said. Beckon.

The first light of dawn found the plains frozen. How strange, she thought, that such a profound earthly change should be revealed in a moment of absolute stillness, and as she looked out she forgot to breathe.

After missing him for two days she woke feeling more peaceful than she had in all the weeks they'd been married. It seemed like such a long time. She could hardly remember how they had got here, how wide the river was, how deep the forests, how long the love. How long had that been going on? All alone in the new bed, she stretched, delicious, languid, letting the syrup of sleep ruin her limbs. Giving in. Waking to eye the progress of sunlight across the floor. It made no sound and she fell asleep again.

The wind shifted. The air was dense and white. Restless. The cow, chewing on one side of her mouth, shook dust out of the grass. Tully rode over. 'Pa says to tell you to watch out, this one might turn into something.'

'A storm?'

'Or a fire. Awful dry over there.' Standing in the stirrups of the old cavalry saddle, he was peering across as far as he could.

She touched the saddle and his boot, its dry hairline cracks, a frieze of dust. As if there were eyes in the pads of her fingers, she focused on nothing farther away than the reach of her hands.

'Were you born here, Tully?'

'No, just the littlest one. I was born back east like you.'

'But you feel at home here now?'

'Sure.'

'You aren't waiting for something else?'

'I am, of course, I'm waiting to grow up and go west to the coast.'

'Just like that.'

'Something's happening out there.'

'But the land.'

'I don't need it.'

The dust was ground right into his skin, he'd take it with him wherever he went away just as she wore the speckled shadow from the leaves of an eastern forest.

'If a fire starts, douse the walls of the soddy and throw water up on the roof. That paper'll burn you down. Then water the ground and beat out any brush that blows near you.'

'Maybe I'll …' but she couldn't leave. Matthew expected her to … she wondered if he expected her to be willing to die for him. Certainly she had those expectations of him.

'Fire jumps. It burns faster than the grass. You gotta make it jump over you.'

His alarm surrounded him like an aura. She tried to imagine such a thing as fire jumping over her. She smelled not burning but the pungent sweat from the shoulders and flanks of the horse.

'I gotta get back.' The moment he separated from her, the sunlight caught him. He shimmered and the hole he left was filled with dust. She drew the cocoon of herself closer, watched the whirling worlds of dust, heard arguments she couldn't understand and wasn't interested in. The circular shapes played around her feet, rising and sinking. She watched for a long time, but it never finished settling. If she were to watch forever, blinking in its indecision, could she avoid making any decisions of her own? The clouds broke more and more slowly until she forgot what she was about and her body bucked, sucking in what it needed.

'So far so good,' said Tully the next day. He had brought an old braided straw hat for her from his mother because this sun was dangerous. 'I thought I smelled smoke last night.' There's no smudge of it in the sky today.

Wearing the hat, she hauled bucket after bucket of water to the garden. She was determined not to lose her vegetables. Lettice needed more and more water. In between trips she filled the bucket at the slough.

At the end of the week it rained. She closed her eyes and let the sound wash over her. Just in time. She thought of Matthew. No one had stopped by with news from town. She didn't like not knowing where he was. She saw him looking out a window somewhere at the rain, the two of them doing the same thing at the same time. He was missing her. At night he dreamed. In the morning he leaned over, but the cot was wide enough for only one. If he walked by a woman in the street, if he touched her sleeve, if her skirt brushed his thigh ...

She couldn't do much inside without supplies of thread and yarn. It was too hot to cook. A single loaf of bread lasted her a long time. She tidied her few belongings, rearranged the chairs, sat at the table and watched the ground steadily soak up all the water the cloud had given it. I am like that, she thought. I will take everything I can. There had always been empty spaces within her, gnawing, snarling, howling hollowly.

It was hot all night now. At about three, when she couldn't stand it any longer, she sat up, peeling herself from the sticky sheet, crossed her legs and fanned herself slowly with a piece of folded paper. The air was too dense to breathe. Just as she inhaled she stirred the air in front of her face. On the chair beside the bed was a dish of water. She dipped a piece of flannel in it and wiped her face, arms and neck, then fumbled for a piece of ribbon, pushed her hair back and tied it. Unable to open the door until dawn for fear of snakes and bats, she waited. How much longer? In that first greying she would be safe and a whisper of air would lift this smother of night heat. Into that empty space and stilled time she would be able to surrender. She should have been able to go with him, have someone to talk to when she couldn't sleep, look into windows on the busy streets, look at the shops, the people, have a place to sit in the shade. Something to do. Someone to watch her doing it. They would eat at a restaurant and look at each other.

She thought about women following men.

The next day she began a letter: 'Dear Mama, Did you follow ...' a long letter, a waste of paper, one she wouldn't send, but would use to start a fire instead.

Six

Because he was moving above the ground, Matthew imagined his thoughts scurrying between the big feet of the horse. He hauled them up hand over hand. Mine, he thought. This ground beneath my feet. One day mine. I will never leave.

He looked around. He was all alone. Beneath him a shadow moved quickly, not disturbing the grass, but when he tried to stop the horse for a moment he couldn't, as if someone were whispering, 'Move on, move along, hurry by.' A rustle in the grass, not real words, though he understood them. A voice rising from inside, setting its hints in the brush, one that came to tell the truth.

Beside him, hidden in the grass, a long snake lay motionless, feeling the horse through the ground.

The horse took the bit in such a way that he could hold his head just above the tips of the grass, allowing him to watch and listen. His wild old soul said, Keep moving, horses don't stand alone, horses herd, they stand head to rump, whisking away flies.

Matthew was looking for the sod corn growing in the wild grass, but it was hard to keep his eyes down. He caught the ripple of tawny bluestem, the pale broad leaves of corn slashing it, tassels swirling in circles. Gnats and pollen foam. A sound came up from the middle, from the chaos, from the smooth inside of a shell, a sound holding all possibility, or the end of it, all potential gathered and sunk in this one last echo over the endless landscape of grass.

Matthew was interested in beginnings. Success wasn't just a matter of luck, it took skill, work, the element of will, the shaping tool of his imagination, the ability to take the land into his mind, chew it, digest it. He wanted this land the way he had wanted Hannah. If he worked hard and carefully, he might have it in five years. Already he'd built a house on land with sweet water. He'd begun a fence. In the fall when the sap had run down he'd dig up a few small elm trees and replant them in the yard. He'd ride out like this over his land and demand of it, 'Grow me corn. Give me grain.' He wiped sweat from his face and threw it down, saying,

'This is the salt of the earth. This is how you get it. I give it to you, and in return you give me fruit to hold in my hand.'

The horse was swimming through the grass. Matthew held the reins loosely. He was the one thing to be seen from far away. He pushed the horse forward, parting the grass. 'Come on, show me what you can do,' he said, tempting, taunting, twisting his fingers in obscene gestures. 'Come on, sweet earth, I'm calling you,' but his voice was thin. The winsome breeze tossed it away and the spears of grass pricked holes in it.

He rode through the buffalo grass, the wind curling on the rise. He rode beside nodding sunflowers gleaming yellow in the tassel-silvered corn. Along bluestem turning in the hollows. By plump milkweed pods, ragweed, broken trumpets of goldenrod, sunlit chaff in the air. When the horse stopped for a moment to shake off flies, the sound of the wind in the grass didn't change. It was as if he and the animal made no difference. He heard his own breath and pushed it just so in his throat, harder. This was the voice he'd heard since the beginning.

As soon as he passed, the grass winked shut behind him, forgetting him, turning peacefully away, like the thoughts of someone dying without expectation or fear. All the old beginnings, remote and indistinct, lived fresh and immediate in him. His dreams rose and hung on the sharp signs of the earth. Hungry insects nibbled under the leaf. A bank of cloud chilled along its edge. The air was indifferent to dreams.

Seven

What an old story it is, of men and women out on the edge, waiting, watching for the perfect pitch and lean in the grain. That year no one could believe the good fortune or remember such a combination of conditions. That stunning movement of sun and water in the seed, leaf, blossom, coming to this moment. In the gardens the tomatoes dragged down their stems, beans strangled their climbing poles, squashes rolled off the rocks on which they'd plumped. In the creek wash, berries ripened and fell into the water with blue plums, yellow currants, waxy wild grapes. Fruit drooped, green striped gooseberries burdened the bush. Plumes of mustard-yellow ragweed bestowed pollen upon the shoulders of the earth. Barefoot children got carried above the prickly weeds and through the oozing drone of insects, the sharp parchment wings of dragonflies, the points of Indian paintbrush, held up to the spongy pocked faces of sunflowers. Dizzy drift, mesmerizing halo of petals, cup of sun. The sky dragged with the gold smear of the snail sun. Pollen and seed swept into the air, sticking to the warmth, the silence of the swollen sky.

The wind shifted to the north, came across, stopped. All over the land the people worked day and night, pausing only to sleep and eat. They watched each sky sign: the height of a flight of birds, the drone of bees. Did the flies bite? Did the fish look up out of the brown water in the creek? Were the magpies quarrelling? Old people were alerted by their bony joints. The wind rose in wet clouds. At night the dew darkened the ground. Hurry. Hurry. Fires kept coffee hot and spread light like a cover over the sleeping children. Everyone began to look the same in uniforms of dust, rusty salt stains, ragged hems and split seams. Faces blanked out from exhaustion. Babies took to any breast. Dust muted the dawn, darkened the sky at noon, obscured the glow of the prairie sunset, made the campfires at dusk sweat through curtains of orange. Wagons straddled weed-clogged roads on their way from field to barn. Seed corn was separated and stored, meal corn ground, feed corn stored on the cob in cribs. The women and children shucked it, its silk withering at their feet. They would save the shucks for mattresses, but for now they put their babies down to sleep in the sweet pale piles of husks.

Addie was due any moment. Though she had had two of her live children by herself, she welcomed all the attention of the women. Someone brought a rocking chair, and she luxuriated in spreading herself, caressing the mound of her stomach. She looked tired. The children gathered around, leaning over the arms of the chair, hanging on her knees. One pressed between her legs to rest his head on the pillow of her stomach. Addie patted his head.

'What do you hear in there?'

'Digesting and beating drums,' he said with alarm, and climbed his arms over her belly. A late show of sunlight through the barn window caught on the dust, making it a thick cloud of gold.

The next day was a flush of Indian summer. The women fed the men an enormous noon meal then sat down themselves. Addie wasn't hungry. 'It won't be long,' she said. A bed was readied for her in the back of the house. They would take turns sitting with her. 'Ohhh.' Addie lay back on the plump of pillows, and propped her legs up.

The women joked with each other and began preparations. Outside, a girl about seven was slowly making her way around the trestle table. At each seat she took the plate and presented it to a spotty dog, who licked it clean.

'Bye, Addie, I'll be in soon again. Come on, kids, you come with me today.'

Hannah didn't know whether to go or stay. She couldn't take her eyes away. Addie's belly had swallowed up the rest of her body. Her hands bottomed up listlessly, empty. Her legs looked withered. 'Mmmm,' her belly pushing out that sound. She had closed her eyes. It didn't matter who was there. She waited.

Another pan of water was put on the stove to heat. The packet of birthing rags was readied. 'Uuuuu.'

And within three hours the baby lay on Addie's chest. She turned him this way and that, lolling his head, looking between his toes and his legs, behind his ears, counting fingers. The children came to welcome him to their ranks. Rosa and Nellie flanked their mother. Rosa hunched up her shoulders and put her fingers close to the mouth as if to help distort her words. 'Awww, look at dat baby, he he baby, be be be be ... tinsie baby.'

'Run and tell yer dad now.'

Nellie sucked her thumb. She was looking carefully, first at the baby, then at her mother. The inside of her arm rested on a plump pillow that had just been aired in the hot sun and covered with a freshly starched slip of white cambric. She would for evermore recall all these things with the smell of fall sun in cotton or its brush on the inside of her arm.

'That wasn't so bad!' said Addie, relieved and gladdened.

'Supposed to get easier each time.'

'Ha!'

'Quicker maybe.'

'Another boy.'

'Todd, we decided on Todd if it was a boy.'

'Nice, same as Mr Lincoln's son.'

Work did not let up. All the next week slough hay was cut. Matthew took the wagon, half full of the cheap hay and half-full bags of corn, to town. After paying his bills he ran up new ones. Besides everything else, he had to buy wool cloth for winter clothes, and try to pick up some scoured fleece. Town was bustling. In anticipation of the long winter everyone was gathering things to themselves, buying up in case snow prevented the trains from getting through. Matthew bought more preserve jars. A parcel was waiting for him at the post office. He added the p.s. to Hannah's letter. He debated and decided to let her open the package. She was angrier this time when she couldn't come with him. The lists were precise. At the bottom of the page she'd written 'dog'. She didn't like having to go out alone in the grass to collect cow patties. Wolves had been sighted. The sluggish snakes came out of the grass to warm themselves this time of year. She didn't like being out of sight. She told him about the time she'd momentarily twisted down on her ankle and couldn't stand up to see above the top of the grass.

She'd been irritable and sick. She smelled different. He lay with his head on her. At first he thought it was the smelter of her body rendering its fluids into sweat that slickered her skin and excited him, but it was more than that. Crawling up, wiping her throat, he told her he thought she was pregnant. She didn't believe him. 'How dare you!' she'd started.

'What do you mean, how dare I?'

But she meant how dare he know before she did. Then she said something else and turned away from him, curling herself into a ball, pulling at her gown until he could see the buttons of her spine.

'Well, go ask Addie, if you don't believe me,' he said the next day, and when he got back she was a different woman, one he would have to get to know.

Because it was late when he got all the errands done, he decided to stay over. Men from surrounding farms and ranches gathered like hyenas at the door of the hotel dining room, licking their chops, sniffing the fumes of beans, steaks, bread, fried potatoes, pie. Matthew followed a girl to a table with the others. She looked too tired to have a night life, but he was assured she did. 'Soiled doves,' they were called. He thought of something damaged, cheesecloth stained purple from the press of berries. She was used to the appetites of men in from the dry prairie. Before any of them had swallowed the last bite she had brought more food. The man at the end of the table tried to touch her as she went by. His fingernails were ragged and filthy.

'Ah ah ah,' she said, ducking his hand. The men darted glances and laughed, showing the food in their mouths. Matthew tried to get her to look at him. He wanted to show her that all men were not so crude. Just then another man pushed out of his chair and grabbed her, pulling her onto his lap.

'Hey, hey, none of that!' shouted the manager. 'Yer here to eat, she's here to work for me.' The man gave her up. Matthew gestured. She came to him. He whispered something in her ear. She smelled like grease. There were small burns on her bare arms, and stains splotched her apron.

Gradually the air had thickened until now he could barely see below the smoke and steam. In the corner a dwarf-sized man was singing the song he used to lullaby to cows through the long nights under a clear black sky. It was having the same effect here. Men rolled cigarettes and tilted back in their chairs. Others left for the saloon down the street. It was dark. Dust blew in the windows on that darkness, mingling with the smoke. Someone started a fire in the potbelly stove.

Matthew walked up and down the street. People bumped into him, but it was early and they were light-headed and frivolous. No one had turned mean yet. When doors opened, light leapt out onto the street, then, as if it were too hot to touch, retreated inside. The echoes left behind blurred and gently stirred the thoughts of dreamers. Matthew had these dreams, these thoughts all mixed up, sticking to each other to keep warm. He shrugged the collar of his jacket up around his neck and put his hands deep in his pockets. He wished he were sleepy. He felt he should have been tired, what with hard work, a heavy meal, the purple night and its chill, but he wasn't. He felt like a camel who can see the wide desert before him and knows, as he stands at the well, that he was to be sent out into it. Hungrily his body soaked up the possibilities. At the end of a parallel row of shacks masquerading as buildings, the railroad tracks cut across. So often it seemed he had stood at the mouth of some sort of transportation, some way out, in, across, some barrier or bridge. When he was home on his land there were no borders except those he designed. The shores were of his making, the frontier, of his foundation. This was the edge. Beyond was wilderness, dark, silent, cold, and something like a breath, huge, hollow, holding. By putting out his hand he could reach into it, touch it, to find out what it was besides this surface that felt like an enemy, to find out what was behind, inside, what it was he couldn't see, wasn't allowed to see. Why did the earth grow dark? Why weren't there two suns, or a side that was always dark? Or perhaps there was. He carried a darkness and was afraid to put his hands in it.

On the way back he heard a thin stringy sob coming from the crack of an open upstairs window. There was nothing to see. He felt this was the way it should be: people crying, talking to God in the dark. The flat board walls between the building leaked. Chimneys, like blow-holes, spewed yellow ash. The mud was freezing beneath his feet. The smell of rust burned in his nose. He passed between the walls into the alley, beneath curtained windows that suppressed detail but showed the shapes of men and women crossing back and forth. Slop and garbage festered in warm plugs beside doorways.

Horses shifted in the corral, steam shooting out their nostrils. Even in the dark he knew how they were feeling, the one with the sour stomach, the shadowy lurch indicating lameness, the breath that tripped on its way out, the first sign of heaves. Once his smell had invaded their ranks, the horses nodded and moved towards him. The first one put his head over the top rail to have his face scratched. He was already shaggy in winter hair. Light shone in their eyes in spots and triangles. He warmed his hands in the circle of their breath. The cold leaned on him from behind. The air thinned and cracked.

Taffeta or ozone? Jittery, blue-black like flame. Fierce. Over there, was that the girl from the hotel or not? A skirt, a wrap, crazy quilt of silk and wool. She must be cold. Her breath exploded around her head and froze, glittering, on her loose hair, which hid her face. She did something exciting and wild with her arms, flinging them out, lifting the shawl, which stretched like skin, a bat's wing, stirring the night around her, switching, cutting clear of cobwebs and rats. What was she doing now? Huddling, hugging herself. Why was she out in the dark like that? What was she waiting for? Who?

Deliberately, treacherously, she turned, drawing a wing across her face, and began to spin something around herself, plucking silk threads, twisting them with static electricity until she slowed and glowed, shuddering in the dark with a brittle blue light. Slowed and hummed and waited. She saw him. Come on. Come on. She turned her back to him. He petted her, his hands cold. She curled and backed up against him. He didn't know where to put his hands. She shifted and began to spread her legs, then jumped away into the shadow under a lean-to. He stumbled after her into the dark, into a deep space that echoed. He found her by following the sound. She found him and pulled him over her back by his breath, hand over hand until his mouth was by her ear. She heard him roaring, holding on. She split her legs, rubbed, tilted. His hands clawed her shoulders, clutched her waist, her hips, reached around her belly. The taffeta there squirmed, smarted and crackled. He burned. She bent down, did just what his body told her, held him on the surface of silk while he reached down, down into the dark.

Before he could see, she was gone. Before he opened his eyes, he was standing by himself shivering, sweat clamping his shirt to his skin. He ran back through to the street. His skin moaned. In the first pool of light he looked at his hands, which weren't scorched, as he'd feared, or smeared with blood.

Smoke backed out the saloon doors like a drunken man and fell in Matthew's arms. A dog snapped at the shape. Noise formed a fog in the street. No one wanted to sleep. He climbed onto the wooden sidewalk. Someone was singing a mournful lament about love, loss and wrong. Or it could have been one of those songs making new legends in a land overloaded with heroes. At night, he decided, you can go either way.

He shoved his hands in his pockets and shouldered his way to the end of the bar. Some of the men were there, rearranged around open bottles, cards and money. A layer of smoke gurgled just above their heads.

Occasionally someone shouted and a bubble burst. Up against a post leaned a man, his body richly carved and solid as wood. Another man slurred his new English. That one, straw chin, roared. Over there another shivered on his new money. Nothing got past the owner overseeing it all.

Folding his arms on the bar, Matthew noticed splinters in the sleeve of his jacket. He tried to remember where they came from. He pushed up his sleeve, but they hadn't penetrated. Picking them out he made a little pile that he brushed onto the floor. He had a drink, another. How long had he been gone? No one had noticed. He overheard talk about loans, new machinery, corn, raccoons and dead children.

'See that,' said the man next to him, moving closer. 'See that,' as if his hand were separate from his body, as if he wished it were, cleanly removed instead of stubbed, brutalized by one of the new machines. 'No old horse-drawn harvester'd do that to a man, take his hand and leave that! That!' In disgust he slid it as far away from himself as he could, to the edge of the bar.

'Put that goddamn thing away,' said the bartender, wiping the spot. 'Don't worry, man, there's always them what can't take progress.'

When Matthew looked around no one was talking, though he was just in time to see a man with flat eyes glaze over into a stupor and sink to the floor.

'He's through. Get him out.'

It was cold along the floor. A dog slunk in the open door and looked around. 'Get him out of here, too!' the bar owner had to shout over an argument that had sprung in the middle of the room. Someone was coughing too hard. 'He'll be dead by spring,' said the man with the mangled hand. 'I'll drink to that.'

Matthew understood every word. There was no mystery in the uncut voices or the silences of these men to interest him. His own voice confused him, kept secrets from him. He paid for his drinks and walked to the hotel.

Inside, the small fire had warmed a space to which a few insomniacs had drawn chairs. Matthew started up the stairs. He wanted to get out of his clothes, which were stale and too tight. The stairs seemed steep and high. He had barely the energy to climb to his room. Halfway up he stopped, exhausted. He took a deep breath to pull himself together, but it didn't work. His legs bandied out, his hands numb. Winded, he sat and leaned over his knees. Downstairs the talk was low, mumbly. He remembered perching on the landing at home, listening to the ends of conversations, the bits and discards of grownup talk. That sweet tantalizing moment, agonizing him to want to grow, to be able to participate in the inner circle, even to be able to stay awake.

Someone threw another piece of wood into the fire and someone else started to sing, accompanying himself on a guitar, a soft jilting strum talking to itself. A song about a new boy and an old kiss, a verse about an old boy and a new kiss, that chaste kiss that bent men down.

He wanted to see who was singing, whose tender voice was triumphing, who dared sing the next to last song. He was feeling better, the weakness having left him. He was hungry and wondered if he could get a piece of pie and cheese from the kitchen at this late hour.

Stopping in the doorway he saw the young man and he smiled, not because he wanted to be noticed, but because the voice was so beautiful, that of a lesser angel, a child. Not of this place, he was clean and shabby. Curls ringed his head. The skull glowing through showed its perfect shape. He balanced on the chair, balanced his song on the short blue flames in the stove. The song was too old for him, the words a witness to some terrible wrong. 'I never dreamed it this way, it shoulda been …' After a while the story didn't matter. It was his voice, a little breathless, a pull of smoke across green water. Behind it, each man censored to suit himself, to fit what he felt should have been in his own life.

It was hard to see clearly in the firelight and dust, but the boy's skin seemed transparent. His song covered it with a second skin. His fingers ticked the strings. The gut in his fingers surfaced of its own strength.

Crossing behind the stairs, Matthew wandered to the kitchen.

'Is there anything I can have to eat?' he said to the small girl in a filthy apron, which on second look was half an old sheet bandaging her chest and knotted high on her back. Besides restraining her it seemed to hold her up. Refocusing, she looked around. On the table was a plate of leftovers.

'Pie? Cheese?' He didn't want that congealed mess.

She put down the rag she was holding and turned to check the cupboard as if she couldn't remember. 'Coffee?' she said, indicating a pot on the stove. It distracted him long enough for her to find something she didn't want and to put it on a plate. 'Ten cents.' Her voice was white and thin, poised in the air like the tail of an antelope. When he gave her the coin, she held it in her hand where he could still see it. What did she want? What was she looking at?

He ate the soggy pastry, knowing it would sit in his stomach, and the stale coffee. The fellow was still singing, humming really, loose motionless isolated notes. It made Matthew feel careless.

'They say he can hear bats.'

'What?'

'Him, in there, they say he can –'

'Oh, yeah?'

It was apparent that she knew the boy, that he had wounded her in some way. It terrified Matthew that there was a whole life in her, that she hungered and thirsted, that someone like her might kick him aside, use up what he needed, and do it without knowing what she had done, blind to him as now, looking through him to her beloved, or looking backwards into her own mind, that pure place furnished by the structural logic of desire. He was frightened that her mind was mindless, that she could walk by him without smiling or crying.

'Who is he?'

'Gabriel,' she said, like a bell. 'Gabriel,' meekly, as if most of the sound she intended was left behind in her heart. She squeezed a wad of apron and skirt.

Matthew shrugged her off and left. The fire was whining on a diet of sapwood. It was dark. Gabriel got up. The guitar hung from a strap and he was still worrying the strings with one hand. The other he extended to Matthew, swiftly, sweetly, saying, 'Gabe.' One hand, on his way out, the handshake earthy after the sleepy mythology of song.

At breakfast the next morning Matthew found himself at a table with a group of men who were discussing a horse race. It was to take place in the early afternoon, starting at the railway tracks, circling once around the town and back to the tracks but not crossing them.

'Who's going to make sure there's no holes?'

'We can all walk it before!'

'Send the kids around with pickaxes.'

Another fellow arrived and yanked back the chair beside Matthew. 'Goddamn kid's laid out ... Oh, I don't know, got into a fight or had too much to drink. I warned him. He's finished, I'll be damned if he gets any more work from me. He can just rot. Here I am with the best horse of all of yuh and no one to ride him!'

The girl brought coffee. 'What do you want?' she asked the newcomer.

'Someone to ride my horse!' he cried, taking off his hat and handing it to her. 'Put that up there for me, will ya, and aaa,' he looked down the length of the table, 'some bacon, flapjacks, a mess of eggs ...' That seemed to be enough. He turned back. 'What the hell'm I going to do!' he said, banging his fist on the table.

'Maybe I could ride your horse,' said Matthew.

All eyes attended. Hadn't they seen him before? New boy this year, came last spring, putting in corn. 'What do you know about horses, boy?'

'I've done some riding back east. All I've got here are plough horses, but I've been sitting on them.' The men laughed.

'Why, yer clothes is too loose to stick on a horse. You'd catch the wind and blow clear away.'

'Oh, I don't think so,' he said, hunching his shoulders and folding his arms. 'Show him to me, Mister ...'

The man leaned back. 'Dobkin.' He was looking to see if Matthew was serious. Matthew picked up his mug of coffee and sniffed the steam that was present only because the room was chilly. He looked the other way.

'You want to see the horse?'

'Yes, sir.'

The girl brought Dobkin's plate and another pot of coffee. 'Uh, huh ...' he said, chewing. He swallowed and said, 'Well, let's go.'

In the tight cold air the sunlight was like thin milk. A white spray of dust covered everything. Dobkin took out a pistol and shot the skin of ice on a watering trough.

'Whew!' Matthew shook his head. Dobkin laughed. They crossed the street to the stable. The horse was in an inside stall. He saw that Dobkin was taking no chances with his investment.

'Well?' Opening the gate he pushed the horse to one side and backed him out. He stepped side to side in a crisp dance, nudging Dobkin and reaching his head forward to inspect Matthew. Cross-tying him in the empty aisle, Dobkin held up a bucket of water. Eagerly the horse buried his nose, spluttered, shook his head, and drank. Matthew walked around him. 'If he cain't whip them others, I'll be ... I'll be ...'

'He looks good.' Matthew ran his hand along the good slope of the shoulder, the solid haunch, the sturdy clean legs. The horse had hardly a mark on him. 'How old is he?'

'Five years. Name's Dragon. Got him on my last trip west. Look, kid, I got money on this horse. Can you ride him to win or not?'

'Could be.' Quickly he brushed Dragon's back. Dobkin handed him a blanket of soft wool. The saddle was the light, spare, army model.

'Never had no metal in his mouth,' said Dobkin, handing him a hackamore. The braided rope and leather adorned Dragon's fine head. Matthew pulled his forelock out and smoothed his ears. It had been such a long time since he'd ridden a horse like this. Although he was warm, shivers skimmed his back and arms. The excitement, that old pent-up feeling. He could already feel the big horse bunched up beneath him, slippery muscles oscillating. He led the horse outside.

The street was filling with rattling wagons and people on foot wading through the dust. Children noticed and stopped to watch. Matthew steadied the horse with his voice. He gathered the reins, snugging them once, took hold of the saddle, and mounted. Dragon shifted and sneezed, tossing his head and rolling his eyes. While Matthew was adjusting the stirrups he talked to him. 'Easy ol' raggedy horse, easy now, whoa.' Dobkin tried to shoo the children back, but anticipating something exciting they wouldn't leave.

They started up the street. Dragon was inhibited by the traffic. He eyed the other horses, avoided dogs, and shuddered at the sound of snapping skirts and loud shouts. In a few minutes, at the edge of town, Matthew urged him on. The horse had a short clever step. Matthew saw that he had to stay off Dragon's neck. He hitched his feet in mid-air to avoid danger.

Before the horse could get hot, Matthew slowed him down. Dobkin was standing on the side of the street, impatient, cold, trying to keep a cigarette lit. The coffee he had drunk was wearing off. He was an ugly man, Matthew noticed, but saw that it had taken Dobkin a long time to become ugly, because parts of him, angles and attitudes, hadn't been altogether buried. He was the type of man who was revealed and aggravated by raw weather and circumstance.

'If you want me to, I'll be pleased to ride your horse.' Settled, then. Dobkin held the rein and they walked quickly so the horse wouldn't get a chill. They agreed on Matthew's share of the winnings and his pay as jockey. 'Just before,' suggested Matthew. 'You can always turn my pockets if I'm killed.'

On top of the conversation he was thinking what he'd do. He counted on getting out in front right away. What did he know about racing? He knew how to stick to a running horse, that was all. What if someone whipped his mount in the face? What if someone cut him off, pushed him aside? He asked Dobkin to tell him everything he could about Dragon's other races and about the horses he'd be racing against.

By one o'clock the sky was low and threatening. If it were to snow, he knew he might not be able to get home. He wondered how he would be able to find his way back with the road buried, the tree branches broken by the shock of cold, the grass shrivelled. It was a land without a memory of itself. He hadn't thought about winter until now. In spaces like this without trees, there must be other ways to tell that winter was coming, but he didn't see them. He didn't want a test of two days' duration or longer, he wanted to be home before the first flake hit the ground.

The horses blew their breath into the cold air. Unafraid, boys drew a starting line in front of their shifting feet. They smacked the dust boiling up into their hands. Their fingers were blue. The owners of the horses shouted at the boys to get back behind the line. Men and women milled at the edges, spoiling the wilderness behind them.

And out there, an undertow of sound was pitched just beyond hearing.

Heat steamed up from the horses. 'Let's go, let's go!' Shouting, stamping, clapping. 'Let's go! Let's go!' they chanted. The twisting horses couldn't wait any longer. The starting shot was fired in the air. 'Haa, haa, haa.' The horses reared and plunged forward, released. Reins threshed and jangled on their necks. Dragon was running on top of the shouts, his hooves jabbering over the ground. He ran with both ears forward, not listening to anything from behind. Sired by a jackrabbit, thought Matthew, holding on with his knees. This was a horse used to racing, born to run. No one owned this horse when he was running like this. Matthew was just tolerated, along for the ride, pointing the way, but Dragon was the one watching the ground, avoiding holes and bumps, holding his head up like a deer.

He was up with the front runners, who had slowed the pace as they approached the halfway curve around the end of town. Glancing over his arm, Matthew noticed just a few people, some on their horses, who wheeled and disappeared to race through the centre of town. On around and he could see the finish line clotted with people. Everyone was yelling, waving hats. Shots were fired into the air. Dragon swivelled one ear back, then the other. He spurted forward, sucking in the excitement. The crowd parted to let him through in his final stretch across the line. Dragon slowed immediately. He knew his job.

Dobkin was already collecting money when Matthew rode up to him and stopped. Dragon stood squarely, heaving and blowing. People reached up to pat him. Dobkin looked up and the elation of victory slipped off his face. He hated to part with any of the money, but there were too many witnesses. Matthew pressed him, staying in the saddle, shouting down, 'I've got your horse! Pay up!' Dragon stepped back as the crowd shifted.

'Here, here,' gestured Dobkin, waving a few bills. Matthew grabbed them, dismounted, and handed the reins to Dobkin. Some of the people were looking at him as if to remember. 'What's your name again?' one said. 'Where do you live?' asked another. 'I've got a horse I race sometimes.'

'Right, right.' He was uncertain, in a hurry to escape. He didn't like the feeling of everyone grabbing at him. He wasn't tall enough to see a way through the crowd. Dobkin, his face red, looped the reins over his arms so he could hold the money with two hands.

Matthew pocketed his money and shoved his way through to the street, which was empty of all but a few storekeepers who stood watching from their doorways. He headed straight to the hotel, where he gathered his purchases and left by the back door. His own horses came out of the pack in the corral. He hitched them up quickly, tied down the load and started for home, waving goodbye if someone looked in his direction.

The wind on the prairie was low down like a sluggish tide lugging itself over detritus. Through its resistance the horses dragged their feet, and the wagon wheels mired and slipped. Matthew squeezed his legs together and tucked his feet under the seat. He shrugged down as far as he could inside his jacket, but was still cold. Hooking the reins over his foot, he dug around just back of the seat for his sleeping bag and pulled out one of the blankets to cover his lap, another to wrap around his shoulders. He tried to knot the wool, but with numb fingers found the tension difficult to gauge. The horses grew quickly tired. If the wind were to shift behind them, he knew they had a chance of getting home by the following night. Otherwise, he couldn't guess how long it would take at this pace. The day after tomorrow? Hannah would worry.

He realized he hadn't been thinking of anything for some time. Once in a while he shook the reins. The horses seemed startled that he was still there. They tossed their heads, then slipped back into their stupor, and he into his, hunched over his useless hands, hypnotized by the rise and fall, the piston shift of the horses' rumps, the ripple of their tails in the descending darkness.

Because she couldn't see the sun, Hannah perceived only one edge to the world, one that lightened and darkened, repelling and attracting her to its surface, swinging her away from itself and pulling her back. Without beginning or end, and most peculiarly without a middle to hold on to, the days slipped away, each one the same. Every day the brown earth was cloaked in the same cold light the colour of ash, a tasteless, thin dark.

Following Addie's suggestion, she opened the old hay mattress, emptied it on the floor, and covered it with the wagon tarp to make a rug. Then she stuffed the muslin casing with corn shucks, making a sound like crackling insects to punctuate the slow moan of the wind. The fire gulped cow patties and mouldy husks, flaring and smouldering. She couldn't tell what time it was. She got up, walked here and there touching things, put on her sweater, Matthew's jacket, a wrap. Knotting a small blanket at her chest she went outside. Her feet interrupted the flow of dust, and it shimmied up her body. She squinted, and covered her mouth with a corner of the blanket.

When they arrived, there had been no paths, not even those single raw paw widths worn down by animals. She had watched with delight, over the months, the grass worn down beneath her feet. Now she could let a whole day go by and it didn't grow back, this path of soft time. This one led to the shed of hay over saplings they had made for Lettice, who was expecting a calf. Hannah got her an ear of corn from the crib. While she ate, Hannah leaned over her shoulders. It felt good to press against something warm and alive. The cow's coat was getting heavier. Close to the skin the hair was soft and clean. Twisting a handful of straw, she began to brush the dust and scrape the manure from her legs. She cleaned the corners of her eyes, wiped her nose, gently scratched the wrinkles of soft skin behind her ears. Lettice, looking for more corn, moved away when Hannah tried to lean on her again. A cold tide of air seeped in.

Hannah retreated, taking the corn cobs back with her to burn. The wind climbed over her and jumped down, pushing and pulling at her clothes, forcing her to close her eyes to slits and breathe under cover. It whirled and wailed in her ears, blew out her hair. She ran to the house, slipped inside and shut the door, but the wind continued to whistle and whine for her, splitting on the corners, spilling over all sides of the soddy.

She threw a cob on the fire and began stuffing shucks in the cracks around the door. A small whistle came from the window and two or three places in the roof. She thought she'd be able to staunch the sound with fleece. The fire needed more fuel before it would boil water. The damper in the stove pipe perked irregularly, a glad sound. She slid the kettle to the hot spot and put a pinch each of catnip and black tea into a pot. She fed the failing fire. Matthew had built her a chair with a back to it. Folding a quilt, she padded the seat and back slats before sitting. Her hands slowed, wandering over the swell of her stomach.

In the sewing box beside her on the floor was a small hand mirror. Her face just fit, half in the cave-like, secure, gloomy darkness of the soddy, half luminous in the filtered wash of light from the window. She touched her dry cheeks. The line of her mouth was unfamiliar, her eyes those of a child waking confused from a disturbing dream. Tipping the mirror down, she looked at her stomach smoothly swelling like a fruit. The fire sputtered. She had woody stalks and cobs for it. When the water boiled, she poured it on the brew of tea.

How many days had it been now? Perhaps Tully would come over. Tomorrow, when the dust, when the wind, if the cold subsided. What did the children do in the long winter without school to go to? Addie and Lewis had to teach them at home. What else did she have to say, to wonder about? The tea was dark and strong. She sliced bread and ladled plum jam on it. Food lasted a long time when Matthew wasn't here. It was dark outside when she had finished. The fire sighed. She poked in twists of hay and encouraged the flame by blowing on it.

Half the mattress was stuffed. By folding the flap underneath she would be able to sleep on it tonight, perhaps nearer the stove and away from the sod wall. He should be home tomorrow, she hoped. Sometimes at night it was so dark she found it difficult to breathe.

In the morning the window was a single eye of light looking in, preventing her from seeing out. The sun looked wan and simple, showing its other side, one she neither feared nor trusted. It was ineffectual, a winter sun.

Chalky brown bone-dry dust covered everything, but in some spots had shifted to exhume the shrivelled and disintegrated ruins of plants she'd never seen before. The September flies were gone, the remaining birds eerily silent. She missed the sweet, sluttish, opaque, golden smell of autumn. The earth's softness had been replaced by lumps, excrescence, protrusions, bumps, pocks, warts and corrugations of wind, all bunched, huddled and battened to disaster. She hadn't been able to see this far into the distance before. Like a small child she had concentrated on the close, the crisp, the minute detail under her eye. Her world had been tangible: the sleek grass, its gloss, the glaze of sun. Now she stood exposed on a desolate stage without an audience.

That night she woke to the sound of dogs barking, but realized they weren't dogs at all but wolves. She imagined them ripping open her stomach and tearing the invisible child right out of her.

First they unloaded the wagon, then Matthew unharnessed the horses and put them in the shed, getting them water and corn. Hannah started undoing the parcels. The third was the package from home from both sets of parents. She touched the paper, the string tied by either her father or his. She had to cut it off. Inside the paper, a box, and inside the box – she stopped: should she wait for him? How could he have waited when she couldn't wait a minute longer? Inside the box were several smaller packets. A tin of taffy candies. Toilet soap wrapped in paper. She held it to her face. A book from Matthew's father. It smelled like the soap. She put the box down on the floor to make room on top of the table. A tin of chocolate, clearly labelled.

Matthew came in starving. His hands were filthy. He tore off a piece of bread and stuffed it in his mouth. It was as if his whole body were eating, fingers kneading the crust, eyes devouring, shoulders grinding up and down. If he could he would have rubbed the bread right through his skin. 'Is there anything to eat?'

'I had no idea when you'd get back.'

'But there must be something, some dried fish or meat, potatoes to fry up?' He looked around, picked up the teapot, which was empty and cold. The kettle, to his relief, was full and simmering.

'Don't you want to see what's in here?' she asked, hovering over the parcels.

'Oh, yeah, I didn't open that, I left it for you,' he said between bites. 'Sure, let's see what they sent.'

'Candy, toilet soap, this book.' He read the spine. 'A ream of paper, raisins, my paper mâché box. Look, I thought I'd never see it again.' She smelled the forgotten fragrance of old trinkets. Inside, her mother had put a paper of pins, hairpins, sewing needles. 'Black, brown, blue, white thread,' she said, standing each beside the others. 'A cheese! No, no, you can't just eat up a whole cheese!' She put it away in her apron pocket. 'A comb, a box of tea, packets of spice: cinnamon, ginger, sage, mustard, allspice. Seeds! Your mother must have sent these from her garden. These are flower seeds! Some tobacco for you! You're father must think you've taken up smoking. Or chewing.' She pulled out some fabric, a soft wool flannelette. 'Why, what's this for?' Her mother had made her a brand new nightgown just before she left.

'Baby clothes.' His mouth was still full.

She didn't say anything.

'It didn't snow.'

'No.' She was still staring at the cloth. 'No, it didn't snow.'

'I thought for sure I was going to get caught.'

'There were wolves howling, they woke me up. I thought – I dreamed,' but she couldn't remember exactly what it was.

He sipped his tea. 'Oh!' he said as he warmed up and remembered. 'I got some canned milk, in that package.'

Milk! Her mind skipped to soups and puddings. He opened one of the cans and poured a touch into his tea, turning it a creamy brown. 'Give me a sip.' She held the cup just below her breasts and leaned back slightly. He stared at the success of her stomach showing under the apron's surface.

'Look at me! You haven't looked at me since you got home. I've been here all by myself for seven days and six nights in the dark with the wolves. I had to do everything by myself. I needed you and you weren't here.'

'I can only be in one place at a time. The railroad doesn't come here, there isn't a store right down the street. What can I do? What do you want me to do?'

'Talk to me.'

'I am talking.'

'Talk about me!'

He had never talked about her. At times he'd thought of nothing else but her. She had inundated the cells of his body like slow poison, altering his moods. On her wings he had felt the best he ever had, better than the land, better than the future, better than dreams or logic. Hannah in his mind.

He started to laugh, but it frightened him. 'Don't kill me, don't kill me,' he wailed, throwing his arms up across his face, as she pounded with her fists until whatever it was that roiled in her was gone.

'Hey, look,' he said, pointing. There seemed to be one more package in the box.

'I thought it was just padding paper.' She opened the packet. 'Letters!' She didn't understand. 'Why did they send them this way instead of faster?'

Dear Hannah and Matthew,

How are you? Your father and I are fine. Joel, Aaron and Sally are fine, too. We are having some hot weather and storms. I will be glad when it gets a little cooler. I work once a week in a lady's house doing work for her since she had a baby. Joel grew 3 inches this summer. Sally moved into your room after you left. Are you taking care of yourself? I hope so.

Love, your Mama

Dear Matthew and Hannah,

I can't imagine what you are doing, what your life must be like! You say your nearest neighbours are several miles away! How do you keep a house made of dirt clean? The first part of your letter, describing the train ride and ferry trip was interesting. I read between the lines for the full effect. We are so far apart now with me at school. Sometimes I worry about Mother and Dad. Life is wonderful here. I may not be the greatest, but there are lots of people who think I have real talent. One day your little sister may surprise you and if not you, Father at least! Is there any chance we will ever see each other again? I can't imagine coming all the way out there, but perhaps one day. There is so much going on, I hate the thought of missing even a minute and am trying to figure out how to stay here for the summer next year. Do you think I'd be able to persuade Mother and Dad to come here? Ha Ha. Well, one never knows. I live in a girls' lodging. Three of us share a huge room so we don't get on each other's nerves. Besides, we are hardly ever there. A group of us share a studio as well. Sometimes we play together if we can stand it. The other thing is, there is nothing like a big city, Hannah you would love it! If only one didn't need to sleep. You could go 24 hours a day here if you could stand the pace. Well, I have a deadline to get this back to mother before they send off the big package. Write!

Love, Molly

As well, Matthew's father had written a long formal discourse, which they read silently in turn.

Winter was a shock. When the land slowed and stopped, snow found it waiting like a corpse. This was not the snow of memory, the cozy white blanket of fluffy flakes. This snow came nailed to the bitter wind. It sifted through invisible cracks, burning, dry, forming ice that cut their fingers through thick woollen mittens, clogged shoelace holes and the gap between scarf and hat. Its cement glued a layer of banked hay to the sides of the house.

Some days Matthew could walk on top of the snow. Other times he broke through and had to bandage his legs so that the edges of ice wouldn't cut his clothing. Each day he drew several buckets of water for the animals, dragged in a couple of bales of hay and a small amount of corn or grain. On his way back he got another bucket and wondered when the calf would come. He thought he might have to sleep out there when the time came. Setting the bucket inside the door, he fetched stalks, cow patties and cobs to burn. He thought how simply his life was arranged. At the moment there were no decisions to make. The snow had left him awake on top of the land, alert, imaginative. He was the purveyor of its aspiration, its possibility, its hope, its excitement. Its substance slept under him. He was the dream of the land.

At night they fastened an old blanket over the door. In the morning it was packed with snow that had filtered in. Curtaining off the back of the house, they moved the bed closer to the stove, each day inching nearer. The window became opaque with hoar frost. They pulled two chairs snug to the stove and ate in a silence they were inventing. They made certain sounds when the wind was too noisy. They made lusty, defiant songs. And they touched in a certain way when they were too cold to feel, watching each other's hands, the fingers stroking down, moving the skin slightly, pressing so that shadows would lie down in it. Caressing, rubbing, tickling. Some days the firelight was stronger than the midday light. When he tapped his shoulders she got up and stood behind him, loosening the layers, peeling back all but his woollen underwear, and began to massage his back, the muscles boasting, releasing beneath her fingers.

Day after day everything was the same, and they held to the patterns tenaciously. Each morning she made a porridge of oatmeal or cornmeal, and tea. He honed his axe on Mondays. Once a week he mended rope. In the evening he read briefly, bent close to the shoulder of deeply glowing ash. A fragile interruption to the cycle was the occasional afternoon when he carved designs into the sides of the crib he had made for the baby. Between sessions Hannah stored her sewing in it, diapers, gowns, bonnets. She was hoping for another parcel from home after the trains resumed regular service. In the afternoons she sat with her feet up on the edge of the stove. It took so long to do each stitch when her fingers were cold. Her growing stomach was proving a good work shelf.

She wondered at her docility, found amazing her ability to sit and contemplate stitches, the manure green fire, her future. The last time she saw herself she had been warm and magnificent. Her belly was flat. There was a certain spring in her curls. She was mean and adventurous, proud and mysterious, even, mostly to herself. Now, the mystery was in her and not of her, taking over, housed in her body. She had become someone unrecognizable to herself, this person who beckoned life out of a germ, who gave up food, hours, thoughts, sleep, control. This woman who sang to her stomach and jumped at the responding kick. This strange person living in her, sitting down with her in front of the fire, hungering with her, sleeping with her. 'Bringing out the best in you,' said Matthew sleepily in the middle of the night.

They listened. Silence. The storm had stopped. After three days the wind had lifted. It must have been what woke them, the awful silence slithering in while they dreamt, lying on them like stealth.

Eight

A large stained apron bunched up over Hannah's belly, a red bandanna encircled her head, and socks wrinkled down her ankles. Beneath the apron her dress was unbuttoned. Nothing was as it would have been if it really had belonged to her. She had put together this costume from her former clothes, as if she were a child playing house. Addie lent her a voluminous jumper, and when she got cold she put it on, too. She had a towel tossed over her shoulder and a damp rag in her hand. Beside the hot stove on the dirt floor a pot of snow melted. She stirred the snow soup, and when it had melted she poured it into another pot on top of the stove. It took a surprisingly long time to heat. Ten pots of snow, from right outside the door, made one pot of water.

Dust formed a skin on the surface of the water, on the snow outside, on the table and the rim of the sugar bowl, dust in the basket's weave and in the shoelace knots. Dust under and over, behind the pillows, between her toes. She ploughed her fingers through it, this constant dandruff, brushed it aside, swept it into the straw under the tarp carpet, rearranged it, drew in it, measured it, wiped it, ate and breathed it.

She moved slowly as if there were nothing but time, time hanging around the small opaque window, time growling in their stomachs and lying down on the lids of their eyes. Time whistled in the wind, but the moment the wind died down, time stopped. Or was it the other way around?

She still heard voices outside in the wind. The first time she heard them she took it seriously, searching the house. Where are you? I'm here, where are you? Round and round, stopping to reverse direction, glancing behind herself. Leaning back against the sod to catch her breath. Looking up. Walking out away from the house to see up on the roof, this side then that. Where are you? Who are you? What are you? Why are you hiding, teasing me? The voices were thin, watered down, scattered into echoes.

She listened, but heard only the fire and Matthew turning the pages of the book his father sent him. Though the old straw was broken down, it made a little sniffly sound beneath her feet as she moved around the table setting a place for each of them: two squares of hemmed cotton, two linen napkins from home. Flatware, knives, spoons. Two bowls left upside down so they wouldn't fill with dust before supper. In the backyard of her childhood she used to make play stews of twigs and small stones. She would crouch over puddles to ladle mud soup, hunker down to lay out leaf plates, bark trays, stick forks. Squares of moss cakes sprinkled with lichen, candies of broken glass.

She brought a kettle of water to the boil on the hot spot of the stove, then poured it over the tea leaves. Back then, when dark, hand-over-hand black clouds threatened in the summer afternoons, she had arranged the children on the porch for tea. Their excitement was no greater than her own, dying to do it right, whatever it was, sitting just so. Here let me help you, politely, there, cross your legs like this. Put your napkin on your lap. Don't smile too much. Now, may I pour your tea? Would you like cream? Sugar? A sweet? Mama's best china out there, the spoons that matched, her own apron. Cats walking by on the edge peering through the pickets, watching her pour sweet water from the well into the teapot for the thirsty guests, who struggled to sit still and balance the teacups while a storm jittered and jangled. Leaves belly up in the trees, bugs frenzy. Hurry, hurry before Mama comes home!

She rubbed in the crease between her breasts and the top of her stomach. The baby was right up there. Way back then … stuffing a pil-low up under her dress, tipping the mirror so that she could see most of herself, the important part, the middle, poking the corners of the pillow up where her breasts would be, holding it there with her arm, the rest of the pillow billowing out, filling her dress. She would tuck the bottom edge of it into her pants. That was it, that was the way it looked. She would lean back, accommodating, noticing the disappearance of her feet, opening her legs to rest the load on the seat when she sat down. Smoothing, petting, adjusting. Trying to lie down on her stomach. Trying to imagine. 'Playing little mama?' said her mother, catching her. But she had done the same thing.

'Do you think it's a boy or a girl?' she asked Matthew.

But he could wait. His lack of curiosity astonished her. 'I don't care what it is,' he said, snuggling her flank. In the middle of the night when she woke him to feel the baby's kicking, she wondered how he could wait so easily.

Whereas with the cow he hovered for three days, coaxing and

curious, tossing a coin, breaking straws, talking to her. He had built a separate space for the animal. He had made plans.

Hannah wanted to watch, but when the calf finally came it was in the night between arteries, eerie moon shows and haloes.

I'm lucky, he thought, and careful. Hannah will be all right because I am. It rubs off, conjoins our destinies. Step right on in here, next to my life, into my life, under my umbrella. 'Come right in,' he said to her the next morning, inviting her to see the calf already standing under its mother.

Lettice reached out with her nose to nuzzle Hannah's belly. Not yet, she thought, it's not my turn yet.

'If it's a boy, Benjamin. If it's a boy with red hair, Jonah. If it's a girl, Emma, unless it's a girl with red hair, then I'll call her Meg.' Under the stoneware sugar jar was a small piece of paper full of names, but these were the ones that had stuck.

Not my turn quite yet, she thought. She was rooted, she was a root. The impulse was downwards. Fleshy, pale, explosive. When?

'Why, the baby hasn't even dropped yet!' exclaimed Addie. 'Here, the baby has to drop down here. That's when it gets ready to come out. It should turn and the head will go down here,' she said, touching her. 'You'll get used to it, honey, you'll be glad of it, a woman's touch when it's only been the man. Some woman who knows what to do, who's been through it. For all those births in the barn, with the hay to soak it up, the men have never been through this,' she said, holding Hannah's hand to add drama, taking her into this private woman's world. Thank God we're here, we who can stand the smell of blood in the sheets, we who can wrap the afterbirth. Don't worry, I'll come.

Hannah daydreamed of blood that was just like water. She thought it would be wonderful, she'd be the whole world, in the centre of the bed, in the flickering light, her hair spread out on the pillows, attendants soothing her brow. Her body strong and wet, heaving, finally warm, even hot, her belly rippling, breasts bursting. She imagined talking to the baby, encouraging it. Mama's here waiting for you, come now, I'm here, Mama's going to catch you, right here, I'm making a place for you. Separating the blizzards with her bare hands. This space is for you, baby. Pushing back the sticky air. Come now, baby, Mama's here waiting.

What time was it? The calendar was white like the window, blinding, a wall rather than a way through. Time was supposed to be – but what it was was slow, down around her swollen ankles. Coming down on this other body that had surrounded her.

Matthew was back from chores. She looked at him. His face was in darkness. In the doorway, for that moment, he was a silhouette cut-out. He was in the dark more often now. Most of the time it was too dark to see. What can he do for me now? she thought. What good was he? Snow and ice coated the window. The lamp burned a small circle, light leaked out cracks in the doors and the grate of the stove. They had precious few candles. Inside, a play house made from the dining room table and pinned blankets.

On a day when there was no wind she followed him out into the sunlight and sky and snow, for that was all there was. The cold snatched her breath. But nothing else! she challenged. It was wonderful, this shrill cold burning her nose, licking her skin. It demanded a sixth sense to wonder at it. She rubbed her belly. Come on, baby, there in the dark, come out and feel this diamond, shocking, blunt block of cold.

The animals burst out blinking, snorting, breaking the ice, but they wouldn't and couldn't walk on the surface. They waited wildly for Matthew, trying to watch his every movement while the sun slid on the ice and danced on the glistening slippery curves of their eyes. Hannah looked at the calf. Today they would begin taking milk for themselves. Her eyes hurt. Tully had warned her about sunlight reflected off the snow. 'Matthew, watch out for your eyes,' she called.

He was standing with his arm over Lettice as he looked way out beyond, but he could barely feel her. Under his eyes he saw the chicken coop, the pigpen, the fence. He could almost see the corn growing through the snow, the wheat yellowing, buttering in the sun. He could almost hear the voices. He couldn't tell if his eyes were open or closed. Hannah called through. He couldn't see her either, the sunlight was overwhelming. No horizon, nothing there. It was better behind his eyes, better to think about that. What he'd do was most interesting to think about. The thoughts made his body stir, his groin. Saliva started in his mouth, a slight mantle of sweat dampened across his shoulders, the muscles in his legs tightened.

'Come on,' she said again, mothering, gathering him into her little play house half-buried in the pure snow.

Within two weeks Addie came calling for Hannah, who could think only of the few extra minutes of light proffered by the sun in its slow progress back from the North. Those few moments were hardly enough to light the way.

They hadn't been able to blind death. It wasn't the baby that had died, what you would think if someone told you one of the children had died. Babies dried up the fastest, burned up in fevers, strangled on the croup.

'Rosa, Rosa is the one who ghosted,' said Tully.

What an odd expression, thought Hannah.

'Rose, the second one, the one right after me. My little Rose, Mama used to say, my little rosy girl. She said she was someone to talk to, girl talk when all there were around were animals and men. She bit me, you know, I stuck my finger in her mouth and she knew it wasn't Mama, so she bit me. She was going to be a mother herself. That's mostly what she wanted, I think. She played dolls with the baby and baby with her dolls.' He didn't tell Hannah how they had spent a lazy afternoon hour in the little play house of hay she'd built.

Hannah expected to see Addie in the same face, but the woman was changed. She had pale hills where the bones lay, swamps where the flesh had begun to sink and hollow. The voice was the same. How could that be? Hannah was too frightened to move. Anything could be too extravagant, dangerous. She might destroy something else. Everything must be so precious now. She was afraid to think.

Then Addie was taking her hand in a display of obstinate lucidity, leading her to the coffin, which lay on the table and was made of the same wood. Nellie, who was barely tall enough, propped her chin and folded her hands on top, hiding her chin. She sucked her thumb. Once in a while she crept one hand towards the coffin as if she wanted to touch it. Before Hannah could see if she did, Addie pulled her around. 'My Mama's girl, see her there, how beautiful she was, how beautiful she always was, from the very beginning. What a plum for heaven, my Rosa,' she said, reaching into the coffin, touching her dead child.

Hannah's breath thickened in her throat. She wondered if it was smoky in the room, if they were burning some incense or herbs or medicine rags against contamination. What had killed Rosa? Her skin was smooth and white, her mouth closed, its curve serene as if it had never had to form itself around a cry of pain. Her hands were folded neatly. Her fingernails looked stained a berry-juice blue. A white dress covered her body, the skirt wrapped, holding her feet together and upright. Hannah didn't know she had owned such nice, soft, flat little shoes with a strap and a bone button. Addie was still talking. She seemed to be saying the same things over and over, all the things she'd ever said to this daughter, reminding her of all the close moments, kind thoughts, things unsaid, as if an accounting would be called before Rosa were allowed into Heaven. Yes, she would be able to say, my mother did love me enough. 'Remember the time, remember, you were caught in the sunflowers, you thought it was the face of the sun, you thought you were too close, your face was all yellow,' she said, turning to Hannah. 'Her face was all yellow and big yellow tears,' she said, tilting over, almost falling, colliding with Hannah, heavily, against her belly. What was it? She got a funny look on her face. Hannah couldn't see what it was.

She shuddered, afraid her belly would explode. 'Don't!' she shouted, igniting. 'You've touched the dead!'

'What! What did you say? I heard you!' Were there no witnesses? Tully elbowed in. He'd heard every word. 'I heard.'

'Stop. Who's talking? Stop!' Hannah gasped, stuffing her fist into her mouth to stop herself. Everything. Slow down a minute, let me see what's going on, what's happened. The touch. That touch!

'I'm so cold,' moaned Addie, going into Tully's arms. Had she heard? She didn't hear, did she?

'Mamam, mamam.'

'Addie,' said Hannah, reaching over her belly.

'Don't you touch her, get away.'

The table rattled. Nellie was pulling down on the corner, making it tip. Tick-tock, tick-tock.

'Stop that!' Hannah slammed her hands down on the surface. Rosa's body jiggled in the coffin. Hannah's eyes retracted tears. The wood burned the palms of her hands. She shrivelled back up inside as far as she could go, past her nerves, up next to her marrow.

'Go home.' It was Tully, comforting his mother, shielding her, thrusting his shoulder towards Hannah.

'She's just a child.' But Addie's voice was cooling. 'I'm cold, Tul, I need to be closer to the stove. She just didn't think.'

'Are you all right, Mama?' He wouldn't forgive. Could not.

'Addie, I …' but Hannah's throat was scorched dry. Tully forced by her and settled his mother in the rocking chair. Hannah lifted her hands from the table. She wanted to reach in the coffin and yank Rosa up in her arms, to kiss her slack lips, the tissue covering her eyes, to brush away the sharp shadows under the slivers in the rough wood. To dig out the deep shadows that threatened to close over little Rosa. Now that there was no chance, she wanted to do it.

'Nellie, go call Papa, he will have to take Hannah home.'

She would never remember how she got out of there. Trying to touch Addie. Tully hitting her hand, her whole arm, pushing her away. Hitting her. Hitting. Attacking, recoiling. Frightening her in the dark crowded shack. Of all the people she knew, he was the one who could kill her. That's what she'd thought, huddled next to the door, her hand on the latch, watching him the way buffalo watch wolves.

Lewis was shrunk up in his seat on the sled. He wore silence like the coarse stubble shrouding his face. He didn't notice his wrists staring like red eyes out of the gap between his sleeves and gloves. He didn't question why he was driving her home so soon. The cold was white and dry. The sky could do no better than a matte grey. The horizon cut severely across their vision. Conceivably a wrong move might have tipped this lid of snow they were on and send them sliding under the edge of the sky.

Hannah started to talk, but she had nothing to say. The scarf, wound around, bandaged her mouth. Out of the corner of her eye she could see him. There was no other contact. No comfort. Just beyond the edge of the sled was the ghost, much closer now, bolder in daylight but invisible without the benefit of night to hold its shadow. The ghost of Lewis's despair. The ghost of her guilt.

She thought about the baby in her dark, then about Rosa. At the end she *had* wanted to touch Rosa. It wouldn't have been for Addie, then. She imagined the magical private moment: Rosa warming in her arms, sitting up, saying, 'See, Mama, I was just sleeping. I was just foolin' you!' Hannah was whispering to herself, relating the miraculous resurrection to Matthew. Her breath dampened the inside of the scarf and filaments of the wool stuck to her tongue. She tried to spit them out.

'Why didn't she forgive me?'

'Forgive?' said Matthew. 'What did you have to do with it?'

'She said something, I can't remember what.' Her face squeezed shut, she couldn't tell him. 'And why did he – 'she tried, pulling up. She didn't want to tell that, either. What if she bruised? How hard had Tully hit her?

141

She'd say she fell against something. 'My arm is sore,' she said, rubbing it.

'Are you hurt?' What was she saying in that high-pitched whine, twisting away though he came with tenderness. 'What's wrong?' He thought of animals who separate themselves from their kind just before giving birth. There was not much space. How much would she need? 'What do you want?' It was difficult to talk without touching her. 'Let me …' he said, coming near, sniffing the mystery, the softness of her arm, her breasts. The hardness of her belly, such a surprise, the wooden tension under her skin. Lacy stretch marks, the sorrel streak down the centre of her body, brown haloing her nipples.

'Be nice to me,' she pouted, out of her depth.

As if he had any intention of being anything else, his thoughts were all pastel in love, expanded, thinned, simple. Single-minded, he petted her, rubbed her ears, loosened her blouse to stroke the cool skin over her bones. He purred.

In the night, inside her, the baby was moving. 'Shhh.' By adjusting the quilts like a tent she raised her knees. Gases rumbled in her. Smoothing the cotton flannel gown over her stomach, she began to massage, round and round, making small circles. Beneath her skin the muscles shivered. She tried to find the baby's head. Matthew turned, but he was still asleep beside her. It was too dark to see him. 'Shhh, there, there,' pressing there with the heel of her hand. Under her fingers, the bloated landscape, the warm shell. Her heart beat through her ribs. That she had lost control was a surprise. She couldn't play in her body any more. Those women she'd seen spread back in chairs like dough rising in containers, pale flesh heaped around the middle of their bodies, eyes receding but sharp and dark, hiding in caves, keeping watch. They became the centre of everything, gathering people to themselves like curiosity to a closed box. They relinquished themselves.

'My baby,' she whispered. When Matthew went to town again she wouldn't be alone. She would never have to be alone again.

An unburned log settled into the bed of ash in the stove. Although it was inky black she could see it, as if memory could jump out in front of her eyes. She caressed its shape in her mind. The hearth and heart of this house, this home. This is my home now, isn't it, she thought, starting with herself, warming her big stomach in the show of heat shimmering from the stove. This was where it began. This was when. 'Baby, my love,' here in the dark, saying strange things to each other.

She relaxed. It was easy to think she was the centre of the whole world. Nothing could hurt her from the outside. She glowed in the dark.

'Why don't you just go and do something. Go outside, there must be something to do.'

'It's cold out there. I'm not going to go out if I don't have to.'

'But I can't stand it when you sit around here doing nothing.'

'I'm not doing nothing. It's just that I can do it sitting down for a change.'

'But you're always where I have to be.'

'That's impossible.'

'I have to do so much before the baby comes. Everything had to be ready. I can't have anything left to do. It'll be too late then.'

'Everything looks done to me.'

'Ha!'

He rode over to see if he and Lewis could pickaxe a hole in the ground to bury Rosa. Tully wouldn't look at him. Matthew supposed it was grief. Addie took him aside. 'I'll still come, you know. You ride over day or night,' she said, as if telling him a secret or confiding in him. He felt as if he were peeking through a crack in a door inadvertently left open, seeing and hearing things he wasn't supposed to.

Before he went home, little Nellie climbed up into his arms. He didn't have to do much to hold on to her, she knew how to cling and grip, and whereas earlier she had been staring at him, once up in his arms she didn't need to any more. He had a dry salty smell to him and strength. She put her hand on his throat to see if she could feel the delicious sound of his voice as well as hear it. When he talked, when he said anything, she thought it was going to be a story. He began with a pause, his voice straining the sounds, and they lost some of their commonness. The words meant more, but she wasn't sure what. It was the same with the stories everyone told her. Something was going on inside the words, something bigger, that the form could barely hold. He put her down. He had to go home before the sky went out.

On February 17, something woke him. He listened. It was Hannah turning.

A dream was beginning in her. It was summer and she was standing out in the bare bright yard. Her skirt billowed and snapped like a sail. It seemed to be pegged down in the dust and was turning the same colour as the ground. She felt a sharp tug. Because she couldn't see anything, she couldn't tell where it came from. The skirt was stretching. It seemed to be made of her skin. Her skin, an extra piece growing out of her waist, she couldn't see how. It didn't hurt. There was another tug, then a sound like barking or wet crying coming from under the skirt. The skin dimpled as if something were pinching it from underneath. Bumps appeared and disappeared. Sharp pokes stretched the skin thin. She could barely see. High noon was grinding in the sky above her. Light glowed from under her hands where there should have been shadows. Someone was calling her, the voices blossoming out of dust. Though she couldn't understand the words, there was no doubt of their claims.

Matthew watched her all morning.

'Should I go now?'

'What?' Hazily.

'Addie. Should I go get her?'

'I was just um ... thinking ... It's too soon, isn't it?' But Matthew was lifting her out of the chair, her skirt and petticoats drenched. He helped her undress and put on fresh wraps. 'I want to wash these things now.'

'For God's sake!'

Using some of the precious hardwood, he built up the fire to warm the back area where the bed was.

'I'm going now.'

'What time is it?'

'Almost noon.'

'It's so dark.'

'Cloudy day.' She had such a funny look on her face.

'I'm hungry.'

'No, don't eat anything.' But she would as soon as he was gone.

First it took several hours for a few minutes to pass. She held her stomach, then her head, between her hands. She sat still, thinking of sudden storms, the sled breaking, Matthew falling off and being run over, wolves eating his body, snow covering his bones. She slowed her breathing and lowered her eyes, helpless.

Burning up from the middle of her back, a fiery pain raced over her bones, its heat seeping into her flesh. Low down another pain gripped her, an old pain, one that knew its work, a hard swift pain reeling in her thighs, sucking her blood for fuel. She tried to watch it, to count the strokes and follow it around, but this was a different language. For her it was a new country like the one outside, deceptive, without edges, colourful. Old, knowing, sure. Her body seemed to recognize the pain and it acquiesced, shuddering, swallowing, sweating, indelicate responses of its own accord, graceless. But she felt that it knew best, that she should trust its sympathy. She should let the pain shrink her down inside. It knew what to do.

She moaned. The dirt walls dissolved. The daylight coming in the window glowed. She had to stare right at something to keep it from fading away, to hold it in place. Things assumed enormous importance: the thick edge of the table, as she crouched on the chair in front of its warm wood, loomed, filling her brain. She could see its open pores, untamed splinters, perfect curves of grain. Light from the lamp streamed down over the edge. The pain's heat leapt up over her shoulders like a fish, fluttering and splashing, almost playfully.

Dropping her arms akimbo on the table, she put her hands near each other, but they didn't touch. Clay cups, broken open, lay in front of her where she could see them. Why did she see herself breaking up when the pain was welding her together? Her white skin was chalky, almost crumbly like dried mucus. Her womb gorged on blood.

How much time had passed? Now the pulse was pain. In between was no pain, a neutral, colourless relief. Her tongue tasted metallic and gritty. She thought she was hungry, but nausea rippled just under her ribs. Then she thought of nothing.

In that moment there was no other reason for her being than to provide energy for the birth. Time as she used it evaporated. She was indifferent to the scratch of scent, uninterested in surfaces. She overlooked the white air. Sounds became isolated, floating by as meaningless as footprints were to sand. She had no questions. There were none.

Before she had anything ready, Matthew was back with Addie, who hurried Hannah behind the blanket. 'Now, let me see.' Hannah lay down and pulled up her gown. Before touching her Addie bent over close to her face and whispered into her ear. She handed her a small wet towel and told her to wipe her face. 'Now, my girl, let's see where this baby is.'

Addie told Matthew to stay out. 'Women's work,' she said, and closed the curtain. 'Looks good. That baby is coming right along.' She appeared suddenly behind Matthew. 'She's closed her eyes for a moment, having a rest before the big push. You got a smoke?'

'Just this,' he said, startled, handing her a crude cob pipe.

'That's fine.' She filled the bowl with tobacco and lit it.

'Why is she so quiet?'

'Gutsy girl.'

It was Hannah against Hannah, he knew that much. This was not for him. She was proving herself to herself. She had not said a word to him about pain or dying. She was going to live forever, he had no doubt. Hannah for Hannah, burning and rising until the world ended.

They heard her wake and gasp. He peeked in. Her face was slick and white. Addie told her to push. Hannah's whole body tensed, flesh bunching and buckling, growing raw and proud. Addie had turned her sideways. She seemed to be pressing on her belly with one hand, digging into her with the other. 'Come on, my old girl, catch your breath now, easy, easy, getting ready to push, not yet, not yet, easy, now it's coming, take a deep breath, now, now, push, harder, harder, push that baby out, I see the head, it's coming,' chanting, pushing and pulling the baby out with her voice, coaxing, 'You can do better than that, my girl, push!' Her belly was arching and rippling, alive on its own like a snake swallowing. Addie's voice deepened, 'Good girl, there's the head, now breathe, steady, let me turn the baby, there, easy now, almost ready, the next push will get this baby born, that's right, deep breath and now let's see this baby.'

He could see it. 'A boy!' Waxy, bloody, squirming upside down, then laid on Hannah's stomach. 'Cover him up, he's cold after being inside you. There, hear that, he's starting to cry, here, let me push you up, see that!' Matthew wanted to come in, but Addie wanted him to wait until she got the placenta. She took a soft towel and wiped the baby a bit more. The women huddled over the boy, sharing a secret, swaying like willows. He couldn't hear what they were saying, and that muffled laugh, why were they laughing? Crying?

'Put him on your breast.'

A few minutes later she opened the curtain. He went to the bed, not knowing what to do. Addie had left them alone, but he still felt like an extra person. His hands hung down in front of him. Hannah was triumphant and inscrutable. She was looking at him, enchanted with his discomfort and an extra emotion new to her, a thick fierce tenderness.

She slid over, making room, and gestured for him to sit. 'Turn the lamp down a bit.' He touched her face, her arm. She uncovered the baby's head, took Matthew's hand and placed it there. He could hide the whole baby under his hand.

'Here,' she said, putting the baby on his arm. 'Here's Benjamin.'

'I think he likes me.'

Addie was mumbling to Hannah, to herself. 'A boy ... well, it's good to have them first. Give your husband his boy then you don't have to worry ... Crazy over that little thing ... "My son," they say it so much easier than, "My daughter". Can't hear it themselves, but they do. Give them the boy so they can relax ... and when the girls come...!' She shrugged.

'Come on, come on,' she said, giving the baby back to Hannah, digging Matthew up off the bed. She took the lamp away and put it on the table.

He followed her out. 'I didn't think it would be like that, so easy I mean.'

'Mmmm,' she said, tilting, nodding. 'For the first, it was. Small head, easy quick labour, her good health. She's a strong girl.'

As they talked, Hannah was overwhelmed with fatigue. Her arms and legs felt like stacked wood. With the last wisp of strength she stroked the baby's cheek with the end of her finger. The baby sucked the tip of his tongue.

She thought that something should be different, there should be more happening, more houses with lights going on in them. More people ought to know. Her mother and father wouldn't know they'd become grandparents for months. Joel an uncle, Sally an aunt. Tomorrow, perhaps, someone on a nearby farm would find out, tomorrow or the next day. On such an important occasion, how could it be only these people she hardly knew? In this lonely place, alone in her body, alone with her baby. Snow, wolves, cold, nowhere. The voices from the other room were so soft she thought she could hear the baby breathing. And though she'd not thought about running away before this, now she did, and it became an alternative that had always been there, except that now the possibility was crushed as soon as it was acknowledged. Now the baby was here. Now she couldn't run.

Addie was going to stay over. For a while she sang to herself, but it was past her bedtime and soon she too was asleep on a makeshift mattress of horse blankets and wagon wraps. Under her ear the straw chuckled like chicken feet.

Matthew was afraid to get into bed with Hannah. He tended the fire and pulled a chair in by the bed so he could watch. Both were asleep. This couldn't be real, surely his eyes deceived him as they did when dust phantoms in the barn scared him into thinking someone else was there. She'd handed the baby to him, put him right into Matthew's hands as if she thought he knew what to do. She was swollen, salty. A halo of light was sunk just below the surface of her skin. She had a new smell, still raw in the centre, waxy like honeycomb.

Picking up his son, Matthew laid him in the furrow between his thighs. Addie had swaddled him, making him look and feel like a sausage. The baby made crackling sounds as if he were drying out. 'Are you really here? Do you miss that warm wet place?'

He hadn't thought about himself as a father. Little by little the baby would have to grow into him as he had grown in Hannah. He laced his fingers together to hold the tiny head. His breath on the little face. Who did he look like? How could he tell? Dough-boy body, pink skin scalp. Does he look like me? he wondered. Did I look like this? Mama, did I? Will he love me – when will it begin? How will I know? This creature made of the same stuff as me. When he closed his eyes, Matthew saw a future self standing side by side with a son. Man-child. One day you'll step into my shoes, one day you'll stand in my place. There's plenty of room.

Outside, the bear of winter rolled over, dragging its claws.

This was one beginning. He thought of others. The oldest beginning, his first memory of himself, seeing his own baby arm reaching out for the forbidden. What did I say, Mama? What did I do? The embroidered stories of his childhood. What did I do after that? And then?

'What was I before then?' Half afraid, half intrigued by shadows that were part of the common knowledge, part of himself that belonged to those big people who laughed so easily at him, whose memories tunnelled back through him. 'Tell me again about the time when I ...' The safe repository of his soul, she hid it under her hands, in her heart. He could picture it almost, hear it in her chest. 'I keep you in my heart,' she had said, but he had seen himself standing there, so she was talking about yet another self, one not allowed to lie around in the hot clean daylight.

'Now, my son, who is there in the bed of her heart?'

148

How much room was in Hannah's heart? Her spirit he'd always been able to see, shaking in the air, but he couldn't recollect ever having seen her heart. He'd had everything else of her, what had that been if not her heart? It didn't matter. It was something disguised as heart, perhaps, something he'd acknowledged. So why was he so cold now?

He was just alone, that was all, awake while everyone slept around him. He had slept alone on the prairie before, the horses nodding over his head, their breath steaming in the black cold air. Here he was warm and dry, there was even a little light, but it wasn't enough, it wasn't right. He touched the baby's face. 'Open your eyes, don't let me be the only one.' He wasn't supposed to be left awake like this. There had always been someone watching over him. He never let his mother sleep if he woke first. He would stand at her side of the bed, harshly whispering, 'Mama. Mama. Mama,' until she opened her eyes. Day and night she was awake listening, hearing all through that sultry afternoon when he'd been feverish, hearing across the wide open desert night of his wild dreams. She'd found the way to him.

His hands were cramped from holding the baby for so long. He put him back under Hannah's nose, where she could smell him. A last drop of root coffee sat in the pot. The air was stale with so many people breathing it. He opened the door for a second to flush out the smoke, and that whiff of fresh air did him in. Moving the chair closer to the bed, he laid his head on a sliver of muslin, and slept.

'Mama Mama Mama,' he heard his childhood voice locked in his mother's mind. She could remember the sound of it, but he couldn't, and when she died she would take it with her forever.

Hannah noticed that the sleeves of her blouse were almost tight, the buttons angling out of their holes. The baby's head sank into her arm, the abundant softness of her flesh. He seemed to know her breast better than she did herself. Matter-of-factly he had taken over her body. Her ears pricked up to his puffs, splutters, squeaks.

Matthew was over there, his same shape, those small pouches under his eyes, the length of his fingers, the double-jointed backward tilt of his knees. She could see him with her eyes closed, the way he stood behind her, looking over her shoulder into the dinner pot, commenting, saying the same thing he always did. He was entirely predictable. She could barely stand to look at him.

The baby was newness, hers, a lush growth feeding on her. 'Where did you come from, baby mine, I mean really come from?' His skin was perfect and delicious, his breath sweet. The inside of his mouth was folded like a flower. 'Are you making me love you? How are you doing it? This soft little place under your chin, is this how? Or this warm little hollow here?' Filling it with her lips, kissing him, laying her ear on his chest to reap the astonishing beat of his heart. She hungered for it, thirsted for his breath, caught it, hooked it with her tongue, tasting it sweet and dry.

They spread out on the bed. There was barely room for Matthew. It was the middle of the night. 'Are you awake? Why are you awake, did something wake you up? Was something wrong? Buffalo? Wolves? You're never awake in the middle of the night.'

'Is it the middle of the night?'

'Yes.'

'Are you?' he whispered.

'Am I what?'

'Awake often in the middle of the night.'

'Of course, for months now. You think pregnant women sleep through the night? You think the baby sleeps through the night?'

'Shhh, talk more softly.'

'Why?'

'You'll wake yourself up.'

Her voice dropped, it was without tone. He could see her face remote from him in the dark. It wasn't happy or unhappy, this different aspect of her face. She just couldn't focus on him. Does the baby look like me? he wanted to ask her. Do you ever look at me the way you look at him? That hard. To himself, barely hearing his own thoughts.

'Do you want to talk about something?' she whispered.

'I don't know what I want to talk about. I don't know what I want to do.' A cold sick feeling in the pit of his stomach. There was too much to do. He couldn't possibly get the fields ready, get the seeds in. Things touched his fingers as they passed by. He reached, wanted to get things going in the right way, the way he wanted, the way he had set his heart. After all. Could he do it? Was this going to be enough? He had to get out of this overheated landscape.

'Well, go then, Matthew, what are you waiting for? Why do you wait?'

The baby snuffled hungrily. He had to get out of the house. When he left in the morning, Hannah didn't even hear him.

The big horse was surprised to be ridden out over the crisp, wind-thinned sheet of snow. Matthew had thought it would be deeper. He couldn't tell anything by looking at it. Light blazed through him, the sun was getting strong again. It burned on the barrel of the gun, which became a wand, a sword touching the horse's shoulder. Putting his nose down in the snow, he shivered and blew. Matthew adjusted the gun on his lap. He'd shot rabbit this close before. This time he wanted something more. Antelope had come down in the break beyond the gravel bed. Stringy, mean-tasting creatures this late in the year, but fresh meat, and Hannah had a way of bruising it, beating it down.

Something moved in the chuck of brush beside him. Stopping the horse with his weight, he raised the gun, his eye moving delicately between the sight and the area to either side of him. A stray cow floundering. He rode over to scare it out. 'Go home, go home.' The cow flushed a scrawny rabbit out onto the bewildering slick of snow. Matthew shot at it. He didn't often miss. He shot again. 'That's got it.' A little dark blood. He'd shot through the whole front of the animal; there was a little meat on the hindquarters. He'd have to do better. For the baby. When the baby was hungry, he curdled up, making a small helpless sound, surprised and hurt, as if to say, What's wrong, why do I feel this way? Everyone was hungry. Everything was still frozen. The hay was almost gone. The animals were eating the straw stable from the inside out. He could see the bottom of the black bean jar. Hannah was pale, the baby was still crying. He had pictures of them in his mind now, and not one of the old ones; there was a whole gallery of the old ones, his favourites. Always Hannah alone. Now she wasn't. He tried to remember exactly what the baby looked like. He put the baby in her arms, at her breast, on her knees. He separated them; the baby cried. Hannah hated him, he wouldn't stay where she put him. She said she was hungry. She picked up the baby. He'd never be able to get enough for them.

Getting down off the horse, he stopped before picking up the rabbit. His face was stiff. He heard Hannah. The baby was hungry, she said. He heard her up front in his mind. And as he listened, a little weight came down on his shoulders. A little extra muscle perhaps, across the back? Something was coming in contact with his flesh, thickening it. (His hands were still at his sides.) It filled his body with something like dread. It wasn't the wind in his ear, after all.

The rabbit's ears were untouched; silken and warm, they lay limp in his fingers. He held it like that until all the blood was out in a slow drizzle through the cold air. In a simple noose, he tightly caught the hind feet and hung it upside down from a harness strap. He climbed back up on the horse, so high in a flat land. Behind him, the sun was wolfing down the pale cloud cover; its heat was on the back of his neck and before him, distorted, diffuse, but recognizable as his own, the commanding staff of his shadow.

Did she ever see that? Did she see the same self he did? What did she see? He kicked the horse forward, faster, turning him to the higher ground where the snow had blown away. The firm footing gave the horse confidence; he broke into a trot, was quickly urged into a canter; Matthew clung, his legs between the horse's shoulder and the girth straps. Drumming the ground, the horse moved faster; Matthew felt him loosening up, warming and relaxing. The air was not so cold now and he could smell the ground. Faster, faster. A getaway. Suddenly an antelope reared and swerved in front of him. It turned back behind him. Swivelling, Matthew raised the gun. Which way was it going next? He wouldn't have another chance. The animal's back was buff-coloured, blending into the snow. He didn't think he could get it through the neck. Aiming lower, he fired. Again. The antelope somersaulted, skidded on its back, tried to rise, splayed and convulsed. Matthew urged the horse forward. Still he could see the deer shuddering. It must be dead by now, he thought. It clawed the snow. He was close enough to see. The bullet had ploughed a furrow right next to the backbone. Blood welled up. Nervously the horse stepped aside; he sneezed. The deer wouldn't stop. It didn't stop twitching. Matthew had to reload the gun. It was taking him forever, his fingers stiff with the cold. He dropped a bullet in the snow. The gun wouldn't break; he had to force it. 'Give up, give up. Die, damn you, Die.' Shouting it down. By itself, the gun wasn't enough. 'Die. Die.' The words exploded out his throat. He was gasping for breath; his stomach turned; jumping down just in time, he vomited. Elbowing the horse out of the way he shovelled the gun barrel against the skull of the animal and shot again. Forever and ever the deer tightened itself up, then slowly, slowly, relaxed. The horse shook his head; Matthew was momentarily worried that he might run away, and so grabbed the rein. He was so cold. He looked for the sun. There it was, so bright he couldn't look at it. Turning, he expected the deer to have moved again. He raised the gun, but this time it was quiet. He poked with the gun.

Reluctantly his body obeyed his demand to walk around the carcass. Round and round he went, unsteadily at first, uneasily, his legs brittle; the fabric of his trousers flapped and rubbed raw, though there was no wind. It might move, he thought, the lungs might lift. 'Keep down.' Grinding between his teeth, 'Stay put, you ...' pointing, circling, the muzzle of the gun close enough to paint, tracing the curves, drawing the outline.

Instead a miasmic steam crept out of the wound, spilling in the clear air. It was one wound. What difference did that make? Dead was dead. His own feet were firmly on the ground. He had no dead-making holes in him.

The horse was pulling on over to a tussock of frozen grass; Matthew let it go. Taking a deep breath, he kicked at the antelope's rump. Dead for sure. Moving closer, he hunkered down and dipped his fingers in the dark blood that lay in the wound's furrow. He looked to one side, the other, then, bringing his fingers to his lips, he tasted the soft blood. Rubbing all over the surface of his tongue, he salted down the taste of vomit.

Beneath the antelope the snow and grass had been mashed down and melted. Wolves would be along later to sniff the spot. Even now they watched hollow-eyed from the deep brake bushes, holding their breath. They stood in such a way that the shadows of their bodies and the blood of the antelope blended into one flat shape.

Riding home, Matthew couldn't stop himself nervously grinning. He was lean and taut. Trembling with energy and hunger, he'd never felt this strong, this good. The world he saw was coming light and fresh; he could drink air through his skin, sunlight washed his face. Letting the reins down on the withers of the horse, he held out his hands; they could hold the heat, use it. He was all alone, not as if he were the last but the first. The first person, dropped by a good god onto the earth in its springtime. Thinking, this is all for me, all for me. Mine.

His mind raced, then, finding something pleasing, slowed. He remembered how the animal had exploded from the bush, its eyes wild and fierce without that snivelling fear domestic animals show as fright. Heat bolted in his body, he was sweating, his smell strong with warning and challenge. The horse turned, slicing its own shadow. His mind overshot, surrounded, danced around his body; appraising, directing, then firing. 'Shoot, shoot,' it said, banging his blood; crazily casting his spirit out, making it look, offering it a feast of blood. He saw the muscles of the animal laid bare in the effort of escape; he became the bullet burying himself in the thick of skin, shrieking, spitting blood, quenching himself, sliding in the flesh as easily as if he were invisible. Then stopping somewhere deep, lying back, exhausted, dizzy with the stress and excitement, gasping for breath. Drained. Safe. Accomplished. Confident. His body relaxed and turned as slow as sleep.

Wonderful illusions of his place in the world moved in his mind, light and full of dream. The antelope was all antelope. He could hold it all together, above ground, in the colourless air, he could do anything he wanted. Make the land thaw and open to him. Make storms stay back and rain fall when he chose. He was the god, he remembered. Watching himself in his own place was the most interesting thing to do, the progress of himself over the earth, the process of his thoughts, the mystery of his own mosaic.

A strange slow grey crept back into the sky. The frozen grass crackled and chuckled. Overlooking. Forgetting; it didn't miss the antelope.

Matthew saw the house. For a moment it was strange to him like something someone had told him about, but he couldn't remember. What was it for? Who lived there? How small it was and low, pressured by the snow and cold; he could see that. How hard it must be to live there; the dark stuffy air, the dirt and dust. Long months, bleak tempers, cold shoulders. He slowed the horse down.

Hannah was there waiting for him. He began to anticipate her approval. They would eat for weeks from this kill. She wasn't crazy about game, the oil, thick smells, worms, gravel; she had to scrub the oil out of her skin, bending over, her arms bare and glistening, frighteningly white, plunged in a tub of soapy water. But they wouldn't be hungry.

'Bring the baby out,' he said. 'I've got something to show him.'

'Matthew, look.' She was waving at the ground as if to brush it away.

'What?' He didn't see anything.

'Look at that, and that ... there, see it, look, the footprints, the hoof prints, for God's sake they were here, right at the door. While you were gone they came. They must have been watching. Maybe they're always watching us, how do we know, what could we see? They were here.' She pulled up short. 'Well. Do something!'

He could see the tracks leading up to the door, stirring and compressing the snow, then there, again, where they had ridden away. 'What did they do to you?'

'Nothing. They scared me. They touched the baby. They took some bread and milk.'

'And did you scare them back?'

'Its not funny, Matthew, there are such things going on as massacres.'

'There are,' he said, nodding. But he didn't want to fight anyone; he didn't want any trouble.

'They talked about me. I know they were talking about me in their own language and I got this funny feeling that if it hadn't been for the baby, they might have ...' She looked sideways. 'Come on.'

'I've got this deer,' he said, stopping her.

'Oh my.' Picking up her skirt, she stepped out to look.

They had a shoulder roast for supper. Hannah was too busy to notice how Matthew was sitting, straight and narrowly on the chair he had made, propped up by the pegs of domesticity. By stretching out his leg he could reach the rocker on the cradle he'd made for his son and give it a little push. Hand-twists of straw burned in the stove. All around him were the solid blocks of sod he'd cut out of the centre of the earth and built up around his wife. His child, keeping warm, he thought, fed, dry. He wiggled his toes inside his socks. Built up to contain his life, to keep it safe. He should have felt better.

Nine

The last snow, a half-hearted surprise, swirled down the high sky and disappeared in the grass. Ice melted down to a transparent skin showing black water underneath, then sank. Frost worked its way out of the ground, a process of silence, but with a scent that stung the air. Pasque-flower, prairie cat's-foot, windflower appeared close to the earth. The creek, swollen with mountain water, slapped from side to side in its bed, clawing out caves, undermining them, toppling seedlings and sending sawyers down into its swiftness. The first rainfall spilled deliciously and darkly; inky black drops slipped down out of the night sky to drum on the well cover and the hard dry ground. Crane and heron, like bare souls, swam the skies north. Ducks wedged through. From time to time they tilted down to feed in the slough water. A blue blush fringed the white bluffs. Silver sage. Saw-toothed mint. Blackflies.

The rain made a mud. When Hannah opened the door, a pulpy sloth of dung-brown mud stretched from her toes to the horizon. The grass was stuck up in it. A stink of algae and carcass. A scum of white leach dried in scallop edges. The sky wouldn't touch it.

Giving in, Hannah tore up the canvas tarp that had served as carpet and let Matthew track in on the dirt floor. Soon they were at sea in their bed, a ship aground on a dirty hard soil, and down there, boots like pairs of twin dinghies ready to ferry them in and out. Diapers drooped in signals. They held a ghostly light soft on their surfaces, which illuminated the inside of the sod house like a white dream. It was too warm to keep the fire inside. Insects that had wintered in the walls left, others wandered in the open door. Boots clogged with slop, she dragged her feet along the memory-worn path. Her mind was an even slick of routine. The drudgery of fire-keeping and water-toting was weighed down by wet diapers, dirt and rotting thawed food. Hannah had to wash and wipe Lettice's legs and udder, then she shed hair into the milk. The baby cried at night, in the late morning, through the afternoon and just at suppertime, no matter when that was.

'You're green,' said Matthew. 'I didn't notice inside there. Your skin is green.'

She'd expected everything to look the same as it had before, but this bleed of colour, this urgency, the fierce growth, shocked her. Last year they'd been too late, they'd missed it all. This was no secret breathing and breeding in a close warm eastern dark; this was a hot explosion, a violent struggle for space, a race from the ground, each plant growing in turn, gasping for sun until, above all, lorded the grass.

In spring, the wind in the trees made a moist weighty sound like flags. Around her, birds swarmed, sable and swift, scooting through the draping sunlight, whirling the heavy warm wind with the tips of their wings. The baby slept in her arms; he wasn't heavy at all. He was sweet and snuggled down; his skin listened; he was glad to be there, she knew. They did everything together. She was used to the weight of him; she would miss it, she did miss it when she put him down to plant the kitchen garden, to milk Lettice, to churn the cream, to wash clothes and diapers, to clean and cook. She wiped the tip of her finger on her skirt to clean it so she could touch him just once more; then again, and there.

When she took a deep breath, it was no longer the stink of scorch, sour milk, urine, the fester of stale straw and smoke, but rather the fruit of grass, melted ice from the mountains and the syrup of strong sun. Hannah stood in deep grass, in the midst of trees, among the trees; they were close; she measured them against the sky, but the trees stood in the water in the elbow of the creek; gold-tipped willows, wild plums, their white blossoms sprinkled in the blue spring water that mirrored the clouds playing in the shallows of the sky.

As soon as the road was set, a peddler arrived on it. He came as if he were long lost, welcoming them into the world he brought with him, that jingling, jangling, clanking, small, weathered wagon, refreshing their memories of the worlds left behind. Opening the wagon as if it were a flower, he lifted the awning, unlocked the door, opened the shutters and lowered the counter.

'I bring you the outside world, madam, nothing less than what you've always needed and wanted, isolated as you are in this lovely spot of God's earth …'

'Madam,' said Hannah aside to Matthew, momentarily interrupting the tinker's trill of monologue.

'… your cozy home, this green land. And that's a fine-looking pair of horses over there, and that must be a new calf this spring. You're lucky, the folks back a-ways lost twin calves, they told me … Oh, 'thank you madam, that cold water is just what I need after the hot dusty road, mighty tasty, I thank you …' He moved on to Matthew, talking about the unions, farmers, ranchers, Indians, roads, politics, renegades, outlaws.

To keep herself from touching everything, Hannah clutched the baby, who yawed back over her arm to see for himself. She leaned over him, eyes hungering, thinking of the thousands of times she had dusted such wares in the general store, hating the endless surfaces. Now she stroked each item with her longing. Plain old speckled tin, it would look so nice on her shelf. She needed a fry pan too. Canisters, colander, measures, milk pans, ladles. He had fly swatters, buckles, candle moulds, scales.

'You wonder where I've come from, where I've been? To all the corners of this earth. Where're you from, folks?' They told him. 'That's nice country, I been through there many times. I've been everywhere, I've seen it all, if not here, then there. There's nothing I haven't seen, nothing surprises me, hell no, pardon me, ma'am, but this world's barking out loud, hummm, I can hear it everywhere I go, things are moving out, the land is filling up, you won't be alone out here for long. Be careful, be careful who your neighbours are, look for the sweat, look for the salt inside their hat brims, look at their hands, don't let them soft-skinned people come next to you, they'll borrow. First they'll borrow, then just steal, they don't care. You be careful, you're a nice family. Why, I can just tell things will go well for you, you've got that look in your eye, son. Yes, you remind me of …' He sighed and seemed to drift off into a reverie that would be disturbed by words dropping into it.

Hannah looked at everything. She backed up beside Matthew, who was standing sleepily, leaning on the tinker's words. She'd overheard what he said, how he saw something else special in Matthew. Maybe she should worry less, the tinker had seen people all up and down the country, all kinds and he said he saw the spark in Matthew. Maybe he was a liar.

She was between her men, the one who could not avoid her, who had come like bear to honey-bee honey, like dizzy bee to deep blossom. He had come. Now, she washed his scent out of his clothes and rubbed in her own. She smiled, the sun was over her shoulder, on her side. Leaning on him, she loved him, and the baby loved her, leaning until there were no pockets of air between them and it was delicious, this moment between moments.

On such a lovely day as this, they set up a sawhorse table and ate outside. Hannah liked a triangle of people at the table, it made a stronger shape, the wider base securing a better balance for the conversation. The tinker, whose name was Josiah, began to tell his own story, the parts about ending up alone, how his soul was slurped up by the evils of the world. 'You think I always looked like this, fat, bald?'

Short, she thought. But listening to them talk reminded her of the bantering around the old black-bellied stove in the store. The edge soon wore off their voices. They told each other truth and lies in equal measure.

'You think I was always alone? It's the vagaries of life that get you, the sluts and the storms, I say, bein' in the wrong place at the wrong time. Fightin' your way out and finding the only talent you have is selling things ... and carrying tales. Like the little county tabloid, a living newspaper, I'm important, you know.' He meant that, but was embarrassed and quickly puffed up his chest.

She slipped away and found herself thinking things about him, knowing, for instance, that he never slept. Even when the horse slumbered in its harness, she saw him awake, leaning on the cold air that hung down from the sky, wide awake, alone in the night, every night. Knowing that if he slept at all it was just a nap, cut off before he dreamed, snatched under the brim of the wagon in the noonday sun. She knew that his feet reddened and throbbed with gout. That salvoes of cluster headaches hammered in his brain, stretching his skin tight with pain. She knew; she overheard. Which was it? It didn't matter. She had to turn her head. She had to get up and fetch something from the cupboard. On his arm were slices of scars like the cuts she made on sausages to keep them from curling. He had no courage. He was ugly, too ugly to look on her baby. She would have to force herself to help him again. She'd have to hold her fist against her stomach to keep the food down. She didn't want him to take off his boot and make her bathe his foot, make her wrap it. He might expect her to rub his head, standing behind him and then he might try to lay his head back between her breasts, he might want to sleep there for the first time.

'Excuse me,' she said, 'I've got to tend to the baby.' She hid with him in the house, cooing to him, 'Bless your heart, rescuing me like that, you sweet soul, clean little perfect baby, that's right, cry a little, let him hear you, have a little cry.'

When the peddler left he leaned into the darkness of the house and said, 'No need to come out, ma'am, I know you're busy with the little one, thank you for the meal, I appreciate it, thank you ... Goodbye.'

'Matthew.' It was a week later. She was still calling him. 'Matthew, as soon as the seeds are in we've got to go to town, to get the baby baptized,' she said in a crisp matter-of-fact way. She had to, he was so reluctant. He wouldn't even answer her now. 'I don't understand; why are you so angry all the time? I'm going to go crazy if I don't get out of here for a while. I want to show off my baby, I want to see some strangers.' The word rolled ruggedly on her tongue. 'I'm so bored.'

Now he tried to see her through the dust he'd been raising with the plough for weeks, through the rainbow of chaff and seeds, through the shudder of sudden storms, the glaze of fatigue. 'It's foolhardy to say such a thing.'

'Oh, you know what I mean, bored in my mind.'

The sun was hot on her back, sweat dribbled down inside her dress. Out of that damp limp body, her mind crawled. It was restless and strong, stamping on the surface that was beginning to feel repetitious underneath her feet. She was getting hungry. She tilted, began to chew at her lip and the silence he had left for her.

'You can't say that to me, you don't know what I mean. You've been out of here. How can you keep me here? You're making me stay – why?'

'I've never even thought about it. I'm not trying to do anything to you, I'm just trying to get the crops in, I'm exhausted.'

'Well, I'm tired too.'

'I didn't say you weren't. I'd be surprised if you weren't!'

'But that's it, you just don't notice.' Elbowing across the table, she moved her head in front of his face. 'See me.'

'See me, see me.' At first he was teasing, making a face, talking through the brace of his teeth; then suddenly he wiped his hand over his eyes and whispered, 'See me.'

She kissed him ever so lightly. 'I asked you first.' It was better up close, she could blow away some of the dust from his eyes. She was more sure of herself. She had always been sure if she could just get it right.

He was going to touch her. 'Can I, can we?' Already with his eyes.

'Can't say no to you, can I?'

160

Her hair was dry and precise in his hand, but her flesh was as lush as freshly turned loam.

'Why did you say that?'

'What?'

'About being bored.'

'Because, because I think about being somewhere else, I imagine hearing another voice, not yours, not mine. I'm tired of the sound of my own voice. Believe it or not.' She was laughing, but she also closed her eyes. She meant it.

'Its just that I couldn't imagine being bored.' She shrugged. 'I was so surprised to hear you say that.'

'Forget it, Matthew.'

'I'm never bored.'

'Aren't you lucky.'

'Its just that I can't imagine ...'

* * *

'My baby leaves me just enough to keep *himself* going.'

The town women regrouped momentarily, looking to each other, trying to figure out if they should laugh or not. Hannah had seen to it that she was in the centre of things. First there was a bouquet of women, then a boundary of wood walls. Surrounding the building outside, polished by sunlight, a white fence, the first picket fence in town. It felt so good around her, she thought it might be the next thing she wanted. A border of red geraniums. Streets and alleys checked the open spaces beyond. Hannah had gathered them all herself. Everywhere she had attracted attention with the baby: old men with moist chins grinned; children pulled on her skirts. Distracting them with promises, women pushed their own children away so they could concentrate on the baby, attracting him successfully with the goos and smiles of long experience.

Hannah hadn't forgotten their first drive through town, the way everyone stared at her. This time she didn't say a word. She let them look, appearing to be fussing with the baby's wrap, making adjustments to the bonnet, turning him so the sun wasn't in his eyes, telling him secrets. Only when they pulled up to the hotel did she seem to notice where she was, with a soft casual surprise and perhaps relief that the wagon trip was over. Holding the baby with one arm, she brushed her hair back under her scarf. By then she'd seen the groups of two and three women stopping back in the shadows and the old men without mystery, sunning themselves in their favourite spots. Loose boys, who earlier would have snatched the breeze from her skirts, chalked her off as having crossed over into matronhood and therefore become too mysterious and mundane for them. But they all turned once. 'Who's that?' they whispered. 'Oh, I remember, he wasn't one of the ones passing through. That must be his ...'

Reflected from the bleached fronts of the buildings, thickened with dust and heat, light cooked in the street. Hannah stepped directly onto the boardwalk. Out there on the prairie she was always small. Here there was a chance to measure herself against the low block buildings that helped to break the horizon and stop the sky from landing on it. Out there, as far as she could see, she could see nothing. Here people bruised the golden air; they saw each other every day. Imagine! Just imagine the company: warm women cosy as teacups, comfortable, close, holding each other's babies, leaning on each other, licking wounds, lighting the long dark hours of winter. Whereas out there she was assailed by the scent of whipped grass, mint, manure and dust, in here she was comforted by the unmistakable aroma of human beings in their stride. Out there, the soft night was deaf; here the walls had ears.

Even though she was hot and dirty and hungry, even though she'd had an idea that the town would be something other than this, she knew she'd stay until someone drove her away.

In the stale close chamber of their room, she said 'I don't remember that it was like this.'

'Sure it was.' He coughed, that cheap dry sound she found irritating. As soon as he'd put down the bags and opened the window, he went back downstairs, leaving her alone.

A thin dust of street dirt slid off the window sill into the air. It didn't matter. She stood in the path of the broken street sounds, plucking them up as they rippled by. After the staggering silences this jittery, unpredictable pulse was delicious and just far enough away. She wasn't ready for the thick of it. Eavesdropping, she could hold at the edge and watch the dart of life beneath her. At any moment she'd be ready to go down; all she had to do was catch her breath.

For the first time her arms were empty and free of work. Folding them she noticed that her breasts rested on the shelf they formed.

Behind her, swimming in under the door was a lush sweet smell of fresh baking, bread, pies, cookies, someone else's cooking. Tonight she'd sit down to the table. Someone would ask her what she wanted, would serve her, take the dirty plate away and wash it. No dirt would sift onto the food from the ceiling; the cups wouldn't be chipped; the napkins, without stains, would perch like white birds. Someone else would have washed them. Like the street below, the dining room would be crowded with people stepping out of their day-to-day lives.

'Hello.'

'Hey there!'

'How's everything?'

'Howdy!'

Touching his hat, tipping it, tucking his head, smiling, shaking hands.

Hannah nudged him.

'Oh, this is my wife.' But she was an aside.

'You're the one rode that crazy Dragon horse, aren't you. Doing any more riding?'

'Not on my old horses.'

Hannah interrupted, 'What are you talking about?'

He touched her elbow and continued, 'But if you've got anything going in the next day or so ...' and trailed off, his gaze moving to a table in a quiet corner away from the street window, which was opaque with dust, and the alley window seeping the reek of garbage.

'What was that about?'

'I told you, remember? ... last fall when I was here ... that race I rode in ...'

Ever so carefully Hannah sat down. The baby in his basket fitted beside her on the floor. Occasionally one of the men in the room glanced at her. Then another. It was a heat that burned her. She should feel like this all the time, she thought, more in the nature of her true self, mirrored in the eyes of others. This was that other Hannah. Had she forgotten already?

Soft and close the baby slept. Matthew was eating, as he did, deliberately, low over his food. Though he was urgent and energetic, there was a rhythm that lulled her; she could imagine him eating forever, the baby sleeping on through this time into another, the flowers on the table never fading.

It was early. People were picking each other out for the evening ahead. That old friend or this new one? Who's got the stories? Who's got the money? Unlucky in cards. A job for tomorrow. A woman for tonight. The heat had not let up a whit; if anything, as the wind dropped it had begun to stack up in the corners. After supper the men would lean back in their easy chairs and smoke until ash-knit doilies embroidered their thighs.

After their meal Hannah and Matthew took a walk. Wooden sidewalks skirted most of the main street establishments. The dust was rose-blue. Horses sneezed out the day's dust and hitched their knees for sleep. Last-minute business transactions ricocheted. In that last light, hands in handshake glinted like fireflies and the moss-green money fluttered softly. What Hannah heard was the thick boot sole thumping on the wooden walk, the resonant hollow clomp, people walking on top of the earth. That space below her feet had room for an echo. Out there – she couldn't look, she could look, safe in the arms of the town – out there the ground soaked up her footsteps.

'Well, excuse me!' The woman who had bumped into them swayed to maintain her balance.

Is she drunk? Hannah wondered in bright surprise, eyes gossiping.

Matthew was between them. Gently gripping the woman's shoulder, he whispered something close in her ear. She chuckled soggily. 'Pretty, pity, pity...'

'What did she say?'

But before he could answer, the woman said, 'What a shame, what a shame,' shaking her head, a motion that unbalanced her.

'She *did* say that, "pity pity", why did she say that to me? Why?' Hannah kept her eye on the woman as she shuffled and bobbed down the sidewalk seeking a welcome in the next saloon. 'What did you say to her? Do you know her? How come everyone knows you and no one even remembers me?' And when they did she couldn't hear them; people were always talking so she couldn't hear them; they turned and twisted away at just that moment, they appeared and disappeared before she could get a look at them.

'That's just old crazy Lizzie.'

'Old!' Had that woman been old? In the twilight she must have made a mistake.

Then for one moment there was a peculiar silence. It reminded her of the awful dry place where she lived. The prairie was too big for her. It was too cold and too hot, too dark at night and in the day too bright to believe. The sun had too much room out there, it was too mean, too lonely.

With a quick slight motion night began. The men put their hands in their pockets to quiet the money, but they still jingled. Hannah noticed it was their spurs; when red light caught them they glinted like cockscomb.

The yawn she felt welling in her throat sank as her breath bubbled up. Yellow light spoke in tongues of the excitements inside; soft smoke floated in obfuscate illusion. Voices jousted and overrode each other.

'What did you say?'

He repeated.

'What?' She couldn't hear through the crush and crowd of music and talk. More than one plinky piano, more than one song contributed to the dissonance.

'I said, are you tired or do you want to go back to the hotel dining room?'

'What's at the hotel?'

'Oh, people sitting around, talking, coffee ... I don't know.'

'Women?'

'Not often, but it's not a saloon.'

'Where are the people like me?'

'Home.'

Hannah moved the baby to her other hip as they went in. The tables and chairs had been rearranged. A feeble glow of coal pulsed in the maw of the black stove. A man snagged a small piece with a pair of tongs and used it to light his cigarette. When he turned he almost bumped into the serving girl, who was mussed and wrung and scurrying with the last of leftovers, washing the table tops and, through the stringy curtains of her hair, keeping an eye for the reach of men's hands. Hannah sat down near the back of the room. A little shadow made room for her. With her foot she pulled another chair over. Leaning back she propped the baby up on her shoulder; as he snuggled and settled she pressed her lips to the side of his head. Across the room, the girl gripped the back of the chair she was moving; she stopped and stared; her eyes turned black.

Matthew brought two cups of coffee. His was laced with brandy.

'That girl is watching me,' Hannah said.

'Tell her to come over, she just wants to see the baby.'

'How do you know?'

Tolerantly, tactfully, Matthew said nothing, merely smiled and beckoned.

Laying the baby in the hammock of her skirts, Hannah watched the girl wipe her raw hands on the rough canvas of her apron and crouch in front of her knees. She had a rough ragged part down the centre of her head; lint or bits of chicken down clung to her hair. The girl's hands were scrawny and scaly like chicken's feet; she wanted to touch the baby. It might hurt him, thought Hannah. She stopped her, and so the girl had to curl her empty hands up under her chin. When she got up she looked at Hannah with a withery, awry smile and put her hair behind her ears. Someone called her. Hannah didn't catch the name.

Matthew swallowed half his cup, put it down and was about to tell her something when she heard the singing, but couldn't see who it was. Men bustled back and forth looking for places to settle. Islands formed, a card game over there, a coffee klatch, a huddle at the bar. From the hall came the sound of loud talking, arrangements being made, comings and goings. There was smoke and confusion, shadows slipping across her. She liked the sound of the song. She could barely hear it, but it had been so long since she'd heard anyone sing. Some of the men were humming. She heard, 'Git along, git along,' a round-up song; they all knew it; it had much the same effect as it did on the cows. Groups formed and quieted down. In a few minutes the cigar smoke was rising straight up to the ceiling as if from campfires. As the men shifted and settled, Hannah caught a glimpse.

'He was here last time I was in town. Gabriel.' Matthew was surprised and uncomfortable. He stood up, reached down, touched Hannah on the arm as if to say he'd be right back, then hurried over to refill his cup.

She leaned back, her head touching the wall. She caught sight of Matthew out of the corner of her eye, but didn't have to watch him. Her whole attention was concentrated on the next song.

'I've been a-travellin' long / travellin' on an' on / unravellin' song on song / just to keep goin' along ...' His voice was touching her as surely as if it were a hand, as gently as the hand of a lover. It was changing the way she breathed.

'Come on with me / we're goin' east to greet the early sun / come on with me.'

'Hey man, is that a song to the cow or the woman?'

'Hold on there, my friend,' he said, interrupting himself, 'read it anyway you want ... come on.'

'Oh, you gotta sing sweet to them cows,' mumbled another, saddened and slipping on down.

'Hold that thought, friend, and let me sing to them for you ...' It was hard to tell when or where the song stopped, his voice was so soothing.

But Hannah was trembling. Beneath her heart the baby was waking, the new rhythm had upset him, and he twisted, arching back over her arm. Any moment he would begin to cry. Surprised, she looked down at him as if he were a stranger. 'Oh you poor little thing,' she said, picking him up, cooing in his ear. 'Did I forget you were here, you poor little soul? Ohhh.' She got up, found Matthew and indicated she was going up to change the baby. 'I need the key,' she mouthed. He reached it out to her without a ripple in his conversation.

Except for the desk clerk, the lobby and halls were deserted. Leaving the door to their room open provided enough light to see what she was doing, and to see the baby looking up at her from the bed. 'You'd like to have us just stay here, wouldn't you, alone in the dark and the quiet, but I've had too much of it. Don't worry, you'll get fed, I'll put you under my blouse, don't worry.' Standing up, she looked at him. 'There's no running away from you, is there?'

Squirming, he frog-legged himself free of the mussed wrap, smiled then stuffed his fist in his mouth in anticipation. 'My little puddle bum.'

Downstairs someone had taken her chair, but another was empty up towards the front. Squeezing by she noticed she had a clear view of the singer. His guitar was sitting in the chair. She tried to find him in the room, but wasn't sure what he looked like. The baby was whining. Loosening her blouse, adjusting the shawl, she slipped him inside, where he grabbed her hungrily and kneaded on her breast in his pleasure. Biting her lips, Hannah winced at the first pull.

When she looked up, Gabriel was back, bending his ear over his instrument, listening to it while the men called out favourites from their corners. Having started four songs, he found what he wanted and began strumming vigorously, 'Yippi ti yi yea, get along ...' Everyone joined in, clapping, foot stomping, knee slapping; it was one of the favourites. The man at the table next to Hannah crossed one leg over the other and spun his decorative spurs to the beat.

'Good-bye, ol' Paint, I'm a-leavin' Cheyenne / My foot in the stirrup, my pony won't stand / I'm a-leavin' Cheyenne, and I'm off for Montan ...'

'Then fare ye well, my own true love / then fare ye well for awhile ...'

Hannah couldn't have been any closer, it would've been too dangerous. Unbuttoning the little pearl buttons at the neck of her blouse, she let her skin breathe out. His voice was in the air, embodied. She shivered; sweat ran down between her breasts into the baby's undershirt. Gabriel tossed his head back showing his white throat, the throat of a child.

I am a child, she thought. She shifted the baby to her other breast, and he took hold, sucking rhythmically. She felt pleasure and dark down deep inside, the blood backing up in swirls and whirlpools, sinking on her pride. The song poured over her, the milk and the music.

Gabriel took a deep breath; the chord slid away from his fingers, letting in a bland silence. In its space Hannah's breath caught. There wasn't enough air for her. Sweat floated up on her skin, making a sleek cocoon. When he stopped she was without sound of her own. She was cold. Touch-up shadows slid in under her feet camouflaging the floor. Rolls of smoke loitered around her thoughts, clouding them close and indistinguishable.

The baby was pinching her as if to say, Come on, Mama, and she did, a rugged shaggy see-saw breath righting her in the world where it was nonetheless hard to tell things apart, where the shoulders of men were as good as boulders and laughter cried out of nowhere. Where without warning a different self had swum up to stare at her.

That cross-looking scrawny girl was up there. Leaning to the side, Hannah could see that the girl was giving him a drink of something as if his legs wouldn't work or he didn't have time to get it himself. As if he were too important to do things for himself. After she handed him the glass, she hung around, or had he put his arm around her hips, holding her there? Was he looking at her? Curls obscured his eyes, but his head was tipped. His lips were moving.

There was too much noise for her to be able to hear. Someone was bent over, laughing helplessly on beer, bringing the manager, who warned, 'I don't want any trouble here.'

Closing in around him, the boy's friends were reassuring. Hannah couldn't see through them. For a moment she tried. The baby slipped off her nipple. He was heavy flesh on her lap. He wanted her to rearrange him; she could feel his fingers clutching the roll of skin on her stomach. She wanted to push him off onto the floor. Just like that, through some knothole, out of her life. He was too damp and demanding. Gimme, gimme, gimme, the little song he sang in her ear, the slow fizz of bubbles. And now, this limp sublime weight, gorged with her milk.

'Give me! Give me!' she repeated to herself.

As night began to break up and more serious groups formed, Matthew collected Hannah. Her lacklustre air surprised him; perhaps it was the yellow smoke and shortage of oxygen. Her blouse was wet and twisted. She leaned against him going up the stairs, the slow slouch and laxness of her body disturbing him. He'd been moving more quickly, dodging the hard bodies of the young men like himself. How easily he forgot. She reminded him of Lettice, her soft hairless udder, milk leaking when he touched her. He helped her climb the stairs. She seemed reluctant. It was as if she were going to say something and couldn't think of what it was, or forgotten something and would have to turn back.

In the hotel room, as she thought about sleep, she pulled the curtains and saw herself fragmented in the black glass panes. In bed she thought about the way the window fitted into the wall, the way the flowers in the wallpaper stopped below the frame and started again above. The thin lamplight shone on the flowers. Even though it was hot, the ceiling was so high, the corners so deep, she could breathe with bewildering freedom.

The baby was in a slovenly soggy sleep beside her. Matthew had to slide in on the other side. The bed shifted and sank. The rank smell of stale smoke rushed her. She thought he might try to touch her, he liked to do that, a habit, absentmindedly, stroking her hair, patting her hip. Putting himself to sleep. She couldn't bear it. Her skin was swollen. When he wasn't looking she rubbed the hollow in her throat. When he put out the lamp, her fingers wandered in wider and wider circles. She remembered her skin lying more smoothly on her bones than it did now.

The night was not as dark as she'd remembered and though she'd swear she didn't doze off, it was in a different sort of consciousness that she woke looking for the laws of nature, for the grip of gravity to hold her down on the bed. But something else was happening. She didn't want to look. The air had stopped moving. A tide of light was frozen where it rose in that last dream. The light flooded in the windows. The walls were full of windows. Once inside the room, the slow light burned white. Hannah had to close her eyes. A whispery sound was stifled before she could tell what it was. Her skin whined and complained. The baby slipped off her breast; she hadn't even felt him. Covering herself, she sat up, and with her hands pushed the air back off. Some of it got in her mouth; it tasted bitter. Reaching down with her toes, she tested to see if the floor was as soft as it looked, but that was another deception. Try as she might, she couldn't hear any other world out there. She slipped out the door. Her thoughts gritted and ground in her head, producing dust.

It was dead and dark at the bottom of the stairs.

'Ma'am ... ma'am, what d'ya want?'

'Who's that?'

'Me, ma'am.'

'I'm not a ma'am.'

'What're ya lookin' for?'

'That singer.'

'Oh ma'am, he's gone along.'

'Where does he go?'

'He goes to his home.'

'And where's that?'

'I'm sure I don't know.'

Hannah hauled up and looked at the girl hard. 'On the contrary, I'm sure you do.'

The girl didn't answer. Her eyes were so sodden with fatigue they looked as if they might sink back into her face and disappear.

'Tell me, tell me,' Hannah said, shaking her by the shoulders. The girl's bones were going to crack inside her grip, bird bones so thin she could easily crush them; disgusted and frightened she pushed the girl away. 'Who are you, anyway?'

Hesitating. 'Suela ... my name ... is that what you mean?'

Hannah backed up, turned to the side and began to walk quickly around the girl in a tight circle, rubbing the palms of her hands on her nightgown. The bottoms of her feet thudded smartly on the bare wood. Suela watched the feet scoot and dart like pale flat fish. She watched the edge of the white nightgown snap and stretch.

'What are you doing?' demanded Hannah.

'Shhh, ma'am, you're going to wake somebody up.'

Hannah glanced around, but she didn't see anything. She repeated.

'What are you doing?'

'Talking to a friend.'

'Who else is here?'

'A friend.'

'Where, where is he?' she said, pushing her out of the way, smacking the kitchen door open. A gust of air whipped out the candle that had been the only light. Nonetheless, she could see the shape of a person sitting at the table.

A soft sullen voice stirred the soup of dead air, oil, dust. 'Take it easy, honey, what's your problem?' A female voice.

'Who's talking at me now?' Turning, she grabbed Suela, who had followed her. 'Who's there?'

'I told you, my friend.'

'What's her name, though?' Squeezing her arm.

'Ow – Oda, her name's Oda. Let go!'

Hannah stumbled forward, the edge of the table catching her sharply across the thighs. She leaned over and her hands splayed open on the rough surface. 'What are you doing, it's the middle of the night!'

'Honey, this is the only time we got.' Oda was laughing a little under the words, jiggling them up and down. Suddenly a match flared and sizzled; she lit the candle, showing herself, a broad fleshy tuber of a woman, sweating through her cotton slip. Before her on the table was a lump of cloth, which she retrieved to wipe her glistening bosom. 'If you're staying, honey, sit down, it's too hot ...' she said, subsiding.

Hannah stood up and turned slightly to watch Suela skid by and sit back down in the chair she'd occupied. Her body was so slight as to be almost gossamer, but the way she moved was ugly, as if some burden or affliction were shifting and attacking her in an unexpected manner.

Hannah looked from one to the other.

Suela said to Oda, 'She's got such a sweet baby, that one does.'

'What are you doing, honey? You don't want any trouble now. You want to go back upstairs to your bed.'

'But what are you doing up like this in the middle of the night?'

'Honey, this little city don't sleep through the night. I've seen every sunrise ...' She sighed. Hannah couldn't tell if they'd pleased her or worn her out. Suela giggled and sprawled in her chair. Reaching down, she hauled up her petticoat and rubbed her face. The candlelight buttered her thighs. Though they were not looking at each other or talking, they were communicating, a shrug, a hum, a drift of scent.

They have left me behind, thought Hannah. No one knows where I am, no one will be able to find me. I will be lost in this place.

Outside, something rattled, clattered and fell.

'Ahhh, cats.'

'Or rats.'

'Or snakes.'

Suela and Oda stared at her, then laughed. 'Come on, honey, sit down there and tell us about yourself.'

Time backed out of the kitchen, leaving them alone. Try as she might, Hannah couldn't tell them anything they didn't already know. Closing her eyes when they weren't looking, she tried to conjure something amusing or different. She hadn't intended to tell them anything and now this, outdoing herself, sweating words, while they roosted and yawned and wiped the damp hair away from their faces.

'Oh God, you'd have to be already asleep to sleep in this heat,' Oda said, rolling her head around. Her neck was warm and moist.

The next words warped and deflected on the pre-dawn wall of acute silence. Overwhelmed, Hannah gathered herself and stole back upstairs, parting the ghostly dark with a sixth sense, disappearing into her bed to sleep through a sunrise of yellow starchy light and a slight breeze that lifted the curtain deliciously and covered her with its daydream of distance.

* * *

Matthew was talking slow horses and fast money.

Hannah interrupted. 'We have an appointment this morning,' she said, raising her eyebrows. Raising the baby in front of his father. Smiling.

It took him a moment. A soft smell murmured in his nostrils before he heard and saw. 'What time are we due there?'

'In an hour. We've just time for breakfast.' She'd talked to the minister, everything was arranged. When they'd first arrived in town, she'd unwrapped the small white baptismal gown from its brown paper and hung it up to air. Matthew's mother had sent the piece of fabric. At first Hannah had thought it was for her. 'Two yards! That's not enough for anything.' Then, realizing, she flung it in the cradle beside the baby. 'Something for you.' Addie helped her measure and adjust a pattern. Small inverted pleats gathered the front. She sewed a tiny round collar, a scalloped hem and blanket-stitched the button holes. She couldn't believe it herself. 'But I'm the one who needs new clothes; what am I going to wear?' But by adding a narrow black ribbon to the throat of her plain old white blouse, the effect was completely changed.

She wore a black cotton twill skirt, its slack folded into a wide belt. Addie had lent her that, too. The polished shoes and cotton lisle stockings were her own, at least, startling her with their cleanliness peeking out beneath the hem. Standing close to Matthew, she nicked his ankle with the sharp tip of her shoe. 'This way.'

Strong sunlight lathered on the floor. Even though she had a vague memory of a sleepless night and distress or disillusion, she felt both ethereal and charged with purpose.

'Coffee, ma'am?'

'Oh yes, thank you.'

'You?' It was an old woman Hannah had never seen before.

'They've got a horse they want me to see.'

This stranger sitting across from her. Part of his life she knew nothing about. She was one part of him, too, yet apart. She was curious now about her inattention to his details.

'I told you about the race, about riding Dragon.'

'Dragon, dragons – what is this? What am I supposed to know? Why are you telling me this? Are you going out there with those men?'

'I'd love to.' Half his face was behind the coffee mug.

'Well go, then.'

'I may be able to pick up some easy money, we need ... we need everything!' His laugh was hard-edged. His eyes wandered the room dreamily, unfocused. Not looking for anything he'd seen before, he felt unsure, slip-shod. Even if he were to find what he was looking for, he might not recognize it in daylight. Here and there his eyes rested, like air, on the baby. He thought, What are you for? What's your life going to be for?

The church was narrow, its lines sharp. Where the road curved away at the edge of town, the building cut clean the cloth of blue stretched across the sky. Dust had basted the peaked roof, and when the wind blew that way, bleached tumbleweeds banked against the windowless walls.

Matthew's head was high and slightly tipped back, Hannah supposed, to keep his eyes in the shadow of the brim of his hat, but it made it difficult for him to see the ground in front of his feet. She was surprised he didn't stumble. Perhaps he wasn't walking on the same rutted road she was. She noted with distaste the soft flare of his nostrils, as if he were sniffing for something or anticipating a race. Why could he never stay, here with her, in the moment?

Across the road, a soft old Indian man had slowed down to set up his summer teepee. He was the colour of gingerbread. He wore a raggedy blue Union uniform, medals dangling off it like loose shingles. Though sentried to the spot, he was nevertheless springing up and down, bending his knees. He was watching them with excitement. Later, during the baptismal service, he began to chant and sing. 'Some heathen song,' Hannah told Addie. 'It had no beginning and no end, as if it was going on inside him all the time and he just let it out once in a while. It was awful, just the bowl of water, the words, no music; I thought at least there'd be music, I thought we'd get a song.'

Because it wasn't yet past ten, the interior was relatively cool. Light swarmed in the doorway, but didn't disturb the dim aisles. The sap smart smell of new wood tingled in her nose; she could see proud splinters. The floor was dirty. She dropped her eyes on the baby; he was looking at her and when she greeted his eyes, he smiled in joy. He must watch me all the time, she thought, all those times when I'm not thinking about my face, when I think I'm alone.

It was difficult to pay attention, the minister's suit of words lulling her. 'Saying, "Ask and ye shall have; seek, and ye shall find; knock, and it shall be opened unto you." So give now unto us who ask; let us who seek find; open the gate unto us who knock; that this child may enjoy. Dost thou, therefore, renounce...?'

Was Matthew listening? He held the paper with the responses.

They read, 'I renounce...'

'Dost thou believe...?'

'I do.'

'It is very meet, right and ... be all honour and glory, now and ever more. Amen.' He reached for the baby. 'Name this child.'

'Benjamin Brede.'

'Benjamin Brede, I baptize thee in the name ...' and the slick of holy water slid on his honeyed brow.

I hope you do a better job than you did with Rosa, thought Hannah, taking him back in her hands. Briefly, she imagined God's face, yawning overhead, the sky inside his mouth. There was too much space. How could He keep an eye on all the little sparrowy children? Lifting Ben to her face, she smelled his milky sweetness. Benjamin. The name was too big for him. What if it's the wrong name, what if it didn't suit him? How was she supposed to know? Now that he had a name, who was he?

'Well?'

'What?'

'He's waiting for me,' said Matthew, indicating out there in the sun-drenched yard, a man sitting in a buckboard, hunched over his knees, smoking and wig-wagging his boot on the edge. The man stared at the Indian. Hannah could see enough of the look in his eye to make her pinch her nose shut. Lost in a pure mindlessness, the man didn't turn until Matthew saluted and slapped his hand down on the horse's flank. 'Ready?'

Sucked in behind the wagon, the dust leapt into funnels and swirls jaggedly across the road. Hannah covered Ben's head with her shawl. When she looked up she couldn't see the Indian man.

In the few minutes it took her to walk back, it had become much hotter. Walking quickly created a breeze on her skin, but it also forced sweat to crawl out and stain her clothes. A chandelier of drops hung at her hairline. It couldn't have been this hot last year. Ben squirmed, the sun in his eyes. She propped him up over her shoulder. Now that he could hold his head up by himself, she folded both arms under his bottom. He pecked at her shoulder with his fingers.

A leftover scrim of cloud in the western sky evaporated. Looking straight ahead she could see the other end of town.

After the soddy, the buildings here were like houses of cards, little more than paper and paste, a mortar of dust and tumbleweed. The sun was lapping up the small shadows that darted out from beneath her skirt. This, she thought, calls itself a town! Only dogs could find this place interesting. They were following her back along the sidewalk. When she was a child, dogs had bothered her bare legs. Even though they'd have to bite through all her layers of cloth, she lifted Ben higher.

Back at the hotel their bags were stacked tidily beside the desk in the lobby.

'Check out time is noon, ma'am.' Matthew had forgotten to tell her.

He'd said nothing about leaving. What was she supposed to do all day?

'Well, I can't do anything until my husband gets back.' Had the manager expected her to remove her bags right away? 'Are you still serving?'

The dining room was empty. Sitting at a far table, she ordered only tea, though the day was too hot for it. She had to make her money last the day. Had he even thought of that? She was tired and there was no place to sleep. Would she have to go to the trough to wash? Change the baby in the stable?

But when she went to the barn she found it to be a deep, golden place. The straw dust had settled and the stale smell was sweetened by the low sun of morning and evening. Weathered barn boards, frozen and thawed, had shifted to accommodate the weather. The horses nudged each other when she entered, then went back to their noon doze. Above all, it was cooler. Beside one of the stalls of sleepy horses was a matted pad of straw. Sitting down, Hannah held Ben up in front of her. His feet scratched on her skirt as he tried to stand up. For a moment he was thrilled until he remembered how hungry he was.

'I know, I know, ol' sweetie pie. Your turn, I know. Mama knows.'

One of the horses stuck his prickly pink and black nose sideways through the slats, sniffed and sneezed, spraying her shoe. 'Git out,' she said, shaking her head at him. 'I got nothin' for you!'

Because it was too tailored, she had to open the front of her blouse to feed him. He watched. Sun coming through a crack in the roof showered his mother's breast. He touched it, pressed his fingers into it, licked the nipple and took hold. The sun warmed his cheek and lips. He closed his eyes. 'Yes, yes,' Hannah sighed, leaning to rest her back, humming, 'Mmmm. Hush little baby don't say a word ...'

* * *

Gabriel yawned. Something was waking him up. He'd been dreaming and hated to lose that late-morning easygoing dream. He'd learned to sleep through the bustle of dawn's comings and goings. An old blanket, tacked on the shack's wall that was shared by the stable, kept out stray dust and muffled the deep feet of the horses. This was a different sound, immature, haphazard, personal. Rolling over, he lifted a trapdoor tear in the blanket. For a moment he couldn't pick her out from the mottled camouflage of shadow and sun that speckled the stable's interior.

Momentarily the voice dropped beneath the deep dozy breath of the horses, then surfaced. Now he could see her nested in the straw. One arm supported her child; she had raised the other above her head and was playing with her hair, idly plucking out strands. Her eyes slipped and lazed.

What he saw was a woman mangered in a soft gold of straw. A baby floated on her body, its head hovering in the dazzle of sun, on the halo of her breast. What he heard under the dreary song was the heart's sigh. This was unexpected. Without her knowing, he was watching every move and enhancing it. This was not a dream but the next best thing. He wasn't awake; his breath was shallow and high. If he let go of his breath this life might drain away. His muffled heartbeat sounded in his ears. Eavesdropping, he was unearthing the silences in his own imagination. I want, he thought, I want that soup of love, that thick green sweet smell, the first the earth gives up in spring. I want to be surrounded by flesh that reflects me as the moon reflects the sun; I want to drown and slide in her sweat, pull the stream of her breath around me; like no other, the mangy mother; I want to suck from those vessels, a suck of the promise, to swim in the forbidden. In the eyrie of all hope, I want a free dream, I want, I want …

When the baby sucked on her, it made her womb pulse. Usually she was too busy or too tired to pay attention. Now she was startled by the strength. As the baby pulled her open, she needed more air, the muscles across her back tightening. She stretched her feet out and curled her toes.

When Gabriel appeared in the doorway, though under the hood of shadow and in a clear silence, she immediately recognized his shape; she had known it forever. It choked her.

The baby stopped nursing and looked up. Hannah made no attempt to cover herself, the nipple and its aureole moist and shining. A glaze of perspiration lay in a triangle on her chest. The stable was hollow, too large a space for this.

Gabriel shook his head, making his curls spring. He knelt so that their eyes were level; he couldn't look away from her. 'No, no, don't,' he said as she started to lift her hand, his in the air, hovering over hers. 'Put the baby back on,' he said eagerly, breathlessly, almost touching her, then his fingers retracted, hiding inside his hand. Hannah thought he might hit her.

He was afraid he'd soil her.

Turning Ben she teased him, wiping his lips, tickling his cheek. Even though she was watching what she was doing, she didn't see. Ben took hold.

'Um hmmm,' Gabriel jerked his head in affirmation and pleasure. Catching her lower lip in her teeth, Hannah bit back a laugh. He was so earnest, almost hypnotized. She could look at him without interruption, only to discover she didn't need to, there were no surprises, not even the curls at his temple riding the tide of his pulse there. The derelict scent of sleep in his clothes. The scoop of his eyelashes. Hazel eyes. Flaws. She knew. His sleeves were too short, the knots of his wrists shone exposed. Square pronounced joints punctuated his fingers. But somehow she knew all about him.

To keep his balance, he reached for her knees. Still as stone she waited. Then patiently, possessively, with both hands, he pushed her legs apart. Her skirt stretched then fell in between. He inched forward until he was there and his hands slid under the baby, around her hips. He held on to the cloth as if afraid he would fall.

'Who? Who?' But it was like a small coo of comfort. She wanted to squeeze him in her thighs. She wanted him to reach up to suck her lips; to lie on her, smother her. Tell her his secrets. She wanted him to sing for her; to blow the word down her throat until she echoed.

Gabriel leaned on the aroma rising from her skin. He was so close, Ben tried to catch his eye, but Gabriel had closed his eyes. He breathed on the soft sigh of her breast; he could smell the baby; he could taste the salt on her skin.

Hannah couldn't look out any longer. Her eyes drooped to the top of his head, then closed. One of his hands was pushing her blouse aside, cupping her breast. He licked it. For a moment the wet skin thrilled, then his breath netted her. Sliding his arm back around her he began to rhythmically press her hips with his hand. With his lips softly closed, he began to rub back and forth on the nipple. His other hand was slowly climbing to her throat. She turned away from it. He waited. In a moment she turned back. Reaching up he covered her face; her breath gilded his hand. Ever so gently he opened his mouth. She could feel his teeth. She tried to twist away, but he was holding her now, sucking the milk out of her body, rubbing his fingers in strange patterns that distracted and interrupted her. Sucking the milk right out of her body!

She tried to get her hands free, but before she knew what he had done, he had withdrawn and was holding her hands in his, looking into her eyes. His own were sad.

'Shhh, shhh,' he consoled. 'You are so beautiful, so perfect. You and your child.' His eyes stayed in hers, but she was frightened. 'No, no, there, shhh, nothing will happen to you, nothing will happen to you; you are the most important person in the whole world, don't you know that?'

Twisting her hands free she gathered the baby up against her, pulling her blouse, tucking it underneath him. Gabriel lifted his hands, opening them in front of her, offering her something. 'You have it now. Don't you know how it works? The men release the love in women. Then the women give the love to their children.' His voice was singing through a valve of pain. He continued to look at her. The way he was doing it lifted a loneliness from her soul; she had felt herself turning into a gift in his hands. 'From the beginning men love women, we drench them in our love, we worship them. We open them and let the love come out.'

'I have to go,' she whispered. Ben was kicking and arching back. 'I have to go.' Gabriel didn't help her up; she saw his hand ready, but couldn't touch it.

All afternoon she paced the boardwalks, changing sides of the street when the sun began to blister. She couldn't talk to anyone. When Oda ambled into her path, catching her by the arms to admire Ben, she stood numb and burning. How could she know? What was there to know? Her mind was a polite blank. Oda tried to take the baby, but Hannah couldn't let go, and so the woman trundled them both to the back pantry for lemonade and a clean diaper. Oda did the talking. 'Look, honey, I'm too tired to be prying into your life, but let me tell you I've seen all kinds and you're not cut for that out there.' Taking a rough wet rag she wiped Hannah's face. 'You're starting for home when your husband gets back, aren't you?' Hannah nodded. 'Well, wash this diaper and it'll be dry by the time you're ready to leave.'

Hannah nodded, then mumbled, 'I want to go home.'

'What? What'd ya say?'

She repeated to Matthew, 'Take me home.' But as soon as the last post and clump of garbage was passed she shrank and shivered. That home was not inside her. Was home supposed to be that pelt of brown and tawny grass, that wave of yellow corn? Not a home those thick dry walls. It wasn't the same sky that had been a bowl over her childhood.

Matthew was talking, twisting words like straw into cat-torches that flared in his excitement and energy. He smelled like a clean hard-run horse. Once in a while she heard him. He had made money. Someone had brought in new horses, a mixed-breed maverick from the southwest that could flick his tail at anyone. There had been fire somewhere, flooding. Dead cows. Indians were being moved again. There was talk of a new kind of fence. The wagon rumbled and creaked.

She had a terrible ache underneath; she didn't know there was a space for anything that deep inside; there'd been the weight of the baby, and before that the weight of Matthew, and before that she'd been at home.

In the thin blue evening air she thought: What was it that Gabriel had said, about her being the most important person in the whole world? That nothing could happen to her? Was there any more?

Ten

She woke at dawn, but he was already gone, leaving the sheet cool to her fingers.

Gone to see the dark ships of trees afloat on the light sea of grass, and above them white cloud whales gently mouthing the diatomaceous stars. He had seen the morning star clear the air until it was pearly and delicious.

This had promised to be the magical country. The seeds in his hand were cool, dry and hard. A few slipped through his fingers. A little dust clung to his fingers, a smell of burlap. The spirits were coming up in him oily and eager. Flavoured. Never the smoky shy whispering wraiths; his howled and hugged. Nudging his hand, they made him spill more of the seed. Not all were old ghosts frozen in an undelivered past, riding in hope on his coattails; some were energetic and shapeless, sniffing a future form, colour, fulfilment. He trusted that this land could handle crowds.

He wished one of those photographers would come along to take a picture of him in the middle of the land; he'd like to see himself, to be sure, to see what he looked like. To see that he really was here. Urging the rawbones horse to the dome of the next hill, he looked over, but there was nothing; as far as he could go there was nothing. Not like the clutter back east of a civilized land where the garbage and the secrets of men surprised travellers; where he'd seen a hog-butchering station hollowed and scorched below the oily lacquer black of strong trees, links of chain rusted through, shell cases, withered rope. The stone stub of the foundation of a house long decayed and softly smothered with prickly nettles and thatch grass. Creosote-stained ground, ribbed with old railroad ties from an abandoned spur. Out here there were no surprises, no tell-tales. The spoor of men disappeared. Breath evaporated. Beneath this solid dense rug of dirt, there were only a few human bones. Their ghosts piled up on his knees, huddled on his shoulders.

He couldn't imagine spirits clinging to Hannah, though when he saw her now he noticed dust on her arms, a faint smell of urine that seemed to come from her hips, where the baby rode, and occasionally a bleak glaze on her eyes as if she were trying not to see something that was too close. It was easier to touch her now; he remembered how difficult it was in the beginning, how her skin was in such extremes he couldn't tell if it would freeze or burn him. Now she was there licking him, panting, watching him when she thought he wasn't looking, as if he might disappear. Lapping him up with her eyes as if her fate depended on him. She tried talking, but there wasn't anything to say. She never did talk much, but now was acting as if she might have something to say.

Way off in the distance, he saw a worm-curl of dust, which could have been antelope, riders, or a hot spot starting a whirlwind. Tully would know what it was. Tully said he didn't want to know anything about this place, that he hated it here. The only thing that didn't bore him was the hardship, and that made him angry. He said he remembered his mother's face before they'd come to the prairie. In the silence that followed, Matthew lost interest and his mind wandered. He was just beginning to think of the past and future of other people. He thought about his son Benjamin now. Benjamin and his father, together, so close they would always be able to hear each other.

As he rode around to the west, his long shadow flushed grouse squatting under the brush. A hawk glanced and glided alongside. Redwinged blackbirds scolded and swung on the tufts of the grass. The sun was sweet and warm, his shirt wasn't sticking to his back yet, he wasn't thirsty, and the light around him was liquid yellow, lit from underneath by the green lush of grass, and above by the blue bowl sky.

Circling back, Matthew looked at the corn in the weeds and grasses. Behind stood the tall elms from the crook in the creek. Sun and shadow dappled through the leaves. His thoughts were mussed up and quiet. The scent of mint and moss broke through. The long-tongued leaves of the corn plants would soon pant in the hot air. He had come out here for some reason. What was it?

He heard something, another kind of language, perhaps. A rush. A rustling. Yesterday they would have been just sounds, twigs crackling underfoot, the soft thud of ripe fruit, the slump of a sandbank into water. But this was something else; this time it meant something. He was overhearing, eavesdropping. His mind began to pull on it, but at once, upon encountering his thought, the sound came apart, and though he lost it, some mystery remained, wordless, as soft memory. He wondered if he was supposed to hear what he had. A secret challenge resided in it.

After all, he reasoned, he hadn't made it up. He'd only dug down a few inches. He'd only sat so high on the back of the horse. It just wasn't enough yet. He'd pay better attention. There was a way farther to go. He had heard something.

Hannah had two thoughts before the baby awoke. Before the air burned her throat. She wanted to reread Molly's letter today, the latest one with the X's and O's deeply embedded in the paper, the one for her new nephew. This thought she brought forward. The other blossomed: I have a secret. I hardly know what it is. It frightens me. It might be a monstrous delicious sin. I'm going die for sure now. God could get her for something. He wouldn't have been interested in her before. She'd never thought about God, really. She'd never done anything that stood out like sin. In the safety of summer's all-warmth, she could entertain God, show Him her sin on the lap of light that was summer.

Leaning over the edge of the bed she lifted Ben in beside her. He didn't wake up. He just twitched his hands into little curls, holding the ends of his favourite dream. She liked him close by to protect her. He wouldn't leave her. She used to know what Matthew was thinking about her. Before that she didn't even care. But now, what if he left her? Out here. Farther than ever. On this edge. She waited for the little luff of wind that she imagined pushed day round and round the earth. The same day over and over again. She waited for the baby to raise his head. She was also waiting for Matthew to come back and kill her, because he knew. He could get another woman to come and take care of Ben. He could give Ben away. He could drop her down the well. Get the horse to stomp on her or pull the wagon over her. She watched him when he wasn't looking.

One morning, she remembered, she had even cried. 'I never cry,' she said to herself as the tears ran softly on her cheeks. Maybe she was still asleep, her mind felt more like dream than day. She wasn't sad; she wasn't thinking about anything just then. The tears were very thin and evaporated before they reached the pillow.

For a moment she hesitated and had to check the date at the top of the page: Spring 1871. Molly was so expansive she needed seasons in which to spread out. This letter began just as the previous one had. 'I can't imagine doing what you're doing. What is it like to have a baby in the middle of nowhere? I must say I certainly don't envy you one moment of your life – yet that is – dear as Matthew is and all that – the baby must be cute though. Next time send a photograph, at least to the family so I can have it sent on. Well, how are things going here, you ask? Just great. I've moved a couple of times as better situations or better friends or different friends come along, but I've been quite consistent about going to class and keeping up with all the work, and so I mean all the work! Incredible. Each professor thinks that his course is the only one you're taking and that if they don't give you tons of work you'll get up to no good. It means some late nights cramming it all in. But I got through! Surprise. Big surprise for Mother and Dad, I think. We are still wrangling over whether I can stay for the summer. I don't even want to do that now, I want to go to New York with Audrey, who has a cousin who lives there (I guess I won't get out to see you this summer! I couldn't be much farther away than NY.) Imagine! The music. Audrey says there's music everywhere in the summer, even on the streets. I want to be everywhere at once. I want to be everything that's possible! I hope I never change and settle for something less than, than, well whatever it is out there. Even if nothing happens right away, New York is the place to meet people. I never daydream about myself being married or having children. I'm always, at minimum, a star! Surrounded by fans. Can you believe it! I wouldn't admit that to everyone. I mean it sounds so outlandish, but I really believe. Everyone says you have to believe in yourself because no one else is going to do it for you. So what do you think they'll say? If you and Matthew had any money I'd ask you – ha ha. No money in farming, I guess. What does he see in it? He did always go to empty places to daydream, but … [that bit was scratched out] Anyway, must go, time's a wasting. Love to my little nephew and Matthew and you. Molly.'

Hannah rubbed her finger tips over the braille of X's and O's filling the rest of the page. Molly never could stand empty space or empty time. Of course, Molly didn't know her very well. Hannah could see herself in the centre. She didn't know what she would have done, but afterwards, when the people came to stare, she wouldn't have minded some of that. What did Molly think of her, anyway?

'Then fare ye well my own true love,

'Then fare ye well for awhile …' How did it go?

Ben woke up; he thought something was going on. Hannah hummed and sang to him all morning. Her voice was light and neat.

In summer half the household was outside: a trestle table, tripod cooking fire, washtubs tipped against the house, and around the corner, propped discreetly in a clump of tall weeds, the chamber pots, airing and bleaching in the sun. The elbow room and fresh air gave an new perspective on things. Matthew had fashioned a tent contraption, four tall poles with a large sheeting of muslin tied at the corners. When the wind wasn't blowing up dust she and Ben could work out there. Ben would lie on his back or his stomach and watch her. The light filtering through the cloth made him look healthy, but she wondered if he really was.

While the garden was growing they went over to visit Addie frequently, and silently she began comparing Ben and Todd. Both babies sat on an old quilt in the shade of an awning and their mothers' eyes.

Lewis and Tully were off looking for thieves. 'Do you think they'll run into Matthew?' But Hannah swivelled her shoulders and shrugged her mouth. There had been this irritation since the corn had begun to show, about the time they'd been ready to put in turnips between the rows. A shifting dusk-to-dawn operation: animals, Indians, overlanders. 'All common thieves, that's what they are!' said Addie. Hannah was watching Nellie inspect the goose bumps on her arm: Nellie growing old with fear because she was no longer small enough to be hidden in the trunk. 'And now that the garden's coming on they'll be right in there as well.' She was picking apart a wool dress to turn inside out and re-sew. 'If they'd just ask, I'd give handouts.' Nellie saw the wolf, with his floured paw and honeyed voice right out of the nursery tale, sitting at the door.

A black spot appeared near the babies. Hannah stared at it to see if it moved and required killing.

'I'm someone who's endured many losses,' mused Addie.

'Hmmm,' said Hannah. Addie was talking to herself with an unusual energy.

'I married him because I didn't get the story right. The one I was supposed to marry was to leave a message for me at the restaurant. We were going to run away, the two of us, and he went first. He said, "I'll tell the girl where I've gone," because there were several choices then and I was to come the next day so no one would suspect and find out. But when I got there the girl was an old dishwasher who was deaf and I couldn't find out anything. He must have thought I'd changed my mind. I never heard another word for a couple of years, then up comes a letter from the west coast, letting me know he was fine and settled and he wished me well in my choice in life, which obviously hadn't been him. As if he knew anything! And do you know I'd been waiting in a way, Lewis and I were almost together, but always in my mind there was something, like I had to leave the door ajar, you know what I mean, just in case, but after, well, there wasn't much point was there. Just imagine having your whole life turned around, sabotaged because of a deaf Dora of an old woman who was a complete stranger! He must have thought she could understand, all that nodding she did, "yes, yes, yes," but it was nothing. And here I am. There wasn't much point, was there, when I lose them, eventually … well, I seem to lose them all.'

The words hung from her lips; she had to keep sucking them back up to reshape between her teeth. She had told this story a thousand times to all her selves. It was a mythology; details were altered now and again, but the underpinnings were firm and irrefutable, and though it was her own story, she had become someone else, so the way it was told now was as if it were about a good friend, someone she knew well, but someone about whom this story might have been the most interesting part. Someone she might have forgotten if it weren't for this incident. In the early days, when there'd been pockets of time, she'd embroidered fantasies about what her life might have been, but now her imagination was engaged by crop failure, illness, dry wells, prairie fire, injury, insects.

Hannah stared at her, an act she thought unusual in itself; as mothers, they looked at the children. Addie couldn't look back because the sun had sneaked into her eyes. She reminded Hannah of no one she'd ever known. Not one association bit the hook she dangled in her brain. Tully, Nellie, Todd, none of her children resembled her. Poor little Rosa, now carrying the baggage of near-perfection like soft obscuring snow, would never be matched with Addie.

Addie was not in the least like Hannah's own dear mother, soft, smelly, worried. She was suddenly overcome. 'I want my mother, I want to see my, my mother.'

'How long has it been, honey?'

'Over a year now, fifteen months.'

'Oh, that's not so long.'

'It's forever. It's too long.'

'As you get older time shrinks so. Why, the whole life of one of my children could be a time I won't even remember!'

186

'I want to go home.'

'What did you imagine?'

'I want my mama to see my baby.'

'You're so young.'

'Age has nothing to do with it.'

She began to think she didn't know Addie at all, none of her insides. Addie seemed to know that old geezer Josiah, the peddler's most intimate habits, things he might have wanted her to do for him, but Addie never wanted anything, did she? She was letting life lie right down on her.

'Be a dear and go inside, ah, and get some scraps of this wool. It's in the trunk at the end of the bed on the, ah, left hand side, that's a dear. I'm tuckered out in this heat.'

The room was cool, the darkness rich and restful. Dust had settled in an elderly grace, a gauze. It was exciting to be in there by herself. When she had been little and alone in the house she would peek in drawers, poke behind the clothes in closets. Without other people in them, rooms took on a difference. They were like a promise in silhouette, waiting, watching.

She studied the arrangements. Now that they were going to stay here, she was becoming more interested in how things could be kept: what could be left on the ground, how to pack bacon in bran, how to do a hundred things to a kernel of corn, how to squeeze water out of sand.

Beside her, greenbottle flies strolled on the cluttered table. None of the furniture had sharp new edges. Beds were piled in bunks so close together that the trunk served as a step-up. Hannah opened it carefully. Her eyes were becoming used to the gloom; she could see the dark slips of wool and smell the reek of stale sage and wormwood. She was looking for secret sorts of things. All she found were old combs, a piece of red glass, scissors, spools looped on a cord, wool socks roiled up like snails. Maybe Addie had nothing left of that life, nothing that showed. Hannah had had a bruise for a couple of weeks. Now that was gone. Sometimes she heard his breathy voice working its way by her ear. Sometimes she thought he'd maybe gotten a fierce hold on her; other times she could barely remember, though she'd had a moment, hadn't she, a moment alone, and no harm came of just thinking, did it?

She touched a tortoise shell, a flannel of darning needles and several magazines.

'Can I borrow these magazines Addie?' she said, bringing the wool.

'Sure, just keep them nice, there's, ah, stuff in there that'll be good for something.' Her voice was filmy. Getting up she folded the dress in on itself and laid it on the chair. 'I'm going inside for a moment.'

Hannah narrowed her field of vision to concentrate the children. Nellie crept steadily in between the babies, then lay low and turned first to one, then the other, touching their cheeks. Her bare feet, bowed out from the ankles, were both filthy and healthy-looking like an animal's paws. Each baby retreated into an idle pre-sleep world of his own. Todd played with his fingers. Ben scraped up some reassuring folds and wrinkles in the soft quilt. She loved it when he slept, his cheek sagging on the sheet in his deep dreams, the curious inactivity of his hands. He was a pale soft baby. His skin reddened under her thumb and her fingers left prints like sucker marks. It was just possible to lick up a curl on the top of his head, but his scalp was flaky.

Eventually she had to move Todd because the sun was lowering. A long time must have passed.

Inside the house she couldn't tell if Addie had meant to nap; the way her body was arranged – exposed – on the bed, she could have been sitting for a moment and been overcome, or she could have deliberately left one leg dangling. The bodice of her dress was stretched tight on her breath. Down in her open mouth Hannah could see that her teeth were bad. Her whole body looked used. How could Hannah depend on her? How helpful would she be able to be? She was glad she hadn't seen Addie like this before the woman had helped with Ben's birth; she would've had no confidence at all. Hannah's own mother was upright; even in the middle of the night, she'd been attentive at the side of her bed, coming to shove out the nightmares, first thing in the morning hollering in her room.

'Oh my God!' It was a cross between a laugh and a drawl. The laugh was to herself. Then she said, as if in passing, as if up from a dream too soon, '… that one first-born, that one won't love you.' So quietly in fact that Hannah wasn't sure she'd said anything at all, but if she had heard correctly, she didn't want to hear it again. Old women, she thought.

In her day-to-day, Addie talked before her thoughts caught up. Her mouth sank on the empty air she exhaled. 'I must've … oh my, well … I can't seem to …' Hannah appeared to be leaning over her. Was something wrong? She sat up. Hannah had an unforgiving look on her face. It was unforgivable to be weak, thought Addie, and to be seen to be weak.

Lewis and Tully rode up with the dust strung out behind them due to an unusual easterly wind. The sun shone through as an uncomfortable reddish colour. They looked to be riding in on the tongue of a dragon.

'We ran into Matthew out there,' Lewis shouted, 'he's coming on, just stopped home to get the rig. Addie! Here, put this in a pot.' He threw a fat rabbit on the ground.

'Good shot, Pa.' Nellie fingered the hole.

'Get me the knife, Nell. Hannah honey ...'

'Hannah honey, Hannah honey, Hannah honey ...' Nellie tied her tongue on it.

'... draw fresh water for the pot, over there.'

Soon Addie and Hannah were shoulder to shoulder on the cool side of the fire. 'He just has to have stew. Stew this, stew that. He brings me all these small animals,' she said, poking the bubbling flesh under at the end of a long spoon. 'Get me something from the far side of the garden will you, Hannah?'

Nellie pulled the giggling babies back on the blanket by their legs. Lewis was around the side of the house, stripped to the waist, washing. Hannah walked across to the clogged outer rows of onions and carrots. The ground was hard and dry on the surface. Onions were splitting and cracking the soil open. Once she got hunkered down on her heels, she could see the yellow flowers on the tomato plants and the gleam of the peppers. Lamb's-quarters and purslane had been judiciously cultivated to grow wild. She picked some. That little distance from the busyness of people let the long notes of birdsong through from the prairie thatch. It was as if the sound were too heavy and mournful to float up over. Wild wood sage and rose were beefing up the pale smells from the garden. The wildness was always close upon them. She wanted Matthew to come in a hurry. She was getting smaller and smaller.

Tully was in the barn. Way back where it was dark, he was rubbing the horses with straw hanks that he had twisted in a particular fashion. The horses were enjoying it and the handful of stale grain he had thrown down. One of the horses had had to be cross-tied. The other lolled in shadow and the rusty dust of old straw. He blew at the grain; it backfired and flew up into his nostrils, making him sneeze. Under Tully's hand the short summer horsehair felt as warm and fluid as silk.

Tully's skin was peppery. He rubbed his eyes on his sleeve. Whacking his heel on its back edge, he dislodged a splat of manure. His eyes kept sliding out of the barn, slithering out the thin throat of light. He wanted to look. He wanted her to look first. He wanted to make her turn and see how much he still hated her. Nothing was forgiven. Between times he forgot, so that when he saw her again what happened beside Rosa's coffin came back to him as a surprise. In between times, as if she wasn't worth it, he didn't think of her.

His heart could go either way so easily. In the beginning he liked her ignorance. Her innocence was equal to his own. He had so many thoughts. She had none. Her butterfly spirit, its inability to light on anything, had startled him.

She'd gotten softer to go along with the stupidity. He couldn't understand how his mother could let her near, how she could have gone to help her have her baby. Maybe it would have died if she hadn't gone. Hannah might have died too.

Now that he thought about it, she couldn't be expected to survive. She had been afraid of the huge space from the start, of snakes and of being alone. If he just kept her out here long enough, he wouldn't have to worry. In a while, in the long term, she would suffer. He might not have to do anything. He could watch. He wore his hat pulled so far down it laid a shadow across his eyes; he could sit back and watch from this shadowy hiding place. He could watch her slowly sinking.

Hannah jumped to her feet. Had something fallen nearby? Was Ben all right? Had she been cut off? For a second she remembered the night she had come home from Matthew's and found her mother riding that dream about dying. It made her feel sick. The picture wasn't very clear. There had been too much smoke in the kitchen. Her mother's voice had been pitched in a way she'd never heard before. Her own mother had turned ugly and strange, scattering her fear like old slippery peel.

No one was looking for her. In another minute the basket was full. While she'd been wiggling carrots loose, her eyes had become used to the darkness between the rows, so that when she'd finished, she could see well across the yard and even through into the mouth of the barn, where, for a moment, she was sure she saw Tully, in silhouette, pointing a long gun at her.

It was almost dark, a purely red twilight, when Matthew and Hannah left for home. Dust rolled out in front of the wagon. On each side vesper sparrows trilled in the coming night and the old owls flattened their feathers. The prairie was so wide open, once the horizon had been lost there was no hope of finding the way. They had to rely on the horses, who had created the road in the first place. As the night woke to flutter with wings and stealth, the creak of the wagon wheels became unbearable. Had they endured this noise all the way out? Incomprehensibly, Ben slept on Hannah's lap as if the sound were music. His face was a blur. Beneath them, the wood and bolts rattled. Matthew was talking with authority, shoving words into place. Their strong edges pushed the darkness back a little. But when he took a breath it rode right back in on his air.

The land didn't yield easily to his foam of words, though they protected the light inside him. Their opacity was the essence he wore like clothing. It kept things just far enough. In the beginning he'd thought that one day he'd be able to go around unclothed, but now he knew better. Still, for all the layers of fabric and care that should have made his skin soft, it was, like his spirit, growing tough and resilient.

'One of the best things about riding a running horse is sharing that energy, lying low, the mane beating, outrunning the dust, running over the sound.' Another was the blur of fence and bush and face; it all became a blur of sideline. He could look and see if he wanted to, but he didn't have to do anything about it. There was no hunger. He wasn't afraid of the dark.

'Who are you talking to?' She couldn't hear a thing.

'As long as I keep talking, things won't – as long as I pester them with my words, the horses will go to home, is what I mean to say.' As long as he kept laughing, the boneless ghosts would remain under the ground. 'And as long as I sweet-talk you, I won't be alone.'

'You know what Addie said once? "If you stick up and stay put, things will begin to cling to you." I don't remember when it was or what made her say it.'

'Yes, dust and –' he said, reaching for her chin in the dark, seeing with his fingers. It had been a long time since he'd touched her there. And under, plucking the skin of her throat.

Calmly, Hannah thought of strangulation. He could strangle her, then run the wagon over her throat. It would look like an accident. The whole thing was in colour in front of her eyes there in the vast soup of darkness. Even as his fingers were around her neck she would lay the baby down safely on the seat. It would be too dark for Matthew to see the look in her eyes; he might be able to go through the whole rest of his life without having that to haunt him, he could just forget her. Maybe Ben's hair would turn red, reminding him of her, and once, a long time in the future, he'd be sorry, but might not even remember why he had killed her. An old man. Unimaginable! She couldn't see him sitting in a rickety rocking chair, chewing over a lifetime.

Matthew had dropped his hand and was tapping his fingernails on the seat between his legs. His stomach was full; the horses were headed right; he wobbled and took a deep breath and was on the back of his running horse.

Even without thinking of strangulation, when Hannah tried to picture herself next to Matthew in something like old age, she couldn't, she wasn't there. It was as if she had no future.

As if she had no past, again and again, she turned to see, but there was nothing there, no memories to fall back on. Surely she'd left home with some. They didn't take up much room, memories. God knows, there was plenty of room out here. Perhaps it was too dry. It was so cold in the winter. So hot now. But she'd thought memories were made of sterner stuff sunk like icebergs and warts below the surface. All the people in her family must look different, it had been so long since she'd seen them, but in her mind's eye they were the same, she couldn't change them. Perhaps she'd been careless with the old memories or perhaps they just weren't that important.

'Ben looks healthy, doesn't he?' Hannah stopped Matthew and pulled him under the muslin tent. He'd been in the sun for so long he had to blink a couple of times.

'What d'ya mean? Of course he does. Look at him.' Ben frog-kicked his excitement.

But that night, she heard him. It wasn't the first time. Sleeping but restless. Each breath a whistly, sniffly little package. She felt his skin: he wasn't any warmer than usual in this hideous August heat, unrelieved for over three weeks by storm. 'For God's sake don't wish for rain now, let the corn set!' Matthew had said as she soaked through another dress.

And another thing, even if there weren't a bright warm moon, she would still be able to see the heaping and overflowing of garden crops, this heaven of food that grew above the ground: tomatoes, cucumbers, peas, celery, spinach, all rotting because it was too hot to eat! Her mouth saying yes, her stomach, no.

Gently she turned the baby over. Maybe that would help, and for a moment it seemed to; he coughed and curled. She pulled the diaper away from his skin. She listened. The prairie was noisy with bickering insects, the scratch of corn leaves, a squawk from the muddy slough. Taking a rag still damp from the line between two chairs, and lifting the cover on the bucket of tepid water, she dunked it in, squeezed the excess and wiped her face and arms. For a couple of seconds, as the water evaporated, her skin felt cool and dry, with that vaguely remembered tightness. She wondered if Molly had got to New York after all. You'd never be able to hear a bug there, snakes had been driven out long ago, she imagined; a city that never got dark, no one would ever be lonely. People were busy inventing ways to stay cool and, for winter, fires that kept going all night long. She should have been used to these nights by now, but she wasn't. If harvest didn't start soon with its excuses to visit, she was going to go crazy.

Ben stirred again, scrunching up the way he had when he was tiny, but that didn't work; he lifted his head in his sleep. Hunching down beside the cradle, Hannah began to rock it. Side to side, creak, crick, creak; the wood was swollen, it had a different sound than it usually did. Ben listened, decided, and tipped his head down. Hannah yawned; all over this land the men and children were sleeping and the women were awake. Rocking, bathing brows, keeping the watch on, keeping an eye out, soothing and singing away the threats and impositions. Without the women, Hannah thought, the whole centre of things would soften, decay and break away beneath. Then one night everyone would simply fall through.

Then it started again, in that infinitesimal moment between rocks, or when she slowed slightly, she heard a raspy breath as if it had been run over a file. What was it? He wasn't sick; no fever, his nose was always a little runny, occasionally he sneezed, no more than the rest of them, though. And if he was sick, she hadn't figured on being unable to recognize it and do something.

Picking him up she tried him in her arms. Their skins stuck together; when she shifted him there was a ripping sound, but shift him she did, this way, that way, peeling him off to apply him to another place that might be better. Each time she moved him he jerked, tensed and waited until she'd settled him again. Finally, stretched up sideways to her shoulder, he seemed comforted.

She got up to go to the window. Deceiving wisps of vapour that would never turn into real clouds trailed east from the cold mountain tops, which she imagined frosted the bottoms of the stars as they passed over. Mountains must have much more character than prairie. Molly would have gone straight on into the mountains and beyond. Why, she hardly knew anyone who would have come here willingly. It was the men. Addie followed Lewis here. She had followed Matthew. That wasn't how things started. He'd been following her since she was a little girl, he said, spying on her, catching glimpses of her. How had this turnabout happened? Had there been one special day when, without her noticing, things had gotten turned around? Had it been that day or that other one? Nothing flew to mind. Maybe when she'd closed her eyes to get kissed he'd turned her, and when she'd opened them things looked different. She hadn't really cared then; now she thought she might. Was she supposed to end up staring out this window at this huge sky and this silvery flat land that compromised her imagination, hoping her baby wasn't choking to death?

The early morning horizon was smoky, smarting with the dust of yet another wagon-load of travellers. Hannah watched from the doorway. Her eyes were dull and she was rubbing a greasy cream into her hands. Absentmindedly she massaged the solution on the knob of each knuckle, between the fingers and over the fan of fine bones in the back of her hand. There were places on her skin that stung of thistle, thorn and sharp grass cuts.

They were just off the beaten track. Only those going straight north to the Dakotas might get stuck on their road. Twice since they'd been here, strangers had assembled stiffly at the door, hungry, dirty, tired. Ugly people who might have been attractive once, but now they and their children had a crust on their limbs, face, eyelids. So many children, one after the other, coming dirty and wary out of nooks and folds in the wagon.

The woman didn't have a bit of trouble calling all their names, and if one popped around another to be named again, she wasn't taken in. Hannah promptly forgot their names, which were unusual, long and formal-sounding, if she'd heard rightly: Hammond, Viola, Butte, Ravenna, Culver, Magnolia, Lanark, except for the baby, Rufus, as if they'd run out of the other names or had wanted a dog by that time and got, instead, a plain, poorly manifested little chap who sat up by resting his belly on the ground between his spindly legs. Ben, lying on his back in front of him, seemed to interest him slightly. His eyes were so dull that Hannah couldn't see what colour they were.

As soon as the other children had been revived by water, they spread out to investigate, tipping over washbuckets, picking the flowers off the tomato plants, jumping on the bed, opening the box of her treasures from home.

'Stop it! Put that back ... and that. Go on now. Out. Don't come in here again, you hear!' she said, out of the hearing of the woman, who frightened her, but who was lethargically unpacking the top layer of the back end of the wagon load, airing out, separating, rearranging.

'Could I trouble you for some soap, dear? A diaper? Pins? Rags?'

Her husband had already gone into the shed beside the barn and was helping himself to the tools. 'And this little piece of rope here?'

'No, I'm sorry you can't.'

'But I've already cut it to just what I need, won't be any good to you this way.'

'Oh, I'll find something to do with it,' said Matthew.

Their feisty little yellow dog was barking around the calf. Lettice began to circle it uneasily, putting down her nose, which the dog snapped at.

Matthew was trying to say that they were welcome to what he gave them, but that they couldn't just help themselves. He was being polite, but no one was listening. He shut and locked the door to the shed.

Hannah shut the door to the house and stood in front of it. The children stood facing her, but the light shone in her face so she couldn't see what they were going to do next. Then, as one they all turned on the smell of their food cooking and gathered scowling and frowning in a beggarly group around their mother.

'Here, Troll, Wooly, Beezus, Sooks, Man.' Nicknames, she supposed, the hidden beginnings of which she was not curious to know. But she did have a lot of milk, which she took over to placate them.

'I'm sorry we haven't room inside for all of you,' she said with what she hoped was enough force to let them know she meant it, but there was too much noise. The children were squawking to be first, the mother, pinching soft places to keep them back, the dog, weaving and nudging ready to get the bits that might fall from a careless bowl.

Hannah didn't know what to do. Were the children being fed now so the parents could eat later with her and Matthew? Were they supposed to cook together, and with whose food? Where was Matthew and where was her husband, what was his name? Hers? Ramona? Isabel? Something astonishingly inappropriate.

Heat wriggled up from the fire trying to escape the earth, which itself had begun to shimmer at the edge of that rude red swollen sun. The shapes of the children sharpened in shadow. They'd eaten everything there was and it wasn't enough. From them, one and all, came the same whiny sound, rehearsed and without feeling. With nothing to do for a moment, they started to throw dirt on the fire. The woman took a stick on which the cooking pot had hung and beat at their hands. 'Get back and get yerselves organized for gettin' bathed right now.'

This seemed to please them and grouping tightly together they began a new, more cheerful sound that could have been giggling. With their mother's shadow poking out from the middle, they bustled off towards the creek.

Hannah started to say something. What was the use? She hiked Ben up on her hip.

'So you've been travelling for a long time?' continued Matthew.

'Oh yes, and before that. Why, we can't even remember where the beginnings were. All the children were born on the road ...' Matthew got a picture of hermit crabs scuttling backwards into empty shells.

'We named 'em for the nearest place to where they'd been born; it keeps a good record of where we've been.' The man was caved-in in the chest, as if he'd always been walking into that harsh, hot-and-cold-running westerly wind.

'So, do you think you'll ever stop and settle?'

'I think of nothin' else!' He ended each sentence on an upward lilt, giving the impression of being surprised by what he'd just said. 'People aren't supposed to run around the country like this; I never grew up but stuck in the same place; it ain't good for you, wears out yer feet; wears out yer brain always figurin' out where you can go next; where you ain't been, but this country's big. Big enough. You like this place, boy?'

'Yes, I do,' he said in the ease of twilight.

'Jeezes, I don't. You can back up out here forever and not bump into anything!'

Matthew tipped his head down, squishing the smile. 'You're right there. Let's go.'

When they reached the yard the man paused to look things over. 'She's got 'em down in the water. Did ya ever notice how kids can smell?'

Hannah was standing where Matthew could see her. She was mouthing words: 'Thank God you're here! Thank God you are here!' He got it the second time.

The man turned. 'Say, you folks haven't eaten yet, have you?'

'Why, no.'

'Well, we all should sit there. Wife'll put the kids down and we can have some grub. So, what've you got?'

It was a long and silent meal. The man had just a few good teeth, and so had to chew in one spot, then another. The woman, Rosalind? Beatrice? never got through one bite without one of the children coughing or crying or calling. And every time either of them got up, Matthew or Hannah would jump up too, ready to follow in case they were going into the dark to steal something.

'Yes, but ...' With coffee Hannah was putting her life down, the sameness, the smallness.

'Sure it's been more interesting than yours, but yer young and you know you can do things either way in this life – go out to look for it or stay home and by 'n by it'll all come to you. It's all the same. You won't miss anything, honey, don't worry.'

But from the outside, the other side, the wrong side, it looked so much better out there.

'But all that travelling you've done. All those places you've been.'

Matthew glared at her in the dark. 'You weren't born here, remember.' Indifferently, indulgently, her eyes, swift and not seeing, swooped over him. 'Oh, you know what I mean.'

In the lime rose wash on the underside of cloud, that long road stretched easily through her mind. It was a different road from the one she'd come on. It had no bumps, no lumpy nights, no wrong turns, misleading signs, mud, ruts, dust. It led nowhere in particular and anywhere she could imagine.

'Blind, deaf and dumb, that's yer majority of people.' The man scratched his head and then unconsciously smelled the tips of his fingers.

Hannah said, 'I'm going to check on the baby.' She thought she'd

197

heard a funny sound. He'd fallen asleep before supper, giving her a rare chance to eat undisturbed. Now she had a funny feeling. The house was darker than it should have been. It was dark and deliberate. It was too quiet. It felt the way an empty house did. The lamp was on the table in its usual place. She lit it. The light made little headway in night's thick pitch.

She could clearly see that Ben wasn't there. He wasn't on the floor either. She swung around. There was no place he could have gone. There just wasn't that much room here. Her heart swelled to fill her throat.

Still holding the lamp, she ran back, waving it so the light swirled dizzily, alarming the group at the fire.

'What's wrong?' It was Matthew up first.

Jerkily rocking an imaginary baby, Hannah flung her arms open. 'Gone! The baby's gone!'

'What?' broke in the woman. 'Oh God, just a minute.' Labouring to her feet, she ambled to the back of their wagon. 'They've probably gone and done it again, look in here. Look in here, will you.' Holding the tarp back, she clutched Hannah's arm, forcing her to peer into the hot gleaming mass of her naked children. 'I could've told you. These love babies. Take 'em right over every time. Why, one of these days we're going to drive right away with an extra one and I've already got so many I'd never notice.'

Ben was wedged between the two oldest children. Hannah didn't even remember seeing them. She reached in, but drew back afraid she might touch one of them. Ben grinned at her.

'Give me my baby.' Her voice was so different she didn't recognize it. Matthew got there. He reached in. The children were squirming. One scratched him. Another tried to kick his hand away.

'Stop!' The woman slapped here and there, the air, skin. 'Stop squawkin'! Ain't they the limit, though.'

'Keep them in there, don't let them get out, keep them away from my baby.' Matthew gave Ben to Hannah. He was crying by then. One of those peculiar children must have sneaked out and stolen him right out of the bed where she had put him. Perhaps skulking behind the stagnant drape of wet clothes, around the edge of her eyes. Had Ben slept through it? Why hadn't he cried? 'You dumb baby, there's lots of bad people who like to steal babies; you gotta learn to holler if strangers try to take you!' Then she was speaking to herself, so softly she could barely hear. 'Everything's getting so dangerous.'

Matthew sat up most of the night, his ears straining for unusual sounds. He felt he might have let the thief right through his door. These folks didn't think anything they did was wrong. They thought every thing in the world should pass through their hands. They owned practically nothing, but Matthew felt they'd touched all the things that had ever been made or used by man. What had he said, that quaint back-roads 'by 'n by?' By 'n by everything would come to him, too. He never doubted it.

Once, when he simply couldn't stay awake, he nudged Hannah and put her in the chair by the window so he could collapse for an hour.

At dawn there were stirrings. All he could see was the woman milking his cow on the other side of their wagon. She didn't stop when she saw him. Like hungry vultures the children perched on clumps of grass. Occasionally the woman squirted them as if they were kittens. Nothing else seemed amiss. Out of his sight they would raid the field for anything that had grown too fast, he was sure but too worn down to care. Just go, he felt like saying, take whatever you need and go.

'Goodbye, goodbye, good luck,' they were all shouting. The woman was actually crying. Because of that, Hannah let her rub her arm and kiss her cheek, but she felt as if a net were being thrown over her. The woman turned Ben around in Hannah's arms, so she could have a look at him. She held his face in her hand. She held his eyes in hers. Then she patted Hannah. It was a conciliatory gesture. And just before she turned away, she pressed a lumpy packet into Hannah's hand. 'Magic seeds,' she said under her breath. 'Plant them next year, it's too late for this year.'

Hannah looked hard at her face in order to remember it after they'd gone; at the same time she hardly looked at all because she knew she'd never see them again.

None rode in the wagon. Each had a place to go. At first there was some running back and forth across the nameless road, but by the time they were halfway out of sight all, even the dog, had settled in drearily, rocking from side to side with the wagon's roll.

In her life, Hannah had first looked with true seriousness at Matthew. Then at the sod house. Now she looked at Ben and at things close by. The vast distances shocked her. They stretched farther than she'd imagined. Thinking about it subdued her, dulled her. She was drowning in her own breath, which was stuck down in the softness of her body. She watched the wind warm itself on the thick fur of grass. She was slightly taller than the grass, but just.

She didn't know names.

'What is that called?' That small bright flower. Thinking, Have I seen that before? Was that here last year? Nothing had a name here. Back home everything had a name. She remembered the gentle calling: McCabe's Road, Blue Nob Hill, Swift's Bridge leading over to Windfall Field.

It was a soft clear night for counting stars, the air a silk, the black a velvet, but the silence was so thin it couldn't hold her song. Still she sang into it, her breath soft in her mouth, the syllables of the song vibrating in her head, around her eyes:

Star shining number number one number two number three
Good Lord, by 'n by, by 'n by, Good Lord, by 'n by
Star shining number number four number five number six
Good Lord, by 'n by, by 'n by, Good Lord – by 'n by
Star shining number number seven number eight number nine
Good Lord, by 'n by, by 'n by, Good Lord, by 'n by
by 'n by, by 'n by, by 'n by …

The only way she could tell the sky was by its stars, those impulses from the dark side. 'Star light, star bright, first star I see tonight, wish I may, wish I might,' but there was no wish. They'd made her sad, those stars, a sadness past that of childhood, as if she'd grown tall enough to see over the edge.

Furled in a shawl and her own skin, which were not enough against the chill of stars, she grew cold and old, and when even the sadness couldn't hold, when it sloughed off, she was left with nothing inside, only a fragile stiffness of dumb bone to hold her up.

She wasn't safe. Neither wolves nor worms could see her, but this wasn't her home, that's what she was afraid of. All along she'd been so sure of herself. But if this wasn't it, if this land wouldn't let her be safe and happy, then where could she go?

The hard packed ground beneath her feet must have been cold underneath, but she couldn't feel it. Nor could she distinguish the wad of cloth in her hand. Her skin slept; the land had done that. She thought of the way Matthew had gripped her, hard, pulling her along the high ridge between his valley and hers, back home. Home, her mouth tried to hold the word inside. Your home is with me, he'd said. There'd been stars, hadn't there? And a moon, that thief of light. There'd been light, a bath of light. She'd been swollen with light and hope and wishes; that's what it had been like. She'd been safe. Someone had been watching her, that was it, watching over her, a guardian angel keeping her from harm, letting her play the games. But there was more to it. The hard spin of sex, a yawn of hunger, dust and babies, the terrible greed of babies, and that strange boy; how he drifted back and forth now like a small flame that she couldn't blow out; a small sharp blade of grass cutting her ankle as she walked by, a thistle, a thorn. Why was it that nothing Matthew had ever done to her had made her think this much?

She took a deep breath; that felt better. What were they again, those thoughts? Should she try to remember? But, dreamlike, they were evaporating into the dry night air. She kicked the ground, nicking it. In the morning she'd be able to find the small crescent marks. Not to worry, there would always be someone along to rescue her, wouldn't there? She wasn't meant to be left alone. So far life had not let her alone; there was almost too much to do. Why, she could barely keep up with it all. To stand still like this was a luxury.

'Where were you?'

'I don't know,' she said, raising her eyebrows, the gesture smoothing her face. 'Nowhere.' Eventually she might forget the desolation. Like pain, it would forbid memory.

Eleven

The morning of November 16, 1871, was soft and sweet. A whimsical sky dotted with playful clouds vaulted over a land harvested of everything but dust. Tawny and subtle, the dust didn't hold Ben's interest the way the oddly baroque, curlicued clouds did. He tried to scrape them out of the sky, and instead of frustrating him the way she thought it would, he laughed.

Dawn was coming later and later; Matthew was sleeping in until light slit the horizon, then rising slowly, lazily, lifting his son into bed with him, lifting him into the air until he squealed in delight.

The morning was quiet. It tasted different. He gave it one small thought, then lost interest. Overnight the dust had settled in a soft grey-brown carpet. He noticed from the look of his footprints that the soles of his boots were worn. He needed new trousers. The shirt seams at his shoulders were stretched, his left elbow almost through the sleeve. He was going to help butcher a pig over at Donnat's in exchange for some smoked ham, and so had intentionally worn his worst clothes. Next spring he'd buy a piglet from them.

The chickens were enough to get set up this fall. And those saplings for the yard just as Hannah had wanted: he'd had to drive two days for them, back breaking in the tight sod to get the long roots out. Immediately all the leaves had fallen off, but they were still alive, bandaged with burlap and corn shuck against the coming winter. And she was still hungering for trees. 'More trees, over there I think, and some to break the wind here.'

The morning was gentle and above board. The ground had hardened; the unforgiving jolt came up through the bones of the horse into his body. Maternally, Hannah had made him take his blanket-lined jacket, tied on behind him with the saddle bags. It was ten miles to Donnat's, an hour on a cavalry horse. More like two on this, his steady old 'mint condition' horse.

It took just over two hours, which was how long the water took to get boiling, and the pig had ideas of its own, running into the stubble of the corn field. He was damned if he'd go in that little bare pen. It took two ropes and two horses plus all the kids screaming behind, pelting him with clods of dirt, to corral him. Snorting angrily, he pulled to one side, then the other, but they got him in and as soon as he'd finished rooting around in some ears of corn and settled to eat them, Robert killed him with one clean shot in the base of his brain.

The kids poked him with sharp sticks. Some parts of him were still jerking. They tried to find every remaining bit of tenacious motion: between his hooves, under his tail, his snout, between his legs.

'Shoo now, get away,' shouted Robert. 'Come on, you kids, we've got work to do. Here now, out of there, you'll get thrown in the boil too if you're not careful, now! Scat! My God, this is a big animal, let's hope the insides are as succulent as the outsides. Heave 'im up, now.'

Chains hoisted, whining and straining. The pig straddled the sky, which was greying evenly. Scalding water sloshed on the dry ground when the pig was lowered in. The children, screaming and squealing, climbed the fence, carefully fitting the heels of their shoes over the next board down to hold them on. The boys leaned forward, arms straight, hands on their knees, waggling them in anticipation. One of the girls stood behind on a board, her hands clutching the edge. Her arms, bare and blotched red, were spattered with mud; her face was tucked beneath her hair. For a while the children shouted encouragingly at the gutting, then they leaned into each other's space to get a rise out of one another. Giggling, they briefly lost interest as the pig drained and dripped. Then one said, 'Ain't that sickening, ain't that the most sickening thing you ever seen?' pointing to the tangle of intestine being milked of its steaming contents.

Matthew wiped the fat from his arms. Mrs Donnat had brought a hot ginger switchel. He was terribly thirsty. For no reason he noticed the reflection of the sky in the cup. It was without blemish, as smooth and clear as liquid. As he puckered the drink up, he could see the little girl over the rim of the cup. Above the noise he couldn't hear what she was saying or singing, but her mouth was moving in a regular way and she was clapping in a solid sharp stroke, her hands beating open and shut, her arms spotted with blood dark mud. Her head snapped and her hair, lank and oily, angrily switched her face.

When the body was stretched and stable, each of the children was given a scraping tool to remove the stubborn hairs left on. They circled to find a good spot, then leaned and grunted vigorously, warming themselves.

Something in the air was making it thick to breathe. A still grey hill stood out on the horizon.

'Sowed any more seed, young man?' asked Robert.

'My ground's not that broken up yet.'

'No, no, in the woman, man! In the woman.'

'Oh, no, he's still a baby. I thought …'

'Well, not necessarily. It depends.'

Matthew listened hopefully, but Robert was on to something else; stroking the huge body of the pig, running his hand flat on the broad back, lifting it until only a finger was left tracing the outlines of future meals. 'I can give you some fat back right now if you want, then this piece when it's smoked, we might as well smoke it, we've got the set up …'

'Sounds good to me. Say, next spring can you –'

'I'm way ahead of you, going to get you the orneriest and hungriest of the litter, or the second hungriest … Say, ah, Matthew, I couldn't interest you in a dog now, could I? We've got these, well, come on over here, let me show you.' In a corner of the barn was a tired-looking bitch with three puppies. 'They're ready to go, I can't keep 'em and feed 'em all winter unless I lose a cow. I don't suppose you have enough to feed –'

'Well, sure, why not, I can get another deer or something. This dog, she doesn't go after chickens, does she?'

'No, there ain't none of that in their blood.'

Stepping over a low board into the manger, Matthew watched the puppies investigate him. The little girl was right beside him. It was clear she had her favourite.

'Was that the best one?' he asked her.

'Yes, sure, this is Roo.'

The girl had picked the puppy up under her front legs. He said, 'She won't bite my little boy, will she?'

'Of course not!'

'Do you think she would take care of him?'

She paused. 'Is Roo going to your house then?'

'Your dad says so.'

'I know he says that.' But her grip on the puppy was weak. He could hardly hear her and at first thought it was because she was feeling bad, but then he found he had to lean towards Robert, too, to catch what he was saying. The air was hanging in heavy cold veils.

'What time was it, anyway?' he asked.

'Can't be that late.' They were all noticing how dark it was suddenly.

'Maybe I'd better –'

At first he could see the shape of the wind blowing gently, then it gusted and billowed with snow. There were streams and eddies twirling back, swirling. The air began to shudder, waves appeared and passed. There was no shore for them; suddenly the wind stopped, the snow drifting, idling, waiting for the next hand of wind to slap it down. The snow looked just like the chaff that blew off wheat. It stopped again; Matthew's clothes relaxed on his body, heat filled the spaces. He couldn't believe how beautiful the snow was, thick and wet, huge flakes sticking to him. The ground had gone under. The feet and whole side of the horse were white. He couldn't hear the horse. Instead he touched him. Once, there on the neck. Another touch behind. The horse didn't have enough hair for this kind of weather. He brushed some snow from the saddle, a lump of it melting and sliding off the horse's rump. More replaced that. He brushed some snow from his leg. By then there was more on his other leg. When he looked back the snow was filling up the crevice between his leg and the stirrup leather. All the buckles were filled in. Snow had built up on his boots. It was becoming a sort of armour on his body. Plates of snow planked his thighs, the sleeves of his jacket. Epaulettes of snow. It made a helmet of his hat. It was having a peculiar effect, he was slowing down. Flakes of snow were going up his nose when he breathed. When he stuck out his tongue, the flakes melted on its surface. In a few moments a cushion of cold descended, accumulating everywhere layer upon layer of snow.

Just before the horse shook his head, Matthew saw how the snow had built up in the curl of his eyelashes. And how he had flattened his ears down and back. How long had they been travelling now? There didn't seem to be any way to tell. It used to be that way. The deep fissure was out there where it had always been, wasn't it? What was that cut of darkness? And on that side, a high wall of blowing snow building itself from the ground up. They had to be careful, there were soft spots. The horse went up to his knees suddenly back there. Perhaps he should be afraid, but he wasn't.

Curiously, the puppy wasn't moving. Snow had followed the contours of her shape inside the burlap bag at his knee. He took the puppy up into his coat, worried that she might be too cold, though the snow was like a warm cover now over them both. His lap was full of snow. The breath of the horse puffed out to the sides.

It was getting colder. Something was happening, a change elbowing, batting his head, icing the plaster of snow on his body. He was in a hurry to get the snow off, standing in the stirrups, shaking, brushing it away, sweeping it off the horse with great gestures. It was sticking to his skin. The weight was dark and sharp. Where it had melted in the wrinkles in his trousers, he could feel it freezing and cutting his soft flesh. It was difficult to brush it out; his fingers felt blunt, the feeling in them thwarted. With his gloves on he couldn't get hold of the kerchief around his neck to pull it over his nose. But there was ice in the air now. He turned his face, hiding it in the upturned collar of his jacket. The horse was beginning to struggle, his hooves breaking a crust. The wind was scudding from behind. When it blew the horse's tail, the coated hairs painfully whipped Matthew's thighs. It was harder to breathe, and whereas a short time ago he had been able to see the clouds of breath from the horse's nostrils, now they had disappeared.

He couldn't see farther than the edges of the horse. Out there, beyond, was a solid, surrounding sound. At first it pushed on his body, then, peculiarly, as if finding no entrance, it rushed by, scalding him, sucking the heat and stir from his blood. The centre of him would freeze if the puppy weren't there beating against him with its own heat. He couldn't squeeze the horse to let him know he was there. He shouted, the wind carrying the sound forward, strangling it, so that the horse heard only a squeak.

The dry granular snow scoured and grated. It got into everything, his pockets, down inside his boots, his gloves. He kept his mouth shut; he felt snow under his tongue, sharp and bitter. Closing his eyes he was startled by the stark screen of white on the insides of his eyelids. Idly he wondered if they were still moving. Reaching out ever so carefully he tried to feel the neck of the horse. It was difficult to tell, but it seemed to be nodding slightly. He tried to lean forward. His body was numb; he didn't want to move it. A large quiet space as white as pure snow was opening up inside his mind. Heat and cold, hunger and thirst, no longer signified. A shimmering aura of eerie sound was close and dreamlike; a howling, hooping syrup was pouring over the curls in his brain. It must have always been so. He couldn't remember a beginning. He couldn't conceive of an end to it. Stalled in the white in his mind, the sound was fascinating, comforting, godlike, alien. It was the only thing holding. It had travelled farther than he had, returning with sounds he'd never heard before. It was delivering signs and signals that he couldn't read. He was being held, hypnotized in a thrall of sound. Moaning white mouths, white lips caressed where he had no skin.

Then, when there was no farther to go, he fell. The horse had stumbled into something deep and soft, his legs buckling stiffly, and rolled to the side, gently, without a sound. Matthew was partly underneath, unhurt. The horse made an impression in the thick snow and Matthew's body made a space beneath it. There was no need to do anything else now. The weight of the horse was pleasant. In a moment or two there seemed to be a change in the wind, a muffled distant sound as if it was far above him, with an edge to it after all, a bottom to stand on.

A strange thought floated into his mind. It had to do with opening his eyes or being born. Such a bizarre idea. Why would he want to do either of those things? He was so peaceful. This was a nice place. Nothing was bothering him. No one wanted him right now. No one was calling his name. A while ago it was different; he was different, someone else, jumping night and day, eyes always open, troubling, anticipating. This was nice, a kind of sleep, but he could see himself. Why did babies want to get born, anyway?

The snow was quickly surrounding him. It piled up against his ears. The sound of the wind was remote, a leaden whine. He listened. It was wonderful.

Then the horse was struggling, throwing his head back and forth in the snow. Trying to get up he thrashed his legs in a purposeful swimming pattern. He was snorting and shuddering. Then, from far away, came a blunt shout. Matthew didn't want to hear; he wasn't curious any more. The organ of curiosity was shrunken and cooled. But the shout blasted again, closer this time. Part of him was being pulled. There was a drastic and sudden change in the intensity of the light, but he couldn't imagine why. Something had hold of him. What could he do? He was being dragged on a rough surface; he didn't like it, the snow was cold down the back of his neck. How long was this going to go on? What had got him? There was more noise. His body was being rolled over. It got dark. Underneath him the puppy squawked; the puppy, of course, that soft brown centre like liquored candy. Abruptly he was rolled again. A shock of cold hit his chest, pushing the air out. He gasped; his own voice, he recognized it with increasing affection. Beginning to curl on his side around the pain, he felt sharp twinges in his arms. Was someone talking? He couldn't understand the words. Someone in the next room or just outside the door. An old voice from mountains, a man hollowing out caves with the raw vowels of his throat.

The man was taking off Matthew's gloves, boots and socks. It seemed to be hard for him, a stiffness or reluctance. Vigorously he rubbed the bare skin then redressed his feet. He'd wedged something hard under Matthew's head and now tucked his hands between his thighs. Burying a dull grumbly sound, Matthew started to open his eyes. The man touched him on the face. His eyes hurt.

'Whaa ... Oooo.' His mouth hurt. He began to shake uncontrollably. Reaching over, the man rubbed his back. Matthew vaguely heard him grunting approvingly and on top of that the wind outside, a shrill screech, an endless hum, but from far away, no longer in his head.

Opening his throat he began to blow air through the sputtering of his lips, making a ridiculous noise. He pushed harder, his blubbering lip muscles distorting the air more and more. The pitch changed; the puppy, who was as warm as a little bun, put her nose close to his and mumbled. Matthew began to laugh. It felt so good. The puppy yapped excitedly.

As soon as he stopped shivering, the cold crept back on him. He saw his body thick and still down there. Sitting up, he looked around. He was in a small place, a bald bank of earth below ice-slickered grasses, hollowed out of the snow beneath a bush. It seemed to have been created out of the frosted clouds of his breath. Reaching up, he was just about to touch. The man stopped his hand.

'Who are you?' His face was thawing. Drops of water slipped down his cheek to converge beneath his chin. He wiped at them. He checked his body, hard and dark under his eyes, the tough skin jittery on top of stiff muscles. He wiggled his toes.

The man seemed attached to the whitewashed dirt wall opposite him, his clothes steeped in a tea of river water sludge: a fashionable black felt Stetson raw-edge, wool trousers, leather fringe jacket, beadwork, braids. Weather-veined face, sharp cheekbones, motionless black eyes.

'Who did you say you were?' The slow smoke signal of his breath punctuated the air. Matthew coaxed him. The puppy was watching. 'Where are we?' he said, looking around, holding the small space up in the palm of his two hands, this swollen light without shadow. 'What happened?' He thought of his horse, and scrambling up on his knees searched for an opening. Behind him perhaps? But there was nothing. The Indian gestured him back down by compressing the cold air between them. All right, all right. What could he do? Maybe the horse had found a windbreak on the other side of the bush.

'How did you get here? Have you got a horse out there?' The man wore riding boots. Between his feet he had spread a saddle blanket. It floated on the snow. Sliding his fingers under, he handed it to Matthew.

'This is mine!'

The Indian had one too, and was sitting on it. Matthew copied him. As he did so, lifting himself up, shifting, repositioning, he was surprised by how stiff his muscles were. Not sore, though he expected to be because the horse had fallen on him. This felt as if he'd slept too long in one position. He didn't want to move. He hung his hands over his knees and tightened the muscles across his back, trying to keep his skin away from the cold damp cloth of his shirt. He didn't know where to look and eventually became engrossed in the regular funnels of steam sliding from his nostrils, accompanied by the hissing wind. Matthew thought about food, imagining brown bubbling clouds of steam, but he couldn't imagine himself into feeling full.

The Indian moved across and shoved a branch aside. Snow swirled. He couldn't stand, and so kneeling he urinated through the opening. The branch snapped back in place. The opening didn't look big enough to fit through. Was that the way they'd come in, was that the way to get out? Matthew smiled weakly. His mind was racing nowhere. What time was it? The white snow was greying, the air was slowing down and thickening. 'I can't stay here. I've got to get home.' He'd have been there by now, he thought, seeing himself curiously patriarchal, leaning back in his chair, toes warming, hooked on the edge of the stove. On a rug at his feet, his son and his dog, gently sniffing each other. And at the table and sink, her strong back holding her straight, his wife, perhaps singing a lullaby or inventing a new song to celebrate his safe return. Soon it was going to be too dark to travel. Tomorrow then. He'd have to get an early start. If the horse was there a quick ride home. If not, he would have to see which way was closest and hitch a ride with the Indian, or walk. If the snow was too deep, he'd have to find the nearest house. The whole thing began to loom like an adventure. He saw himself as some buckskin-clad, bearded mountain man who had lost his perfect peak. For the moment. Closing his eyes, holding his cold hands over his ears, he heard the various versions of the story. A rapt older Ben and Hannah, altered by a romantic, marinating firelight, listening. A long story about loss and gain, hardship and luck, cold and colder, the weight of wet snow, the locust hum of ice in the wind. 'Were you afraid, Daddy?' 'Nooo,' Ohhh, the cutting wind, blocking breath, dealing death without curiosity or courage. The deaf and senseless wind.

The Indian was lying in a stoic little ball. His body numb in the syrup of cold, Matthew felt his ears opening like flowers. 'Are you asleep? Hey, are you?' The Indian man grumbled between wind sobs. 'Will I freeze if I go to sleep? Are you going to sleep?'

The moment Matthew stopped talking, the wind backed up in his ear and drained down inside until there was no room for another sound, until he was alone with the wind and couldn't hear the sound of his own voice. Dozing on saddlebags and a pad of snow, his other ear to the ground, he listened to the earth. The wail of the wind hammered his head to the ground. His breath dripped under its own weight.

'Arrgghh!' He gasped up out of a clog, breaking it up, chopping the air away from his throat where it had collared him.

The Indian struck a match and lit a coil of wick in a dish of fat. Its sooty flame thrilled on the ice wall. Matthew was panting. Sweat shone on his face. The Indian stared at him.

'It's not getting to you, is it?' Matthew asked in a high helpless stutter. Studying him, the Indian took a deep breath and motioned him to lie down.

Was he crazy or was it actually warmer in here? The heat from their bodies couldn't escape. He'd heard about igloos. Curling up, hands between his thighs he peeked at the other man, who continued to watch him. The air between them flattened the light. It flickered on his eyelids; he could hardly stay awake. He could hear the wind pumping.

Once in the dark he woke to change dreams. By greying dawn he saw he had survived and promptly fell back into a deep thirsty sleep. He dreamed he had a new part to his body. At first it seemed a burden, riding on his back, fitting itself against him, then he got used to its weight, and the warmth was comforting. A warmth belonging to him; a birthright, blood brother, bedfellow.

'Mm, mum, mummm …' His lips were dry. Flexing his fingers he could just barely scratch some snow to his mouth. It melted and burned. The pink of his flesh surprised him. He held his fingers close to his eyes. The snow stretched endlessly away from his face as white as a bed sheet.

The Indian was shaking him, showing him something in his hand, offering him something to eat. He was eating it, stringy skin stuff. His stomach reared in anticipation. Just seeing the Indian sitting there eating made his blood warm. The jerky tasted of smoke. Once he got it between his teeth his saliva gushed in friendly recognition.

'You're just full of surprises, aren't you?' His mouth was full. He's not afraid of me, he thought. Probably checked me for weapons when he first pulled me in. But I'm not afraid of him either. He knows what's going on. He knows the rules better than I do. If he loves me he'll take care of me. He won't let anything hurt me. Matthew lay down, rolling, showing his belly, the insides of his thighs, wrists, palms, tilting his head back so that his throat shone.

They sat across from each other. The Indian rubbed his hand over his face; Matthew rubbed his eyes, up under his hair, and scratched the back of his neck. He reached over his shoulder, helping one arm with the other, pushing it farther down his back; the Indian wriggled inside his shirt. Matthew yawned; the other man scratched the corners of his mouth. He slid his tongue over his teeth; The Indian broke off a small twig and began to dig at his gums. Crumbs of icy snow fell on the Indian's leg. He brushed them off and inspected other areas of his clothing; Matthew plucked up wrinkles in his shirt where it bunched around his wrist.

It was colder. He wanted his clothes. There was enough for one but not two. Each wanted the other's.

Stiff from the cold, his fingers didn't bend. The Indian gestured for him to come closer. Matthew could tell this from the hesitation, barely perceptible, of the man's hand when it was nearer himself. If the hesitation were on the other end, it would have meant, 'go farther, go away', but he didn't dare; there was no place to go but out into the snow. Go to death. Who would say that to another man in a storm? There were rules about such things. Between men.

Outside the wind rapped and unwrapped.

I've heard this before, thought Matthew. All my life. How different could it be? The wind was the wind. I've lived through it. But this time it wasn't the same. It didn't stop. Before, it would stop in a minute or a few hours, overnight at most. He remembered a ravaged night, wind rearranging the crops, and in the morning, the explorations and discoveries. His father and mother lamenting the torn branches, the shale off the roof, the baby birds torn from their nests.

He thought, I've listened to the wind, watched it in the distance making whorls, raising Cain, I've listened to it as if it had my future in it, the night wind rapping, calling me to the window to see it unattainable in the tree tops. I was so small, but I would grow up to reach it. I listened to it getting ready to make a storm, that whispery sigh in the weeds. Saw it throw pollen. I heard it suck on the chimney damper and rattle the porch door. I saw it roll on the grass and push through the squeaky gate. It blew birds' feathers backwards and caught the winter breath of horses. It has roughened and reddened my Hannah's cheeks.

But her face faded. He rubbed his eyes, as if that might help keep her in focus. Strangely enough he could clearly see distinct lines from her body. As if in silhouette, the arch of her foot, a swollen breast, the rise of her belly. Deep inside where he was still warm, he ached.

The puppy, singing and crying, struggled out of Matthew's jacket to pee on the snow. Matthew chipped off nubbins of snow and placed them in her mouth. She whimpered from hunger. He smoothed her fluffy coat. He liked the way the puppy looked, her fat soft muzzle that flattened when she put her head down on his leg. Trust. Maybe he could soothe her hunger by rubbing her tummy. Turning her over in his arm he kneaded her body with his other hand. Under her caramel coat of hair was a layer of cream-coloured down. She grabbed hold of his hand with her short legs, his fingers with her sharp teeth, tried to curl her tail around his arm.

Matthew wanted to look outside. Where was that branch? There, he pushed it open. He could see exactly nothing through a sluggish ice fog soup. Leaden air sank in his lungs, so cold it burned. He put his hand out; it disappeared; when he pulled back it wore a glove of ice.

There was nothing to do. The cave protected them from the wind, which thinned the fog into a devilish snow mist. Matthew imagined that the horses were dead from the inside out. He worried about the air; it was already hard to breathe, and the snow seemed to be getting through.

He turned to the Indian and said, 'Does it seem darker in here to you, I mean thicker; is there ice in here yet? Talk to me even if I can't understand you. Please talk to me.'

Still the Indian said nothing. Maybe he understood perfectly, maybe he was just waiting. Could he be one of the group who'd been at his house that time when he'd gone deer hunting? Was this one of the men who'd scared Hannah? What was it they'd done? He couldn't remember. Had they hurt her? What had she said?

'Come on, there must be something.' He was cramped and freezing again. He rubbed his arms and legs and beat the backs of his feet, cracking the packed snow. It was getting dimmer, he was sure of it. Was this going to be the second night? By God, this was crazy. Hannah would think he was dead. Did she have enough fuel? Could she get out to feed the animals? She was alone in the house, in bed. She'd take Ben to bed with her. The two of them, without him. This was closer to the edge than he'd ever been. He didn't remember there ever being doubt; Hannah had always been a sure thing. He'd never imagined danger to himself or to her. The thought was brand new. Immediately it filled the space emptied by the disappearing light. It flooded his body until he was too swollen to move. His muscles tensed tight as boards, a sturdy fence to hold him inside. His breath was slow and careful in the shallows at the top of his lungs. One false move. If the thoughts got out they could upset the way things were. Snow could stuff the chimney, they could freeze or smother. The stove could burn. She could be reduced to breaking up the furniture for fuel. Wolves and bears might try to get in, they might lean on the walls of the house and dig in the sod, and when she went out to the sheds to feed and water the animals, they could bring her down. Her face would be invisible in the white of the snow. He might never find her.

Up till now, the endings in life had all belonged to others. They hadn't required him. No one had ever left him; nothing that he wanted to continue had ever ended. So far he had not looked back.

Sideways out of the corner of his eye he got one last impression, blurred, beautiful, discrete, as if he had pasted his shadow up where he could see it keeping an eye on him, keeping company. He had grown accustomed to it. As night came on, a cool velvet deep-water current of black, it melded with the shadows of the men and became one thing, a comfort, as the wind honed itself on ice and deep spaces, reforging its strength.

How long could this keep up? Tomorrow he'd have to decide whether or not to try heading out. His stomach growled. By wriggling just so, he could create a pocket of air warmed by his body and trapped inside his shirt. The puppy had given up crying from hunger. She was smaller, a little famine in the hollow of his stomach.

Then he thought he must be dreaming, rolling back over the shore of sleep. He was beginning to recognize the landscape as warmer, friendlier, more vivid than the shrouded world of this internment.

He'd been given a green cloak and a high horse golden in colour and mythology. Just above him floated desirably soft clouds. Beneath, a bleak, unrealized promise of earth. Behind him was his shadow.

'I bring the land!' he shouted, stopping the horse, who two-stepped nervously. It was rolled up like carpet under his arm. Taking the corners he stood in the stirrups and flung it out over the barren ground. Like a ribbon it unfurled in a long sensuous sequence. At the same time, making a peculiar sound, its surface sucked the clouds right out of the sky, leaving a bland blue. This seemed to weigh it down and, sinking comfortably, it began to spread out in a graceful fan of grass. The area was predominantly flat, but when reaching an irregularity, it tossed up all kinds of flowers, berries and trees, which grew rapidly.

'I bring …' he repeated, but no one was there. Only the horse and his shadow. The horse had put its head down, snatching and tasting this new grass. The shadow was whispering into the wind. 'It's hard without an audience, isn't it?'

'Where are they?'

'Not here yet.'

He was going to cry.

'Now, now, take it easy; don't get in a huff. Let's see what we can do.' Shadow got down, or rather lifted off into the air.

'Where're you going?'

'Nowhere.

'Don't leave me.'

Shadow licked its invisible lips. It opened the hole where its mouth would have been. Matthew hadn't noticed before but Shadow's breath stank like a dog's. He didn't let on. One of the first rules was, Don't antagonize Shadow. By twisting to the side he could see right through the opening.

'Well.'

'Well, what?'

'Are you going to get them for me?'

'Don't rush me.' Appearing as bored as possible, Shadow tugged Matthew's boots off and after sniffing and making a face began to pull and squeeze his toes. Shadow's fingers were wet and rubbery, and as strong as tongues.

'Hey,' but before Matthew could continue, a soft lizard dropped to the ground and slithered away. Reaching for his ankles Shadow managed to get a frog; his kneecap gave a turtle. Taking his hand, Shadow gently milked mice and rabbits.

'You're sure you want to go ahead with this?' said Shadow.

'The People, get to the People.'

'First this.' Shadow plucked a cricket from his ear, an owl from his wrist; Shadow eased a bear from his elbow, a buffalo from his stomach. An eagle leapt from his forehead, knocking off his hat.

'Stop, stop, leave me alone. Can't you use the horse?'

Shadow was circling quickly, round and round, one way, then the other, getting more and more excited despite itself. Shadow loved the rush of creation.

A snake slid out of his spine.

'One last thing,' Shadow squealed, flopping up and down. With great flourish and mystery, Shadow reached into Matthew's mouth, rummaged around and, after a dramatic pause, extracted a coyote. Shadow displayed it proudly.

'That's it?'

'What did you expect?'

'Human beings.'

'Oh yes,' clearly uninterested, 'the lesser beings. You're sure you can't wait? I'm so tired.' Shadow dropped coyote, swooned effectively, then drifted to the ground. Shadow sighed and peeked at Matthew.

'Get on with it.'

Shadow dragged itself up into a long thin smoky shape and coughed. A tiny wizened creature fell.

'No, from me, in my image. You know what I mean.' He waited. 'Come on, you promised.'

'Did I? I did, didn't I? Shadow always honours its promises, that's one thing can be said about Shadow ...'

'Just and strong and brave and free.'

'What?'

'That's how they should be. The human beings.'

Coyote curled his lip and largely suppressed himself. The other animals peeked up out of the long wavering grass. Things were tense and interesting.

'Where would you like them to come from?' Shadow asked, smiling. This was Shadow's favourite question. For every creation it got a different answer.

The curious sun came around to watch. It shone in Matthew's eyes as it tried to see better. 'Ow, ow,' he said and Shadow jumped on his back and hid. 'Wait, wait, what's happening? What am I going to do? What am I going to get? I'm not going to get it, am I? Take this back, I wanted something else. Is it too late? I had in mind something else; what is it … I used to know.' As he tried to think of it his eyes skimmed and skittered back and forth. All that they touched was erased. Until the animals figured it out, they vanished, but as soon as they caught on to what was happening, they fled as before prairie fire, yelping and crying. Matthew's stomach turned cold.

His back was cold. He opened his eyes. He was inside a closed mouth of ice. There was no throat. But there was all this light where there should have been the limp imp darkness of Shadow. This was a black world bleached blinding white. Unnatural. It should have been dark; this called for a brew of magical, sinister dark.

His head hurt. It was gone now, the crooked little dream leaving a feeling of company and discomfort. His stomach was hollow. He squeezed his body around it. Perhaps he could go back to sleep. The pain in his belly held little promise. He yawned. His eyes opened. He was slept out. The dull air hardened and built up against the walls. Lying on his back, he looked for the slick ice underneath, but was unable to locate its surface. The waxen air thickened on him. Time, on the other hand, was thin and watery.

He figured Hannah would be talking to God by now, making deals, doing whatever it was she did to fix things. He hid in her folds and listened. He'd never seen her do it. She said, 'Oh my God!' He'd never heard her pray. She said, 'For God's sake!' He'd never smelt the dust of angels on her. She pursed her hands and lips.

'Do it for me,' he said, whispering from behind her, 'talk straight to God; get me out of this mess; make it right.' She could burn through this ice all by herself, she had a core of fire. Why, there was so much fire in her, the surplus bled out her hair; her red tongues swarmed him. What else on earth was there besides heat? Without it he was going to die.

And fresh air, her breath a twist of citrus, crushed berries. 'Hannah!' She was full of plump warm round seeds. Round like tears before they start falling. What colour would they be? Clear as crystals, opaque opals, moonstone, lustrous milky pearls. She had a whole world inside her. He didn't know if she needed God. In the beginning was the egg. The cave walls curved over him.

The wind sizzled. Hard snow bounced and fried on the roof. They were being buried for good. He had visions of feast, despair, famine, the flanks of fast horses, all weighing false like hollow-hearted apples. He tried to touch his thumb to his forefinger. Where was that man? Where was his face in the dark?

Matthew couldn't catch hold of him. Not afraid of all of him, he was afraid to look in his eyes, which had pressed up against the ice. Holding his breath, Matthew strained to hear. His heart beat in his ears, pounding at the door the wind had closed on his head. Backing down, it panted in his throat. He turned the collar of his shirt to keep his pulse warm and safe. He couldn't think that way. His eyes wandered, but they didn't see. He began to log his possessions: boots, socks, long-johns, trousers, shirt, jacket, scarf, hat, more than he realized, considering how cold he was. Deep in his pocket a handkerchief, coins, lint. What an impoverished person he was. In the saddlebags: rope, matches, knife. He had an awful thought: What if they could no longer hear each other. The Indian's lips were moving. What was he saying? Matthew wanted to crawl over so their breath could mingle.

The Indian started talking out loud. His voice was too familiar, not unlike Matthew's own; resonant and remote, a bit raspy from the cold. Matthew listened for one single word that he might recognize, one he'd be able to pick out in the ripple of vowels. He knew the man wasn't really talking to him or, if he was, it was as if to an infant, soothing a restlessness with round syllables. It's a story, he thought, he's telling a tale, one he knows well, one that's so old, it has its own life, its own form. Coming from an old land that has just begun to sing.

Outside, the wind shredded itself on edges of ice.

He was aware of pause and emphasis. Perhaps a chant. As Matthew listened, the twist in his stomach began to unwind. Then the song was story, rolling in deep sweet sound, uncovering the truth with a mantle of cadence. Perhaps prayer, its breath reeling in incense. From that word Matthew caught a scent of swinging, smoking grass; from the next, underground water, cloudburst, and later wild rose and snake hole.

And even though he wanted to know and wasn't allowed, he didn't care. Someone else had taken responsibility. He floated on the word, the simple breath. It masked the subtleties of wind, the creaking weight of growing ice. Each gesture the man made on the white wall was a silhouette that was as dense and endless and green as death by drowning.

If he could just have the time to learn the language, if he could just listen long enough, he'd find out. This man knew what to do. Calling the friend and the enemy, he was naming names.

Then unexpectedly, he finished. He nodded. It was Matthew's turn.

He knew I was there all along. He dragged me into a cave made of snow, and together we ...

But I have no stories, thought Matthew, or said out loud without hearing himself, because suddenly the Indian looked at him sharply. Or could he read his thoughts? What did he want him for? Who was this other man as dark as earth, the fields of his face as flat as the prairie?

'What are we going to do?'

Shadow lay in placid slough ...

'How are we going to get out?'

... a drawn gorge of lips ...

'Where are we? Do you know that?'

... climbing cut banks of bone ...

'Which day is it now?'

... low bluffs of his brow ...

'When is it going to stop?'

... knuckles rising in knolls ...

'Who are you, anyway?'

The Indian reached beside himself and lifting a piece of pale meat handed it to Matthew, who took it greedily, eagerly, without question.

'Full of surprises aren't you!' But cautious in his dependence, he smiled softly. 'Just how much have you got stashed away there?' His eyes swung slowly. He could eat a horse. Maybe he was.

The Indian was staring at him.

'What do you want?' Nervously chewing. The meat was raw. Did an animal crawl in here? What is this?' He looked at the last bite pinched between his fingers. The Indian offered another piece. Matthew pointed at it. 'What is that?' The Indian picked up a limp pelt. For a moment Matthew couldn't make out what it was, then startling, he felt the packed snow around his body. 'The dog! That's my dog!' His mouth hung open, but no words fell out of it. A cold fear flooded his chest. The Indian popped the streamer of meat into his own mouth, licked his lips and gestured as if to say, That just hits the spot, doesn't it? But Matthew's blood watered. His hands curled meekly. He couldn't feed himself or keep warm or defend himself, much less vent his anger.

The Indian jerked his hands up and froze; he stopped chewing. Matthew looked, held his breath. He couldn't hear anything. Something had happened to the wind, the air. He couldn't breathe. Scrambling to the place where the branch moved, he shoved weakly on it. Nothing happened. Turning his back, he leaned and pushed. 'Come on, you old geezer, help me or we'll be dead in here.' Magically they broke the skin of ice and toppled out into silent brilliance.

The light slammed Matthew back. It was too stunning to live out there. It hurt. He wanted the walls. Up against the wall, the wall at his back, he was used to it. The silence stripped him down. It was a pure land-scape, airless and abysmal. As far as he could see was grey horizon, with-out merit or interest, deep frozen, merciless, the underside of the world.

Was he supposed to send a noise into this sleep? Was that why it had become so still? The silence giving him room to say, 'Here I am!' How dismal this world was without the sound of his voice. How empty. But he didn't know how to start singing those songs that once woke this kind of world.

The Indian narrowed his eyes. His feet screeched on the crust of snow as he stomped a place. The noise was overwhelming, deafening. In some places the snow was packed, in others he broke through. As soon as he had made a flat space, he began snapping off the brittle branches of bush and started a small fire with Matthew's matches. The invisible fire boiled a small can of snow water into which he dropped a few dried leaves to make a bitter brew of tea. But it warmed. Matthew shivered vio-lently as he drank. The sun's circle floated in a soup of sky. It had been three days.

He was beginning to feel a little better. Then they found the horses, stark frozen, standing up. The eyes were brazen. Clearing away some of the snow, they took their gear.

Unbelievably, once they'd climbed to high, wind-blown bare ground, they saw the slow smoke of the half-buried soddy. 'It was here all along! Just out of sight. I don't believe it.' He started to run stiffly, broke through crust, and so slowed to a careful walk. 'Come on, then,' he said, but the Indian veered away. 'Hey, where're you going?'

The man glanced back with a wry smile.

'Do you know where to…?' Matthew began to say. He listened to him crackling and crunching across the proud flesh of snow, then turned and hurried towards the house without looking back.

* * *

On the first day Hannah said, 'Oh-oh, I'll bet your ol' daddy's stuck over at Donnat's now with this blizzard on. It looks to be a fierce one, listen to that wind howling out there. Don't you worry though, Mama'll keep you safe …'

On the second day, when there was no change except for the worse, Hannah said, 'Come on, my little one, don't fret, there there. Look, we've got plenty to eat and plenty of fuel. I wonder … I wonder when … Let's see if we can sing this old storm on its way. Come on now, let's sing so loud Daddy'll be able to hear us all the way over there …'

On the third day, after not sleeping very well, she placed Ben on her lap facing her and put his arms around her body, his head between her breasts. Up and down his back she rubbed small circles around the vertebrae, then slid her hands down to cup his bottom. When he'd been inside she'd felt him like this, his snaky spine. All by herself she'd been able to keep him safe. 'Oh baby mine, hold on to Mama.' She'd never seen anything like this before. She couldn't get out to feed the animals. She thought, I just hope they've got enough sense to go get at the hay … I wonder when?… I wonder if?…'

Later on that third day the storm melted away. Hannah had a brief surge of hope. Although the snow was blown away from the door, allowing her to get out, she saw immediately that travel would be impossible in the frozen sculpture of snow, its sharp edges, swept and swirled, smothering and sinister. Nothing was marked, no mistakes visited upon the vacant, impassable land.

The bottoms of her feet set off the crust of snow like buckshot. The noise blew holes in the thin casing of sweat that had inexplicably formed a second skin on her body. She burned. The cold scorched her cheeks. A strong clear light pooled with snow to bank the side of the shed. She opened the top of the double door.

The animals smiled. They crowded expectantly and sniffed the fresh air warily. Inside was a yellowy brown cardboard colour. They shivered. The steam from their manure cooled and dripped back down. Edging closer, they blew like bellows and encouraged her to rearrange things. She hauled water and measured out oats and corn.

But deep among them, while they shouldered and squeezed, she became increasingly uneasy. Their breath was too strong, its sound coming from too deep inside. They were raw, the openings into their bodies glistened with mucus. They'd been talking behind her back.

The rank air began to boil in her lungs. Fluids in her body wavered uncomfortably. The animals had conspired to get her and press her between them. The muck sucked on her boots. They'd stomp on her if she made a wrong move.

Covering her head with a corner of a plaid wool fichu, she closed the door behind her and set the latch on it. Clutching her chest she tried to run. She threw up what she had eaten. It wasn't digested. She ran. Behind her she saw the wolves come around the snow bank to eat it. She saw them smell her footprints. She heard the low sounds in their throats. She ran to the soddy.

Bolting the door wasn't enough; she leaned back on it, rolled her spine up and down, kicked it with the heels of her boots, smoothed the wood down with the flat of her hand. Light shone through the hoarfrost on the window. Rushing over to it, she dragged the small curtain across its face. She was burning. She took off her wrap and boots, unbuttoned the wool jacket of her dress, took it off, the skirt, petticoats, chemise, stockings, underwear.

With her own body burning up she couldn't tell if Ben was feverish. He slept on his back. Once he opened his eyes, then closed them again. Hannah pushed on the wall above his bed. It was dry and cold. She fed the fire though it hurt her skin. Plucking her hair out of its pins she began to sob. Going to each wall in turn she touched it, tickled it, pressed her palm on it. Her hair was ringing in the steam of her fever. When she plucked the curls out, they sprung back. Ben was still sleeping. She had nothing to do but listen for wolves and pretend she was someone else, someone wolves and shifting animals weren't interested in. Perhaps someone without a child. Without a husband who had abandoned her. In the bottom of her papier-mâché box under the keepsakes and treasures that reminded her of yet another person, she found a folded piece of red tissue. Tearing a small square, she wet it and began to rub the colour on her cheeks. Before it was all used up, she wiped her lips, nipples and the palms of her hands. Using soot from the lamp, she outlined her eyes. There was a shiny green ribbon, a strip of old petticoat, but even that soft worn old thing irritated the flush on her skin. She needed another mirror. She became invisible.

She tossed her hair, but there was no wind. She smiled, but no one saw it. Threw kisses, no one caught them. Sang a shrill song, but no one was awake to hear it. The heat swam out of her body, but there was no one to burn.

She climbed on top of the bed. The dry dusty cold circled around her. This was no longer home. Home was her own bed, that old room she'd left behind. Home. That past shaped itself up around her: a string tied on the rung of the chair, the carve of corner moulding, bruised floor, June bug carcass. Closing her eyes she saw it all there in the same old way, smelled the tang of her body on the thrown-back covers. Window smoking in dusk. The rhythmic shrill of crickets. Wind sucking on the bottom of the limp curtains. Her dreams draped on the bed posts.

A curtain pulled across the doorway to the kitchen had muffled the voices of the big people, whose night talk mysteriously kept the world turning. Whose never closing eyes watched over her so she could sleep. Who tasted her food with their forked tongues, heard her cry above all others, and walked the edge so she wouldn't fall off.

Everything, just as if she were still there; it felt so good she didn't want to come back. It was a bath of memory, warm, clear and quiet. She wondered if that quiet place had always been this close? Was this all she had to do?

A hot mirage emanated from the stove. The heat was a stone wall with things buried in it. She listened for the small crackling cries of hurt animals, colicky babies, people making love. The heat used the sounds of live things to mortar itself, to give itself shape. It was trying to fit her in. She held her breath, she didn't move. Sweat slid down to soak the sheet beneath her. The salt stain spread in an erratic landscape. The man would come there to lie on her. He would misunderstand. He wouldn't talk about it, but she knew he wanted to straighten her out as he did his fields, which he ploughed in a straight line, lines all up and down and back and forth across the land, railroad tracks, roads, fences, house foundations, irrigation ditches. Only the creek ran crookedly. The past and the future could look at each other from bends in the creek. It wasn't natural to plant them in straight rows, to have the past hidden and falling away in these echoes. It wasn't right to have the future stretching away to a vanishing point, invisible.

She got Ben up in bed with her. He cried out at her burning touch. He had a stuffy smell like the insides of stale milk pans. She held his small hands, unfolded his fingers one by one, let them curl back, then selected one and slipping it between her lips began to nibble on the nail.

Ben began to play with her, pulling himself over her arm, giggling, crawling up on her stomach. Her skin was so hot. He sprawled on her chest and fastened onto her breast. The milk burned his mouth. He pinched the other nipple, tapped it, flicked it. He rolled his face from side to side on the pillow of her breast, laughed, munched on it with his tiny sharp teeth. His strong rubbery tongue curled and licked. His hands kneaded and crimped her dough. He closed his eyes and curled his toes. He was going to eat her up. She was his honey, all warm, all his.

Hannah was wide awake. Her mouth had set in a thin line. She seemed to be looking at the ceiling, but she had focused beyond the peak of the roof. Her body, thick and unwilling, didn't move. She was different. She saw herself differently. She was going to ripen her flesh like fruit in the heat of the fire. In the white flour ash, smoothing it on her thighs, belly.

When he got home, Matthew thought he saw her. He wasn't sure; a silken dust shrouded everything. He looked outside then back inside making sure it was his house. What if she were dead? He didn't know how to talk to the dead. The firelight trembled on the edge of the body so that he couldn't see if it was breathing or not. It was her shape, but it was also the shape of a drift of snow. Beside him a container of water idled; he watched it throwing circles from the centre as if it were being disturbed from inside. He held his breath. It wasn't fair. He'd come so far. 'Look at me,' he whispered. 'I made it. Hannah. Look.' He waited.

The dark seeped out from behind and inside and underneath. Shadows pooled one into another.

'Hannah?'

She rolled over. The baby was fastened to her. She hunched up in relief, looming over him like a creature with a sprung spine. Her arms

223

and legs caged him. The fleece of her hair hung down like a shaggy tail reversing her body; her breasts were pointed teats. Her haunch, a headless shoulder, shifted threateningly. She growled. The baby let go.

The firelight splayed and splashed on the other side of her body; she fed it. The fire was hungry. The baby was hungry. The wolves were hungry.

'Hannah!' Matthew was shouting; his voice just slipped between the loud reports from the stove. She bent her head straight back as far as it would go, but still couldn't see who was there, and so she twisted from one side to the other, tucked her shoulder in, beckoned.

He dropped his pack. She crawled back on the bed. Shovelling his son into his hands, he put him down in the crib, and then stripped out of his stinking clothes. She was glistening.

He touched her. Her flesh scalded; he wanted to burn, he wanted in. He'd been so cold, colder than he ever imagined it was possible to be. He wanted to tell her about it, but first he wanted to wrap her around himself.

She smiled; he swallowed it. She threw him a new kiss; it bruised his lips. A tune rumbled in the back of her throat; he put his ear down to listen.

Over his shoulder, into the everlasting dark, Hannah's fever-bright eyes glittered like stars. She was grateful because she was afraid. Even now she thought she might be changed into someone she didn't know and wouldn't be comfortable with, someone she wouldn't recognize and who might embarrass her in an emergency. Someone she might have to look out for, a fragile person who didn't always have control, who could get sick, who didn't know what was going on.

She was holding on to him, but he couldn't feel her grip. He was sinking in; the centre was soft syrup, molten, and just as he seemed to reach it, it dissolved. She was bottomless. He was nowhere near. This was supposed to be the place he had settled; the place of all others where he would be safe, comfortable and sure, where there was no change, where he knew his way in the dark.

He propped up on his elbows to look at her. A paste of chalky ash was between them.

'Hannah?'

She closed her eyes. She didn't speak.

Climbing down he stood in front of the stove.

'God, but I'm cold.'

Turning he saw her lying transparent and boneless, without pride. He stared down. Had he touched her?

'I – I never expected to see you lie down like this.' What he saw was her spirit lying down, not the flesh, which had rolled between his hands. The ash was drying on her thighs and belly.

'I have a new story to tell you.' But he couldn't look at her any more. Huddling down before the stove, he noticed that the fire looked like a hole to hell.

This was a country without old tales, without hearth.

Twelve

Within a few weeks Matthew had told Hannah what had happened so many times that, although she hadn't listened once from beginning to end, she now knew six versions. Each had more weight than the last; when he talked she felt her face flatten.

A film of frostbite scalloped his ear and white spots polka-dotted his cheek. He shone. He stood over there talking, building himself, celebrating the fact of his body as it surrounded him. He found himself gazing at the hills of snow, the silt of his imagination whitening it to an uncommon brilliance, not unlike what he imagined the inside of possibility to be. It seemed to drink his energy in slow deep draughts.

She insisted that they go to the barn dance. 'Everyone's going ... I'm going.'

He remembered how he would follow her anywhere when she was like this, switching her will as if it were a tail, cracking the air. And through the cold, her sharp scent.

It was already dark when they arrived, the shape of the large barn blurred by a rippling edge of steam. For a moment, when the doors opened, the block of human-heated air and the black wall of winter met and shuddered. The dancers hesitated, looking to the newcomers, then brightened in recognition or curiosity. One by one they turned back to their partners.

'... whirl your partner ... allemande left ...'

The air was sweet with cider and laughter. Lamp glow stirred by the dancers swirled in smoke. As it warmed, the women shed their swaddle of extra wraps, which soon draped the posts and rails like moths. Fiddle and flute music ran like an undercurrent tugging on their legs. Mouths softened, a moustache of sweat glistening their upper lips. As the music retreated, chatter rose so that there was always a dear noise.

Mrs Bradley, her placid face holding her hair around like a pink pin cushion was saying, 'Well, I was the first one to know ...' A yeasty smell of well-being rose from her.

Sitting nearby, a woman took off her white gloves and folded them in half before placing one on top of the other in a little sandwich. She slid them into her purse, centred the purse on her lap, and covered it neatly with her two hands. Simultaneously her feet, side by side, toed an imaginary line. Her shoulders trimmed and her head settled slightly, an old house on its foundation.

Hannah handed the baby to childless Evelyn. He was content there, one hand braced on her dry breast as he reached for a pearly cameo nestled in ruffles at her throat. She let him. 'Gently, don't pull on it.' He looked at her face, stretched one arm back, and turned to be sure Hannah was watching. She smiled. She might not have to hold him again until he was ready to go to sleep. With his weight gone she had to consciously straighten up. She plucked her dress away from her skin where it had been glued by his heat.

The music was starting again. Glancing softly, the women wondered if the men were coming back from their corners and secret circles. Each time, they emerged warmer and more forward, expansive even, doing their best to play someone who might surprise or frighten them. As the anticipation grew, a lively flush and flirt of red coloured their cheeks.

'Let's keep things moving, ladies and gentlemen. Old Man Winter is just outside the door, let's not let him in. Come on now, get your partners and form your squares. I'm going to throw an easy one at you, you won't have to be on your toes for this one, so how about trying a new partner this round, that gal you've had your eye on …' The crowd shifted uneasily. A man shrugged, closed his eyes and reached out one long arm like a scythe catching Hannah around the waist. 'This little gal!' He bowed. As he swept off his hat to toss it up on a hook, she saw that the skull of a rattlesnake was fastened at the centre front of the hat band, a red bandanna, and looked like clotted evil inside the eye sockets. Before she could touch it the man grabbed her hand and pulled her over to the platform-built dance floor. Others moved in quickly. The fiddler was already stomping the boards to establish the beat. Looking around the square, Hannah saw a young man she remembered from harvest time; and that one, the soft unmarried brother of the railway man. The fiddle squirted. 'Honour your partner …' Hannah felt the wisps of hair swing out away from her head. Tiny flames of her hair burned through the gold in the air and the fine straw dust swirled. She let her body bend over the arms of the men. While they held her she leaned back and looked at the ceiling, the same vault of bat air and blindness as the barn she and Matthew used to hide in, throwing secrets up into the webs that buttressed the huge beams. Just outside it was cold and sad and dark. The secrets had been so enormous she didn't think the world could hold them, or her, but it did.

This, the present she had always worn with élan, was clutching and riding her. She was feeding everyone, keeping them clean, tending hurts, brooding. This time to dance and dream was more what she had in mind. To throw her skirt over the air so it billowed, and to flick her eyes at a man until he blinked.

He was laughing, 'Switch your partners, give her away, keep the next till a rainy day …' Another slid his arm around her. And another until she had been with each fellow.

The fiddler smacked the strings quiet. Spirited clapping and cheers burst the sudden silence, and those who'd been dancing and had worked up an appetite rushed to the tables. Hannah saw her biscuits. By now they must have thawed. There was glazed smoked ham scored with diamond cuts framing dark cloves, green bean and corn relish, johnnycake, baked chicken, cole slaw, pickles, wild red berry jams, braided breads, yellowed cheeses and more.

Matthew had something in his coffee; she could tell by the way he held it, swirling the liquid up around the inside of the cup. A new crowd had gathered to him. As she looked she saw that it was true, he was different. It there hadn't been this length of time to stare at him, she might have missed him altogether. And whereas to her he had lost substance, to others this translucence shimmered new mystery. No wonder! As she looked around at the winter-tired people, she saw that the sharp stories on Matthew's tongue were better than the old earth-tolling songs retold.

The women were fussing over the food, replenishing, rearranging, brushing crumbs to the floor where a couple of dogs had been waiting stoically. Between the women's hips small children insinuated silently and sent their small fingers out to snatch the biscuits, pickles and nuts close to the edge. 'Mama, Mama, when are the cakes coming?' Wiping the pickle juice from his fingers onto her skirt. 'Tommy!' Plunking the bowl down. 'Stop that. My best dress. Oh, will you look at that now!' 'Mama, Ma-ma, when?' She pushed his hands away. 'Get away with you.' Picking up a napkin she snapped it at him.

'Don't stop with only one helping. Come on back for seconds, there's plenty here for everyone.'

Hannah held her plate up close to her face and rubbed her fingers around in the jungle of juice, then licked it off. Putting her finger back in she slid it in tight little circles. As she did, her tongue concentrated between her lips. Was someone looking at her? She was still hungry. Spooning some of the brown sugar and mustard syrup from the platter of ham, she crumbled a wedge of cornbread onto it.

Tully was watching her now, leaning with his tumid belly against the broad boards of an empty stall, peeking through a knothole, his cheek hard on the rough wood, his breath small and soft, saliva frothing in his throat. Would he have the courage to stick to her?

Bales of straw had been dragged down in front of the stalls, and the ladies were sitting upon them, arranging their skirts like florists. Relaxed by now with food, warmth and gossip, they swayed and leaned, overhearing each other. When the men came to invite them to dance they exclaimed that they would have to sit this one out, showing their empty plates. 'But a coffee would be nice.' The men wondered if they had permission to pick other partners, especially from among the younger wives. Though they worried about their big boots, that everlasting youth with the dancing-fool feet was just under the surface. Without noticing that others were doing the same, they looked at Hannah waiting in the lamplight. She had cocked one foot on its heel so that it stuck out from beneath her petticoat, spicy and red in slippers so soft they could have been mistaken for skin. And the tilt of her foot left no mistaking she wanted to dance again. They wanted to lift her right off the floor, get their hands tangled in her clothes.

With one finger Hannah brushed her lips clean of crumbs, licked them and then, feeling that they were dry, soothed them with a dab of butter and pressed them together. Her eyes were focused on the thin air just in front of her face. She listened. Something was missing. She heard the hoarse overlap of voices, people shifting, bumping into each other. Unshadowed sounds of delight, surprise, relief. Over there people were starting to sing. Different words were emphasized as they were remembered. No one knew the middle part, and the song slid away, finishing with a rouse. Everyone laughed. The fiddle player sawed his bow on the strings so that it sounded like laughing. One of the dogs howled. Other people were clattering dirty plates. Beneath her feet the floorboards creaked and groaned. The sounds swarmed up into the empty space above, swelling it with blast and pomp. What was missing? What had she grown used to without knowing it?

Addie was smiling and closing in. She touched Hannah's toe with her own. 'They look so nice.'

Hannah looked down. 'Yes, but why did she send them to me?'

'Didn't you always want them?'

Putting her hand on Addie's arm, Hannah stared at her. 'I don't know.'

'When you were a little girl, perhaps?'

'But if I always wanted them, why didn't she give them to me then?'

'Maybe she couldn't afford them or maybe you didn't need them so much.' Lifting her foot sideways, Hannah studied the shoe, which was the Mary Jane style, red with a gold buckle, the dyed leather pleated underneath and tucked into a thin sole. Impractical and frivolous, they decorated her feet, changing them into magic hooves of bright flexible horn.

'You don't give your baby everything he wants when he wants it, do you?' Hannah looked at the other side of her foot. 'Where is he?'

'Agatha has him over there. He's still going strong.'

Hannah wished Addie would go away now so somebody else could see her. 'Umhum,' she said, looking over her shoulder to see if anything was happening. One of the fellows had whimpered that he wanted to dance with her again. 'Umhum.'

Behind her, things were stirring. Trays of soft cakes and cookies, bowls of ice cream, toffees and hard candies; peppermints, lemon drops, tarts with deep purple-berried centres. Immediately the table was surrounded by the children and, reaching over their heads, their fathers.

With fistfuls of sticky sweets the children crowded in a semicircle around the fiddler, who had crouched down and was playing snatches of nursery songs. Silently the sugar foamed in their mouths. They stared and licked their fingers. Soon the littlest ones were sashaying their hips from side to side, unable to keep still. Others began to clap and cheer; older children gathered. Everyone was amused and laughing. The children were now inventing antic moves to hold the attention of the adults; they began to think they could do anything, poking their behinds out, making ugly faces. Addie was reaching around her little Nellie's face, feeling it to see if she was making herself foolish. Nellie turned and bit her mother's apron, then nervously tilted her head back, leaning, smiling, nudging in the warm nest of Addie's skirts. Hannah thought she was a cute little girl. Addie had done her hair up in a tight knot of braid that made her head look tidy and small. She hadn't noticed before, but some of the older children had large adult-shaped heads; they didn't appeal like a baby's, and looked strange, top-heavy. For instance, Cyril Hoffman over there.

He wasn't the one, though. She sensed someone watching her but glancing around quickly didn't catch anybody. Pretending a noise had distracted her she looked over her shoulder. Whatever it was, it wasn't there any more. She turned her head the other way.

The dark, which was doing things back there, froze. She kept looking at it, daring it to move. After a moment, when her eyes got used to it, she picked out the shapes of some things and make them familiar. But there were more, things content to hold still and wait undetected, that watched without eyes, tasting the air and smelling the cold on her skin. A chill shrunk to the bones in her back.

Even though there was noise and commotion, her ears were stopped with a silence as thick as wax. She hunched her shoulder and pressed it to her cheek. She bit the air as it slid. Her heart beat up the length of her neck.

A lantern was struck by laughter; as it swung, the bursts of light blinded and drove the shadows.

'May I…?' Alex Lowie, his hand near hers, asked, but she was blank. 'This dance?' he said. 'Will you?' He smiled, pleased that he had caught her unaware.

Beyond him Hannah saw others gathering. She was stiff. When she moved to accept, a salty crust of sweat disintegrated and powdered her skin, making it feel unpleasantly dry. The people were forming two lines. She didn't know how to do this one. She coaxed Alex Lowie to the middle of the line because she wasn't sure which end would start. All the men were on one side, all the women on the other. She smiled at no one. Once or twice she started to look over her shoulder. The aprons of the women caught and threw the wonderful lights. Some of the men were wearing white shirts. It was almost impossible to believe that this was the same colour as snow.

Nothing was still any more. On both sides of her, the women were turning to each other, bobbing their heads together in brief intimate exchange. Across from them, the men were stepping backward then forward again, looking at their feet, then looking at the women. Hannah tilted her head; she was warming up and had forgotten how clammy she had been before. Leaning into the open space between the columns of people, she tried to see what was holding things up. The fiddler was tuning his instrument. She leaned forward just a bit more. Behind the caller, who was standing with his back towards her, was someone else. She couldn't make out who it was.

The fiddler placed the bow and began. Without wasting any time the caller shouted his instructions. Everyone straightened, turned and, taking hands, raised them high in an arch. The first couple, ducking their heads, executed the gauntlet in a quick sliding sidestep. When they got to the end they locked fingers and continued the arch. 'Just the girls,' someone called. Others clapped smartly for a few seconds then fell into the rhythm of the music. A little boy sneaked in behind the next couple and ran down with them. Two girls were skipping up and down outside the ranks. It was almost Hannah's turn. The couple before them had just ducked down. It was happening so fast now. Her partner was trying to catch her eye; he was counting strenuously, out loud; he had her firmly by the hands. In a second it would be their turn. As they lowered their hands, she glanced up to the stage; that other person was Gabriel, the one she hadn't been able to see, hidden as he'd been by the caller. There wasn't time. Energetically, her partner yanked her down the centre. She held her breath; her knees were buckling, Alex had to grab her; he thought she'd got off balance; he grabbed her around the waist. When they got to the end he apologized. Hannah stared at him. He looked frightened. Since they'd stopped, she tried to stand up by locking her knees, but that didn't work. Backing away she pulled her hands in and curled them. Alex came with her. 'I just want to sit down,' she said in his ear. A couple of women closed in on each side of her and helped her to a bale of straw. They patted her hands in her lap and while one went to get her a cold drink, the other was distracted by the dancing. Hannah swallowed air. Her shoulders were hitched up. Putting her hands flat beside her thighs and straightening her arms gave her some room to breathe. Cautiously she looked over there, which was so far away. The distance made her sick and sleepy. Was he looking at her? How long had he been looking at her?

Matthew squatted down in front of her, his face at her knees, and put his hands on hers. 'What is it?' He looked like one of the big-headed children dwarfed there at her knees. She shook her head. 'Nothing, I just ... I just ...' She shook her head and made a thin line with her mouth.

'Here.' The woman had brought water. Matthew handed it to her.

'Thanks, it's nothing, really. I don't know what happened, I just felt funny, I'm all right, really.' Matthew was still crouched. He loves me, she thought. His eyes were wide open. 'I just want to sit here for a minute.' Matthew sat beside her. His arm was comforting at her back. The women nodded to each other. Everything was as it should be and hardly ever was.

Matthew was in the way. She would have to lean forward and look around him to see Gabriel. He was half turned towards her, one hand kneading her fingers, playing with them, weaving, pressing, undoing. They both stared down. The way his head was tilted, she could feel his breath, which he was using instead of words. She noticed the soft bloom of his hair: the weather had made it dry and fluffy. She blew a path through it. She blew in his ear. Rolling her head back slightly, she discovered she could see over his shoulder. Lifting one hand, she placed it absently, tenderly on his back and rubbed a wrinkle of cloth up between two fingers. The warmth of him came through her fingers. He had always done that.

To the right side, on the stage, Gabriel was strumming chords on a banjo. He didn't have to pay attention to what he was doing. When Hannah looked, he was shining softly to her a smile without beginning, one that would never end. She wanted to dream this dream.

His thigh was next to her, his hip, the cover of his body; he was so close, but she couldn't feel him. She opened her hand on his shirt, moved her arm over and laid it down the curve of his back, brought her shoulder near. Her body was heavy, she couldn't move it fast enough. Even though he was still beside her, she couldn't reach. She wanted him; it had never been too far before, his heat all the length of her. The taste of him, what was that like? The smell of him before, then after; that was something. The air so cold she didn't think she could tell and then she could. In the dark, knowing just where every part of him was; knowing what he'd do next and then it being a surprise. Wanting him. For some time he'd been digging out, digesting that hollow inside her for himself. She let him. She said yes. Following him. She said yes standing up and lying down. Yes. Holding on for dear life.

Yes. Gabriel was nodding his head to the music. Yes. Nodding to her. He meant business. The curls of his hair were striking his face. When he had touched her, his hair had coiled and burned her skin. All the eyes of her body were turned towards him: the one that witnessed, the one that spied, the eye for an eye, the one that watched and the one that saw danger. The hungry eye. 'What do you want?' she whispered.

'What?' Matthew turned his face up to hers. It was so familiar, a mirror image, that she didn't recognize it. 'Something?'

'Excuse me?' Agatha was bringing the baby to her. 'I think he needs you.' She smiled, a little sadly, but it was an old familiar feeling, one she was used to.

The baby stretched in his excitement, then began to cry angrily, grabbing her as hard as he could. Clucking and shushing, Hannah smothered him against herself. 'What did you think, you silly baby, did you think your mama had left you and run off? Is that what you think of your mama? Hasn't she always been here for you? What a silly baby you are!' Jostling him tightly in her arms, prying his fingers from her. While she pulled out her blouse to slip the baby underneath, Matthew stood and stretched, rubbed his cheeks, tucked in his shirt, yawned. He was so sure he knew what was there that he didn't need to look over his shoulder.

He's that sure of us, Hannah thought, the weight of the baby on her. Of himself. Hadn't he come back from the maw of death? They'd argued:

What did you think happened to me?

Weren't you worried?

Don't you trust me?

It was trying to get you, Matthew.

What do you mean?

That storm, it was trying ...

Well, it didn't, did it?

No. Not this time.

Not ever.

But you aren't paying attention, are you?

To what? What are you talking about ... aw, come on, come on over here to me.

I just don't know you.

I know, I know. Slurping her ears.

Do you think about how lucky you were?

Why?

Someone was there to save you.

But he couldn't imagine. Or could he? He had expected. He did expect. Oh, come on, it was just an accident. A freak storm.

In the night he awakened. 'I did it!' shouting, skin peeling. 'I survived! Of course.' He saw *that.*

Hannah saw ruins, a dead horse, chickens with their legs frozen off, onions that broke like glass. While she got breakfast, he told her the story. His voice hadn't returned to its usual timbre after being roughed up over the ice. He doesn't care if I hear it, she thought, he just wants to tell me. As long as I keep asking, he'll take care of me. This is the way it works.

Ever since, she'd been keeping an eye on him as if the cold and dark might get up and catch him. But then she began to think he could do anything. This thought might have given her confidence, though it wasn't *that* she'd missed. She felt like she'd been awake for a long time, surrounded by light, hard edges, interference. If Matthew nudged her in the middle of the night, she was instantly wide awake. There were wolves howling on the cold bright plain. Snakes lay coiled in the sod walls. White ashes stoked the fire. In the darkest drape of the year, she just needed more sleep, but if she lost sight of him, he might disappear. She had to keep an eye on him as all the women did, looking at their men, always watching them, afraid they'd vanish. She had to love him more but with greater caution.

Someone was trying to organize the children into a square dance. They kept changing partners. The adults said, 'Well, all right.' Then they switched again. 'Make up your minds and stay put. Now ...' When the music started one of the boys changed his mind. 'May I?' said Matthew, who had gone over to watch. Bending in half he executed a princely bow to the young lady, who pulled her apron up over half her face. The caller started again. With a little bit of luck ...

Hannah played with the baby's foot, which was striking out from beneath her blouse. Tensed with hunger, his toes grabbed her finger, his hands held her breast. The noises of his hungry sucking crept up to her through the neck of her blouse. Even though they were well used to each other, he was doing it too hard. Trying to distract him by petting his cheek through the fabric didn't work; he pushed her hand away. 'Hey!' she said and rearranged him. He thought that meant he was going to move to the other side, and it was enough to get him settled with one hand hiding under her breast and his legs going limp on her lap.

Addie came over and sat down next to Hannah. Her Todd, still unsteady, came and went from the safety of her skirt. Hannah wondered if she could tell the difference, or if all the little hands felt the same, picking and plucking, absently tapping on her knee as Todd's did now.

'I can't get warm this winter,' Addie said. She was pale and tired-looking. 'I get to feeling this way every winter, but this year it seems worse; maybe because it started so early.'

Hannah had almost forgotten about the winter, but it was there, wrapped around the barn, sleeping like a bear while she was inside, the music frisking on her red shoes, the breath of neighbours warm, her stomach full of flavours. Then she heard Addie.

'I said, no, Mama, I won't mind going at all! Then she said, if you have to go with him without the reason of love you'll have to live with your decision. I never suspected she thought that much of love.'

Hannah saw that Gabriel had undone the top button on his collar and had folded up the sleeves of his shirt in soft rolls.

A large tear was banked on Addie's eye. Rummaging under her apron in the pocket of her dress, she pulled out a small brown bottle of tonic, unscrewed the cap and gulped down a mouthful. 'I did better than I would have, that's plain, isn't it? Where would I be now? What could have been, I wonder. California...'

Hannah was thinking, What is he doing?

And over there Matthew was looking over the heads of the children to his mountains. What will I do next? he wondered, licking his lips, rubbing the sweat from the palms of his hands onto his trousers.

'Why, there are parts of my past like that that don't seem to belong to me any more. I can remember, but it's like a different person did it ... Ah, I'm going too far,' she moaned. 'I don't want to go that far ...' and she headed off to tell the simpler stories to someone she barely knew.

Hannah felt Ben slip from her into sleep, his body sodden and warm. He jerked and curled when his head tipped back, then sank his chin in close to his neck and oozed into a deep swollen slumber. Sometimes when he was so still Hannah had difficulty recognizing him. Not that she wasn't glad to be free of him, but once he closed his eyes she seemed to lose sight of him.

The clutch of women sitting over to the side was all too happy to take him in among them while Hannah excused herself. One made a pillow of her shawl, another covered him and held his limp fingers. When small children wandered by they didn't notice him.

As Hannah walked around the edge of the floor, tucking in the tails of her blouse, she was looking through everyone else. An undercurrent of the music slowed around her ankles, the clapping broke and splashed. The children's stumbling, clomping shoes rumbled under her feet like loose river stones. She smoothed her skirt over her hips. Lamps swung and swayed. A mud brown dog nudged in front of her.

At the farthest point, just before she risked disappearing, she stopped and looked back over the frenzy of dancing children. Layers of light made a circus of the heat rising from their bodies. Behind them, what she saw was shaken and radiant. It was air to breathe and with each breath she took him in. Clear across the room she could smell him.

A woman was just coming back along the aisle from the privy. When she saw Hannah she made a face, tossed her gaze behind her and pinched her nose. Hannah hadn't expected to see anyone; she wanted to be alone for a moment. Not very far away, she should still be able to hear the comfort of voices and music like a sweet ragged reminder, but with a good blizzard this might be made to last forever. The light would change as it already had. On the inside of the snow cover, a soft cold sponge of air would force everyone to circle and sing to keep their spirits up. She would dance in the centre of them all, picking one, then another of the men as partners, giving each a turn. She would twirl until she was afraid she'd burst apart. Until the soles of the red shoes wore through and the new barn boards were as thin as paper. And as she whirled around, her hair would come undone and the people would raise their hands to warm themselves on the red flames. She closed her eyes and smiled.

She remembered warm mushrooms spilling out circles in the short damp grass. Fairy rings in diamonds of dew. Stones thrown into the still green pond. Spirals drawn in soft dust on a hot afternoon. The round tops of hills. Whorls of wind gathering the dry crisp of leaves. Haloes round the moon. Lying under the ring of its light, rubbing an angel in the memory of snow, on the sleeping secrets of the earth. The eye of the moon. She had lain there until the moon winked. Peculiar that she should think about that now. The past did not interest her. It sank beneath, and once the surface was calm again, she saw her reflection with the sun overhead just as it was, and round and round on the slick rigid skin bustled the spiky-legged water bugs.

Out there, the sharp cutting edge of the barn was splitting the wind, opening it to its cold centre, honing its throat to a howl. A slow ice chill creaked up inside the massive studs of wood.

She saw the trees again thick around her, staining the air brown, pillaring between the white snow and the white sky. She'd never gotten lost there. Bending her head back into the folds of woollen scarf, she'd held her face up to the icy daylight and still it was pinned and pricked by the thorn tips of the top branches. And when she lay on her stomach blowing snow from in front of her nose, licking the cold sweet crystals from beneath her chin, the trees caught her eye. Around and around they grew; she could always touch them by just reaching out. She did it and the world held together.

Back in the barn it was dry and dark. The music had stopped. Tongues were unrolling low along the floor. Walking back she couldn't see her feet scuffing beneath the straw. Their shapes pushed up the dust, scattering the chaff, which slid like small bright coins. Thin gold dust tarnished the hem of her skirt. One wrong step and she'd fall into a deep sleep that would last a hundred years, and just beyond, circling on the scent, unravelling the warp of her dreams, the mad gallant pursuit of princes. And in the deep, high, golden halls of hay, dust grated from stars got in her eyes, so that at first she couldn't see him standing in her way.

'Some women let their bodies forget they've carried children. Don't you do that. Don't you ever forget. I like to see what the children did.' His eyes grazed her body. 'This soft shape,' he stroked her belly.

'And this,' sweeping the wings of her hips around.

'Here,' sliding his hands up under her breasts.

She was remembering. He was close.

'There.' The pressure of his fingers between her legs. Gently gathering the cloth, which brushed against her skin. Holding her by the clutch of cloth.

'… and these,' touching her lips. Her breath filled the hollow of his curved palm, heated her face. 'Once a woman has kissed her own children, her lips change. You can feel it. They are honest; they have tasted the earth and immortality. They are heavy; they burn …' His voice shivered. He rubbed her lips until they opened. He watched her face until she had to close her eyes. He was so heavy. His words grew around her like broad corn leaves, folding her in their thick green.

His breath was drenching her like rain after a dry spell, warm, soaking, until she was swollen and muddy and her blood, watered down, was moving her bones out of the way. A thin slick glue of sweat was out on her skin. Where he touched her, he stuck fast. He was holding on like a drowning man. He was downed in front of her, his hands clutching inside her skirt; farther, to her belly, his fingers kneading as if to bury something there. Her skirt made a halo around his head.

He was saying something else, but it was muffled. He gagged.

'Is something going to happen to me?' she gasped, stretching her hands open over his head, trying to cover it, to push him under or pull him up.

But he was going, slipping from her.

'Gabriel!' As he separated from her she called him by name, quickly, again, to hold him. Or thrust him away. Naming him, pushing him out there. He put his ear to me, she thought, the way the Indians do when they want messages through the earth.

A column of dust signalled and swirled, filling the space where he stood. The straw crackled in his footprints. A barn rat leapt over the fresh spoor. Hannah grabbed her skirt, gathering it in her arms, holding herself with it, reluctant, afraid that if the heat drained so would her life. 'Stay,' she whispered with breath and hope.

'Popcorn! Popcorn! Come and get it!' The shout ricocheted, flushing soft cats and another of those lean coarse dogs who, barely lifting his nose, trotted by Hannah. She watched him for as long as she could. Two kids whooped and ran by without looking.

Numbed, she walked towards the light and noise. Behind, there was no trace of her. Nothing was disturbed. She thought she saw a curled black hair embedded in her skirt, but it turned out to be a wrinkle. Turned another way, pressed open, exposed to the light, it disappeared.

Just before she reached the end of the corridor and barely preceded by a slight scraping sound, she saw Tully crouched at the edge of the loft above her. He was biting his lips back from any identifiable expression. How strange he looked hooked over his knee bones, a crow. His eyelashes were long enough to cast shadows and blank out the surface of his eye so she couldn't see what he was looking at. He didn't talk to her the way he used to. That was when? He had killed the snake; she wouldn't forget that. To steady herself she put one hand flat on the post; the other wouldn't reach. She stretched. On each side the support and splinters of the wall were beyond the tips of her fingers.

'Hannah, Hannah, I got you some!' Nellie was poking a small brown bag of popcorn under her nose. 'Mmmmm, smell it.' In her exuberance some of the kernels hopped out. Hannah thought of the rats. 'Can your baby have some?'

'No, no honey, he's too small, he'd choke, he doesn't know how ...'

'Yeah, that's right, I remember.'

'Did Tully ...' she began, turning, but he wasn't there any more. What was happening here? Bending over, she put her arm around Nellie's shoulders, held her, nuzzled her forehead. She smelled the snow-water scent in her freshly washed hair, and the singed sharp popcorn. Nellie fed her. As they chewed they looked down at their shoes peeking out from beneath their skirts. Nellie stopped eating. 'I like them shoes,' she sighed, 'they're too big for me.'

'Why, when I was your age, that's just what they said to me!' Standing, Nellie came up just as far as her waist. That's a place I was, she thought. I used to be one whole thing, I'm sure. Memories were becoming heavier.

'Can you imagine being that small?' Addie had said, squinting through the hot sun. And 'Can you imagine ever doing that?' Or, 'What do they see, do you suppose?' They'd been watching the babies, sweet buns, eyeing each other in a languid sleepy stare on their blankets.

That world is lost to me now, isn't it? she thought. There was just this: A steep view down, watching over the children; squeezing, patting, turning them towards the sun. She'd always thought of the freedoms and privileges. What were these things coming her way? Instead of following her, irresistibly, in a bright agitated wake, the love in her life was breaching in front of her, a shimmering mirage, beckoning, building itself out of her breath. Instead of panting behind her, love cried and butchered, calling her by its own name. Instead of sniffing at her heels, it sprang up and convulsed, gripping her in its molten imagination.

Nellie was pulling on her. There was laughter, then a commotion. An argument. She couldn't hear the details. They didn't matter, but the loud voices of the men excited her as they swore and hunched against each other. 'By God!' shouted one of the men, his voice like a big white arm raised in the air. 'Stop!' Was that a woman's voice? The women were looking to see whose men were involved, then looking to each other, growling and shaking their heads.

Suddenly Hannah wanted her baby. She wanted out. This place was dangerous. Here were vultures and snakes. There was sport and bad temper and carelessness and hunger.

The woman holding Ben was craning up from her seat to see what was happening. She had let him slip down on the bale. He was trying not to wake up. Hannah could see him curling his feet to regain his equilibrium. A pale dog stood up, one paw on the straw, and licked the baby's face. Hannah hollered, but it was too noisy. She shook her skirt and kicked at the dog. 'Git, git – you gimme my baby!' snatching him up, scaring him awake. He gasped and started to cry. 'Look what you did!' No one heard her. Muffling the baby she began to dodge in and out of the knots of people gathered to see what was going on.

'Matthew, Matthew,' she called and called, her voice sliding shrill. Where was he? Was he in the fight? Was it a fight? Maybe someone didn't believe his story and had challenged him. Maybe he fought when he drank. Or maybe it was about her! Had Matthew followed her? He'd been worried. But he wouldn't have waited if he'd seen her in trouble. It would've looked like trouble to him. Standing still she began to twist from side to side. The baby held on for dear life. People crushed around her. Someone slipped a hand around her waist and squeezed her back. He whispered in her ear, 'Follow me.' He was holding her so tightly that she couldn't turn around. She tripped backwards. He caught her. 'Tully!' It had felt like a bigger person. 'Tully, who's in there? Who's fighting? What's happening?'

'Someone else must've seen you,' he mumbled. His lip curled. 'It's just cattlemen versus farmers, they're talkin' fences and ...'

'What?'

'You heard.'

'Oh,' she said, burying her cheek in the baby's neck. 'Oh that.'

Tully was taller than Hannah now. He leaned over her, smiling a soft sort of sly smile that she hadn't seen before, a smile that was older than he was.

'I didn't have any idea at all.' She stared at him. 'It was just so sudden it frightened me. Didn't it scare you?'

He smiled, this time to himself. 'Not much scares me any more.'

'Well, more and more scares me.' She didn't like him. She started to move away, but he snatched her arm, then put his hands on her shoulders. His hands were enormous. He slid them over the baby, completely covering him, arranging them in a way that stopped her. He put his hand right around the back of the baby's head and turned it so he could see his face. The pressure from his fingers seemed to depress the soft flesh and hair. The baby stopped crying. A tear stuck on his cheek. The way the light glistened, it resembled a tiny eye, little splits of light, a cat's eye. With the thumb of his other hand, Tully blotted the tear.

'Don't,' said Hannah, sweating, under her breath. 'Please don't.'

People were breaking apart, milling about, trying to find family. Matthew saw her. He was making his way through, gesturing. 'Come on, cookie, whatcha doing?' He was bright, flushed.

'Where were you?' she said, grabbing him in her eyes.

'Where were *you*?' Touching her cheek. Touching the baby's cheek. For the expression of his son, for the strong curve of her arms at work, for her creamy centre, Matthew loved her more than ever. He was full of outrageous love.

Exhausted but reluctant, people began to leave. It was dark morning. The cold was brittle and black. Everyone was still talking, the words shooting through the emptiness like bullets and disappearing. Hannah kept her head down. It was hard to remember what someone had just said. The words echoed in the well of darkness. Away out there in the night she imagined she heard the soft circular breath of her animals waiting for her.

She sat back on the seat, feeling the roll of the wheels, the ping of the horses' hooves up through the wagon. Voices spun. There was so much space between the people out there, but they had been smiling, hadn't they, in the beginning?

Each wagon veered in a slightly different direction, choosing the straightest, shortest way home. The roads were not firmed. Hannah liked roads already laid down by history and worn in by use. Stripped clean of snow by the last wind, the ground here was stretched out bare and dusty, a flat, hard, dull, indifferent surface, but inside the artlessness was a land of ambush, risk and manoeuvring. And it was the people who ambushed as well. Her eyes were growing used to this dark. She wouldn't need light again. A good thing, for there was no more light in the world.

'We have to get on the right side of things, you know.'

'What?' It was hard to hear over the noise of the wagon, and he was distracted by the rush of his breath into the cold air. She moved a little closer, but didn't repeat what she'd said.

A little later she said, 'You've always been my best friend.'

'That's what this is? Pooh.' A huff of frost.

'Well, you have to be now.'

But he was thinking and then said, 'Did you ever have a best friend?'

'I must have!' she said, patting her mouth with her big woolly-mittened fingers.

'Best friends walk side by side, you know.'

'What's that supposed to mean?'

'You've always been two jumps ahead.'

The air was dead cold on her cheeks. She faced front. She couldn't stand anyone so close they couldn't see her. 'But someone might step on me.' Her skin shivered and tightened.

Still later she said, 'Matthew, do you remember when I was little?'

'But I was little then too.'

'I know, but do you?'

'Remember – like what?' Knowing this wouldn't do.

'I don't know, just things about me that I can't remember.'

'Well, I'm sure I can't.' He blew a long thin breath to the cold, where it froze. Then, as if someone were walking over his grave, 'You know, sometimes I feel as if the past was eating up my footsteps as fast as I can lay them down and maybe even that isn't fast enough and it's going to suck the ground right out from under me.' The marrow in his bones shrivelled.

'Oh, I don't mind that.' In fact it was a comfort to her, what was past, so accomplished. You could see the beginnings and the ends of things. You could imagine how they could have been different but weren't. It was a safe place, the past, round and reassuring. It must have been something else that was gathering inside of her. Opening her coat, she pulled the baby against herself. Her body was sweetened by the heat of his body.

Wriggling over as close as she could, she spread her blanket over Matthew as well.

'Cold?'

It seemed inconceivable, now, that she had ever fallen asleep on the prairie at night. Somewhere else, anywhere else, she could sleep for a hundred years, but as she thought these thoughts she drifted off against the rattle creak groan of the wagon and Matthew slipped his arm around her as he felt her slouch.

He had to gently wake her when they arrived home. The barn was chilly without the horse's heat. The circle of light from the lamp was so small. The cow and her calf stirred and blinked in their stall. They thought something was wrong. Matthew rubbed the horse with straw and gave him a few handfuls of oats. Folding his arms, he leaned on the top of the manger and watched the horse eat. Bits of grain clung to a wet spot between his nostrils, and he rolled his eyes trying to see down his long Roman nose. This spring Matthew would have to get himself a fast horse. Stretching his back he thought how good that would feel. Just before the run, the crisp edge of anticipation, the ripple of energy back and forth in the muscles, the glistening start of sweat. A clean-limbed, deep-chested colt. He was partial to browns and bays, their legs were stronger. He had been listening as well as talking at the dance. Macons were breeding, and some folks from the sand hills. There was going to be more competition. A lot of people seemed to know about his ride last year. There was interest. Certainly he was interested. And if he fenced in that piece that ran the other side of the creek, there was good grass and the cottonwood shade. He could already feel the hot noonday sun.

On the way from the barn to the house, he stopped, hunched his shoulders, curled his hands in the pockets of his jacket. All around, the cold was holding bitter and bright. There was a sort of beauty to it, a purity, a possibility of thought, of counting stars, gracing the universe. For a moment he held time. The thousand dreams were sweet.

Inside, Hannah was hurrying. In just a few hours the air had thinned and dried. She used it to restart the fire. She hated it when the hearth was cold. It was as if her heart had stopped and the blood drained away. Angrily she banked the cold ash and watched the poor flame thread through the twist of straw. 'Come on, come-on come-on,' under her breath so as not to wake the baby, who was in the hammock of her skirt. She added husk and corncob. Soft waves of yellow light smoked up.

Though the baby had just a flush of hair, she brushed her hand over and over it. She wiped his head as if it had been soiled, and examined the soft spots at his temples as if for bruises.

Because his bed was cold, she wrapped him in another quilt, made a pillow of the warm corner and, brushing aside the dead air, laid him down in the cradle. Matthew was taking his time. She remembered how the furrow of earth had cradled her; that was with Matthew, down in there under Matthew; it was a kind of ritual and death. '... and you, my little fallen angel, my punishment. Revenge.'

'What are your dreams?' Matthew had asked in broad daylight.

The ground beneath her feet had trembled; her eyes had swung uneasily from side to side as if something might be loose, unattended and free.

'I used to be your dream,' she had said, finally. 'It's full-time!' Had he laughed then?

Now she was sweating, looking at her life as it lay around her.

Poised over the baby she whispered, 'Are you what he was dreaming then? Whose dream are you, anyway?'

Rhythmically she started brushing the front of her skirt. Soon she was rubbing it down hard as if there were something stuck that she had to push out. The heels of her hands ground back and forth. She squeezed the fabric; she would have ripped it, but it was too coarse. Her arms straightened and worked up and down. Again and again until she couldn't feel her hands, and when she looked they were bloodless white tools that wouldn't do what she wanted, that she didn't even know how to use. And still the clutch was up inside her.

Matthew opened the door. 'Fire went out, didn't it? Well, I didn't really expect ... wouldn't it be nice to come back to a warm house? Just imagine ...' He yawned. 'Too damn cold to take off my clothes,' though he did drop his boots before getting into bed. 'God, it's colder here than it was under the ice!' Shuddering between the chilled bolsters of fabric. 'Are you coming?' He couldn't see her face; she was turned. The light from the fire fussed around her.

'In a minute. Just a minute.' Whipped little words from the unknown place where she had dredged up breath to speak. And shiver. Moving closer to the stove she leaned over to wash the heat up into the curve of her body. Then she was too hot. She wanted to take off these clothes. The blouse, the skirt. She threw them on the trunk, her fingers still and fumbling. Kicked out of her drawers. She stared at them. There was fresh bright blood. From her astonished body. She stepped on it, but it wouldn't go away. It wouldn't be the last. And it wouldn't be enough. It would never be enough. Taking her. Making her give bit by bit. Nails, teeth, hair, skin. Blood. There would never be an end to it until she was all gone. It wanted her baby, too, this hunger did. It wanted to bend and break and swallow.

She gathered the hem of her petticoat up through her hand as if it were a drawstring and tightening it might keep any more of her from falling out.

'What are you doing?'

'Nothing, nothing.'

'Well, get over here.' And stop changing your shape, he wanted to add. A balloon of petticoat, arms folded like chicken wings, a crest of hair. 'Come in here where it's warm. Come in, said the spider to the fly.' He was silly with fatigue and firewater.

'Yes. Yes,' she said, darting to the web, because for just a moment, when she reached out, it was like reaching into the dark with nothing there.

Thirteen

One day, when they had forgotten there was any softness in the earth, it gave way beneath their boots. The third year on the land had begun. As they stood at the edge, they felt the land giving in. The whole prairie, all around them, rocked with green. The field lay down quiet and soft and waited for them. This very spot, this corner was where they'd begun. This year they would back-set the field and put in small grains, oats, wheat and rye; a strip of sweet corn with turnips in between, then push out the boundaries with sod corn.

When Hannah opened the barn door the animals came out, rushing and pushing. How anxious they were to get out of the stale close stalls. She saw how they held their heads up to see as far as they could, and sniff the smell of distances on the loose wind. Testing the quality of ground, they began to run, clenching their skins around them. They thrilled and plunged, shaking their heads, clomping on the hard spot of dried mud, scissoring into the switch of tall grass, and swinging their faces through the swollen heads of grass. In their wake, moths rushed whitely into the sunlight as if the sun had shed.

There was so much space for them. They were not afraid of it. She remembered Matthew in the morning, that look in his eyes. She hadn't known what it was. But now she did; it was forgetting. Abandoning the bottom of the earth for the back of a horse, for the wind pushing him. For joy.

But from where she stood, as he rode away, getting smaller and smaller, it was as if the earth were eating him up after all.

By this third summer, she had recognized the prairie chicken booming, 'Whoom-ah-who-m', and hopping in courtship, and the horned lark singing from the air its slow solo song. The quail woke her at dawn, and at the edge of the sloughs the trumpet and dance of the cranes fascinated her. She didn't step on the pale pasqueflower growing on the gravel to get the April sun, but collected its root for headache. There was wild onion, the lavender of sheepsorrel over clover-shaped leaves; Indian paintbrush, groundplum. Now she called the daffodil, yellow star-grass, and iris, the blue-eyed grass.

Hollyhock splashed up the front of the soddy clutching sun. Sweetpeas flushed and unfurled. Sticky-leaved petunias and adored pansies basked and baked in the yard, pushing the wildness back. There were fence posts without fencing, and she hung on to them one by one: they were all that stood between her and oblivion. The chickens were fenced in; this year she would have to have the yard done to keep Ben in. And the garden would also have to be enclosed.

When she rubbed clots of dirt between her hands, it felt familiar. The paths she walked had worn through the grass. Things they'd brought with them were gone now. She didn't feel quite as bad as she thought she would, in the heat and with Ben on her hip, behind her new belly. Matthew no longer waited for her, and where they used to walk together, speckled with kisses, she now followed Ben as he boiled over the bumpy ground.

She listened for Ben's breath because he wasn't much better. She'd thought he would be out of the dust and fumes of the house by now. Even with the window open she was up in the night, a diaper on her chest absorbing his exertion and damp wheezes. Occasionally he tried to nurse to comfort himself, but finding he couldn't breathe, pushed back from her in disbelief, then anger and frustration. She hummed a monotonous tune. Matthew didn't wake up.

After she got him to nap, tipped up so a breath of air went under his tummy, his arms turned out at the shoulders pulling his chest open just enough, she washed her face, then her arms, then, taking off the blouse, her chest and back. Tying the sleeves of the blouse around her breasts, she took the pan of water out for the pansies. A tub of water had been warming on the bench beside the house. Bending over, she ladled it into her hair and lathered the soap up. Her nose itched; it always did the moment her hands were wet.

High in the sky, the haze was sizzling. She put on an old white blouse worn through the elbows and as thin as gauze everyplace else. Drops of water slid down the ringlets of her hair and spotted the cloth for a moment, then evaporated. Ben was in a deeper sleep.

Hannah crossed the light in the yard. Before this place, she couldn't imagine there being too much sunlight. She had always thought of herself as a creature of the light. Now, holding her hand in a salute, she shaded her eyes and ducked beneath it. Delicious air held in darkness under the reach of the grove of trees; around her feet a drowse of warm grass, gnats in swarm, bees divining for nectar from the wells of prairie blossoms. The air was warm, animal, swollen on summer; it dozed in the thick shade, slumbered against the cage of sunlight, saturate, sinful. She tried to catch the leaves slipping, lolling. She tried to imagine what it was like under the grass, if it might be cooler, tickly. In the early morning, ducked down on the damp hem of her petticoat, she had stripped beaded dew from the cool surfaces of leaves and licked it from her fingers.

Riding south, sideways to the rising sun, Matthew watched his long thin shadow scythe over the grass. Rapid and flickering, the movement hypnotized him and even reminded him of something. A joke on him, a telling, a bad dream. What was it?

He stretched up and back so the sun rolled down his throat. Reaching behind his head, he poked his felt hat forward until it rested on the bridge of his nose, almost on the slight smile pressing his lips. The reins rested across the insides of his fingers. Through them he could feel the sway and bob of the horse's head. Between his legs, the body of the horse shifted and rocked. The energy rippled up Matthew's spine. Occasionally the horse ducked his head, wrapped his mouth around the sweet green morning rustle of grass, ripped off a bite, and chewed the air into a green froth, flinging it out in long streamers that lassoed the lace of wild flowers. A little breeze sweet-talked in the grass, scattering a shivery sort of sound that could be mistaken for rain or the skit of insects on the wing. When the legs of the horse kicked through, midges burst, whitening the air. An iridescent green old geezer of a fly buzzed loudly and lazily in the drench of soft hot air. Another fly came and went.

Faint and far, combed through the plumes of the tufted bluestem, was the exasperated song of birds rushing to get the morning's work done. Crows strolled the bare places. There was the red-winged wink of the blackbird. Matthew took a deep breath. The cool of the night and its dew, still clinging to the air, freshened. Well-being and calm flooded through him.

Before the sun, the bunt of the sky stretched and relaxed open. Wisps of cloud appeared in the new distances. The sky-blue thinned.

So complete was the warmth, so bright the light, so persistent the rhythm, that Matthew uneasily began to forget himself. He pushed himself back in the shadow of his hat brim. Strange things could happen to him out here. He was alone on all sides. The wash and wave of the grasses had swallowed everything in their swells. He caught his face thickening as it did when no one was looking at him, when he had lost sight of himself.

What would happen if he disappeared riding like this? Just a turn into the sun. It was a good distance. This was still the early morning in his life and that was why he was so hungry. All the things that hadn't happened yet – there was plenty of time, plenty of room here. Colour of daydreams, their bright amorphous daring, smarted on the insides of his closed lids.

The sun was midway up. Thick and hot it sank against him. It happened like that. Suddenly the air, heated to a solid, weightless, invisible silence stinking of the forge, plastered itself to his skin. Dry and hard, the air scraped down his throat. Sweat began to leach out where his skin was thin.

He was talking to himself now, in his head. He knew it had to be his voice, but the sound was distorted. Sometimes, without real shape, it rode the rhythm in his pulse. Or stretched and hummed as if crossing a wide hollow place. It was not the crisp of words with their edges burnt back and contained, recognizable. Not the names of things with their warm comfort fitting objects like old clothes. Rather, this was a loose slow swirl of sound, unravelling in his head, between his ears, mindless, without curiosity, an undulating vapour of ancient memories. Formed of all possible sounds, oddly it approached a silence that levelled his breath, thinned his blood and made him forget what he was seeing. And even though he couldn't remember when or how, he knew he had been there before.

'Whoa, whoa!' his voice raspy from disuse and distance. The big horse had almost gone out from under him, stumbling over the deep rut cut by the wagon wheels, but had recovered and climbed onto the high hard centre of the road. His hooves clomped on it. Tucking his thick neck, he watched his feet, which raised no dust. To one side, a midway of bees. To the other, the small dusty break in the prairie, indicating settlers. Someone Matthew didn't know, awfully close to the road. A tent still, and children not used to knowing where to hide. Their horses: two stood at attention carefully sniffing and snorting the air. Matthew patted his horse. 'Are you lonely old fellow?'

Hannah had said, 'This isn't a very fancy place, is it?' in passing, to herself. He had overheard. It endeared her to him. He saw that it was true. Tent pegs in the prairie. As long as the wind wasn't blowing!

The woman came to the flap of the tent, which was stiff with dust. Her hands stopped in her apron where she was wiping them. In the next moment she stepped back just inside, where the shadow protected her. The sun still shone on the twist of cloth in her fists. Matthew waved. He said hello. It didn't reach. He noticed that the ragged triangular opening to the tent was shaped like a woman.

A sharp noise ripped loose. Startled, he thought it could be a dog guarding the little skins of the children. He didn't want the legs of his horse torn. But it was nothing. The children stood there soaking in the unbearable silence. He couldn't tell if they were boys or girls. Their arms and legs, sticking out of their clothes, had been burnt sharp by the sun. Glancing from one to another, he couldn't count them all. Their eyes did not move smoothly in their heads but jerked sideways watching him ride by. He feared for himself in their bland gelatin eyes.

Unless something got them discouraged he'd pass by them each time, and likely, in a while, the house they'd build would become known as the turn-off point. It could become a crossroads. Other buildings would be built, a trading post, a blacksmith, hitching rails. People would stop, tie up and start to talk. The stories. Adding wooden sidewalks and awnings would encourage groups. Women – not that one, though – would plant eastern flowers in grim little picketed gardens, soon banked and buried in dust. And the children, those back there, already practising, sullen and pitiless, would be quenched and reheated in these seasons to something new and startling. Old men would dine on their best memories. Old women would wring out the salt and blood. Matthew, on the other hand, would be changing for the better.

It was a country for the imagination. Everyone said, 'You need a strong back and good feet. You have to love monotony, gloom and loneliness.' Matthew loved the light and the sky. The thin infinite horizon; he loved to cast his shadow in the morning and the evening. He liked the sound of the plough cutting new ground, the gunfire burst of roots as the blade sliced them through. He loved his seed. The breadth of air. There were spaces where, if he turned his back and rode away, he was the tallest and strongest and fastest thing in the world. He loved to hope and dream. He loved distances.

And he loved a fast horse.

In a while they came to a shallow creek, but the water was clear and welcome. Upstream, Matthew refilled his canteen. He splashed his face and poured a hatful of water over the back of his head. Downstream, some cattle were standing and switching in the shade of willows; every eye was on him. Once in a while their lower jaws shifted from one side to the other. Plucking his rifle from its sheath, he popped them off one at a time to the accompaniment of the throaty explosions he had practised since childhood. Getting back up on the horse, he rested the rifle across the top of his shoulders and as soon as they were on their way, knotted the reins, dropped them and hung his hands over the ends of the weapon, which stretched his arms in a way that he liked.

There were a few more settlements since the last time he'd been along this route. The spring migrations. Wagons gaping open, oxen standing together from force of habit, lines of laundry. People were spilling out all over. Sad hot people who looked like this was their last chance but were willing to work for it. Tiredly they came in waves over the great distances that were new to them. Matthew was glad he went farther to a place where he couldn't see his neighbours or hear them slamming things and coughing. He saw what he saw from here and wasn't curious beyond that. They were saving all their strength for the breaking work ahead, and even though they were waving their new turkey-red calico bandannas at him and watching, he didn't want to stop for the stories of life back home, the friends and families left behind, by God, the blessed dark between trees, the soft low sky. As long as no one was actually in sight on the land, he could imagine that it was his, all of it, as far as he could see, which was a giant's stride.

By rights he should tell them about the electric green sky of a tornado, the dry whim and whine of the wind, how the sun sharpened itself. He should tell these good people. Rumour was they'd need each other: politically, things were going to get sticky out here.

Had they noticed that there were no echoes, that their shadow was the only one, that contrary to prediction the prairie didn't make one humble?

Farther on, where the land suddenly folded and sank to a wide dry bed that supported soap weed and sweet pea and a tumble of small rocks, Matthew turned to the left instead of continuing along the old road. There used to be a renegade family of Indians camping for the summer, but he'd heard they'd been moved because this way was a short cut, taking a good hour off the usual travel time. Already, the narrow single-footed path was being widened by riders abreast, by carts and wagons. From time to time, a swath of flattened grass veered off and over the rise. After a while he left the path to ride along the ridge where he could see.

Towards evening, he decided to stop. He should push on, he thought, but it was not much farther and it was nice out here. All over the land was that smell of quiet accomplishment. The day's work was finished.

Hobbling the horse, he stripped off the saddle and blanket, turning them out to the air. He pulled peppered sausage, bread, mustard from his bag. The water in the canteen was warm. By the time he got in and was settled he'd want something else.

He walked back and forth on the crest of the hill, and kicked rough rocks down the incline. Wind and the weight of ice had eroded the ground here. In the back of his mind a little song was playing itself over. It sounded pretty good in there. He didn't remember all the words; his tongue shaped those that he did. When Molly fiddled and his father sang and slapped his thigh, he never did pay much attention. What a long time ago that seemed. A penumbral, perfect image. He saw himself small, pale and new. Then curiously he noticed that other than the see-saw of the bow and the whack-dance of his father's hand nothing was moving in his memory. It was their parlour, but everything was faded and slightly flattened like one of those new photographs, and could have been anyone's image. This lasted for just a moment and he decided it wasn't very important, but *was* why it seemed perfect. Besides, if he needed to remember something, he did.

He had never been disappointed in a big way.

He felt someone staring at him. Glancing around, the sun flooding his eyes, he couldn't make out who it was. Moving to one side he put the sun behind the figure, which shone out like a halo or a solar eclipse. It was a man on a horse. The horse's feet were so small that the sun seemed to get under them and it looked as if the horse was standing on sunlight. It tossed its head, splitting the light off in a shower of white. The rider took a slight hold and eased the horse forward along the top of the hill towards him. They were in no rush.

Matthew grabbed his hat. Picking up the saddle blanket he slapped it against his leg and flipped it on the back of his horse, who tried to walk away. Stepping on the rein to hold him, Matthew threw the saddle up, wiggled it and reached under for the cinch. The horse hopped sideways. Matthew loosened the cinch ring. 'Damn you, whoa, stand there now! Whoa!' He didn't want to be on the ground out here. The shadow of the rider was pumping ahead of him like a long searching arm. Matthew didn't want it to touch him. Hauling the rifle up he held the end of the barrel in one hand and leaned the stock against his leg. He adjusted his hat. Beneath the horse's belly, the cinch lolled and twisted.

When the rider finally stopped, a little scuff of dust rolled on until it bumped up against Matthew's boots, but it wasn't until the other man readjusted his position, moving his horse to the left, that he saw who it was. Someone he recognized but couldn't place. 'Don't I know you?' he said. Gradually his eyes adjusted.

'Yes, you do. Instead of a gun I carry a fiddle!' He laughed. For a moment he was laughing by himself, then Matthew caught on and pushed the gun away from himself self-consciously.

'You were coming right out of the sun. I couldn't see who you were.'

Gabriel let his horse sniff Matthew's.

'What are you doing out here?' Matthew asked. In the middle of nowhere on that extraordinary animal.

'Riding this one.' He pointed from at least two feet out.

'Yeah, I see that. Where'd she come from?'

'South. They say she's got Spanish blood.'

'Really!' Stepping back and around to the side, Matthew looked. He wanted to touch, but the horse was watching him. 'Whoa there, lady, whoa, easy now.' She switched her tail smartly and moved one foot over, planting herself on a wider base. 'Where you going, sweetheart? No place to go now, easy now.'

'So?' Gabriel crossed his arms and rested on the saddle horn.

'Nice,' said Matthew, his breath too fast and frantic. He had to swallow it. His throat, dry and cautious, tensed. Slipping his hands into his pockets, he rubbed them on the soft cotton. 'Damn good lookin' horse.'

'The best.' Gabriel smiled gently. Matthew looked at him. He'd never seen him in the daylight before. He finished saddling his horse.

Matthew said, 'If you're on your way back, I'll ride with you.'

'Going to work, actually.'

Was that a yes or a no?

For a while, side by side, they rode in silence. Matthew's horse hung back just enough for him to keep his eye comfortably on the mare.

Despite the dry heat, her coat was sleek. The colour shimmered dark brown, but he had the feeling that if rubbed the wrong way like velvet, it would reveal a rich black. Tiny veins arched and beaded on her shoulders and face. Except for a soft tremor where the long muscles crossed the width of her flank, she was lean, almost stringy. Her shoulder blades slid back and forth under the sheath of skin. She was watching him out of the corner of her eye, flicking her ears. The edges of her nostrils flared and fluted to catch his scent. Any sound, any movement, shivered on her skin. She lifted her feet carefully.

Matthew was hungry again. This was hunger, wasn't it, the pit of his stomach crumpling in?

'Is it a living, what you do?' Gabriel was shaping a cigarette paper to hold loose tobacco. Expertly, he rolled and tucked, tapering the ends, then with a quick light lick along the length, glued it. 'Out there,' squinting his eyes to look.

'Oh, barely. But it depends on what you want. I don't seem to want the same things that other people do.' A hint of pride in his voice.

Gabriel turned; he was interested. 'Is that so?'

'What I have in my hand doesn't matter as much as, well, what I still want.'

'And what is that?'

Matthew shrugged.

But Gabriel had missed it.

In a while, they crossed the edge of a stagnant slough, then turned onto the flat back of the road into town. Here the beaten ground gave up dust that ruffled low before them. The mare kept her nose in the clear air. Matthew noticed how she reached with her feet, getting a few extra inches each step.

As soon as the sun had blossomed orange, the heat dropped out of it and the air became still. Gabriel removed his hat, rolled it up and scratched his hair.

'You'd like to ride her, wouldn't you?'

Matthew sucked a deep breath; it slowed him down. 'Sure, who wouldn't?'

Gabriel rode on a way before saying, 'Maybe tomorrow.' Matthew's eyes fell naturally to the horse.

They circled around the wagons parked at the back of the church and headed into the hotel from behind. Unable to take his eyes off her,

Matthew dismounted first and took the reins of the mare. On the ground he was surprised at how small and perfect she was. He touched the slope of her neck.

'She's keeping her eye on you. She must know you have designs on her.'

Together they put their horses up. Gabriel waited for Matthew to collect his things. While waiting he moved so that he could play his shadow over Matthew's back. Squeezing through the door, Gabriel put his hand on Matthew's shoulder. Inside, he said he'd get them some supper and made sure that Matthew was seated.

For the moment the room was quiet; a few hangers-on sipped their coffee. The women waited for the men to finish their cigars, and looked on disparagingly as the lazy little girl swept around the chairs.

In a few minutes she brought a tray.

When he joined him, Gabriel crossed his arms and leaned forward over the table, intimately, as if he had secrets.

'Aren't you hungry?' Matthew asked over the plate of beef, boiled vegetables and bread. Arched over the food, he could barely stop to talk.

'Just thirsty.' Gabriel rhythmically tapped his beer glass with his fingernails.

'I don't know what's wrong with me,' said Matthew, glancing up between bites, 'why I'm so hungry.'

'Go on, go on, there's more of everything.' Gabriel took a drink and continued to watch him eat. Once in a while, he looked down at his wrists and hands, which displayed little chains of white powdery dust. A smile started and stopped on his lips. As if grazing, he slowly raised his eyes over Matthew's arms, up the buttons on his shirt one by one to where the collar opened on a pale triangle of flesh, the throat working like an accordion as it swallowed. It was admirable, enviable, that simple straightforward hunger. Entering to satisfy itself, it had a life of its own, interrupting the body, taking over. If you weren't careful, it could eat you up, instead, from the inside out, leaving an old skin deflated and shrivelled. He'd seen that, a maggot-eaten carcass hollowed out except for the bones, hair, a dull flat pelt of skin. And the terrible aching hunger, moving on. All the corridors of the body opening and closing, surging and sucking, rippling in spasms, in warm recognition around the desire he felt at night. He felt it coming in the dark when he was soft and lost, oozing out of the places where it slept in his body, his flesh pulled up around as if to hide itself. The way it pretended it wasn't there so that sometimes he felt completely free of it, actually lighter in body and spirit, and began to dream of apples and sleep.

He envied Matthew his ease, the way he kept his head above the horizon, and his woman.

Sometimes it took his breath as well, snatching it just at his throat so his speech was broken and distorted. He had to catch himself, hold himself back behind, waiting for it to let go. He had to pause as if he didn't know what he wanted to say.

Across the table Matthew was settling down. Rounding up the last juice with a crust, he slowly put it in his mouth and swallowed, then took a deep breath. The room around was pink in twilight and skins. He was dopey with fatigue. Resting the ends of his fingers on the edge of the table, he pushed back, indecisive as to what to do next. 'Well?' Suddenly he yawned, his body tensed.

Gabriel didn't dare tighten his skin; if he did, it would crack and steam. He had to keep it soft and elastic over the angles, the uncertainties. He moved slowly and didn't get off balance. He didn't reach for things. His grin was stylish and ready. From behind it he watched and waited. Beside himself. Despite himself. Always hungry. Hunting eyelids heavy, half folded. The little girls told him he looked sleepy; they wanted to stroke the sleep and bandage him in their arms, but he didn't like their hard narrow laps. He rubbed his hand through his hair.

Generously Matthew tilted back in his chair. 'Mind if I ask you a question?'

'No, I don't mind.'

'Where, er, how, did you get that horse?'

'Won her.'

An exaggerated, unbelieving sigh escaped his chest. 'That hurts, whoa, that really hurts.'

'Right time, right place.' Gabriel clasped his hands under his chin and leaned on them. 'And the luck.'

'That was all there was to it, the game?'

Nodding, Gabriel slipped a finger up over his lips.

'Did you lose anything first?'

'Nothing I had.'

Matthew didn't understand that, but it didn't matter. I'm a lucky person, he thought, but I'm not in the right place at the right time.

'That's a once-in-a-lifetime thing to happen, you know.' How inappropriate, he thought, for this swollen boy to have such a wonderful creature. She should be his. He could feel her between his legs, his calves nestled in the muscles of her shoulder, the wide leap of her ribs, the wrinkle of the skin just in front of her withers when she raised her head. Listening to him. Coiling her ears to catch his whisper. Holding herself ready and responsive. The light line of rein to her mouth. She tossed froth on her legs, at her feet. He would paint her hooves with oil to make them flash in the sun as she ran, and run she would, to the edge of the earth for him. When he had touched her, in just that little moment, he knew she would do anything for him. Some people said horses were stupid for doing that. But in return he would take care of her. In return she would have someone who knew everything about her. After a race, he would wash her down, squeezing the water over her flanks, the way he did for Hannah when she stood in the tub shivering with delight, shaking her head, flicking the water from her fingers, switching her hair, showering him. Then she held out her arms and let him dribble water all along the length and under her raised chin, down the centre of her back, spreading it on the wings of her hips; watching the ribbons of water slowly streaking.

'I have to go to bed,' he said. 'I'm beat. See you in the morning?'

'I'll walk out with you. I've got to get my guitar and go to work.'

Gabriel didn't go back immediately. He stood at the bottom of the stairs and watched Matthew climb to the top. It wasn't until he was out of sight that he turned.

For a few minutes while the room was empty and dark, Gabriel laid himself open. He was in the shadow, as black as shadow.

Matthew's room was just around the corner. Locking the door he stripped to his shirt and climbed into bed. It wasn't at all like it used to be, but in the dusk before sleep, surprised by the degree of his fatigue, the muffled brush of song and the gust of voices reminded him of being put to bed in the other room before the grown-ups were finished. Listening, at first to the words, humming the tunes, then, later, merely absorbing the good humour and the syllables. Drifting on a raft built of voices until reaching the rapids of his own dreams, violent and glorious. The loose-tongued curtains lolled at the window.

* * *

The clouds moulded on the northern horizon until they looked like mountains. They made distant bogus thunder. The ground beneath the clouds cooled and pulled the hot air away from its sunny bath on the golden grass. As it travelled, it swept and blended the grasses, which chattered noisily in Tully's ears. It didn't matter, he didn't have to hear anything. He just wanted to hide and see. Crouching in the grass he caught his breath. Last time he looked she was standing in the shade of a tree, but whatever else she was doing was unclear. He wiped the sweat from his forehead and jerked his shirt in and out a few times to fan himself. Parting a hank of dense shoots, he peeked through. She wasn't there any more, must have gone back inside the dusty little soddy. He started to circle back. It would be too easy for her to see him if he crossed the creek by the slope of the hill. There was a blind spot where the ramshackle cow shed was aligned with the house. Sidling like a monkey, he began to pant. It was hard on his hands, too, the sharp broken stubs of grass. The dust he scuffed up stuck in his nose. He rested again, giving his knees a chance to recover.

Edging closer, he saw the usual summer junk strewn all about: table, butter churn airing, washtub, buckets, rope and tools, a constant flutter of diapers signalling from the line. Her flowers were doing well. That was a surprise; he thought the seeds would have been poisoned by her touch.

The old letters lay on the table in front of Hannah. She smoothed the edges. This was the life Molly had put on paper. Which one was this? Which year? For a moment she thought it might have been lost in the post, but it was the same old letter, the same place in Molly's life. The scenery had changed. The streets ran north/south instead of east/west. The horses wore green instead of blue, and the names of the men were Patrick and Sean instead of Alrik and Peder. But she hadn't given in. It isn't my life, thought Hannah, but she had imagined herself in it, someone with a swift and furious talent. She rearranged the letters: '… the usual frantic search for a place to live … I'm getting sick of studying even though … getting on with it … you wouldn't believe what they'll hire a musician to do!'

Hannah thought of Matthew walking out in front of her to be beyond her shadow. The dust he kicked up dirtied everything in the path. Fanning her fingers open, she rubbed pinwheel designs on the smooth mount of her belly. '… one night on a boat, in some sort of a costume, while they rowed their ladies up and down in the darkness and the white dresses made of moonlight ... I sleep till noon ... I have breakfast on a tray, silver teapot, napkin ring, a pink rose in a crystal bud vase, a peach, yellow cornmeal muffins ... sometimes I don't want to get up ...' Hannah had read that letter twice, but couldn't figure out which way to take it. It could be sad, a mistake, because Molly only paraded her coloured lights. Her smile dazzled and razor-slashed whatever it opened on. By thrusting the notes of music and the warmth of her breath in front, she made a fragile bridge that trembled even as she walked across it and dissolved as soon as it cooled. But her feet didn't get dirty.

Flattening the letters, Hannah patted them into a neat pile. She leaned forward until her belly bumped into the table. This was the kind of place that could make a person discontent, yearning for release from the present season. It was always an extreme. Now she longed for the clean cold of winter; in six months she'd wish for the open air heat of summer. With the tips of her fingers she swept a small spot clear of dust, but it had dulled and coloured the wood, and she could hardly tell the difference. The sun was at noon now, retreating from her window, climbing. Once it got overhead she was protected. Its weight was there on the roof. So far she trusted the roof. The baby shifted and sighed.

In the beginning she'd been able to stay here alone, in ignorance, hating it, but bearing what she had thought was emptiness. No longer. Now she knew how close and disguised everything was. It could look like neighbours or old women, a pink plump child, what she imagined love to be, adventure, life. Her own or someone else's. It could make sounds in a language she thought she understood. It could look like something simple and dull, something dropped in the dirt. It could be in her hand. In her head. In her heart. It hurt. It didn't even care and it hurt. It didn't know her. It didn't look where it was going. If she yelled, 'Watch out!' it wouldn't hear her. It wasn't fair. It was supposed to know she was here and keep an eye on her. She didn't know where to look, but knew she'd better be watching all the time.

Glancing up, she thought she saw Matthew walking away again, his back straight, in a hurry, but as if uninterested in the real destination. The place he was going couldn't be seen, but he couldn't take his inner eye off it. It might vanish, but if it did, she noticed, it was only to sneak around and jump up behind him, screeching in the delight of having scared him. From behind, where she stood, she could see this. She never warned him. It was a conspiracy or perhaps she thought, one of the times he turned, he would see her again in the old way when she wasn't looking. She yearned. Gripping her hands up to her mouth, she bit them. Perhaps the women had to walk behind the men so they could keep an eye out for things that might sneak up and jump them. Matthew probably didn't trust her any more. But if that was true he wasn't letting on.

She loved the shape of his back in his blue shirt. She ironed out the wrinkles, but they reappeared to caress him. He filled her thoughts. To the basic outline of her he added colour, texture, fragrance, heat. By pushing all the air out of her lungs, she could get him even closer, an ache, a lump in her chest. She closed her eyes: she was washing his hair in the spring water that had come down smelling of the mountains; laying her cheek on his bare shoulder after the sun had been soaking in it all day; hearing his voice in the air close to her ear, and the murmur of it through his body, the other words he didn't know he was speaking. When he listened at her belly she said, 'What was it? I can't hear that.' Parting the silky waves of his hair. He stood and sucking in his stomach pressed her against him to fill the hollow, and she pushed in until she was all along the length of him, sticky. 'Gotcha,' he said. 'Gotcha,' she said.

Tully couldn't decide what to do. Sitting down on the hump of weeds by the shed, he put his head in his hands. His face felt funny, the bones too sharp and hard. When he squeezed his skull it didn't budge, he couldn't tap the pressure inside. The noon sun spread. The chickens had stopped pecking. Wiping the weep of sweat from his brow, he tensed all his muscles, relaxed them, tightened them again, trying to force out some of the terrible energy backed up inside him. He had to be careful. But what he could see of his body, his arms and legs, surprised him, though they looked as they always had. Maybe his secrets didn't show after all, and he wouldn't have to think about hiding them. He'd thought everyone was looking at him all the time. His mother could see through walls, he didn't doubt that. But she didn't know about this; if she had, she wouldn't have let him go. Kid stuff, she knew all about kid stuff, but not this. A sudden whack startled him. Something fallen over. He shook his arms loose. The silence resettled like birds after a fright.

Lurching forward, he checked the deserted yard. Nothing to either side. He knew she had a table near the window and could be there. He sneaked into the thin curtain of shade on the side of the house. Wind was eating the sod away; he started to crumble a loose piece, then froze. What if she could hear? How stupid! He leaned on the dirt wall. It was still hot. He straightened, dizzily pulling away. Could she hear that? He had to be careful. He worked along the edge, skinning the corner. There were so many obstacles: he could sneeze on the dust, bump into that coiled rope hanging from a hook, upset that rusty old washtub.

The sweat was running down the insides of his legs, pasting the cloth to his skin. If he could get to the door and peek in, find out exactly where she was, see what she was doing ... One thing about the prairie, there was no place to hide. Once he was there, she'd see him. The silence and the light exploded when touched. It wasn't going to be the way he'd planned; he'd have to do something else.

'Oh, Tully!' She was flushed, moving slightly as if to hide something. 'You scared me.' Her hands clutched then unwound. 'What do you want?' Stepping forward, extending her hand. 'I'm glad to see you. I hate being here by myself, well, with just the baby,' gesturing off-handedly, openly, toward the crib. 'It's just, I didn't see you.' She stared at him. 'I didn't hear you.' The thought was incomplete. 'I must have been thinking of something else. It doesn't matter, you're here. What can I get you?' Wondering what it would be. 'I haven't seen you for a while.'

'I see you.'

At once she remembered him crouched like a vulture in the hayloft. She looked at his hands. Had he taken hers a moment ago? No, he hadn't. He hadn't touched her yet.

'Well, let me ...' Turning quickly, nervously, she scooped the letters up off the table.

'Who are all those from?'

'They're from ...' She stopped; his tone had been authoritative. 'Who do you think they're from?'

'Oh, I don't know; a secret admirer.'

'What makes you think there are secrets here?' She meant to tease, but her voice was tense and defensive.

'Aren't there any?'

'Everyone has some, I suppose.' He was making her tired. 'I'm not interested in secrets.' She put the table between them and spread her fingers along the edge for balance. 'What do you want, Tully?'

'That's no secret.'

'I told you I'm not interested in secrets. Why do you keep saying that?'

'I see what you are.'

She opened her mouth but couldn't think of anything to say. Exasperated, she closed her eyes and sighed.

'I know what kind of a person you are,' he said.

'What can I say?' Jokingly, smiling. But she had to leave the smile there, pasted insecurely.

'You're a special kind of person.'

'I don't know what you're saying.' She was thinking how damn big he was. When had he done all that growing? His body blocked all light from the doorway. He was as big as a man. 'What are you saying?' Her voice sounded small, as if coming from a pinched place.

'What? What was that? I can't quite hear you.'

'I said, what are you trying to say?' Giving each word its own air.

'I'm sorry.' He broke sideways, throwing his hands up a little ways, looking around apologetically. 'I guess I'm not trying hard enough.' He walked. His steps were too big. Almost crashing into the stove, he halted mid-stride, turned, turned again. Before he knew it, he was standing at the crib. 'To be able to sleep like that. Just look at that.' He found Hannah where he'd left her. 'The next time I sleep like that I'll probably be dead.' He laughed. 'Has he been sick again?' His face opened. 'I just remembered, he's not a well baby, is he? Probably something touched him. Yes, that could be it, something touched him a long time ago. Can you think of when it would have been? That's one thing about mothers, they're there all the time; if anything happens they know – right? Right? Isn't that right!'

'Right. Right,' she whispered.

'Can't you remember anything? You're a smart girl, Hannah, can't you –'

'And you're a smart boy.'

His lips thinned and spread into a smile. He turned on her, but one hand slowly reached for the crib behind him.

'Don't.'

'Don't what?'

'Don't wake him up.' Don't touch him. Don't hurt him.

'Ah! Mother's fears.' He brightened. 'And furies!' Glancing to see what he was doing, he extended one finger and lightly traced the smooth

263

stones of the baby's spine. He smiled at Hannah, cocking his head to one side.

She was watching his hand. 'I asked you not to do that.' She was gathered. 'Please.' The smile clenched. She hesitated. Her throat was too tight.

'You see, you see, you're a rude person.' He swung his arm up and pointed at her.

'Tully, why – why have you come here?'

'You're curious.'

Gently and evenly she measured the words. 'Yes. Of course.'

'You scared?' He was whispering.

'I don't know who you are.'

'You know exactly who I am. I'm the one who watches you when you think you're alone. Don't you remember, didn't you feel it? You must have. Once in our garden. At the dance, I know you remember, you saw me. Maybe you only thought you saw me, but that was real.'

'But why?'

Her mouth looked so soft and helpless, open like that.

'What? What is it?' Now she tucked her lips in, closing her mouth, closing herself in again. He'd have to get closer.

'I'm the one who's going to steal it back from you.'

Her chest heaved painfully.

'Come out. Stand here in the middle.'

She wouldn't have believed that she could move, but she did.

He circled around her, sniffing. There was a strong scent. He'd smelt it on himself when he was afraid. It smelled good on her. He could see it in waves rising from her skin in the heated air. It rose and floated up into the dark underside of the roof. He knew this, but he didn't watch it. He was keeping his eyes on her. As he circled around her he imagined that he was wearing out the floorboards, that his feet were digging a deep trench and that when it was finished he would climb out and fill it with fierce creatures that would lay their chins on the bank and smile up at her. He stopped in front of her. 'Open your eyes. Look at me. Do it!'

She did.

'I didn't think I could get this close.' He was right there in her eyes. She was going to fall. He grabbed her shoulders. Fear had made her heavy, but he could still hold her up. A thick breathy sound was coming from her, not crying though her whole face was now gleaming and unearthly pale. And he could feel her heart too, beating wildly through her body into his hands. I've got it, he thought, I've got her heart between my hands.

'You know what I thought?' What was she saying? What was she doing talking to him? 'I – I thought you'd come to help me. You always help me, Tully. You always come when I need you.'

'No! No! You're a thief. I came to tell you you're a thief. I don't want to hear anything from you. You steal life. You steal it and lose it. Stop crying. Stop it. Shut up. I came to tell you –'

'Please, you're hurting me. Please let go, don't hurt me, don't hurt me any more.' She got her hands up against him. They were weak and cool, fluttering like white birds. He crushed them between their bodies. It was easy, he was so much bigger than she was. He put his arms around her, slid one hand up under her hair. It was like putting his hand into fire. But he grabbed it and held her face against his bones where she couldn't hurt him. 'I came to take something, but you're going to steal this too, aren't you?' His voice was shaking and getting louder. He threw her away from him. 'You're not hurt. You're tough. I didn't hurt you at all.' He could hardly stand to look at her. 'There's not one mark on you. Not one single mark.'

She didn't dare turn her back. She could feel the end of the table against her legs. Reaching back she got hold of it with her hands. She dropped her eyes to the floor.

'I'm going now. You won't say anything. There's nothing to say.' He stopped at the door. 'Maybe I can come again and see you. There might be something you need help with. One of the times when you're alone and you want some company.'

As soon as he was gone she locked the door and shuttered the window. She tried to wake Ben and finally gathered him, still drowsily sleeping, into her arms. She sat in the sweltering dark to watch the thin lines of light from the cracks in the door for sudden breaks.

* * *

Gabriel and Matthew left messages for each other at the desk. Gabriel's said, 'Don't look for me before noon. Sleeping in.' Matthew's said, 'Doing all the errands first, meet you back here?'

Matthew was no longer a stranger. Around town, people took his word and gave him credit. They told him about newcomers and wiled away the time with him. The news of his miraculous ordeal in the snow was still topical, though filtered. Men and boys gathered to hear it directly from him, and after appropriate reverence offer their own tales of recovery, of being lost and found. It was a popular form of trade and was time-consuming. It was mid-afternoon when he returned to the hotel.

'It's still on, isn't it? Do you think it's too hot? I don't know, I don't think so, they're used to it, don't you think?'

Using his bare-bones army model, the one he was used to, Matthew saddled the mare. 'What's her name?'

'Gracia.'

He tried it out. 'Gra-c-ia.'

'He told me it had to do with grace. But more than that, something about the way men feel about her, her peculiar ability to charm and fascinate. No, seriously, that's what he told me. He didn't want to give her up.'

'But he was an honourable man.'

'No, he was in too much of a hurry.' Gabriel leaned over the fence rail, exhausted by the memory. 'He couldn't do her justice.'

'And you?'

Gabriel smiled. 'Don't push it.'

Matthew creased the reins in his fingers.

Gabriel signalled thumbs-up. 'You ready?'

Matthew was sitting tight, one hand on her neck, the other jiggling the reins. To Gabriel he looked like a little boy about to unfold new wings. 'She knows something's happening.' He preferred to walk beside them. Every now and then, he placed his hand on her shoulder where it came up damp and he rubbed the sweat off on his trousers. Not used to his walking beside her, she ducked her head and poked him in the stomach. 'Here, here, stop that.' She'd slobbered on the front of his shirt. Matthew lifted the reins. 'Stop that,' he repeated, but she was everything he'd hoped for.

Just the other side of the railroad tracks was a warren of holding pens and loading chutes. Beyond that, a haphazard fence, beginning to enclose a bare field, suggested a large circular track. 'We'll start from over there,' said Gabriel, pointing to a high open gate. 'Can you see where it goes? Why don't you take a turn around to warm up and get used to each other.'

Matthew nodded. His throat was working, his mouth opening and closing as he tried to swallow. Gabriel put his hand on Matthew's boot. 'You know.'

'I do, I know what to do.' The mare jumped to the side. 'Not yet girl, not yet, easy.'

'But she knows what you want.' Raising his eyebrows, wagging his finger, Gabriel liked what he saw.

But it wasn't until he couldn't see them very well, for the dust and distance, that he reluctantly climbed the gate. He hated to leave the ground. He was best in his bare feet with the dirt filling in the cracks, the soft tides of earth rising between his toes. The land held him down, he felt its pull. A long time ago he dug a hole, stood in it and buried his feet. He asked his mother to pull him out and she did. He wouldn't fall off if he stayed low and remembered what he'd learned.

Matthew was urging the mare forward, then circling to the right, to the left, bringing her to a stop, making her back up, then walk until she went on a loose rein. Gabriel could tell he was talking to her all the time, from the movements of his head, scolding, cajoling, coaxing, playing her out to her limits. At the far turn he dismounted, led her around himself, dropped her rein, and walked away. Surprisingly she had been taught to ground-tie. He crouched to talk to her. After sniffing the air, she put her head down.

'She listens to you. I could see it,' Gabriel said when they got back to the gate.

The next time around, Matthew jumped her several times as if starting a race and let her gallop on the soft edge of the circle to see if she was clever with her feet, which she was and more.

'This round, I'll time her.' As she ran away from him, Gabriel listened to the drum of her hooves, at first beating loudly on the ground as if to break it open, then gradually fading until he could barely hear, and he wondered if she had left the earth and really was flying.

'Again?' Matthew's face was feverish, his shirt soaked and sticking to his arms and back. Bright thrill glittered in his eyes. His breath was full of force and excitement. Gabriel liked the harsh noise of it. He could see heat waves when the mare bellowed the air out from deep within her body. The energy spilled from them, and he licked it up, tasting it as if it were something he'd been deprived of. There was excess of it, they were so reckless and powerful together.

'Again.' He had them on the tether of his stop watch. He played them out on the long line of time he had up his sleeve, then reeled them in, slowly, quickly, letting them think they were free. He let them begin their own dreams, then pulled them back. Let himself out of their sight so they thought they were alone. He could even imagine that there was nothing that didn't happen except by the brute execution of his will, so much so that when he climbed the gate again, it was easier to stand high.

It was a pale sultry evening. The air had thickened and become purposeful, gathering moisture for a rain. Sounds carried up as if calling the clouds in, and the sun was already coming and going. Instead of their usual chatter and trill, the children were fierce and wild, beating picket fences wherever they found them, shooting tin cans and the occasional old bucket to a dismal well-ventilated death. Dogs defended their half acres, cats stiffened as the electricity danced off the ends of their fur. Out back in the paddock, the horses pranced from one side to the other, stretching their necks over the rails, snorting, tossing their heads at each other, spinning on their heels, rushing to the other side again. Women throwing dishwater out on the flowers paused as if thinking about something, but when they tried to remember what, it turned out to be nothing.

Matthew was sitting in a tub of water, knees drawn to his chest. Just when he thought she'd finished bringing kettles of boiling water, the girl appeared once more. He thought he'd locked the door. He had, but she had a key. He'd just put one foot in the tub when she pushed in. 'Jesus,' he said and squatted down, hoping to raise as much water as possible around his pearly pink flanks.

She didn't even hesitate. 'How hot is that?' he asked, scrunching tighter.

'Not so much by the time I get it up here.' But she poured it carefully around the edges.

'Do you want me to scrub your back?'

'Is that part of the service?' He was beginning to feel sorry for her.

'You might pay me something.'

'Honey, for your nerve alone.'

'What does that mean? Do you want me to or not?'

'Get your brush.'

She produced a wicker tray fitted with brush, soap and sponge. After another brief disappearance, during which she got a last bucket of water, she was ready.

'Wait a minute, maybe this is over my ...' But she was dunking the sponge in the water and scrubbing its surface with the soap. 'Well, you look like you know what you're doing.'

Bending sharply at the waist, she rubbed circles across his back. He could feel the lather change from coarse crisp bubbles to a fine froth. Dropping his head forward, she pressed her fingers through the sponge to massage the back of his neck. Blowing on the water, he could dent it. She took his arms one by one. She lifted his feet. Tilting his head back onto the thin edge of her arm, she placed a small white folded cloth over his eyes, then soaped his hair. He let her do all this. He began to expect it, this being carefully groomed as if to prepare him for some special event. When she was finished, she handed him the sponge and turned her back to him. Her hands hung at the sides of her skirts. Water slid to the ends of her wrinkled fingers and dropped to the floor. He guessed he should say something, but was arrested by the way her white clothes draped like southern moss from the acute shape of her body. Her immobility, boredom, indifference. He couldn't think of anything to ask her.

Fetching the pitcher from the dresser, she filled it from the bucket. 'Up,' she said. He hesitated, then in inspiration shook out the small cloth to its full dimensions, and covering himself rose slowly and carefully in profile. In just the right amounts, she poured the cool refreshing water over his shoulders.

He was alone, sitting in a chair that he had pulled over to the window. There wasn't much to see. The horses were quieting under the thrust of darkness. He could still see the clouds, ghostly lit by anaemic yellow lanterns. The air was pasty and lumpy like papier-mâché. Drifting up the stairs were the tin and silver sounds of kitchens closing up. He hadn't put on his clothes yet. No one could see in. He'd dried himself with the towel, and now he sat on it. The fresh smells were soap, wet wood and skin. For a moment it was as if he'd been killed by perfection.

The way he saw it was as a surprise: the dark horse, the unknown element, the xyz of it. He could feel Gabriel looking at them, looking at Gracia. We both see her, he thought, as if it is dark and a colour has been liberated, the true colour of the other side, one unable to be revealed in stark daylight.

He felt an odd mixture of daring and tenderness. His confidence in the mare was so complete he felt he could do anything with her, turn her to any dream of his, push her, pull out her best, but he wanted to do it in a soft voice, gently, and not have anyone speak badly of her.

Adventure awaited them. He imagined being in danger, riding to get help, carrying an indispensable message in a fateful gallop leading to heroic rescue.

His life was more than his own. He had dreamed of this in his young blood, felt he'd been chosen a long time ago. Each time it had been better. Fed by underground streams, idle moments, he'd laid the back of his hand on the dense mossy surface of consciousness, depressing it, and up between his fingers seeped the clear, cold, liquid imagination he drank to keep his life. He held it close, holy and happy.

All around him the air was electric, stretched, elastic. The invisible fire of lightning in a cloud crackled. The cloud blossomed.

Curiously his hands lit up glove-white on his knees. How like claws they were, holding on to an edge, flexing, ready to jump. He was inured to endurance, but savoured sharp explosive moments like this.

He was riding the prairie, which quivered and twitched and looked at itself uneasily in the bleach of sheet lightning spreading itself across the sky. It didn't see him, and when the grass tossed, it threatened to throw them over. In front of him, a bank of black smoke shuddered and creased the horizon. Inside it, a red-orange rash of flame detonated and jumped forward. A single animal howl surged then split around them, driven by the fire, which was a long whip cracking in the heat highway of the wind. The burnt air roared into the sky. Blackened and punched from the inside, it boiled and ballooned. Juices sizzled and burst from the grass. Digging with his heels, he wheeled the mare around. She leapt out, lather rising like a nap of velvet. She moaned in fear and with each stride forward galloped faster. The wind bent the grass down before them. She was running like a deer now, not having to touch ground so often. Even so, he could hear the fury, and occasionally a wild cat of flame ploughed ahead trying to strike them. Gracia jumped it. Each breath tasted of smoke. He grabbed a handful of her whipping mane. They were shrieking, but couldn't hear it. The fire was more intense now and, pushed down by the wind, it streaked forward hissing, startling the earth. A moment later the wind shoved back. The sky was shattered by sparks that climbed to the top of the sky, cooled, and rained down a blizzard of soft suffocating white ash from the smudged black sky. They became ghosts. They became larger and stronger. The ground sank away beneath them. One stride was the length of two, then three. Gracia kicked up clouds of dust that smothered the swift flames. The dust mixed with the ash and the smoke. Matthew closed his eyes. His skin was cool.

He got dressed with the intention of going downstairs to hear Gabriel sing, but fell asleep on the bed. Deeply relaxed, he lay flung open to sleep, legs apart, arms stretched, the palms of his hands softly turned. He slept through all the rowdy churning and now awoke to a smooth silky silence. The bed sheet crinkled. His bare feet peeled up from the floor with little sticky sounds. He let his head loll back, which had the odd effect of putting him back to sleep for a few seconds. He glanced at his watch: a witching time, the killing hour. The smart thing to do would be to turn over. There was a crack of light coming in the door. He yawned and rubbed his face. He missed Hannah, who crowded him and smelled up the bed.

The air in the hall was stuffy. He wondered if it had rained already, but all he could smell was the tobacco smoke. It lingered in uncertainty around the heat of the lamps posted in blind corners. At the bottom of the stairs, he looked to the right at the desk. Some papers were strewn about, but no one was attending to them. Ahead, the front doors were closed and bolted. He didn't want the street. He hitched his trousers, patted the buttons on the front of his shirt, and tapped his bare toes in a worn place on the floor. He was thirsty.

The dining room was dark. The smoke was mixed with straw as if the air had been beaten with brooms. Underfoot the wood was damp and sticky. The kitchen door was ajar. He thought he heard a low forced laugh or the growl of an animal. In an abrupt tense silence he knew whatever was there had heard him. On purpose he bumped into a chair and pushed it a little bit, scraping the floor, and said, 'Excuse me.' The silence persisted, baiting him. Leaning into the thin yellow strip of light he said, 'Excuse me?'

A huge woman held up her hand, raised her whole arm, the flesh on it waving heavily then wobbling to a stop. She pushed a handful of the thick light in his direction.

Gabriel gestured, reached for her. 'Hey wait, that's my pard-ner!' He flopped his arm down on his lap, ducked his head, smiled. 'You don't know about that yet.'

Matthew slid into the room. He put his hands behind him and leaned back on them. 'Is this where you keep yourself?'

'This is where we keep time,' said Oda.

'Welcome to the night kitchen,' said Gabriel.

Matthew looked over. The room was moody. It took him a minute to get used to the pulse of light from the feeding hole on top of the stove. Its cone shape was like the presence of an extra person. Besides the big woman and Gabriel, that peculiar little girl was here. She had folded her arms across her bony chest. All she had on was her camisole and petticoats.

'Do you know Oda? Who, who cooks all your meals here,' offered Gabriel.

Matthew nodded shyly. When he looked at her she caught his eyes and held them. The rest of her was lost in a soft moving swell of white and flesh that began to swallow him.

'Have a beer, pard-ner.' This time when he said it, it sounded sarcastic.

Matthew broke and looked around as if he expected someone to get it for him. The girl didn't move. He pushed himself off the wall. Where were they hiding it?

'He's *your* friend,' said the girl.

'Hey, hey,' scolded Gabriel and pointed to the barrel, then pointed at her, waggling his finger.

Now Matthew remembered. She'd never said it outright, but he'd known. There had been a meagre admiration, a wistful sigh. He remembered her dirty fingernails, her sleight of mood. She was poking out her jaw, chewing her lip. He couldn't tell if she was sucking up tears or biting her skin.

'Come here, honey.' Oda patted the girl as if she were a puppy, and rolled her eyes in messages that he couldn't decipher.

The girl was sullen and hungry.

'What's your name?'

'Suela,' she glared and dared him.

'So what's this partner stuff?' Oda interrupted.

'This boy can ride horses.' Tipping back in his chair, Gabriel balanced his beer on his stomach.

'I know that. I remember that race. What's this partner stuff?'

'Let me get to it. Take it easy. Don't rush me.'

Oda dropped her head down on her chest and peered out the tops of her eyes.

'So this was what I see. I got this horse that can run. But I can't ride a running horse. He can. So we work something out.' He hoists a bowl of air up above himself.

'That's it?'

'That's it. Isn't that it?' He turned to Matthew.

'I guess something like that.' Fumes from the beer made him feel warm and woozy. 'Just what do you want from me?'

'Only what you want for yourself.'

'I guess I'm not sure what that is.'

'You want to ride.'

'Well, yes, but ...'

'That's it.'

'But that's not all.'

'Of course not, who's saying that?' he said, gesturing and gathering a hurt expression on his face. 'Am I wrong? I thought you told me you wanted ...'

'I did.'

'So.'

'So, I guess I didn't think it could really happen.'

Gabriel pressed his next words evenly and convincingly. 'But you never doubted that it would.'

Matthew wondered if it was true. What was real to him? He shook the hair back out of his eyes.

'Isn't that so?'

'I guess I thought the horse would belong to me.'

'But she does,' grabbing it, 'in a way. You know she can't run without you. That belongs to you. No one else can do what you do with her, I saw that.' The chair clomped the floor as he leaned forward breathlessly. 'When I tried ...' Slowly, deliberately, almost dramatically, he shook his head and scrunched his lips. 'But when you sat in that saddle!' He straightened his back, not a posture he was used to. 'When you do it – it ...' stuck in disbelief, belief, and satisfaction all at once, as if he couldn't think of the words, as if there weren't words.

Matthew's sense of pleasure teetered in the eerie stillness.

273

'Nothing can happen without you.' Gabriel smiled into Matthew's eyes. He could see himself gently laid over the surface of the iris, just where he wanted to be.

Clouds of dust scudded across the window. They thickened and coalesced, letting the pale light play on their surfaces, which looked like faces, then blew away. It must not have rained yet. He pulled out his watch and started to look at it, then stopped. A moustache of sweat prickled. Squeezing the bottle in his hand, he lifted it to his forehead and rolled it from side to side. While his eyes were closed, he listened. No one was breathing out loud. The wind chuckled and rubbed itself through the grate. He thought he could hear other things, too: a sort of hissing and rustling and damp dragging.

'But she's mine, remember. You must always keep that in mind. I can do whatever I want. Kill her if I want to. I can do even that. I have a small gun. It doesn't take much, you know, one well-placed bullet, you just have to know where to put it.'

'Hey, hey, what kind of thing is –?'

Oda interrupted, warning him, 'Don't ask. Ach, he's such a brute.' She was exasperated. 'He's teasing you!'

But she's protecting him, Matthew thought, his warm fragile skin, while my own is rough, windburned and scorched. There was a small raw wound on his arm he hadn't even noticed until now. Gabriel was pale even in the summer. His wrists were soft. He sweated easily. The curls in his hair stuck to his skin. When he sang he shook them loose and they sprang out to make a wreath of dark thorns. Beneath that, the smooth mask of his face. The skin on his bones had remained plump and newborn. It was a surprise that he could speak. The words as they came were like snowballs with rocks inside. They hit and burned, then melted down and slid off leaving a wet cold wake.

He rubbed his eyes. Gabriel had slid down to the floor and was leaning against Oda's knee. The hammock of fabric in her petticoat held him. Suela had moved behind them. Her white hands rested on the glistening dunes of Oda's shoulders. They burrowed the flesh like small self-burying rodents. Oda opened and closed her eyes; smiles oozed up and trembled in her lips. Her head rolled on the girl's arms. A soft feline tremor ruffled her skin. Pleasure percolated in her throat. 'You take it where you find it,' she said.

Matthew focused on the air in front of his face. He could still see everything. The light was flickering all up and down him, little wet tongues, slick, licking the skin off, basting him, tenderizing him, drawing the salt out of his body, laying it on the surface and drying it just enough to cake so that if he moved, he'd crack it. If he breathed too deeply or too suddenly, if something startled him, he'd swell up and burst.

Suela stepped still closer. She took Oda's head. Her fingers spider-gripped, sinking in the soft flesh at the hairline. She pressed Oda's head back into her stomach as if she would ingest it.

In an instinctive groping motion Gabriel reached for Oda's hand and pulled it down over his shoulder. He tucked it under his chin and sniffed it. He squeezed the fingers then arranged them one on top of the next.

'There's plenty children, there's plenty, mmmmm.'

Matthew hung on the wall. Beneath him, they were becoming one massive shape. Having shed the outer skin, they were using an inside layer, lifting and wrapping its silk to build a cocoon, and underneath that, merging the cells of their bodies, they were changing into something else he might not recognize. There were faces behind these faces. They weren't going to show him. He'd seen this kind of thing before. Sidelong glances, knowing smiles, an intimate flush, tics and tensions of the skin, gestures, flights, fancies. It didn't matter to him; they were strangers and he could walk away. These faces were moving and magical. Their eyes passed him from one to another. They blurred and faded, but they wanted him to watch. They wouldn't keep him if they didn't want him here. Watching. And he wouldn't stay if he didn't want to.

* * *

Addie was waving madly from the top of the hill. She was still quite far away. Hannah squinted to be sure that it was her. Who else would it be? And the thick warm early morning air was resistant to sudden movement. Hannah shaded her eyes with one hand. When he lost that support, Ben grabbed hold of her. She hadn't put him down yet. Last night she'd set traps of pots and pans and finally did sleep under the security of their tin triggers and the unforgiving dead weight of her eyelids. 'I don't care if he kills me,' she lied to herself, hiding Ben on the other side of her body. During the night she woke once, tense and coiled, amazed that she'd been asleep and would sleep again until the ordinary display of dawn, the cock's crow. In the morning, a moment of disorientation, delicious, nostalgic. She turned onto her back, stretched, stared at the ceiling, yawned. For the first time in days, her skin felt cool. For a few seconds the world was comfort and light. And even if all things did not seem possible, her energy stranded cold at the bottom of a deep well, she had gotten through to morning.

Ben was happy. He loved waking up in her bed. Propped up on his elbows, arms folded, he stared solemnly then gasped in delight. 'Benjamin!' she laughed at him. 'Benjamin, you ol' so 'n so, you can just do your baby sleep through everything, can't you?' He rolled into the new hollowed place that had been developing between her belly and breast. She didn't always want him there, but this morning she didn't seem to mind. Lounging back, he rummaged under her loose chemise and pinched up her nipple. The milk wouldn't come. He stared curiously, got closer, put it in his mouth. Hannah stroked his head. It seemed like hours had passed since she woke up, but the sun through the crack in the shutter was stalled on the same stain. She was listening. Another still hot day. Cicadas hummed shrilly under the window where the heat was already blistering. She thought she could hear other things, but when she got up and put her ear to the door it was nothing. Ben put his ear to the door, then fitted his fingers in the crack and tried to pull it open. He called Hannah and made a face just in case she didn't know what he wanted.

Now Addie was gesturing, 'Come!' and maybe shouting, but the air was peculiar in the way it held back sound. Hannah couldn't see anyone else. Nellie must be taking care of Todd. She was looking forward to that time, the children taking care of each other. Then inwardly, wanly, she smiled at such a thought with so much future in it. Maybe she could get Addie to come to her. She beckoned. Addie shook her hands no, waving them back and forth like rags, then, grabbing up her apron, seemed to sob into it.

Ben wanted down. There was something interesting in the grass. If she went, he'd want to stay in her arms. To let Addie know, she thrust her arm up once. 'All right, Ben, we'll go, just let me get your bonnet,' which was hanging on the hook just inside the door. She started to walk away leaving the door open, turned, looked, then shut it and draped the latchstring in a precarious tell-tale fashion. Addie was still there, waiting.

The creek was low. They crossed in an inch of water on a bar of sand.

Following the cow path on the other side gave them a few minutes in the steeple shade of the trees. It was a peculiar distance, a protection. She could live here forever with the smell of water, the deepened colours, the shivering white chatter of leaves. She could just stay in here and not come out and not let anyone in.

The climb up the hill was harder and hotter than it had ever been. Addie never made one move down towards her. What kind of a mother was she, anyway?

'Hannah! Hannah?' Her voice direct and desperate.

Hannah was afraid to get too close. Addie had been crying. She started again. 'You've got to do something. He's leaving. He's decided to go. Now. Without any warning. Without talking about it. He doesn't care what I think. He doesn't listen to what I'm saying.' She choked. Hannah put her hand on her arm. 'He thinks he can go now, this time of year.'

'Addie. Addie, what are you saying?'

'Tully, he says he's leaving.'

'Where, where's he going?'

'As far as he can. The ocean. Did you ever hear of such a thing? For God's sake, what are we supposed to do? There's too much work for one man.'

'What does Lewis say?'

'He says the same as me. But he's envious, I can feel it. All men want to run off to adventure.' She dropped her voice. 'Tully knows it, too. He knows Lewis won't chase after him if he goes. He thinks he can do anything he wants. He's grown right out from under me.'

'Well, what are you going to do?'

'Not me, it's past me now. It's you. Hannah, you've got to talk to him. You're my last hope. He's always liked you. Ever since the beginning when you first came.'

Hannah was pushing her away to arm's length. 'But –!' Her mouth gaped.

'He thinks you're something special. I know you can do it. You've got to talk to him. At least try – please. For me, Hannah. It's too soon.' She was gulping. 'I – I ...'

'Addie, wait, wait a minute. When did this happen?' She leaned as she asked so that she wouldn't be pushed off her feet by the vibrations.

'Happen? Yesterday. He came back from somewhere and said he was going. That's when it happened. Out of the blue. Nobody was even thinking of such a thing.' Throwing her hands up. 'Look at the fields, weeks to harvest, what can he be thinking of?'

'Did he seem like himself?' she asked, pressing sideways.

'No, no, of course not – he isn't himself. My boy wouldn't do this.'

'But you know what? A long time ago he told me that he wasn't staying here forever.'

'Years ago. Kids talk like that, you'll find out. When they're mad at you they threaten to run away. They put everything important in a little sack and off they go and hide until they get hungry.'

'No, I think he really meant it, Addie. There was something in his voice.'

'Hannah. Come. Come with me, please.'

'Where is he?'

'There,' she said, pointing to the house.

'Does he know you came to get me?' Hannah was holding her arm.

'Yes. I said, "It's no good me talking any more to you. Maybe you'll listen to her."'

'What did he say?'

'Nothing. He doesn't say anything. He just sits there not saying a word. He said, "I already said it, I told you what I'm going to do." Then he said, "She's a traitor." I thought, What a funny thing to say. A traitor to who? Then he said, "It won't make any difference. Go ahead, do what you want. It won't make any difference to me." I said, "Fine, I will. I couldn't live with myself if I didn't try."'

'But he didn't say anything else?'

'About what?'

'About where he'd been yesterday.'

'No, I don't know where he was – come,' she said, hauling her down the path.

Hannah felt herself to be surprisingly weightless. Any moment she might fly, just give a little push with her black-footed boots and be airborne. She imagined that Addie had seen through Tully's eyes, whatever it was he saw, and that she was helping him capture her. Both were working together and had made all this up with a perfect logic that she would believe. She was going with Addie right down into her house, her lair. Under her feet was the sticky stuff, but until she got there she could still run away. No one could catch her the way she felt now, light and shivery. They didn't know that. They thought she was just her big belly, an easy prey, but she was nothing like that. As each moment passed, her body became less substantial, perhaps even dispensable. It shimmered around an essence that was at once unrecognized in this exposed form, yet entirely familiar, something she knew she'd hatched, an egg ripened within, waiting. As well, she had a whimsical courage. She might start laughing. After all, why would a mother abandon her son or not believe what he told her? It was so unlikely. If you didn't believe the people who lived in your house, it would be dangerous. Hannah believed the little cocoon of a person living in her body, its magical flutter.

'Oooo, don't you feel that prickly air? It's going to rain.' Addie shook her shoulders up and down. 'Ugh, I hate that feeling, it's like something bad's going to happen. Everybody gets jittery, then they get real quiet. I don't like this beating around the bush. If it's going to rain then it should get on with it, not hang in the air for hours making everyone crazy.'

Hannah buried her face in Ben. He giggled for her. The bubbles burst in her head and escaped into the air, where they might become the clouds that would drop the rain, making Addie both right and wet. Now the sky was pure and pale and empty.

Closer and closer they got. Hannah could hardly feel the ground. The mat of roots uncovered near the surface by the march of feet massaged her soles. A few steps more and Addie would be able to put her arm around Hannah's back, they'd be able to walk side by side on the wide path. But Hannah wasn't worried; even if Addie attached something to her, one leap, one kick would break her free. One good shake like a wet dog.

Rubbing their arms, bumping their hips, panting like schoolgirls, they rushed through the centre of the garden and into the yard, which was a flat pan cooking dust and a few weeds.

Nellie was there kneading her jumper under her hands. Todd was hunkered down with a catch of beetle under a box. When he realized he couldn't see it, he lifted the box and the bug scurried in escape. He squealed and gave chase. Ben was squirming rigorously to get down now that things were getting interesting.

Hannah went behind Addie. It looked like she was hiding. She put her hand on Addie's shoulder. A thick warm dark molasses of fatigue ran down inside her skin. Gravity was sucking her down through the solid packed dirt as if it were a soft quicksand.

Hot sunlight blinked and flashed from the bottoms of tin tubs, nail-heads, the bits and buckles in old harness hung on the wall, silver bells, brass, the iridescent green backs of beetles, the yellow beaks of chickens.

'There.' Addie trumpeted, pointing.

Tully turned his face from one side to the other as if his eyes had migrated to the sides of his head and this was the only way he could see. Hannah thought he was looking at her with one eye at a time and saw no difference. She didn't trust him any more. When she looked closely, she realized his eyes were flat, his gaze turned inward.

Addie sat Hannah on the bench next to Tully, so close that when the sun moved, his shadow would touch her.

'Talk, my children,' she said, a hand on each shoulder. 'Don't be shy.' Hannah glanced at her. 'Oh!' Addie turned to leave them alone.

Hannah was looking straight ahead. 'You're not going to do anything to me, are you?' In a pool of sunlight, in broad daylight, as if dark deeds could be done only at night, she thought, I hate you, I hope you do go away. Anything I might say to persuade you to stay would be a lie.

She said, 'Your mother thought you'd care about what I'd say to you.'

'I've outgrown you, Hannah.' Until he pronounced her name, his voice was dull, without curiosity or interest. 'You're stuck here. This'll never be your home; you'll never be comfortable here, this land'll eat you up. Look at you already. You're getting old. Your skin is drying up. You'll lose your teeth and watch your hands get thick. And your hair.' He lifted his hand as if to touch it, then flattened and arched his fingers back away from her as if she were too hot. Tipping his head, smiling, he said, 'Ohhh, I've never touched you!'

'You don't believe that. I'll show you the bruises,' she said, starting to pull up her sleeves.

His voice deepened and saddened. 'I don't mean that kind of touch.'

Anything she might have wanted to say sank back down her throat.

'You should come with me, right to the edge. It's not like this nothing, being surrounded on all sides by nothingness. There's an ocean. You can stand right on the edge of it. Everything's possible. Maybe you could even get rid of that ugliness that's inside you.' His voice was loving and gentle.

'You're crazy,' she whispered. The blood was uneasy in her veins and she was gulping on the dryness in her mouth. Her feet were stuck to the ground.

'Say it out loud so she can hear you, why don't you.'

'She doesn't want you to go.'

'I know that.' He was tired and softening in the sun.

'Are you running away?'

'From what? From you?' He almost laughed. 'If you remember, I was talking about getting away from here when you first came.'

'I just thought –'

'Well, don't think.' He looked at her steadily. 'You should come with me.' He wanted to loosen her hair. He imagined it netting on a sparkling sea, spread out on a breast of beach sand, blazing in his hands. She stands between him and the setting sun, her hair rivalling red. Then, fading in a fog of darkness, it leaves its heat in his hands, burning them, strengthening him. 'It would be an adventure.'

She did think of it, nervously and alone, refusing to believe that he could see into her imagination, his own so littered with chameleon creatures. It was not a rich place, her imagination. A future, crumpled and embryonic, lay in a shadow that stretched out without boundaries. As she watched, the shadow seemed to shiver and turn green and golden like a field of grass. Soon the separate weight of the sky pressed down until it had most of the space and only a thin undulating layer of gold remained beneath her feet. Absorbing the sun, it was almost too hot to stand on. The sky swelled. Nothing could be seen but sky. Rapidly it diminished her.

'Think of the great barriers of mountains, mad rivers on black rocks. Everything there is clear and sharp and hard. Brilliant eagles. To get there you have to climb until you can't breathe any more, then slide down the other side between the arms of the mountains, and the farther down you go the smaller the sky is, and at night you can watch the mountains bite pieces out of the sky. Think about it: bears and mountain lions. Moose and snakes that climb trees. And there are trees so tall the birds can't fly over them. I don't think you've gone far enough. I don't think this is where you meant to stop.'

But Hannah, shrunken and tired, wrapped her arms over her belly. 'Your voice will be stronger in the mountains, Tully.'

Curling his fingers over the edge of the bench, he straightened his arms and, swinging forward between them, stood up. Turning, he showed her his hand palm up, open, safe, then slowly, as if approaching a shivering crouched animal to offer his scent, he put his fingers under her chin and lifted it to make her look at him.

Her skin tensed against his.

'What will touch you, I wonder?'

She wasn't looking.

'Will you look at me when I ride away?' Adding, 'Into the sunset?' It was a picture he'd had in his mind for a long time, his silhouette splitting a reddening sun. Behind him, the flood of his shadow smothered the past, dimmed it into dream, then kept it smouldering overnight in warm white ash until he could fire it up with his imagination.

'I'll turn and wave and everyone will think it's for them, but I tell you now that it'll be just for you. How would you like a secret like that? I bet you've never had a secret like that?' Turning slowly, he bowed his hand to each quarter, a smooth conciliatory movement, even graceful. Inside, against the beat of his own heart, the hooves of the getaway horse were sounding. 'Has anyone ever left you?'

'No, I've never had anyone leave me, Tully.' Thinking back, surprised. It was true, no one she'd cared about.

'So I'll be the first.'

Would he be sure to go if she said yes?

'You'll be the first,' she said. It pleased him, she saw. He stepped back as if released. Exhausted. Triumphant. Taller. Inside her the baby rolled. She pressed in reassuringly and rubbed the hard round part that was the head. Bending forward, she cast a small shadow on the faded calico swell of her belly, and wondered what it must be like to be in there, rocked in the warm moist dark, safe, thinking that was the world. The baby was due sometime in October. It could be snowing by then, an almost unimaginable thought in this heat, beneath the weight of this sun.

'Addie wants you to stay until harvest.'

'No.' Turning his back on her, digging dust with his toe. 'No, it'd be too late. By then it's winter in the mountains.'

'Next spring, then.'

'She'll say it's planting time.'

'Just after that?'

'There would always be some reason.'

'But, Tully, there always is some reason!'

Addie rushed out. She'd seen Tully face the west and shove his hands deep in his pockets, a sure sign.

'What's happened? It didn't work, he didn't listen to you either. I was so hopeful. What happened?'

'Ask him.'

'Ask him, ask her,' Tully said sing-song over his shoulder. He was so many people. One of them could have killed her in a dirty way. Another in a clean dainty way on behalf of small dead Rosa. He'd burned Hannah in his brain. He'd deserted her in empty places, defiled the well by drowning her. And he was this light-hearted person, buoyant, excessive, light-headed with decision, already tasting the sharp clear mountain air. He could only imagine the colours, gold-splashed drifts of snow, the blue draped sky close enough to touch, eagles sliding on the ice-white air.

Ben, walking behind Hannah, stopped briefly to put his hand on her hip. His touch might make her cry. His trust was perfect, complete, without judgement. She closed her eyes. He reassured her. Nothing could happen as long as he needed her. Idly he poked his finger in the plump of her hip. It was something he did when he was thinking of what to do next. When he walked away, she got up and followed him in his wandering. This soft dance they did, one leading the other, glancing, testing the distance. He turned to see where she was.

He loved Tully, went to him to be picked up and held in the air above his head, screeching and screaming.

'Me! Me!' bleated Nellie hopping from one foot to the other.

Addie and Hannah stood side by side in the shade, saving themselves. Their faces were still. Hannah folded her arms. Addie folded her arms and stretched her back up between her shoulders. For just a moment she was tired. She had to think of what to do next.

Fourteen

'I have something to tell you.'

'No, I have to tell you something.' Clasping each other by the eyes because their hands were full.

'No, me first.' Stomping the words.

'Well then?' He couldn't stop beaming. 'Hurry up.' Sucking her lips in, she said, 'Tully's going away.'

'Is he?' Smiling. He was interested. Everyone's life was changing.

'He's going on farther.'

'Is he?' Licking the dust from his lips while visions of w e s t bled into his mind.

Hannah wanted to grab Matthew and drag him back to the present moment. 'He wants me to go with him,' she said crisply, trimming her tongue, tucking her lips.

'Does he now?' Gently. Amused.

'He wants me to have … an adventure.' She parted her lips at the end of the word, softly.

To tease her, he chilled his voice and pushed it down. Frowned. 'So, are you going?'

'Don't laugh!' Her face darkened. 'You just want me to stay here and grind my babies into this ground.' Her voice was raw and undigested. 'And raise fences out of their bones.'

'I'm not laughing at you. I'm just excited because I've got this thing going, I want to tell you about it, that's all. Tully's a neighbour, that's his decision. I've got news. Now I want you to turn around.'

Her shoulder was tender. 'Don't touch me.' The bruises. He might see the marks. What would she say?

He drew small circles on her sleeve until she took a deep breath and unfolded her arms.

'What is it then, Matthew?' He wasn't going to listen. Tully's leaving was of passing interest only, an aside, though for a moment she remembered times he'd looked as if he'd thought of it himself.

'Something's happening,' he said breathlessly, touching her face lightly, gently, with precision.

But as soon as he started to tell her the story, he found he was leaving things out, talking around and about, over her head, behind her back. Between the words were spaces. He started, then stopped. Turned. Talked about something else, abstractions. 'It's just the beginning. It's my dream coming ...' The old dream, pure and without definition, moulded by circumstance, the soft edges sharpened, the colours darkened and starting to vibrate.

His eyes drifted out over the shivery field grass. Heat wavered on the tips of the grass, a haze of dust and sunlight. Cloud thinned in the sky blurring distinctions. His wishes were moist and charged, grown in the sweet soil, up, waving in the long sways of fertile white light, an electric exchange of light and longing.

Alone with his thoughts, he saw how they came, strong, sharp like crushed sage. A bright taste on his tongue. The body he was in became gauze, allowing the passage of angels fallen from a lost green world. Sometimes it seemed as if he hadn't been the first to hold such thoughts, that the grey brain in his skull was made from the reheated ashes of the many men before him who had stopped at the edge of grass.

Hannah went around to stand in front of him because he was not looking at her. His eyes, dark circles smudging them, were focused inward upon the pools of their own fluids. She thought, He doesn't have to love me any more to survive. He was changed, or not so much changed as revealed. Something he'd been holding inside was showing through or about to surface. A light film of dust made him translucent, ghostly.

'No,' she said, reaching for him. 'Don't move. Don't go. Don't go any farther.' She slipped her finger along the band of his shirt. Inside, hooking on a button, she pulled him to the edge of her belly.

'An extraordinary thing ...' He was excited, tense.

She looked closely at him and beyond to the image of his profile, silken, figured at the rail of the ferry boat, looking out into the big river dawn, so long ago when he thought he was someone else. She saw this picture: his full face, the sun squirting through his hair, the freckles of frostbite, a scorch of beard. It seemed only the land was on his face now.

She thought that by now she'd have gotten to know him better, been better able to read the look in his eye, that eventually she'd come to see what he saw more clearly, that side by side in the slant of the sun they'd share choice secrets.

She hauled him forward over the hills of her body. 'You mean you're not going to lean on me any more?' she said, nuzzling her hair under his nose. 'You mean you don't want to put your head down on here?' smoothing the limp ruffle on her blouse.

'I want,' he said, licking her lips. And I still want more, he thought, licking his own.

Licking her off his lips, he swallowed as if something was stuck in his throat. She was stuck inside him, indigestible.

'Who is it, then?'

'What?

'Who is it that's got this wonder horse?'

'Didn't I tell you that? The most unlikely fellow. I hardly know him – well, I know him to see him, that's all, but I don't think I've ever spoken to him before.'

'Who! Who is it?'

'That guy who sings at the hotel, Gabriel. You know the one. And he was at the dance last winter, too, I think.'

'You're kidding.' Her heart pulled the blood back.

'No,' he said, shaking his head. 'Why?'

She made a face as if something was tickling in her nose. 'I – I don't know. I suppose ... well, how do you know you can trust him? Or ... '

'Oh, come on, how do you know if you can trust anybody? How do I know I can trust you?' Stroking her under the chin, grinning. 'Hey, are you going to try to ruin this for me?'

'I just think you're crazy – you don't know how to do this.'

'But he does.' Tenderly. 'You can't hang around the edges of a town and not learn something.'

'I don't want you hanging around with people like that,' she said, tilting her head, sparking.

'People like what?'

'Oh, gambling men, bums, drunks, like that.'

'The men who bet on that race last year were your neighbours. They just want a little excitement in their lives, a change. You can understand that.'

Her stomach filled with cold. 'I'm scared.'

'Of what?'

'I just have a feeling.' Between them they'll kill me, she thought.

'Oh no! Not a feeling.' He posed and put out his hands to catch the feeling.

'Stop it,' she slapped his hand. 'You think it's funny!'

'I think you're funny.'

'Because I'm worried about you, that's funny?' she said, trembling now, close to tears. 'Don't look at me that way.' Shivering, shrivelling.

'It's all right. Look again. Closely. Here.' Gentling, gathering her up into his eyes.

'When you sleep, I lean over you,' she said. 'I watch. I warm you when you come back from the cold earth. I dry you. When you sleep, I lean over you and reflect the firelight onto your face so the shadows won't dig in too deep.'

Is there ever a choice? Is there ever a choice in anything? he wondered. Am I ever free of her?

'I'm afraid you might be wrong this time,' she said.

'This fits me, I know that much. I feel I've climbed right up on top of life, as if I were a hobo right up on top of the fast freight. The wind is blowing in my eyes, drying them up ...' He was blinking and standing back as if he weren't used to having to see things close up.

Hannah was whispering evenly, trying to suppress the whimper in her voice. 'You think you know what's going on, you think you know what this place is, but you don't. Look at me, this is what it is, look at my skin, look at my soul. I am become this ... this land. Look! You think this is something wonderful? This is the truth of it. You think you know. But this is what it is. Right now. It makes you what it is, once you touch it, you belong to it. It takes you and shapes you as it pleases. You don't see that, do you? Do you see what happens to people? Look. This wind is the wind out of my soul. This ground is the earth of my body. How else did it get this way?'

'I want this so much,' he said, hungrily, for the faraway places that were deep inside him.

'You're crazy.' But she felt protective as one does towards those who show their soft underbellies when they think no one is hungry.

There was a blue wind at the back of the sunflowers. Blowing up, it shook the petals, which strained and twirled and snatched the white-washed sun in from behind and dropped into the bowl of yellow light before them.

'You see!' In his hand the grain from the harvest was light and dry. 'We'd have needed more.' He was on his way to the fair in Clearwater to join Gabriel. With the take from one of the races he'd been able to buy a plump clever roan pony who was easy to ride. Hannah pictured Ben sitting up there in a tiny saddle while she led him around the yard. With his winnings Matthew bought a pig, a plough he could sit on, yard goods, scales and tools. After each race he came back with two saddlebags full, one on one side, one on the other.

That summer he finished the fence. They stood and leaned on the top rail when Tully left. They watched him for a long time until he was too small to see any more. When he was gone, Hannah felt the part of her that he had taken with him start to grow again.

'Do you think he'll ever come back?'

Matthew took a moment to answer as if it were difficult to get out of his own skin and into Tully's, but once there he smiled. 'No. Why would he? I wouldn't.'

She watched closely, how the weight of his body, pressing on the heels of his hands, turned them white.

Other details were crisp and important. Ben was imitating Matthew, leaning over the bottom rail, but he couldn't see what was going on and soon bent his head down to investigate the slippery trail of a snail. He dangled his arms. His fingertips just reached the ground. Flicking them, he brushed a hole in the dust. His shirt hiked up revealing a strip of pink; none of his shirts stayed tucked in. She did the best she could. Matthew's mother had written to her with an old recipe for an infusion of buttercups for his chest. Reaching over, she tickled and tipped him with the toe of her shoe. He looked way up at her and chirped his high-pitched pleasure. A moment later he climbed out of the fence and grabbed her ankle. She picked him up and placed him on Matthew's shoulders. Ben snatched a handful of his father's hair. Hannah held her hand on his back. When she looked out, the horizon had sealed itself shut. 'No, I don't think he'll come back.'

The morning Matthew was going to leave, he looked out the window and saw Gabriel waiting at the turn in the road. His wave beckoned. Gabriel waved back, but didn't come. He swung one leg over the saddle and rolled a cigarette.

'What the hell – d'you suppose he was riding all night? Why won't he come in? I'll take a flask of coffee ... How strange.' He went to the window again. 'What's he doing now?'

'Nothing,' said Hannah, looking over his shoulder. Staring at Gabriel, she squinted her eyes, sharpening him. The air was so still she could see the threat of smoke from the cigarette jogging around the brim of his cowboy hat and righting itself. He was unmistakable. He wouldn't come any closer.

'What do you know about him, Matthew?' He would have told her, wouldn't he? In the deep long summer evening, standing in the dapple of sun, the grass shaking out shadow. If there had been anything to tell. After Ben had gone to sleep in the middle of the night and she had woken Matthew to go back to sleep with her. At midday over a second coffee.

'Not much. I do most of the talking.'

'That's no surprise to me.'

'It's probably either very mundane or very mysterious.' Hurriedly he tucked his shirt in. 'I'm off. Wish me luck.' A quick touch to Ben. 'Be back in five days.'

'This is the last time until the baby comes,' she warned.

He rubbed her arm. 'Don't give me that hangdog look.'

Deep in the shadow inside the window, she was watching him go again. It started peculiar thoughts in her head about how lightly men move on the earth. Their bodies always free. How little they needed: clothes on their backs, a few tools. Easy above the ground, they shouted and laughed filling the air with their plans. The sounds swelling and floating. Light surrounded, attracted to them. They rode it high displaying the colours of their skins. They needed so much room.

She held Ben. They watched the rolling gait of the roan pony. Forever she could hear the clay echo of the pony's hooves on the hard high middle ground of the road. When Matthew and Gabriel met they circled each other, but she couldn't hear what they were saying.

Matthew gestured towards her. Gabriel looked. She held Ben up to wave. He wanted down. As soon as he was on his feet he started off after them. 'Oh no you don't.' Hannah picked him up. They went as far as the fence. Matthew and Gabriel were jogging now. A little flutter of dust rumbled out from under the feet of the horses. It rose gently and disappeared. On either side, the fields were the same colour as the dust. Then at last, they were gone.

Something stuck in her mind. The shape of them side by side, like a two-humped beast or a mirror held at the middle of a body to duplicate the half. Gabriel might have been Matthew turned inside out. Just before they vanished she couldn't tell them apart.

Hannah was lying in bed. It was well past dawn. Earlier a bored Nellie had come and asked to take Ben over to play with Todd. The sun had been slanting through the dawn hour. After tying up a bandanna of essentials and watching them over the hill, she went back to bed. She couldn't believe it herself, lying there on the cool coarse sheet, eyes closed, feeling the sun creep up on the bed with her, soft and warm and yellow. The shutter creaked. Outside, the cicadas were grazing in the weeds. Lacklustre clucks from the chickens banked under the window. The dust was down. The air was saturated with the bruised smells of harvest. In the distance where all she could hear was the occasional clonk of a cow bell, the animals were loose in the golden stalks and rubble, salvaging.

A sweet and stupid boredom buoyed her. She examined its smooth surface with the tips of her fingers: little resistance, colourless, the same temperature as the air. At first her thoughts seemed drowsy and small. Sun-touched, drying, shrivelling like grapes to raisins. They wouldn't stay in order. They clumped and tangled, crumpled and wrinkled as if they were brand new and didn't know how to behave. She was watching them and was close enough to feel the air puff when they batted back and forth between her ears, coating themselves with old sounds and smells, memories. She thought they might get free. Without them she would be alone and mad.

She had worn a swatch of ground bald and hard around the soddy. It was a moat, a halo, a magic circle. A comfort. Today she crossed it. Wasps rose drunkenly from the rotting fruit to see what she was.

Beyond that the paths splayed out like the spokes from the hub on the old wagon wheel. She picked the one that skirted the edges of the fields. Way at the end, it turned abruptly, but this time she walked on, thin gold dust tarnishing the hem of her skirt, beside the slough, which was covered with green scum and a lazy lather of mist. The sun was still warming the earth, adding sizing to the air, thickening it. Straggles of geese smacked the rheumy surface of slough water with the long feathers of their wings.

Passing a brackish spike of cattails at the far end of the water, she reached a bluff that was cut deeply and invisibly, intimately, holding silver-grey strips of buffalo berry bush and clumps of blood-red creeper. Above, a golden leaf of ash. From the crenellated bank, the dull, glassy eyes of frogs anticipated their hibernation.

This was not a regular season. Motionless, like a quiet mind, the eye in the hurricane of weathers, this breathless light, a soft monotony, made her believe there was no such thing as winter.

An old spring sawyer, tossed up, had settled in mud and gravel, becoming a low bench. Holding her belly with one hand, reaching with the other, she eased herself down. She'd never been in this place before. The bed of the creek might have changed, but that whip of willows was several years old. She had her back to the sun. It laid its big hands of warmth on her shoulders. A prickle of sweat started out. She put her finger in the neck of the blouse to pull it out. When the air lifted the moisture, she felt a chill just below the surface of her skin.

A little distance from her feet, a beetle in a sleek brown coat scuttled over the ground from twig to weed to shadow. Hannah watched thoughtfully. It didn't know she was there.

No one knew where she was. Behind her was the cut bank, the withy filigree, a rust of yellow; close in the draping air, the heavy scent of sinking water; overhead, a seamless sky.

She had disappeared. Or could. Just get up and walk (waddle, she corrected herself) underneath the sun, in its trail, its slime, as if it were the long train of the moon on wide water. She could follow her whim. Shed the past, this present, her name. For a while she had thought of going east, finding Molly and standing next to her until she became something else, exotic. Now that held little interest for her and no allure.

And she didn't miss her mother very much any more; her letters were a surprise and Hannah had to think how long it had been since the last one. Her sister and brothers were faint and childlike, living in a small grey house made of fragrant wood. It was always late in a summer's eve. Aaron was leaning his head on his arm at the table. Joel was sticking to his mother's front like a folded moth. Sally was sweet and sleepy, balancing herself on the blue kitchen chair. Each time this picture came to her mind, it was clearer and quieter. She had to look for the breath rising in them. She had to force them alive as if it was too dense in her memory to move. At the same time she could taste blackberries juicier than real, hear the whine of mosquitoes and the deep-throated toads, smell the moist muslin evening.

But even when she tried, she couldn't remember the shape of her mother's mouth when she was laughing, and she must have laughed. While she'd been thinking, her shadow had shortened, ebbing under her body, which had been a shallow island. She shook and shifted her skirt. From a distance she heard someone trying to sing, a crooked, dissonant sound cracking the way a boy's voice did on its way to manhood. She turned one ear to it, then the other. It was not English. The singer stroked syllables only to abandon them, using breathy whistles as filler, lapsing into breakaway babbling. Then a small silence. Hannah raised herself forward, climbed to the lid of the bank and peeked over. Her stomach was cold. Though she hadn't eaten all day, she wasn't hungry.

Half hidden in the thick of berry bush and herb grass was a big Indian woman. The tawny colour of her buckskin dress blended in; its yoke of bright blue swung to and fro like a fragment of sky caught on thorns. The Indian stood up. The blade of a short knife caught and threw the sun into Hannah's eyes. She blinked and crouched. Then, just as if the knife had made a clean poke into her, she felt her water break and splash on the hard ground beneath her.

'Oh,' a sharp, surprised sound.

The Indian woman turned. Hannah glanced up. Clutching her belly she crawled over the edge of the bank and sat heavily, rolled onto one haunch. The woman looked around, cutting the air around her open, gesturing with the knife, and said something in a questioning tone. What's she asking me? Hannah wondered. Does she want to know if I'm alone?

'Over there, I live over there,' she pointed into the emptiness.

The woman approached. Standing squarely in front of Hannah, she put down her gathering sack and squatted on her heels a few moments, watching, listening. Hannah was breathing quickly from the top of her lungs. Sweat prickled out of her skin. Her hands were splayed and taut.

'Oww ohhh,' she blew.

Stretching out her fingers, the woman touched Hannah's. Turning her hand over, Hannah took the woman's palm to her belly. 'I'm scared,' she gasped. 'Too quick, it's too quick.' The woman's hand, large and soft, lay on the curve of her belly. The woman switched her eyes from side to side, sweeping the pebbles out of the way. She smelled the warm sticky seep of fluids in Hannah's clothes, the creek water and dust in the hem of her skirt. Leaning over slightly, she sniffed the red fuzz of her hair and touched it.

Comforted, Hannah bent her head down, closed her eyes. The pain subsided. Inside her head she saw a bright fish split the silver surface of her mind, burn in the air, then slice back through into her warm dark blood, which swallowed it like a finished thought.

Light jingled on water, flooded the blue air. When she opened her eyes she saw that the light had mixed with dust, turning it gold, that it had saturated the soft skins of the woman's dress. She laid her cheek on the sleeve. Beneath the buttery suede the woman's arm was firm and seemed to have extra bone. She could hold Hannah, cradle her right in her arms.

Pain began a fireworks low in her back. She gritted her lips and shifted. The woman dragged her gathering sack and shoved it behind Hannah's head, then, sitting down, she wiped her forehead on her sleeve.

Hannah lay back and turned her head away from the sun. The design on the woman's leggings was a rhythmical row of warm, red-beaded tipis piped in blue. In the air between them hovered upside-down blue eagles with piercing ebony eyes. Underneath, a supporting border of pasque flowers, and beneath the burst of white blossoms were little black figures stroking through their underworld.

The woman had crossed her feet. Beneath the dust on her moccasins, Hannah could see perfect rows of yellow beads. She wanted to count them. Hundreds. One by one. Even if it took forever. She had all the time in the world. The sun was stuck on her, cooking the baby, who was almost done now. She started to chuckle. She'd never heard herself chuckle before. On the flap of the moccasin she was sure she saw teeth marks. Maybe the Indian woman wanted to take her baby and eat it. Or pick out small pieces of baby and rub them into little lumps of white dough to make more beads.

In a faint burn, pain girded her hips. She started to push. She rolled up, straightened her legs out, bent them back. Whimpering inside her breath, she scraped at her skirts, gathering the fabric. The Indian woman put her hand across Hannah's back, which was sticky with salty sweat. When she moved her hand, the shape of it remained like a dark imprint of paint on white fabric. She said something else, her voice deep and soothing. Soon the syllables grouped into phrases, a chant. Beneath it Hannah panted and blew, weaving her breath into the refrain, until the only reason for being was to get this baby out.

Cramps quirked in her legs. She climbed on each slowly, using the sounds. Her body bunched in behind. She pushed. Again. Swayed. Pushed. The baby was hard.

In her fist she gripped dust. It must be my hand, she thought, there at the end of my arm, dirty, mottled blue, cold. Her feet were cold too. The centre of her body was sucking in the heat, collapsing the veins behind it so the blood couldn't get back out. Pins and needles numbed her legs and arms. She licked her upper lip, reclaiming the salt. To maintain her strength she nibbled skin and sunlight.

The voice of the Indian woman butted in, boring holes in the hot places in Hannah's brain, filling them until her mind subsided, quiescent, and she surrendered a body no longer hers.

You need me, kid, she hollered down inside. Don't kill me now. She had dreamed the colour of the baby's eyes before, a new colour able to hold the sky, tolerate distances, shrug loneliness, turn aside dreams.

She began to repeat the sounds, not knowing where they began or end as words or if they were like regular words. Soon she and the Indian woman were chanting together. At first Hannah wasn't in the same key. She could hear her own voice, but the breath of the Indian woman was large, and soon they were breathing together and neither could tell whose voice was whose as they overlapped. With each moment their voices grew deeper and darker. It was how the earth would sound, Hannah thought, if it were to open its throat to tell her something. Then only the woman was chanting, but it didn't matter; their voices were the same. They were one voice with different echoes.

The Indian woman was bent over Hannah's knees now. In a dull detached way, Hannah noticed how her face swept back, softly and beautifully, like smooth brown hills. She was a woman made out of mud and clay, blended earths from huge and invisible pasts. She was enormously strong and patient. She was waiting.

Hannah closed her eyes and pushed the baby towards the woman's hands. Her pores sweated and squeaked. Inside, her breath leaned back against her ribs, and pushed. Her womb rippled and urged. Skin stretched, whitened, tore. Fresh blood spurted. The baby's head. A shine of mucus. The hands of the woman closed around it, and in a moment they were wet. She turned the baby. Hannah pushed the baby out. It lay in the hands of the Indian woman. Its face was down. Vigorously, the woman rubbed the baby's back. Hannah reached between her legs to touch it. It was a long way; she stretched. The baby scrunched and started to cry. The woman could hold it in one hand. With the other she wiped its face. Hannah spread her hand over. The baby was drying. Together they smoothed Hannah's skirt and laid the baby on it. A girl. Using her hand as a blanket, she covered it. Looking up, Hannah saw the black head of the woman bent down. It was nodding slightly. It reminded Hannah of a bird of prey. A wing, sleek and piercingly beautiful.

The woman was speaking. Hannah held the baby tighter. Rummaging in her belongings, the woman took out a skin bag. She pointed to the creek. For a moment Hannah watched her go, then leaned over the baby and sniffed. Lifting her blouse, she held the baby under her breast in the warmth of her body. The baby had thick black hair, which she smoothed to one side. She began to think, Just barely here. Where do you think you are, baby? Where am I? The Indian woman had disappeared down the cleft in the earth. We are all alone, she thought sadly. What if no one came? What if someone did and saw us from the other side of the creek, and when they tried to cross they were swallowed up or washed away? What if the snows came and covered us and in the spring the grass grew up all around? The thoughts flooded with despair and longing. You have no name, she thought, hopelessly. You are too soon.

'She isn't mine,' she said to the Indian woman who had brought water and was washing her. The woman nodded and wiped Hannah's face. She didn't look into her eyes, which were anxious. She washed the tears. Using the cloth, she dampened the sweat-starched hair around Hannah's face and tried to press it down. Putting the cloth aside, she curved her large hand to the shape of Hannah's head and touched the red halo of her hair carefully, as if it might burn. She placed her other hand on Hannah's breast, which was as white as fresh snow or the petal of a flower, warm and sweet.

'I'm so tired,' Hannah whispered. 'May I sleep a little?' she pleaded. 'Here,' she said, curling over, laying her head down on the woman's thigh. 'For just a minute.' Cradling the baby. But her eyes were propped wide open, mesmerized by the soft golden skin of the woman's dress. It was the colour of pulled taffy and smelled of crushed herb and grass. 'I'm cold,' she murmured.

The Indian woman, who was stroking her arm, felt a shiver in her skin. She looked all around. Ants were intensifying at the afterbirth, and some crows were walking the bare ground. In the distance, trees were carding thin cloud. The sun was bald, its light watery. There was no breeze and she could smell the birth in folds of cloth. She hadn't seen them, hadn't heard them, but the animals had been catching odour out of the air, had been talking. As soon as they leave, the animals will come close.

Meanwhile, she gathered Hannah and the baby into her arms, onto her lap.

The moment, the warmth surrounding her, Hannah slept.

Above her, the Indian woman's face thickened, saddened. Liquid shadows seeped from the creases in her skin, muting its bronze. In her mouth, a stilled breath softened. The pupils of her eyes dilated as if to release a troubled soul. It was a face the woman herself had never seen, one which, if she did, would be alien to her.

The mother's blood was already soaking into the ground. That will make her think it was hers. It *was* her story now, told without uttering a word. But the Indian understood. She will be hungry.

She held Hannah coiled against her belly, close, while she cooled. She picked scales of dried perspiration from Hannah's skin as she hummed her the windy chant.

Hannah whimpered in her sleep, stretched. Groggily, she opened her eyes. Her body felt as if it had been in the lap of sleep for a century. From underneath, the woman's face was square and strong; she had a slight Adam's apple. Hannah sat up. The baby was on her thigh. She plucked at her skirts, which were stained and caked with dirt. She pointed to the creek.

Hannah sat in the sun in the warm hollow down by the water. Sliding out of her petticoats, she dragged them in the shallow water. The Indian woman helped her cleanse herself. She began to feel better. Different.

* * *

Matthew and Gabriel were riding abreast and laughing. Above them, the sky glowed. Their fortune had been good. No, better than that. They rode along a narrow shortcut through the range grass, the light withered straw shivering along the horses' flanks. At times one or the other of the horses tried to get ahead, but the men wanted to stay side by side, and so they reined and cajoled until the animals behaved.

Matthew's heart was full. In spite of himself he was relaxed, almost carefree. It was uncanny, Gabriel seemed to know what he was thinking, what he was going to say before he did himself. He knows me better than I do myself, he thought. I can say anything to him and he knows what I mean. None of my ideas are too far-fetched. Nothing surprises him, but everything I say is new to him. He loves me.

The horses quickened. They were thirsty and could smell the creek. Their hooves brisked the ground. Behind them the yellow dust smoked low. They swayed their heads from side to side, jangling the bits on their tongues. Beneath their necks, the reins criss-crossed.

The air was soft and foolish. Matthew and Gabriel got a little drunk on it and had sultry daydreams. Gabriel hummed a new tune that he'd been thinking of. Matthew smiled to himself. His head was bulging with iridescent, unformed thoughts that bubbled in his head, slipped lazily against each other, and burst, giving him a feeling of indolent pleasure. And it pleasured him to watch the slide of shoulder muscle on bone beneath the rusty skin of the roan horse, the luff of mane on his neck, the lop of ears, and listen for meaning in the twinge and creak of saddle leather. Between his fingers, the loops of rein were cool and pliable.

Matthew yawned. The sunlight was thin and soaking. His muscles were rendering around his bones. He made minute adjustments, crossing his toes, stretching his spine, sighing. He gave in to the slouch and sway of the horse, and his head bobbed sleepily. When his hat tipped back, the sun nudged under, where, like stardust, he thought, it made him see things that might not be there.

Hannah, for example, there in front of them, squatting over a broad sawyer, when they looked up from their reveries. She was wet, her skirt dishevelled, shoved up between her knees, her hair loose and matted. Beside her a bundle. She had disturbed the mud in the creek bed. A stain of brown water had bloodied the ground around her.

She saw him back.

For a moment he thought she didn't recognize him or was looking at Gabriel instead. Before he could change his mind he saw an Indian woman standing in the water holding something up in her hand. Matthew pushed his horse into the water and across the creek. Dismounting, he dropped the reins into the water and stepped the stones to

Hannah. 'What is this?' he said, touching her shoulder, her knee, moving his hand close to the bulge in her skirt. With two fingers, she pulled the fabric away so he could see.

'Here?' he said, beaming, incredulous.

'I knew you'd like it.'

He couldn't stop looking at her.

'You make me tired, Matthew,' she said, smiling affectionately, taking his hand in hers and putting it on the baby.

A spot inside him began to soften and swell. She was small enough to fit in his hand. Small enough to sink beneath his skin and grow, coating herself with his mineral essence until she glowed, pearl-like, and he imagined he'd have to be killed to let her loose. For his son he had expectations and a conspiratorial smile. For a daughter he would sweat and lose sleep. His soul would shiver and sigh, and her growing would be a wonder and a sadness to him.

Hannah liked the awkward, intent way his face looked as he tried on tenderness the way he might a tuxedo.

The long wet legs of Gabriel's horse, stabbing the pale water like dark spears, were between her and the Indian woman, whose body was split into stripes behind the cage of legs.

'Hey, Matthew.' Gabriel's voice was floating back over his shoulder.

'What?'

'Come here.'

'What was it?' He didn't want to stop.

'You have to come here for a minute.'

'Why? What is it?'

'Something.'

'No. You come here and look at this.' Matthew started to lift his daughter, but Hannah stayed his hand. She wouldn't let go yet. He called again. 'Come, look at this!'

But Gabriel was moving the mare forward. She snorted and shook her head. He pushed her close to the Indian. He picked up one of her braids, raised it, let it fall. The woman froze. Once, then twice, he circled her. The water splashed, making white noise. The mare's hooves stirred the water, which muddied and swirled.

'Matthew,' Gabriel called to him.

Hannah cringed. The tone in his voice was peculiar, sweet and drawn out, rolling on the surface of the water, slithering like warm oil.

'You're in too deep,' said Matthew.

'Matthew.'

'All right.'

Gabriel was leaning over, delicately reaching for the swatch of white cloth, which still dragged in the water. He didn't want to touch it very much, but caught it on the hook of one finger, then held it, gently swaying, moving it under the nose of the Indian as if to make her smell it. He was hardly breathing, his head tilted curiously.

Matthew stood in a couple of inches of water, reluctant to go in over the tops of his boots. He was watching, his eyes, wide and uncertain, reflecting the shaking light off the creek.

Snatching the wet cloth, Gabriel squeezed it. Drops fell on the bright blue bodice of the woman's dress. Then, lifting it high, he draped the fabric on the Indian's shoulders and coiled it into a scarf around her neck. He had to stand up in the stirrups to loop it over her head. She had to close her eyes when the heavy rope of cloth bumped against her cheek. Her hands flew to her neck, groped at the choking cloth. Though she wasn't looking at him, he was holding her down.

Swinging the mare's head abruptly to get it out of his way, he just missed hitting the woman in the face. Then, when he was close enough to her, he leaned down out of the saddle, smoothly, even gallantly, and insinuated his fingers under hers. Before she could snatch them back, he wove his into hers so they were held fast. He raised their hands and examined the pattern of their fingers: the parallel brown and white bars. He was squeezing so hard that the tips of his fingers were red. As if too hot to touch, he snapped his hands open, but hers didn't drop away. He tensed his hand so he couldn't feel it, so it didn't belong to him. He waited, staying like that until the Indian lifted her hand away so gently he had to look to make sure it was gone. And look to see if his skin was burned.

'Matthew!' more urgently.

Matthew watched a stain spread down the woman's dress. 'What?

'Come on.'

'I don't want to.'

'What? I can't hear you.'

Matthew took a deep breath, his body having pushed out all its air.

'I want to show you something.' Gabriel dismounted suddenly, leaned down and dunked his hands. He gestured for Matthew to come closer.

The water wasn't very deep. Matthew waded in. Gabriel nodded to him. He didn't stop long enough for the water to smooth itself out. As soon as Matthew was close enough, he bent down and plucked the hem of the Indian's dress between his thumb and forefinger. He began to pull it up. He was on one side, Matthew on the other. It was too hard to lift the leather, so he turned his hand and gathered the skirt beneath his fingers.

'Hey!' Matthew frowned.

'Just hold on a minute, hold on.'

Her legs were not shaped like a woman's. Gabriel glanced at Matthew. 'What do you think?'

'What is it? What's going on? What are you doing?'

'This isn't what it seems.'

Matthew watched.

Hannah stood up on the edge of the shore.

Gabriel tugged the skirt of the dress, but it was stuck. 'Help me.'

'No.' He didn't want to touch.

'Do you know what this is?' Using both hands now, he roughed the leather up the Indian's thighs until Matthew could see it was a man.

'A berdache!' Gabriel was triumphant. 'The berdache. It's a man ...' The Indian tried to shove the skirt down between his legs. '... who dresses like a woman.' Gabriel grabbed tighter, pulling the skirt up. The Indian lunged to the side into Matthew.

Putting his hands out, Matthew clapped them down on his shoulders and clutched a fist of cloth. The Indian wrenched to try and free himself. Gabriel was pushing the dress up farther. He was making a sound that got mixed up in the splashing of the water, so that Matthew couldn't tell if he was grunting with exertion or giggling. All at once he pulled on the dress, hauling it over the Indian's head and arms. From behind, Gabriel was shoving the dress up. The Indian humped his back.

'What are you doing?' Hannah saw his pale fleshy buttocks. 'Stop it! She helped me!' The baby started to cry, a thin newborn cry that Hannah couldn't hear over her own.

Naked except for moccasins and the cowl of petticoat, the Indian twisted and ducked. Matthew snatched at him, got the end of the petticoat, and put his other hand flat on his side. Gabriel grabbed his other arm and pulled him around. Strung between them the man wrenched, humiliated, from one to the other, his body purposeless, soft, struck pink by the late afternoon sun.

Hannah kept swallowing. Her mouth was dry, the sides of her throat sticking to each other. Her knees were going to go. Wobbling, she sat back down. What's going on here? Who is that? She snuggled the baby close to her breast, looked down at her. The baby was crying. With her fingertip Hannah smoothed the forehead, tiny wrinkles. Tears from her own eyes dropped on the baby. A place in her chest burned. Pulling her knees up, she curled over the baby and her own consciousness. She put her hands up covering her ears so she couldn't hear the shouting and laughing from the creek.

Matthew clawed a handful of the Indian's flesh. It disgusted him. This savage had been touching his wife. He felt the hunk of fat in his hand. Gabriel was giggling hysterically; throwing his head back, almost losing his balance, catching himself just in time, laughing at his own clumsiness. Side kicking at the water, he splashed the Indian's thighs and belly. The water was a froth of mud by now. It coated his boots and trousers.

Together, thinking the same thought, they snagged his legs out from under him and began to roll him over in the water from one to the other. They jumped over him, straddled his fat belly, pushed him under, Matthew's hand flat on his face, and then raised him up, spluttering, helping him, slapping his back.

'What's so funny?' Matthew gulped.

Gabriel panted and stopped for a moment, stared at the long shadows lying out on the water. It was impossible to tell where one ended and another began. 'Creep.' He swore as he twisted the Indian's arm.

Matthew was soaking wet and weak. He was losing his grip. He bent down to catch his breath, and let go.

The Indian's body sloshed to the side. He wasn't in it any more. The big bones lifted him. Turning, his eyes bored into the place where Gabriel was still holding him.

Gabriel's hand was white, luminous, the bones in the back of it shaped like an open fan. 'Get away from me.' Quick, thready, his voice was shredded with disgust. He broke his fingers off into a fist.

For such a large man, the Indian moved with grace and strength. His feet punched holes in the water. The sound startled birds out of the berry brush. They flew up into the huge sky and scolded. The two sounds cracked into each other. He ran up the creek bed, cutting his feet

301

on rocks that had broken off from the mountains to become buried teeth in the mud.

Miraculously, he thought, he still had his skin.

Having sent his self on ahead, he chased it down, catching it just before it evaporated. Then, with it back in place, he ran into the whips of yellow willow reddening in the bath of the sun. He looked over his shoulder.

Matthew and Gabriel were bent over in exhaustion. The muddy water that dripped from the tips of their claws was bloodied. They peeked at each other sideways; Hannah could see their heads turn. Something passed between them, a complicity of silence and forgetfulness. She rocked herself over the raw underbelly of their appetite. She was keeping her eye on them. And deciding she wouldn't go with them any more.

'I won't go with you,' she whispered, trying a voice that didn't go very far, but they heard something. Matthew stood up. The water was soaking up his trousers, sticking them to his skin. He wiped his face on the sleeve of his shirt. His body was relaxed and warm as if he'd been cold and had shivered himself back to health and comfort.

He waded towards Hannah, who wouldn't look at him. 'I want to go home.'

He said, 'Yes, let's go home,' and put his hands one on each side of her face, and she could hear the sound of the sea in there, his blood, she'd been listening to it forever, it seemed. His hands smelled like strawberries and salt. They were larger and stronger than they used to be. She was frightened of him. From his clothes came a stink of sweat and mud slime. His body blocked the sun. He could do that and other terrible things.

'You're wonderful,' he whispered, bending over and rubbing his face in her hair. Bringing the roan pony around, he lifted her up so she was sitting sideways. She made a shawl out of her petticoat and tied the baby around her chest.

Carefully Matthew led the pony up the embankment. There was no wind now. The clop of the pony's hooves was muffled in the dust and did little to disturb the mammoth silence.

Heading home, Hannah was overwhelmed by the sadness of people who had no home to go to, who were hungry when the sun was spreading across the horizon. A soft gnawing disturbed her stomach. Loose thoughts tumbled, wouldn't finish what they started, pulled her eyes back into her head and tied her tongue behind her teeth. The red sun would be setting on her house, falling in over the window sill in a gentle way, reminding the stove to start up, warming the bed covers. A chill spread from inside her skin and she imagined the soft swill of cloth on her skin. Then darkness, the velvet swarm of night. The baby close. Ben. Her hands on them. There would be stars. And the scent of the first frost, which would make her sleep better. If Matthew would stay beside her, covering her again and again when the quilt slipped down, if he would rub the soft spots that she was growing, then she'd forgive him.

Every once in a while, he turned to glance up at her. For a few steps he put his hand on her thigh. He was still smiling, as if he'd had a good meal and his imagination was mellowing in the marinade of all that had been happening. She felt his confidence clothing her.

Gabriel was wading back and forth as if he were looking for something. He was humming or whistling under his breath. The mare had come down to the edge of the water, carefully dragging the ground tie of reins between her hooves, tossing her head, trolling the air as it rose from the warm water into the cool of evening. For a few minutes Gabriel stood by her head, rubbing a length of the rein between his fingers and thumb. Matthew and Hannah and her baby stood out silhouetted on the crest of the bank, the strong saturated light radiating around them, blurring the edges, blinding him, burning the image into that deep place in him where he stored perfection.

'Come on,' Matthew called to him.

The sun was a molten red eye. Beneath it the land was darkening, cooling under their feet. The thin scraping of the insect underworld faded into dark space.

While Matthew rode over to Lewis and Addie's to pick up Ben, Hannah put the baby on the bed, where she began to clean her. Squeezing the water from a cloth, she gently washed her head. 'You're not used to being loose, are you, small soul? I'll wrap you up in just a minute.' In her hands the baby shivered. When Hannah swaddled her, she drifted back to sleep.

Hannah changed her own clothes and sat on the bed next to the baby. She thought about Ben, his little bed with its crumpled quilt. She picked up the baby and breathed kisses on her, pressed her cheek. She waited for someone to come.

After Gabriel stabled the mare, he came back to the house and stood in the doorway. With eyes that were deep inside his body, he watched her, licking a taste of mud off his lips. Words started across his tongue, but there was nothing to say and the air between them was thin. He had put on a jacket.

Hannah in white was ethereal, pure essence. The infant floated on her body. Her hair was a frozen fire. Around her was a magic space. She didn't come out of it. He could see in, but couldn't hear or taste or smell. Except with his mind, he couldn't touch her.

A perfect fatigue had taken over her body, sweetening and softening her bones. She had become warm, the same temperature as the air. She was all body, no part of her unpleasant. Inside she was alert and calm. Things around her hovered in silence as if they might be lost out of a dream and have no purpose.

The sun set. Out across the land, the wind began to move again, picking up the heat from the earth and lifting it into the cool sky. It bumped the shutter, banged a coil of rope against the sod wall of her house. Up on the roof it sucked on the chimney and started a fire in the ashen heart of a piece of coal in the stove. In the middle of the pipe, the damper wobbled: t-pock, t-pock.

She'd heard it all before. The sounds were still strange, but not new any more. She was neither frightened nor curious.

But she didn't take her eyes off Gabriel. Her mind rested on him, a heavy hand holding him at a distance. Even at that, in the dark, she knew how he was looking at her, what his face was like. He didn't lie. None of them lied. All she ever saw were their bare truths. They had no shame. They were innocent and terrible, opening her up to jump inside, shouting and crying, the fierce hunger of them. Joyfully, excitedly, they breathed at her knees, her breasts, her throat. They drank at her lips and nibbled on her belly.

Getting in front of her, they smiled softly and ignited their eyes. They flickered their tongues between their teeth. They opened the palms of their hands to show her the pathways of fate, and invited her to go with them.

And she did, her brain shuddering with the nerve and camouflage of their energy, stunned by their lush love and bright promise. It had been like that.

But how could they have?

Matthew was outside. He'd put on his wool plaid shirt. 'Hey, go on in,' he insisted, pushing Gabriel through the door. He was holding Ben, who was pointing and saying 'Baby, baby,' and looking uneasily at Hannah. 'Mum mum.' They were all crowded at the door, almost stuck there. Matthew put Ben down. 'You don't mind, do you?' he asked, indicating Gabriel. 'I'll do everything.'

Hannah rolled her eyes.

Matthew stoked the fire with twists of grass. He filled the kettle, put it at the back of the stove, then moved it again, over the hot spot. He pushed another pot next to it. 'What should I put in it?'

Hannah was looking at Ben. She patted the mattress, called him gently, smiled. Softly, deliberately, he toddled across the floor to her, put his face to her knee, flicked his tongue through a small part between his teeth, and tasted her skin. He pressed a little more and she felt the hardness of his teeth.

She'd been walking with Matthew for a long time. They'd met with some manners and curiosity in a safe place. The road had been wide and dry enough. She'd trusted him – just because. She wore the trust. It felt good. There were no holes it in. His hand had been warm. She had put her hand in its shelter.

She didn't understand how his hands could do what they had done. How his voice could throw up those ugly sounds of glee. She hadn't thought that was part of him.

Now, she was thinking all the time: I could bar the door, but they could dig through the sod walls. I could run away – to Tully? But the children. Diapers. Food. I don't know the way out, not really, only the paths around the house, worn to the bone now, familiar, comfortable but circular. I could write to Molly to come and get me. Matthew might read the letter on the way to the post. I could send them on a wild goose chase. I couldn't. Because I can't be alone out here. Or any more. I'm going to let them get away with it, aren't I? Aren't I.

Ben had climbed up on the bed. She put her hand on him as he lay down next to the baby to touch the small parts of her face. She tried to see what he was thinking, but her gaze soon drifted away and her thoughts ran out like small battered kites on taut string. She closed her eyes. Matthew and Gabriel were talking, but their voices were so low she couldn't hear the words. They laughed in another language. They produced honey in their mouths and let it drip off the ends of their tongues.

The fire crackled. The leg of a chair scraped the floor. She heard shuffling noises, and the light changed. Matthew came to bed.

'How could you?' she hissed.

He didn't want to, but he turned over, his back to her. Lying on his side, he drew his legs up together and flattened his hands between his thighs. For a while he listened, trying to separate the sound of the baby's breathing from all the others, which had become close to one, a family of sound, familiar and caressing.

A little after midnight she went outside. She was able to crawl out the end of the bed without waking Matthew. She had been sleeping, perhaps even dreaming, but the sudden icy sway of the northern lights woke her.

'Star shining, number number one, number ...' but the stars were swept behind the drapery of shimmering light. 'Good Lord, by 'n by, by 'n by ...' but the song stopped in her throat. She thought that she would have recognized herself by now and things would be clearer, that the space around her wouldn't stretch and swell so, defying her sense of proportion, that it would hold.

The sky leapt. She'd seen it before, but not like this with her eyes wide open. Something was wrong. It felt wrong to be awake. She didn't know what it was, why she had awakened so suddenly in the silent night, overwhelmed with resignation. She had a feeling she wasn't supposed to see this.

Veils of colour rushed through the magic curtain that seemed to demand she play before it, and she would have but for the fear of performing a disfiguring, acquiescent dance. Behind it was the clear black sky, too cold, too pure. Her eyes tried to focus in it, but there was only an emptiness. It had few words to name it, which so frightened and saddened her that she had to lighten her breath and close herself to it slightly.

This was a bare country of unusual size, of smooth, subtle, open space without hiding places, and yet things could spring up and surprise. The skies blasted from behind bland blue-white surfaces. Clouds built mountains that erupted.

Thinking to catch the dry rustle of grass, the scratch of the night hawk on the air, the downwind howl of the wolf, Hannah listened for anything she might recognize, even the wild sounds, the dark familiars, but there was nothing. And the sky was moving, actually pressing the circular horizon of the earth down out of the way, leaving her high and exposed in the swirling centre. She gathered her gown around her as she might the soft white shift of her grief. It fitted differently on her. She was different, not as large and possible and unblemished as she used to be, not as good.

So when Gabriel, smelling of sleep and horses and cold dust, came beside her, nudging into the small round space, she was both glad for the human warmth and disappointed in herself.

'I think I need to be by myself.'

'Uh-uhn, not safe, not safe at all,' he said, shaking his head solemnly. Electricity ran and jumped in his hair.

'You're ugly inside, you know. It's good I can't see you very well.'

'Close your eyes then.'

'Yes. That's an idea.'

But his eyes were fat and satisfied, the surface dull. He doesn't see the same things as I do, she thought. 'You're tired and dirty,' she said.

'I sure am.'

'Were you sleeping?'

'Yes.'

'What woke you?'

'I don't know. Maybe I couldn't –' but he didn't know what the word was, what sense had been tripped. 'Maybe I just knew ... '

'Knew what?'

'That you were up.'

'You were watching me.'

'Not with my eyes.' His sleeves fluttered when the air moved.

Hannah wondered if it was dust that made up the mutating sheets of light shuddering in the sky, thin clouds of dust that blew too high and got bleached near the sun, then frozen in the north, and which now waved in the stare of stars.

'I want to know what you're doing to Matthew.'

A grin unravelled his mouth. He couldn't stop himself. He laughed out loud, a curious sound salt-stained with desperation.

'He needs me,' Gabriel said triumphantly.

'I don't understand that.'

'Then, maybe I need him.'

'What for?

'Oh, I don't know – maybe because I'm too clumsy to race my own horse.'

'You should leave him alone.'

Gabriel put his hands in his pockets, turned, slightly away from her, and hunching his shoulders ducked his head down. He said softly, 'But he doesn't want to be left alone.'

Hannah looked at him while he stared at the ground. His lips were still and it appeared that his eyes were closed. Once or twice the flush of scattering light revealed his face. His skin was plump and untroubled. It didn't show him for what he was. She waited for him to speak again.

When he did, his voice was breathy and furrowed. The words broke off the end of his tongue like clumps of thick warm earth.

'I will die young, but you, you will become an old woman. You'll have the stories and the songs ...'

'How do you know you'll die young?'

He slid his hand along her arm, sadly. 'Tell the stories about us. Whisper in the children's ears. Sweeten the gossip of the women. And when you're very old, gather the babies around your knees and tell them. You know, I can see you as an old woman; a shawl around your shoulders. Like this one ...' He pinched it between his fingers, dropped it, picked up the tail of it that lay like a widow's peak down her flank. 'Then you'll have the stories and the songs – and you can change them. You can lie all you want and no one will know the difference. Your hair will be pale and invisible like a fire in the sunlight. I see you folding your hands in your lap like this.' He showed her, but she couldn't quite see. 'This way. May I?' he said, as his hands came as close to cupping hers as they could without touching. 'No, I don't think so. You do it again, there,' he instructed, gathering one hand into the other, then nestling his thumbs. 'Like this, as if you are hiding something.'

He was talking in his old voice, the one that thickened the air into a fog around her. How had that other one sounded? In strong light, without nuance, it had been shrill, thoughtless, an uprooted voice.

'As if I have something to hide from you?' she said.

'Oh, I don't think you're hiding anything from me. I know what you are, remember.'

'Maybe I'm just this much,' she said, pulling the shawl tighter, making herself smaller. But she had given over her body to itself. She floated above it, looking down from a perch of bliss where she observed ache and fatigue with the detachment of pure thought. Looking down, she saw that her hands had become white. She had been standing there for a thousand years. She was someone who had peopled the world.

'You need me too, don't you?'

'We all do. Don't you know that I've carried you around inside for my whole life. You are one of the oldest parts of me.'

'But what is that?'

He shrugged.

'If you knew, would you do something about it?'

'Oh, God forbid!'

She smiled chivalrously. His imagination had a cold sweet smell.

'Without you I'd be leaning over the edge, howling into the void. I sang and sang and you were listening.'

She still was. The song was less powerful, more mysterious. And she could hear her own life rustling in accommodation.

'I know you hear me. You've always heard, even before, when there wasn't any sound. Softly, softly, before, when it was a kind of dreaming, and now it lathers your blood.'

She lifted one hand to her throat. This country was hard on skin, necessarily crisping and thickening to keep the green person inside moist and slippery.

'Sometimes I think you made me up.'

'Nothing wrong with that. I'm doing the same with this one, too.' In the glow, with a flourish, he swept his hand open up and down the front of his body. 'There's this space and we're filling it up –'

'– as if it were empty.' She had the uneasy feeling that he might rip off his skin, and that if he did he'd be made of thick jellied smoke.

The baby was crying, such a thin new sound that Hannah turned her head in surprise. Matthew was flung back on the pillow. 'Where are you?' he said. He opened his eyes. 'Oh, there you are.' He swallowed and fell back asleep.

Sitting cross-legged in the middle of the bed, Hannah nursed the baby, who had a grip on her finger. She thought, these children of ours, born to this landscape, will know when the changes are coming. The prairie would be their memory and their knowledge, as hers were of the forest, farm and city. She had seen Ben lift the dust and let it trickle between his fingers. He had stirred it, smacked it. It was his. He wouldn't be upset out there where the only shadow was his own. He'd understand the grumble of clouds and know what the colours of different skies promised. Of all places on earth, he had been here first.

And the baby, who would be called Emma, would warm herself on the hearth of Hannah's breast. Hannah would get to tell her everything she knew and it wouldn't be enough. But she would belong. She was from here.

Then to Gabriel, who was watching her from his silence, and to Matthew, who slept deep and curled, she said, 'These will replace you.'

She dreamed of the thin high cries of children being run through the thick deep voices of men.

Matthew had a soft smile. He was stirring the ashes in the stove and filling the coffee pot. Even at this late hour of seven, he had surprised a profound silence, and the morning sky was drained of colour. The first sun promised nothing. It was a small white paper sun. The chill of the air beneath it steamed as far as the horizon. Each drop of moisture coated itself in dull pewter-yellow light. A fetid green scent wafted from the slough.

Only when he was home did he allow his body this delicious lethargy. Behind him, still in the shroud of sleep, were the people he loved most, but they were at a great distance from him. He'd noticed it whenever Ben slept in his arms, giving him his body to hold, trustingly, he'd thought, but the truth was that not much of Ben was still there inside.

Being awake in the midst of sleeping people made him conscious of his own skin, as if he had just gotten into it again and the inside felt unnatural, like the iron stove when it had been allowed to grow cold. Now the stove's heat warmed his thighs. The kettle was sweating; the drops skidded and scorched. A soft draw pulled the thin, thready smoke up the chimney pipe, indicating across all the bare land the place where his hearth was.

The water was boiling. Before long the aroma of coffee suffused. He shrugged his shirt up around his shoulders, put his hands in his pockets and shifted his trousers side to side. He yawned and scratched one foot on the back of his other leg. For a moment he was off balance.

With a mug of coffee to his mouth, he turned. Hannah was barely awake, looking at the ceiling from the dreamy place she had just left. After a while she looked towards the window. A leaf, its broad yellow face thinned to an invisible edge, floated by. Matthew reached out to catch it. She pulled him gently to the edge of the bed. She opened his hand and put it over her face, and inhaled the funk of coffee and smoke. She moved it to the side of her head. His fingers, roughened, splintered her hair, abraded her skin. He was not ignorant of the necessary work any more, no longer innocent in her eyes. They had fallen together to this common place.

For a while they were together like that. From time to time Hannah moved his hand to a different part of her. He pressed just hard enough to raise heat from her into his palm.

Her belly was soft loam.

'What's it like?' he whispered.

'What?'

'You know,' his voice nudging.

She smiled broadly at the bewilderment in his face, and put her finger to an odd button on his shirt. It had been dark when she'd sewn it.

He was crouched for her words, wistful, as one who was going to be left out.

'Secrets.'

He heard the sound deflected, coming at him from one side, then the other, as if two people were talking, as if Hannah were split into two: one old girl he knew well; and growing around that, opaque and oozing musk, sticky to the touch, another, dusted in ashes, stretched by children, bleached, burned arid, tempered by the light in his eyes. This was as sweet as daylight to his soul, this knowing and not knowing who she was.

Perhaps because of that, and despite the fact that the muck of night was settling out, there was an uneasy residue of darkness around them. He'd ridden over it in the past, seen it rag-tag and mixed with the dust around his horse's hooves, seen it watery and thin, retreating before his bold glance, barely noticing it in the scallop shadows of snake holes. This morning he had a feeling they were huddled together listening for something out there to betray itself, to breathe audibly. They were waiting for it to move just enough to be seen, for them to identify if it was dangerous or not. He was worried the thing didn't know they were here, and might overlook them, or show indifference to their struggle with the land.

'Keep talking,' he said. Her words were stepping stones; he balanced on one, then the next, concentrating. He didn't just hear; he was breathing the words, swallowing the sounds; they made him hungrier. She was pressing the buttons on his shirt against his skin. He grabbed her hand, tucked it in his, gathered it to his face. He smelled cold stars. 'Keep talking,' muffled, mumbled into her palm.

She said his name, her voice close, intimate. She smiled, safe, strong.

For a while Gabriel watched them. From the mat on the floor his perspective was childlike. They were big and divine. He was like their child.

Ben found them, his eyes large and relentless, raising them from the dead place they must have been without him. The baby slept through morning as if the unusual light seeping through her eyelids was a pretentious dream of worlds to come, and she squinched, wrinkling the skin of blanket around herself.

Matthew was quiet at breakfast. Gabriel was going on to town without him. Ben was sitting on his father's lap, eating from the same plate. If Ben didn't like something, he took it out of his mouth and put it into Matthew's. Matthew's appetite waffled. Ben didn't want to get down to go play. Reproachfully he looked at Hannah, who was propped up on pillows serenely. She smiled at him, winked. He blinked before he could stop himself, but wouldn't give her the smile puckered in his mouth. He leaned back into Matthew. They stuck together. Matthew was surprised by the sleep and sweat smell clouding from his son. He smoothed a switch of Ben's hair.

'Pee, pee ... pee.' Ben was bouncing and urgent.

'Let's go.' He let him slide down between his knees, took his hand, and they went outside.

'Toast,' said Hannah from her pillows.

'It's cold,' said Gabriel, his hands folded over his stomach.

'Doesn't matter. Toast, toast,' she said, enjoying the choo-choo sound of the word.

Gabriel buttered the stiff brown bread and decorated it with a scoop of current jam. He licked the spoon.

'Thank you,' she said when he brought it to her. 'Let me see your tongue ... Aha!' He stuffed his odds and ends into a duffel bag. 'Getting ready to go?'

'Uh, huh.'

'Where *do* you go?'

'To a place I've made, a sort of nest: some lint, bluestem, milkweed, cracker crumbs, rose petals, thorns …'

'Stop!'

'No, it's true. Why do you say that?'

She didn't say anything, then she shrugged.

'One day,' he said, 'I'll be as safe as you are.'

His skin was lit from behind in the doorway the way light comes around the wings of birds of prey when they are grazing the big sky.

Matthew was three times as tall as his son. The low gauze of cloud was a hundred times taller than he was. Above that, the sky, ten thousand times higher, as far as his eye could see.

The warm cows were standing at the fence, the air around their bodies steaming like an aura. They prodded the sluggish air. In the domesticity of day, they were relieved, wide-eyed, grateful.

Ben said, 'Oh!' and pointed to the hens, who wouldn't come down because their feet would disappear in the ground mist. He was noticing differences, instances when things were not as they should be, as he'd seen them before. Matthew put his hat on his foot. Ben straightened his finger and said, 'Oh!'

The low shred of cloud coloured delicately. Soon it would burn away to expose the clean empty day.

Gabriel tied his thin roll of blanket on the back of the saddle. Still not comfortable riding the mare, he consoled himself, singing to her, old songs, new songs, in four-four time, matching the strike of her hooves on the ground, casting his songs out to be caught in her silken ears.

A brown pungent day.

Matthew put his hand on the top rail of the fence he had built around his house. When he pushed it, it rattled, and he saw that from being bound and weathered the sapling wood was stiff and strong. When he hung the gate, he'd make sure the latch would slip and shine.

A crisp yellow day.

The baby, freshened with oxygen, cried and was comforted. Hannah, standing beside Matthew, eventually leaned against him. Together they watched Gabriel, each wondering if he would glance back over his shoulder at them.

As the sun shone, it cast their shadow as one shape, not one they'd imagined making: thick, lumpy, a surprise, such an odd shape, the result of struggle, impossible to identify if they hadn't already known. As the

313

sun rose in the sky, the shadow receded, shrinking back under them. They thought of ancestors, about where they had stood, how far they had wanted to go. Matthew slid his hand down Hannah's flank because the repetitive gesture reminded him of comfort.

A familiar fall day.

Then, sometime later, there came a day when he said, 'We are still the same after all these years,' and she touched him, having come there to that point in the only way possible, through the long stretch of time, the pains and the triumphs. Her touch was both softer and heavier. And what they thought would never end, had, and had been replaced. And what they thought could not be borne, was. And what they thought would not endure, did, unchanged.

Born in Chicago, Susan Kerslake has lived in Halifax since 1966. Her previous books are *Middlewatch, Penumbra, Blind Date* and *Book of Fears,* which was short-listed for the Governor General's Award. For the past twenty years she has worked as a volunteer with children with cystic fibrosis. *Seasoning Fever* is her first novel in twelve years.